MW00757424

OPERATION LUNA

Tor Books by Poul Anderson

Alight in the Void
All One Universe
The Armies of Elfland
The Boat of a Million Years
The Dancer from Atlantis
The Day of Their Return
Explorations
The Fleet of Stars
Harvest of Stars
Harvest the Fire
Hoka! (with Gordon R. Dickson)
Kinship with the Stars
A Knight of Ghosts and Shadows
The Long Night
The Longest Voyage
Maurai and Kith
A Midsummer Tempest
No Truce with Kings
Operation Luna
Past Times
The Saturn Game
The Shield of Time
Starfarers
The Stars Are Also Fire
Tales of the Flying Mountains
The Time Patrol
There Will Be Time
War of the Gods

OPERATION LUNA

POUL ANDERSON

A Tom Doherty Associates Book
New York

This is a work of fiction. All the characters and events portrayed in this novel are either fictitious or are used fictitiously.

OPERATION LUNA

Copyright © 1999 by Trigonier Trust

All rights reserved, including the right to reproduce this book, or portions thereof, in any form.

Book design by Scott Levine

This book is printed on acid-free paper.

A Tor Book
Published by Tom Doherty Associates, LLC
175 Fifth Avenue
New York, NY 10010

www.tor.com

Tor® is a registered trademark of Tom Doherty Associates, LLC.

Library of Congress Cataloging-in-Publication Data

Anderson, Poul, date
    Operation Luna / Poul Anderson. — 1st ed.
        p.   cm.
    ISBN 0-312-86706-9
    I. Title.
    PS3551.N378O54 1999
    813'.54—dc21   99–24483

First Edition: August 1999

Printed in the United States of America

0 9 8 7 6 5 4 3 2 1

To Janet, Jeff, and Kathy,
who in their different ways are all magicians

ACKNOWLEDGMENTS

As always, Karen Anderson has been first and foremost among those who helped me, in her case with ideas, research, criticism, encouragement, and companionship.

We thank Steve and Jan Stirling for kindness and hospitality; Laura Frankos for admission to the church in her novel *St. Oswald's Niche*; David Eck, Jim Moore, and Ken Seowtewa for guidance and information. None of these people is in any way responsible for any errors of fact, mistaken interpretations, important omissions, and other infelicities that may remain, but without them there would have been many more.

The verses quoted in Chapters 40 and 41 are from "The Childish Edda," which was largely composed by Ron Ellik and me on an overnight drive long years ago. He was a great guy. It's been a pleasure to bring back this memory of him.

OPERATION LUNA

I

WITCHLIGHTS GLOWED BLUE ALONG THE FENCE, OUTLINING CARDINAL POINT AGAINST
night. Earth lay darker than heaven. There stars gleamed and the Milky
Way glimmered. A moon one day past full, climbing out of the east, veiled
many of them behind its own brightness. It cast pallor and long shadows
across the malpais. Northward, Mount Taylor bulked ghost gray.

When Ginny and I looked ahead and down, the glare near the middle
of the great pentacle, searchbeams focused on the spacecraft, drove most
of this from our eyes. My heart jumped to see that splendor.

Somewhere inside me I felt something different stir. The shiver
strengthened as we drew closer. It wasn't happening for the first time.
Earlier, though, it had been rare, faint and fleeting, no more than the
uneasiness everybody gets once in a while for no good reason. You don't
rub an amulet or make a religious sign or ask whatever witch or warlock
may be nearby if it means anything. No, you shrug it off as a passing
nerve-twitch. You're modern, scientific, free of superstitions. Aren't you?

What touched me now was stronger, too vague to be a foreboding
but not just a collywobble. I'd had enough experience to know that. A
hunch? I turned my head to and fro. All I saw besides sky was the head-
lights of a few other broomsticks, belated like ours. I took a long, slow
breath. Even in human shape, my nose is pretty keen. The air that flowed
in was pure and chill; temperature in New Mexico generally drops fast
after sunset. I did catch a slight ozonelike tang of goetic forces at work,
but that was to be expected hereabouts, especially tonight.

Wait, wait—a bare hint of strangeness, outsideness such as I couldn't
put a name to? Wolf, I might have been more nearly sure.

My look went back to Ginny. Since it would be only us two, we'd
taken her Jaguar instead of the family Ford. We'd left the windfield off
except in front, and breeze got by to flutter the skirt she'd chosen to wear
for this occasion. It was pressed around the downcurve of the shaft and
across a pair of long, trim legs. The sweater above hugged a figure as
good at age forty-two as it'd been when we met.

My attention stayed above the neck. Moonlight made her aristocratic
features into an ivory carving. It whitened and rippled the shoulder-length

hair. On her left breast, the silver owl emblem of her order seemed icily afire. I saw not only her usual alertness upon her, but a sudden wariness.

My voice sounded loud through the air whispering past us. "You feel a spooky whiff too?"

She nodded. Her contralto had gone metallic. "Uncanny might be a better word. Or—" I couldn't make out the rest. As a licensed witch, she has a wide vocabulary from exotic languages. I guessed this was Zuni. "Powers are abroad. Coyote is certainly on the prowl."

"And nearby, watching for a chance?"

"Of course. He always is."

"Oh, well, then." I didn't intend bravado. The Trickster is a bad enemy, and not exactly a reliable friend. He'd wrought havoc in the early days here, like when one test vehicle, a flying wing, molted in midair, or when moths got at a still more expensive experimental model, a super-carpet, and ate it full of holes.

However, I recalled, before there was any actual fatality, the National Astral Spellcraft Administration had grown smart for the nonce and consulted the local Indians. They informed it that Coyote had declared feud on it. He didn't like this invasion of his stamping grounds, not to speak of stunts more spectacular than any of his. The medicine men weren't very happy about it either.

So NASA's chief had a talk with President Lambert in Washington. Project Selene had been Lambert's way of pulling his political chestnuts out of the fire after the Brazilian crisis, when he'd fearlessly told the people of Rio de Janeiro he was one of them—"*¡Yo soy un carioca!*"— in Spanish. Also, it would mean considerable pork for his Southwestern power base. Therefore he twisted arms, and possibly other body parts, in Congress, and the Indians got a more decent deal from the givernment than they'd had before, and the priests invoked their gods and kachinas to protect Cardinal Point. . . .

I hauled my mind back. Had the outlaw influences caused it to wander? Those things had happened seven or eight years ago. My family and I had been here for only two. Ginny was correcting me: "Not him alone, though I do feel he's more . . . eager . . . than anytime I've known since I first learned a little about such things. Something else also."

"Like the Blue Flint Boys?" I ventured. I'd picked up odds and ends of lore, nothing like the education she'd set herself to acquire. Mischievous but not malignant spirits shouldn't be cause for worry.

She dashed my hopes. "Something much more powerful, something I—" She seldom hesitated. "—I can half guess at, though not really—"

If I'd been wolf, I'd have bristled. As it was, chill tiptoed along my spine and out to my nerve ends. "Can you discover what?"

"Maybe. But not without cantrips, and we aren't allowed any tonight. This is just sensitivity," like mine, but way sharper.

She shook herself, always an interesting sight, straightened in her seat, and, slowly, smiled. "Well, it's probably nothing to fear. The 'chantments stand strong. I'd know if they didn't. Quite likely a troop of Beings have simply come to watch, same as us."

She gestured downward. Our broom was descending. We could see hundreds of others below, across the landscape, and their dismounted riders, saintelmos shining on the ground or bobbing in hands, people talking or snacking or smoking or tilting a bottle or staring, staring at the vision. They'd come from Grants, Gallup, the pueblos, farms, ranches, as far as Albuquerque and Santa Fe, maybe farther. Sure, they could've stayed home and watched on the farseer, but this was history happening, the first real flight of the beast that should eventually land humans on yonder moon.

"If the Beings aren't friendly to what we're doing, why, neither are a lot of our fellow Americans," Ginny went on. "In either case, they can't help being fascinated." Her laughter chimed. "After all, what a show!"

That whipped my dim dreads off me. The crowd below was heartening, too. They weren't ideologues yammering about Tower-of-Babel technoarrogance, or demagogues whining about money that ought to be spent on their own admirers, or intellectuals oh, so superior to everything less than the critical deconstruction of James Joyce's *Odysseus*. They were ordinary, working men and women, along with kids, students, dreamers— and quite a few tribesfolk, I saw—here because they'd decided for themselves that going to the stars was a great idea.

In a way, too many had. Ruefulness quirked my lips. At the nth hour, Ginny and I found that no babysitters would be available, not for any price, not even her housecleaner, Audrey Becker, or Audrey's elderly mother. Once we might have entrusted the job to her familiar, but Svartalf was old and dozy, Edgar's sense of responsibility still unproven.

So Valeria got stuck with riding herd on Ben and Chryssa. She'd looked forward to witnessing the launch in person, with a fourteen-year-old's intensity, and didn't take kindly to the change in plans. What we offered in return hardly appeased her. We tried to be fair, but didn't believe in begging or bribing children to do their duty. Not that Val exploded, much. It wasn't her style. She'd brood, I knew. What would come of that, I didn't know.

Our broom stopped in midair. After a moment the air said, "Pass" and we continued. The checkspell had verified that we were entitled to go within the perimeter. Its effectiveness was reassuring. In fact, I lost my sense of outside presences, and soon more or less forgot about them.

My wife told me later that she did likewise, though I suspect she never really became quite unaware of anything that ever come to her attention.

As late as our frantic search had made us, we were lucky to find a place at the edge of the employees' parking lot. It was jammed. Besides their vehicles, we spied those of journalists, VIPs, and Lord knows who else had wangled admission. We barely eased in between a chrome-plated Cadillac and an old Honda with a sweep of withered but real straw. As we settled it into the rack and got off, our Jaguar waggled its shaft. The sprite in it never had liked close quarters. Ginny bent over to stroke the spotty-furry rear end and make soothing noises. It calmed down. We hiked off fast across the paving, through the cold. Our footfalls clattered beneath the Swan, the Dragon, and the ascending moon.

As we neared the gate, illumination took most night away from us. The chain-link fence stretched right and left for a mile or more, its witch-lights dwindling off into darkness. Here the edisons glared. Though the physical barrier was just fifteen feet high, I winded a little of the forces that charged it and warded the compound on every quarter, zenith and nadir included.

Since we already wore badges spelled to our identities, we had no rigmarole to go through. They were special, of course. I didn't draw my pay from NASA but from Nornwell Scryotronics back in the Midwest, which had a contract to develop space communication systems. It had gotten me seconded to Cardinal Point as an engineer. My boss, Barney Sturlason, knew well that my lifelong dream had been to work on celestonautics. He also knew that a happy man is a productive man. As for Ginny, who ran her Artemis Consultancy out of our home, we'd more than once had occasion to sic her onto some or other weird problem.

One of the guards knew us. "Why, hello, Mr. and Mrs.—uh, Dr. Matuchek," he greeted. "I was getting afraid you wouldn't make it. You're barely in time, unless they put a hold on the countdown."

"I know," I said.

"Wasn't your daughter coming along? And what about Dr. Graylock, ma'am?"

"We had babysitter woes," Ginny explained, "and my brother isn't feeling well."

"Too bad. Sure wish I could watch from where you're going to. A medicine man from Acoma Pueblo who's here, I heard him mention sensing how even spirits have come to see, heap big spirits."

"Leave that to the professionals," I snapped, "and let us by, for God's sake."

Immediatedly I regretted my impatience. He'd intended friendliness. Hurt, he retorted, "Well, Mr. Matuchek, you remember the rules. The moon *is* up, but nobody's supposed to change shape."

Ginny laid a cautionary hand on mine and a smile on the janus. "Of course," she murmured. "No offense. Excuse us if we're in a hurry, Mr. Gitling. Actually, once the beast rises, what you see ought to be better than the mere liftoff." He dissolved into amiability and waved us through.

The paths beyond lay dim, almost deserted. Everybody not in Mission Control wanted to be at a viewing station. Buildings enclosed us, murky against the sky-sheen from the launch paddock ahead. Off on the left, rising above roofs, the great onion dome of the VAB caught some of that light. The moon barely cleared the walls opposite; its cold, blue-blazoned shield still looked huge.

I did not plan on skinturning. In fact, I seldom transformed at all anymore, aside from an occasional romp out in the desert or, once in a while, to amuse little Chryssa. Her siblings had long since taken Daddy's trick for granted. Nevertheless, as the moonbeams caught me, I felt a strong urge. Excitement, no doubt, weakening inhibitions, stirring ancient instincts.

I quelled the lust by asking, quite sincerely, "What is the trouble with Will, anyway? In the hullabaloo, I didn't get a chance to find out."

"I'm not sure either," Ginny replied. "Nor is he, I suppose. He phoned to say he felt terrible and would stay home and try to sleep off whatever it is."

"A dirty shame. He's probably as responsible for getting a space program started as any man alive."

"Yes, and has it as dear to his heart." Hearing the trouble in Ginny's tone, I glanced at her and saw how she bit her lip. "Steve, I've been worried about him."

"Um-m, yeah, he has seemed a bit odd lately, now and then. Sort of . . . absent. But I figured he was preoccupied."

"No, it's not his research, his instruments. He's hardly said a word about them, which in itself is peculiar. I have an impression he's actually neglecting them, or at best tinkering without making progress. But he doesn't volunteer any information, he's dodged my few questions—"

If anyone would have sound intuitions about Will Graylock, I thought, *it'd be his sister.* She was nine years old, he twenty-one when an accident orphaned them. Circumstances then kept them more apart than together, but he was always kind and caring, the closest figure to a father she had. We'd been delighted when he resigned from Flagstaff and moved out here shortly after we did, with a National Parascience Foundation grant to concentrate on his lunar studies. Soon our kids also were.

Her inner steeliness came back to Ginny. "And I won't pry," she finished. "He'll tell me what and when he chooses."

"Maybe a love affair isn't going so well," I suggested.

"At his age?"

"Hell, I don't expect to be a dodderer when I get there. You'd better keep me satisfied, woman."

She grinned. "Same to you, man." Seriously again: "Okay, I've been assuming it's a personal matter. After all, it doesn't often show; mostly he's his usual self. Simply short bouts of moodiness and—and maybe, now, a touch of flu."

"Still, a pity."

"Yes, but this isn't the big event." Merely the first piloted test of the type of vessel meant to land the first humans on the moon. Seven orbits around Earth, if everything went well, mainly to try out the control spells and life-support systems. Will would have plenty more launches to behold, each different, more venturesome, inching toward yonder globe and the mysteries on it that he himself had revealed.

I didn't remark on how unnecessarily complicated and expensive a way to go I thought this was. Ginny had heard her fill of me on that subject. Besides, she'd repeatedly given the little Operation Luna Company help more valuable than it could have paid for.

And meanwhile, maybe forever, NASA's was the only game in town.

And— We came out onto open ground. Ahead of us a viewing stand raised white bleachers into black night. Beyond stretched half a mile of lava. Short paved roads cut through that jumble, converging on a central spot. There loomed the beast, waiting to leap, ablaze with the light upon it, a magnificence that my humble dream could never match.

2

WE'D HAD A FEW QUALMS ABOUT MAKING FOR THE JOURNALISTIC OBSERVATION AREA. Employees not on duty generally did so, because the site was better than that given the VIPs. We, though, had been famous ourselves for a while, headline material. That was eleven years ago. The sensation had ebbed like a sticky tide, till for the most part we were again contentedly obscure. Nevertheless, once in a while some complete and usually boring stranger or some interviewer desperate for copy hunted us down.

We couldn't readily disappear into the crowd that seethed along the benches and spilled out onto the rocks. My six-foot height and football shoulders are nothing unusual, nor does a wide Slavic face with snub nose, blue eyes, and hair-colored hair stand out especially. But Ginny needs a Tarnkappe, if not a transformation spell, to pass unnoticed by men; and right now any goetics not required for the project or for communications was, naturally, forbidden. We didn't want a farseer bezel and a string of banal questions thrust at us. We wanted to enjoy the event, unpestered.

Well, the press would also swarm thick at the other grandstand, where politicians, pundits, movie stars, self-appointed leaders of this or that self-defined underclass, corporate executives, evangelists, et cetera really did hope to grandstand. Our chances were better among people interested in the adventure for its own sake. In fact, we wouldn't mind encountering certain of the science writers and reporters. We liked and trusted them. But probably they'd be too busy doing their jobs to chat.

Chance favored us, or else we'd overestimated what notoriety remained ours. As we squirmed up the aisles between the tiers of benches, a few friends saw us and waved—maybe they hollered hello through the babble—and male gazes tracked Ginny, but nothing else occurred. We spied what seemed to be a vacant spot in a good location next to a couple of artificers from the project, Miguel Santos and Jim Franklin. Jim's glance met mine. His chocolate-hued phiz split in a wide grin as he gestured. Ginny and I started that way.

Our course took us past a knot of newsies. There our luck nearly broke down. Haris ed-Din al-Bunni himself had chosen to watch from here. Of course they came at him in a feeding frenzy. He didn't care. No, he basked.

Don't get me wrong. He was a good man who'd done tremendous work. Without his vision, genius, and drive, NASA would be mucking around yet with whiskbrooms and muttering about maybe trying for the moon in fifty or a hundred years. He convinced Lambert and the public that it could be done in our own lifetimes. Now his leadership was making it happen.

If some of us believed it could be done smaller, faster, and cheaper, none of us denied that Project Selene's pioneering had brought us knowledge, technology and paratechnology, vital to any space venture. If he courted personal publicity, I'm sure that was mainly for the sake of his program, keeping Congress and the taxpayers happy; his pleasure in it was incidental. To him, everything was incidental to the goal.

Oh, sure, he worked for the Caliphate during the war, when his flying bronze horses gave us a lot of grief. But he didn't subscribe to its fanatical heresy. He'd have been among our orthodox Muslim allies if he'd been born in the right country—though space was his true religion, and he liked his beer and Scotch as well as I did. He actually got into trouble in those days by remarking that his horses were galloping above the wrong planet. At the end of hostilities, the United States Army fell over itself recruiting him for defense research, and later was mighty reluctant about releasing him to the civilian agency where he really wanted to be.

Besides, hell, the war ended twenty years ago.

Big and beefy as he was, he glimpsed us across the heads and lifted a hand. "Ah, Virginia Matuchek!" he boomed. "The beauty titer and charm quotient have risen to where they should be. And Steven, fortunate man, hail also to you." His gallantries were well-meant, though I'd gathered they often got results.

Stares flew at us. Al-Bunni immediately went on with what he'd been saying. Nobody left that. I couldn't hear what it was. Probably a variation on his favorite theme of how the marriage of Eastern and Western Art was bearing fruit that would seed the stars.

Relieved, we pushed on and took our seats. "Hi. Welcome," greeted Miguel through the hubbub, and Jim: "Howdy. Had trouble? Glad you made it, even if just barely."

I told them what had happened. "Improvident, man," said Jim with a bachelor's smugness. "But it's nice that people are this interested, huh?"

"My Juanita is," Miguel put in, half defensively. "She does not like crowds. And if the children are too little to be allowed in, she wants to be in front of the farseer, sharing with them." In haste: "Not that you do wrong, Dr. Matuchek. Each family has its style, no?" She gave him a gracious nod and smile.

"Everything seems Aleph-OK," Jim said. "What you've lost is just time for admiring."

Our gazes locked onto the beast.

Beautiful it was indeed. The paddock stood emerald green, its low fence golden, above the jumbled dark rock. Broad though it was, it barely accommodated the hundred-foot length of the great bronze stallion. Seen at such distance, the figure revealed itself as the work of art, as well as Art, that it was. The head lifted high and proud, eyes turned heavenward, nostrils dilated to drink ethereal winds, and it was as if those winds tossed the streaming mane and tail, as if muscles tautened and quivered beneath the ruddy-sheening coat. The four giant broomstick strap-ons were no disfigurement; they belonged, the way a lance belongs with a knight's destrier. Likewise did the crew capsule on the back, a saddle of domed crystal.

"Here," Jim offered, handed me a pair of binoculars, and got busy with his camera. Witch-sight was permitted none but the tracking team. Ginny already had our glasses up. I focused Jim's.

They were powerful. Through the clear capsule shell, I could pick out accommodations, equipment, and stores for an intended crew of three. The pilot went alone this trip. I saw that she had taken her post at the front, buckled into her seat, and gripped the two pegs that jutted out of the neck, ready to ride.

"*Por Dios*, I envy her," Miguel muttered.

Ginny grinned. "A good masculinist like you?" she gently gibed.

"Well, there should be more men in the celestonaut corps. It is only prejudice that says women fly better."

"No, tradition, I think," I put in. "European. Countless old stories about witches. In other cultures, before the thing started truly happening, it was mostly men, warlocks, and to this day—"

"Captain Newton is where she is because she earned it," Ginny clipped. "You'll see equal numbers of men when they have qualified."

"Hey, I was just talking academese, honey," I said. "You know I respect Curtice." She'd become a pretty good friend of ours, ever since she sought out my wife for extracurricular lessons in dealing with Others. Not that anybody knew anything for certain except that *something* haunted the moon. Yet Ginny had had closer experience than most, clear to Hell and back. Me too; but mainly, I sort of got dragged along, without her education or intuition to enlighten me.

"Oh, *asimismo*," Miguel added. "I envy, but I am not jealous." Mexican-born or no, he understood the difference, which few native English speakers do anymore in these days of progressive education. "I marvel, like the whole world."

Now clear of the buildings, the moon no longer appeared swollen. It was small, cold, and beckoning. I realized what shrewd public relations al-Bunni exercised in scheduling the launch for tonight. Since Luna was the ultimate destination, the sympathetics would always work best—the piece of lunar meteorite in the horse's head would influence most efficiently—if the moon was in the sky. For this short trial run, any phase, any hour would serve about as well. But how dramatic a scene!

A male voice tolled through the noise, which died away beneath it. "All systems are do. Repeat, all systems are do. Final countdown is about to commence."

A kind of gasp went over the tiers and lost itself in the dark. The binoculars fell to Ginny's and my laps. Nor did we bother with cameras. This was a thing to see directly and engrave in living memory. I heard myself whisper, "Do, yes, do. Go with God."

"*Decem*," boomed forth.

"*Novem. Octo.*" I wondered momentarily if Arabic wouldn't have been better. But no, it was al-Bunni's mother tongue. His being in charge made Latin more esoteric, more powerful, than it would otherwise have been in a Western undertaking. "*Septem.*" Navajo, Shoshonean, Zuni? No, they hadn't been well studied—by whites—and our team might have lost some measure of control. "*Sex.*"

Right now? I thought crazily.

Ginny's fingers clamped on my arm. "Steve," she hissed, "something's wrong, terribly wrong."

"*Quinque.*" I turned my head and saw her face bloodless, the green eyes wide.

"*Quattuor.*" The sense of it came on me, not as keenly as to her, but like a barely captured smell. The odor wasn't foul, it was sweet and sharp, dizzying. Nobody else in the crowd or in Mission Control seemed aware. None had had the experiences that sensitized us beyond the normal threshold of perception. "*Tria.*" If anyone did feel a touch of alienness, he or she ignored it, lost in the sight of the moon horse.

"*Duo.*" The stallion trembled.

"*Unum.*" The bronze rolled and rippled, like muscles beneath skin. "*Nihil!*"

The beast reared. His neigh clanged from horizon to horizon. He sprang toward the sky.

He screamed. The booster brooms uncoupled. They fell to earth and started sweeping. The sound crackled and swished, monstrous. Clouds of grit whirled gray-black aloft from their titanium straws. They knocked over the searchlights. Night clamped down on the field.

I scarcely noticed. The stallion held my horror. Moonbeams bounced off him where he bucked like a bronco, two or three hundred feet in the air. Then he fell.

The crash belled and thundered. A huge, twisted, broken wreck sprawled near the paddock, among the berserk brooms. Not pausing to think, I raised Jim's binoculars. The lenses gave me sight of the shattered capsule. I saw nothing of the pilot. She couldn't have gotten to her ejection system, or she'd have ridden the brass eagle down to earth by now.

"Oh, no, no," I heard Jim groan. "The energy—"

Yes, the energy that was to have carried our beast on high and home again was goetically evoked and stored, but that made no difference. The conservation laws of physics said it had to escape somewhere. Yonder metal would soon be incandescent.

Ginny grabbed my arm once more—not in alarm, in command. "Steve," she yelled through the uproar around us, "go get her!"

My wits came awake. Christ, I should have been on my way already. Moonlight poured icy over the screaming, surging, clawing mob on the benches. As I kicked off my shoes and peeled off my clothes, my body drank the radiance down. Flesh and bone went fluid, awareness whirled, soul rejoiced in the pangs that were half ecstasy, the old carnivore came to life and I howled aloud.

I was animal.

Being a fairly big man, I'm quite a big wolf; and the were condition gives added strength. I went through the crowd like a buzzsaw through a bowl of Jell-O. If I knocked down whoever didn't move aside fast enough, too bad. Several times I leaped, to arc over heads and land on a lower tier. I felt some blows—yes, a heavy camera on a tripod—but vaguely. The were condition also means near-instant recovery from injuries that don't outright maim or kill. Nobody was packing a firearm loaded with silver bullets.

I hit the ground and sped on over the lava. A wolf's brain, even a werewolf's, isn't very bright by human standards, but I kept sufficient knowledge of who I was and what I meant to try. And, though I was now nearsighted and colorblind, my nose gave me a worldful of smells, my ears captured sounds a man never hears, every hair on my pelt was a feeler feeding into my nerves.

So rich were my senses that I even noticed I was naked. Not expecting this, I hadn't worn the knitsuit under my clothes that lets me run free as a wolf without embarrassment when I turn back to human. I had thought to leave my shorts on. They fitted reasonably well, since a war wound has left me bobtailed. But somehow they'd gotten torn off in the ruckus.

To hell with that. *Aou-ow-w!* Gangway!

Dust grated my nostrils, plastered my tongue, stung my eyes. A broom forty feet high came at me. The metal rattled horribly. I dodged past, right into another. It sent me flying. I thumped down, recovered, and loped on. The fallen beast loomed ahead. The heat in it billowed over me.

This would be no fun at all. Well, I'd encountered Fire in a worse form before. What was human in me grabbed hold of the lupine. Up over the alloy I bounded. Fur scorched, pads blistered. I howled for pain, yet I kept going. My body drew on its reserves to repair itself almost as fast as the harm was done. Almost.

There were limits—dehydration, if nothing else. I had to be quick. Across a flank I went, along the crumpled mass, to the forequarters and the capsule.

Through dust and smoke off my fur I peered past the crystal. It had shattered when the strength spell on it was annulled, or perverted, or whatever had been done. Yes, Curtice Newton crouched under the touchstone panel. The cabin deck, oak from Dodona, protected her for this while. But if she tried to climb over the sharded crystal, it would slash her like swords, while the metal outside was by now as hot as a medieval heretic's pyre.

But if she didn't escape pronto, she'd bake. Rearward I saw the door of the toilet compartment, burst open. The little Hydro there had collapsed into a puddle of plain water, steaming away beneath the Kheper mural.

No time to waste. I sprang over the rim, onto those blessed hardwood boards. The cuts I'd taken as I crossed knitted before I really felt them.

The pilot stared dazedly at me. Blood ran copious from a scalp wound. The damage seemed worse than that. Crumpling, the horse's mass had absorbed most of the impact, but something had torn loose and hit her. She'd recovered enough to unbuckle and creep out of her seat, then slumped to the deck. I saw that the eagle which could have swung her free hung in its brackets with one wing broken.

I licked her hand. My muzzle jerked sideways. She pounced on the idea, stunned though she was. "Steve Matuchek?" I heard through the racket, a faltering note of amazed hope. I nodded and braced myself. She straddled my back, clutched my shaggy neck, and held her legs close against my flanks.

The expectation of more pain was harder to take than the pain itself. I mastered it somehow and bore her away, out of the capsule and down off the wreck. I don't much remember this.

I do remember us reaching the ground, and a broom bound for us, and how I stumbled beneath my burden. All at once the sticks fell. With a last huge clatter, they bounced across the rocks and lay inert.

The ruin behind us started to glow, but we were well clear of it. I felt only a dull warmth. Mainly, I felt the agony leave me as I healed, and an awful thirst and hunger after what the healing had demanded, and utter exhaustion. I collapsed. Curtice got off and sat down at my side. A shaky hand stroked my head.

The rescue squad arrived. They were a good outfit. They simply hadn't been supplied or trained to cope with anything as grotesque as this. Their warlock had handily exorcised whatever possessed the brooms, considering that he had no idea what it was. It had already left the horse. Its mission of ruin was accomplished.

The team carried Curtice and me off to the infirmary. Unfortunately, it was as fully equipped as most hospitals. Turning back to human, I demanded a pair of pants and immediate release. What I got was one of those silly gowns and a lot of medics giving me every test known to man and some that I think man was never meant to know.

Eventually Ginny arrived and sprung me. I'd never seen a more glorious sight than her when she entered, the telescoping wand from her purse star-gleaming at the tip. (Well, there had been times to match this, also involving her, but they're none of your business.) She'd promptly offered her services to al-Bunni, and, before he could reply more than, "Yes," headed off in search of clues to what had happened.

"I'll tell you later," she said. A weariness greater than mine loaded her shoulders and voice. "Not that I've really discovered anything. Let's go home." We arrived as dawn was silvering the eastern sky.

3

WE WOKE AT MID-MORNING. SUNLIGHT FILTERED SOFTLY PAST VENETIAN BLINDS, touching bedroom furniture, Hiroshige and Charlie Russell reproductions framed on the walls, assorted oddments and souvenirs from our years together. It made flame of Ginny's hair over her pillow. We'd showered before we turned in, of course, and she smelled all fresh and—

"Not so fast, wolfie," she murmured with a wry grin.

Her hand stroked my cheek. I felt the stubble stir. "Yeah, I ought to shave."

"Later. You've got a great idea, but the kids are up and about, along with everything else."

I sighed and stretched. In spite of what we'd been through and the short rest afterward, we felt reasonably lively. Lycanthropes generally recover fast from stress, and Ginny had laid a quick fettling spell on herself. She'd have to pay nature's price, but ten or twelve hours' sleep tonight should do that, and meanwhile this day bade fair to be hectic.

"Speak of the devil," she added as a knock sounded on the door. "Come in," she called. We sat up against the headboard.

Valeria appeared. "Hi, reverend ancestors," she greeted. "I've been crouching for you to come a-conscious."

No surprise. Officially our older daughter had no more goetic skills than the schools had taught her so far, mild stuff proper to her age. But it was plain she had a Gift at least equal to her mother's. She won every spelling bee hands down, and a couple of her experiments in alchemy lab had alarmed the teacher. She was also smart, observant, and more self-guided than was entirely safe. We knew darn well she'd sneaked looks at advanced textbooks—easily wheedled from a boyfriend—and the part of Ginny's library that wasn't under seal. Since Ginny hadn't set any geas on the house last night, it was no trick for Val to play peekaboo with an incantation and a mirror.

Ordinarily we'd have administered a stern lecture about respect for privacy and set some dull chore as a penance. But under these circumstances, chaos at Cardinal Point and, I did believe, anxiety on our account, her surveillance was pardonable, even touching. Besides, she was turning on the charm—the real charm, not a mere cantrip—at full dazzlement.

There she stood, not in the usual grubby sweater, faded jeans, and torn sneakers of vacation time: no, in frilly white blouse and wide plaid skirt. They were exactly right for a figure withy-slim, not yet as tall as Ginny's but stacked like two state capitols. The eyes shone huge and turquoise in a pert, tip-tilted face. With the rest of her female cohort, she wore her hair long, but today the ruddy-brown locks weren't coiled against her head in the currently *de rigueur* Hopi style, like two pieces of Danish pastry. They fell straight down to her waist. She knew my weakness for that Alice in Wonderland look, the minx.

This was our little Valeria, our first-born, whom we'd snatched back from Hell itself when she was only three, and watched grow into an active, happy child with a wacky sense of humor. How suddenly and well I remembered one early morning when she was five: Ginny happened to be away, I was making breakfast for the two of us and dropped an egg on the kitchen floor—how she looked at me struggling to curb my tongue, and murmured in a tone of infinite compassion, "Daddy, don't you want to say, 'Shit!'?"

Then she turned twelve, and the boys were buzzing around her. She enjoyed it but, from all I could gather, she kept them—including those several years older—from going off the reservation, with the same cool competence she'd shown for horses, canyon hikes, and dry camping since we moved to these parts.

Not that she didn't carry high explosive in her spirit— Enough for now.

She beamed. "I've been fixing your breakfast," she said. "I'll bring it." She slipped out the door.

Ginny and I exchanged a look. We both considered breakfast in bed a much overrated pleasure. However, this time we had no choice. I brought my lips close to ear. Stray hairs tickled. "Quick," I whispered, "what's the real situation and the official story? Why aren't reporters trampling our grass flat?"

"I saw to that before I fetched you," she said as fast and low. "The management agreed a hundred percent. The project's suffered a catastrophe nobody understands. The witches and warlocks who cast about for clues along with me found nothing except what's so obvious it may as well be made public today. Oh, traces, suggestions— But you know the basic law of military intelligence as well as I do, Steve. You don't let the enemy know what you know about him, nor what your own capabilities are. Your rescue of Curtice may or may not have strategic implications. Sure, it's a story the agency's image boys would dearly love to build up, but it's being kept from them. The word is, she got away on her own before the metal was too hot, but then had to keep clear of the brooms till they'd been dischanted. The rescue squad's under strict security gag too. The FBI will take over the investigation. We'll hear from them."

"Good work, sweetheart!" I patted her hip.

"You did mighty well yourself, lover." She patted back.

Valeria returned with a tray.

Ben followed, carrying the other. At ten, he'd outgrown a lot of rambunctiousness—or rather, I suspected, figured out that it didn't pay. These days he was a quiet, well-mannered, somewhat studious boy, though he liked exploring our new environs as well as the rest of us. Slender, dark blond, he was a ferocious basketball player at school, made excellent grades, and got along well with his fellow kids. His main interest was dinosaurs. If he stayed by his wish to become a paleontologist, he'd have to master some spooky thaumaturgics, but I felt confident it wouldn't faze him.

Chryssa stumped behind. Four, she was chubby but starting to lengthen out: with her features and curly yellow hair, much like Val at that same age. Where her brother looked serious and her sister blazingly eager, she was quite simply glad to see Mommy and Daddy home. About the single break in her sunny disposition had been a year or so back, when for some reason she'd developed a hatred of baths. She'd submit, but only under protest.

This family reunion, after the savagery last night, roused more and more irrelevant memories in me. Like Val, assigned once to bathe the little one, and the song that floated out of the bathroom to the tune of "Yankee Doodle."

> "Chryssa's hair is moldy green.
> Her skin is gray and awful.
> She has toadstools in her scalp.
> Her ears are full of fungus.
> We will make our Chryssa clean,
> We will scrub our Chryssa,
> We will polish Chryssa up
> Until she shines like onions!"

Though the phase was past and we'd had no more such trouble, sometimes I still heard Val refer to her sister as "Moldylocks." Both of them thought it was funny.

Edgar, Ginny's new familiar, had ridden in on Val's shoulder. The big black raven hopped off onto the bed and walked to his witch. "Gruk," he croaked, half uneasily, half indignantly. He'd missed out on all the hijinks.

Ginny stroked him under his beak and down his shimmery back. "I'm sorry, Edgar," she said. "They wouldn't have let you in. You'll get plenty of action, believe me."

"Gronk," he answered, flapped up onto the headboard, and perched. The knowledge that looked out of his beady eyes was benign—toward us—but somehow, indescribably, colder than what had ever been in tomcat Svartalf's. Well, Ben had told me that birds are the last surviving dinosaurs.

Val plunked her tray down in front of me. I saw coffee, ham, hash browns, buttered toast, marmalade, tomato juice, and a shot of chilled vodka. "Thanks, pony," I mumbled. My girl was reaching womanhood fast. In some respects, anyhow.

She settled down on the edge of the bed. "You're welcome. When you're *quite* ready, Padrito, we'd like to hear what actually happened. We really-o truly-o would."

Ben gave Ginny her tray and took a chair. Chryssa climbed up and snuggled next to her, spilling some juice. Edgar rocked forward and reached for her toast. She glared. He sat back. "Who, me?" he croaked. After she'd had a few sips of coffee, she was able to smile and give him a hash brown.

As the life-giving alkaloid soothed me, too, I could ask Val, "What do you know? What did you kids see on the crystal?"

"First a lot of views," she sneered. "A *scabrous* lot of reporters talking to anybody they could catch, or to each other." She wrinkled her nose. " 'This is a historic occasion, isn't it, Sam?' 'Yes, it sure is historic, Connie. Our first step toward the moon and those mysterious Beings on it.' 'Do you think they're omegans, souls who've achieved perfect clarity, like the Psychontologists claim, Sam?' 'I don't know, Connie. Who does? But we'll be back in a moment after this message.' Meaning commercials for HP dowsers, and Elfland tours, and Audhumla Cream Cheese—'the food of the gods'—as if we hadn't heard all that blat a *million* times before."

I squeezed a small hand. "I am sorry you got stuck here, princess. Though I'm also glad. It became a tad dangerous out there. What did you see and hear right after the launch?"

"Well, how the horse rose and bucked and nosedived, and the brooms went wild, and then just all sorts of chatter and patter and shots of the wreckage, till I plain old *had* to go to bed. Ben and Moldylocks caved in way before." She looked hard into my eyes. "What were you and Mother up to?"

"Uh, helping where we could. Wasn't much."

"I heard mention of some people who claimed they'd seen a wolf run across the ground."

"Rumors, rumors."

"NASA isn't saying anything except that somehow the guard spells got broken and something came in and viked the launch. 'The proper authorities will investigate and report their findings in due course.' Yee-ork!"

"You and Mother didn't sit still, did you, Dad?" Ben asked quietly.

I collected what *gravitas* was available to me. "No, of course not. We aren't at liberty to discuss it yet, though. All we can say is that for us it was no big deal, and we're home safe, and nobody got seriously hurt." Other than Haris ed-Din al-Bunni and all of us who'd longed beyond the sky. "Let's give thanks for this and get on with our work. When we have a real story to tell, you'll hear it." If the government permitted.

"Will we?" Val challenged.

"When it's possible, yes, you will," I promised, regardless of what the goddamn government permitted.

"This isn't the end of the world, you know," Ginny said. "A setback, but we can hope the project will recover."

"Or Operation Luna will take over," Ben said, as softly as before.

Val raised her arms. "Yay for Operation Luna!" she cried.

"Operation Loony, Operation Loony," Chryssa chortled.

"Hey, hold on, kids," I protested. "It's only a sideline, don't forget. A kind of hobby. What we need is to set Project Selene back on its feet."

"What we need immediately," Ginny declared, "is to finish this nice meal you made before it gets soggy and hard to light."

That quieted conversation down to what she and I could more easily handle. We were finishing when the telephone spoiled our carefully rebuilt family harmony. Telephones have a way of doing such things.

The partial animation meant well, of course—especially when the sympathetic vibrations were to be between *simpático* persons. For an instant I was even pleased. The phone flitted to the open door, hung there, and said, "A call from Dr. Graylock."

"Whee, Unca Will!" Chryssa exulted, bouncing on the mattress. To her he meant fun, jokes, comic songs, stories, maybe a toy or a treat. Val and Ben brightened too. He talked and played games with them, always interestingly, never the least condescendingly. Ginny sounded less joyful. "Well, come on," she said. The phone floated to the bed and settled between us. She gestured acceptance.

Her brother's face showed wan in the screen. *Aged*, I thought. *Overnight?* His voice dragged. "Ginny, Steve, you're all right, aren't you? I've just heard the news. Terrible. But it said there were no casualties."

"You've slept this late?" she asked. "What's wrong? You look like clabbered oatmeal."

"Bad night. Could I come see you? I've a notion, maybe clear off orbit, but a notion my trouble might tie in with what's happened at the Point."

A shiver passed through my skin. Considering what Will Graylock's work meant to the whole undertaking— And furthermore— "In any case, the investigation can use your advice and ideas," I blurted.

Ginny made a shushing motion at me. "We're barely back in action ourselves," she said. "How about eleven o'clock? Try to arrive inconspicuously. Currently we need the attentions of the press as much as we need cholla in the toilet paper." He nodded agreement. She disempathed.

I glanced around at our offspring. "Hear that, kids?" I said. "I'm afraid you'll have to be elsewhere while he's here."

Chryssa clouded up. "Poor Unca Will, he's sick? I c'd pick him some flowers."

"No, thank you, darling," Ginny told her. "He has to talk about something private. You know, like when you whisper a secret to Daddy or me."

"He wasn't at the launch last night?" Ben inquired sharply. "Hey, what *is* the matter, anyway?"

"That's what we're trying to find out," I replied. "Secret and Urgent." That farseer show about spies was among his favorites. I plagiarized from it: "What you don't know can't be wrung out of you." *You can't innocently blab* would doubtless be more accurate, but counterproductive.

"Hoy, there, don't scare them," Ginny said. "It's nothing to be frightened of, dears."

Ben rose, stiff-backed. "I know my duty," he said, wounded in his machismo.

"Uh, Val, maybe the three of you could go to the park," I suggested.

Our oldest was also on her feet. The veneer of sweetness had cracked apart. I damn near heard the pieces of it tinkle to the floor. "You mean I get to babysit *again*?" she exclaimed, fire-faced. "While everything interesting happens? Nixway!"

"But—"

"You promised last night! You promised I wouldn't get stuck like that again! This is unseelie! It's scabrous!" She clenched her fists. She clenched her fists. "You're a, a, a wereliar!"

In our theory, we should have disciplined her for disrespect. But, well, she'd been so hopeful of getting the exciting truth straight from us, and instead we'd pussyfooted like NASA itself—no, we'd heard her refer to NASA's public relations as "cowfoot"—and now we not only wanted her out of the way as if she were an infant, we proposed to saddle her once more with that same infant.

"Okay, okay, it was a passing notion," I said. "Not compulsory. Why don't you give Larry Weller a call and maybe go have a hamburger or see a movie?" The last I'd heard, he was the closest to a steady boyfriend she'd yet acquired. The competition seemed to be fierce.

"Him?" she yelled. "That mudhead?" She collected her dignity. "No, thank you very much," she said, hailstone by slowly pattering hailstone.

"I'll stay in my room, if you please." The way she stalked out, all she needed to be Svartalf in his heyday was a tail straight up in the air.

"Women," said Ben with the loftiness of ten-year-old masculinity.

"I'm one," Ginny pointed out mildly.

"Well, girls. Raging hormones."

Wait till yours kick in, I thought, *and God help us, every one.*

"I'll take care of Chryssa," Ben offered. "How 'bout it, sis? We'll go down to the rumpus room and animate my model Cretaceous."

That was manfully done of him. "Jolly shrewd," I said, also out of *Secret and Urgent*. "You may have to keep her amused for two or three hours, though."

"Aw, I can always play a Howleglass show on the farseer. She can't see those often enough, can you, sis? And me, I've got this neat new reckoner game."

"Splendid," Ginny said. "I'll arrange snacks and stuff for you, and lunch if necessary." And for Valeria if possible. "You don't have to disappear before, oh, quarter to eleven, you know—unless we have another emergency," she added, probably to liven things up for him. "Meanwhile, we two had better make ourselves presentable. We'll join you shortly."

"I wanna see the t'rannosaur attack the tri*cera*tops right now," Chryssa said. "Please?"

"Okay," Ben agreed. She jumped off the bed and took his hand. They left. Good kids, both of them.

Val, though, she wasn't only good—at heart—but remarkable. "Hey, what's this problem with Larry?" I demanded.

"I shouldn't tell you," Ginny answered low. "She confided in me, with tears, the other evening. But under the circumstances— His hands got too busy. She had to cast a minor geas to make him stop. I'm glad I taught her how."

It was knowledge legally reserved for older, more responsible children. But Val blossomed early.

"He brought her straight home, but didn't deign to speak a word," Ginny finished. "You were out playing poker."

Rage erupted. "That whelp! That swine! Why didn't you tell me before?"

"I wasn't supposed to. But this is an uncanny situation all around, and you may need to understand everything—"

"When I catch him, by Loki—"

"—understand everything, so you can see what's not important and dismiss it. Steve, hark back. Moonlight on the desert, stars, and a pretty and full-blooded girl—what would you have tried for? I gather Larry had plenty of encouragement, up to a point. By then he wasn't exactly a pointillist. Valeria curbed her own emotions suddenly, violently. It amounted to reacting against him. She hasn't gotten over it yet. I'll bet he's hurting worse."

"Um, well, yeah, maybe," I grumbled as I subsided. True, nothing irrevocable had happened. None of those louts who hung around my daughter were worthy of her anyway. Larry was among the less obnoxious. And, yes, I remembered my own teens. Wretched time of life, especially since it tends to turn off all compassion for it from those of us who've served our sentences.

"Take pride in her," Ginny said. "It's more than—than not being cheap. It's looking ahead and hewing to a purpose."

I nodded, a little jerkily. If Val was to fully master the female side of the Art like her mother, as her genes and her dreams alike called for, she must stay virgin till she had her magistra's degree. "Not easy," Ginny ended. "I know."

In one supple movement, she left the bed and stood beside it. "Well, c'mon, lazybones," she urged.

I followed along. Her familar followed us. My shaving, dressing, and so forth were mechanical. The raven brooded over them. He didn't mean to be sinister; mostly he was a rather genial sort. But though he could more or less pronounce a number of human words, he hadn't said, "Howdy" this morning, only croaked. Now he sat on the shower curtain rod, limned against luminous blinds, like a piece of night, reminding me that he was in rapport with strange things. What was due to hit us next?

And—a silly question maybe, but very natural for a father—how might a young girl, witchy-gifted and in turmoil, bollix everything up for everybody, wizards and demons and angels alike?

4

THE SECOND DAY OF AUGUST WAS GETTING DOWN TO BUSINESS WHEN WE REACHED THE living room. Svartalf sprawled on a broad windowsill. Sunlight flooded his blackness. He absorbed it like a rug.

Ginny went over to give him his due fondling around the throat and ears. He opened an indolent yellow eye and half purred. Edgar, back on her shoulder, leaned over and said quite distinctly, "Greetings, old garbage diver."

"Mind your manners, bird!" Ginny snapped. She swatted the raven, not hard but with plenty of meaning. Svartalf bared a worn-down fang and snarled a bit. Fortunately, he didn't otherwise react. Maybe, being a little hard of hearing these days, he hadn't actually caught the insult; or maybe he didn't feel like leaving his comfortable location. Ginny's Art kept him healthy, but she couldn't turn time backward. Though not senile, he was venerable for a cat, or would have been had anybody venerated him. If he still domineered in the feline neighborhood, it was more by bluff and cunning than prowess. Certainly he was too stiff of joints and short of wind to go on any serious witch-venture—or so she deemed, and gave him honorable retirement.

I don't say he and his successor hated one another. Call it professional jealousy, which now and then led to a squabble. Early on, Edgar had laid a dropping on Svartalf's head. I don't say, either, that was deliberate, though it sure was precise. The tom gathered his muscles to leap and do murder. Ginny intervened. Svartalf stalked off. He returned with a medal in his mouth, one of the several he'd received for his share in past exploits from such outfits as the United States Army, Trismegistus University, the Evangelical Lutheran Church, and the American Mathematical Society. He put it down on the floor by Edgar's perch. When the raven had had a good look at the shiny object, such as his breed love to collect, Svartalf bore it away and came back with the next. And the next and the next and the next. Edgar was fairly subdued for a while afterward.

I went to another window and glanced out. Our back yard had a big old cottonwood to shade it, together with a garden, but in front a patch of brownish grass ran along a sidewalk and a street whose asphalt would beget heat shimmers this afternoon. The houses beyond huddled close, fake ranch style, devoid of trees, under a stark blue sky. The Eskimo dolls in them must already be hard at work cooling them off.

We'd been lucky when we moved here. The place we acquired had stood for a long while on the edge of town, red-tiled, tawny-walled, spacious, honestly built. The suburb was mushrooming around it, if mushroom growth is accompanied by the sound of hammers and cement mixers.

Grants was booming worse, being near Cardinal Point—employees, tourists, and everything that that implied. We'd chosen to settle in Gallup, some fifty miles west. I didn't mind the commute. Flying along, you saw awesome scenery, in spite of what people were doing to it. Gallup kept part of the genuine Southwest, offered the kids a wholesome environment for school and play, and gave Ginny an excellent base in which to reestablish her consulting service. It's the rendezvous for the annual ceremonial gathering of the Indian tribes. That meant paranatural phenomena to observe and goetic work to do, even for a female paleface if she had the skill. Also, what had become more important yet, not far south lay the Zuni pueblo.

"Peaceful scene," I said, for lack of any inspired remark. "Last night hardly seems real."

"You have the order of things reversed," Ginny replied. "Peace is not a natural condition. Your own body is a battleground, every moment of your life. How can you expect the world or any of the universes except Heaven—if Heaven is another continuum, which I doubt—any of them to be different? I should think you'd learned better."

It wasn't like her to lecture me. "You're pretty worried, aren't you?" I said.

"Are you shrugging this off?"

"No, no, of course not. But looking back, I wonder if we're up against any force more formidable than old man Coyote. The business had a certain humor to it—brutal, yes, but not completely malign." As I spoke, I wished I hadn't. My careless words recalled to me the absolute evil we did once confront.

Ginny saw me shiver and came to stand beside me. "Coyote alone would be trouble enough. But he couldn't have gotten in and done his mischief by himself. If it was he, somebody or something else aided and abetted him. How? Who? Why? That last is probably the most basic question of the three." The cheerfulness she'd maintained began to waver. Her voice thinned. "What's been plaguing Will?"

I laid an arm about her waist. We stood silent. Occasional wains trundled down the street or broomsticks slid above; pedestrians and dogs passed along the sidewalk. Then a Völve, staid and sturdy, descended to our parking rack. "There he is!" Ginny cried. She ran to open the front door.

I kept aside and studied my brother-in-law more narrowly than ever before. He stood a couple of inches shorter than me, had grown portly in his fifties, but remained light on his feet. Today the shoulders slumped and he moved heavily. The normal liveliness was likewise gone from the roundish, hooknosed face. Suddenly I noticed more white than gray in the brush-cut hair and Vandyke beard.

Yet when he shook my hand the clasp was firm, the eyes behind their steel-rimmed glasses as bright a green as his sister's. Above the Southwest's ubiquitous jeans, his shirt of yellow silk shantung and Longevity pendant bespoke a sort of defiance. China and its culture were among his many interests. He knew the history and the Mandarin language, had visited the country several times both as guest astronomer and tourist in spite of its current turmoil, and maintained connections with friends and colleagues over there.

"Welcome," I said. "Sit down. Coffee, lemonade, beer? We hope you can stay for lunch."

"Nothing now, thanks." His tone was leaden. "Except, mind if I smoke?"

"Not at all," we told him, routine response to routine courtesy. An ashtray waited. Ginny and I quit years ago, but we don't take the Christer attitude of too many ex-puffers. Just don't blow it straight at us, or most particularly at our children.

He settled into an armchair, took out pipe and tobacco pouch, and lit up. To tell the truth, I kind of liked the aroma of the Russell's Mixture he used. "Is this an inconvenient time for you?" he asked. "I imagine you're both overwhelmed."

"On the contrary," Ginny said. "Before turning in last night, or rather this morning, I gave every client scheduled for today a message on the phone canceling the appointment. Three or four, none of them anything big." In order that she could help my work in its hour of need.

"And, obviously, engineering-type operations are suspended till further notice," I put in. "We're both at your service, Will."

"You're very kind." He sighed. "I feel presumptuous, shoving my petty woes forward."

"Nonsense," said Ginny. "They aren't, and you should have earlier."

"Besides," I added, "you think they may be related to ours."

He frowned through a blue cloud. "That may be the most ridiculous presumption of the lot." After a pause: "However, my physician has checked me over and found nothing, nor did the warlock I consulted."

"I might have," said Ginny a trifle stiffly.

"My dear, in the first place, I knew you wouldn't charge me, and we Graylocks don't freeload unless we get desperate—do we? In the second and more obvious place, Hosteen Yazzie *is* a Navajo Singer, and I thought I might have run afoul of some local influence."

"Ah, Yazzie. A good man, yes. I'd be the first to admit I'm no expert on Southwestern paranature, after only two years. I have learned a little something from the Zuni, but not enough, I'm afraid, to give you much more than a referral."

"And there're a lot more Navajo and Hopi hereabouts, with their assorted gods, ghosts, and goblins," was my banal contribution.

Will couldn't help correcting me: "In spite of their linguistic differences, I've gathered that those peoples have remarkably similar beliefs. Which, in this day and age, means 'measure of understanding.' But since I happened to be on the Navajo reservation south of Ramah when . . . it . . . may have happened . . . it was natural, later on, to check with a shaman of that background."

Ginny leaned forward. "You haven't told us anything about the matter."

"I didn't know it was relevant to you. I still don't. Merely a guess, *faute de mieux*. But, well, you may remember my mentioning to you last year that I'd begun to get some peculiar and . . . somewhat disturbing . . . data in my observations."

I nodded. "That was after you'd made the improvements on your instrument, wasn't it?" I meant the specterscope, his invention, which ten years ago shook the science of astronomy and broomboosted public interest in spaceflight when it found spoor of invisible creatures alive on the moon.

"Not quite. Even before then, I'd caught indications that, whatever they are, those Beings are not all benign, as they'd appeared at first. Several fellow researchers in various countries reported similar results. None of us published, we kept it confidential between us, because the traces were so slight, so ambiguous. Variations in the polarization of moonlight are damnably hard to measure, point by point, let alone their changes with time and the interpretation of the figures." Will's pipe trembled in his hand. "But you've heard this from me before, and seen it amply in magazines like *Goetic American* and *Paranatural History*. What you haven't heard is how the variations went chaotic, and fractal analysis seemed, *seemed*, to show that the attractors may be of the diabolical sort."

I caught my breath. Ginny sat glacier-calm. "This caused you to try for a 'scope with more sensitivity?" she prompted.

"Yes. Well, of course I wanted one anyway. Larger aperture and, for the spectral part, a dragonskin diffraction grating—"

She quelled the professional enthusiasm that had for a moment made him happy again. "Skip the details. Why didn't you give me a look at those patterns? I've acquired more sense for deviltry that I ever really wanted to."

"I told you, they're too vague. The data points wander over the chart, the probable error is absurdly large, the whole thing could as easily be used to prove that the lunar Beings have established a casino or a stock market. I had little more than a hunch that something yonder had gone seriously wrong. Some of my colleagues agreed this is possible, some didn't. Everybody agreed we need better data.

"I had funds at my disposal, and ideas. So I worked, alone and uncommunicative because you know how easily any fool can disrupt such delicate spells. By June this year, I had my new instrument built, rebuilt, and calibrated against the Ankh, the Tetragrammaton, and the Pentacle Reversed. Obviously, it'd require tinkering to get the kobolds out. On the full moon nearest the equinox, I took it into the desert for some preliminary tests."

Will stopped. His pipe smoked like Siegfried's funeral pyre. Ginny gauged when he had mustered strength to continue. "What exactly happened?" she asked low.

He sighed once more. "I don't know. Maybe a, uh, a blob of undigested mustard, or whatever Scrooge said Marley's ghost might be. It wasn't like that first time—" His voice broke. "You know, Virginia. It wasn't like that at all."

"Tell us, though," his sister prompted softly. "You need to."

"I can't very well, because I don't understand it. Perhaps—oh, I'd been brooding somewhat over Princess Tamako of Japan. Who didn't, back at that time?"

Me, for one. I'd thought those several days of global grief and display were mainly hysteria. True, so violent an end to so stormy and embittered a life was tragic; but tragedy happens somewhere along the line to all of us.

Will hauled himself back to the subject. "In any case, I did my early observations, then got into my sleeping bag for a nap before resuming toward moonset. The moonlight lay like ice over the sage and sand and rock; the stars seemed oddly cold and strange, far away— Never mind. I drowsed off. Into nightmares. I must have threshed and struggled, because when I finally lurched back to consciousness, I'd rolled clear off my air mattress. I wasn't in fit shape to carry on; tried, but kept fumbling, making gross errors. And since then, this past couple of months, well, nothing has gone right for me in my research. I can't get up any energy, I can't come up with any ideas, I klutz up every experiment or observation I attempt—"

He shrugged. "The doctor thinks it's depression, and wrote me a prescription. It hasn't helped. The Singer said it might be a curse or some other malign influence, and tried Enemy Way, but that didn't help either, so now he's baffled too."

"Beauty Way would have to wait for winter," Ginny said. "Too long, and maybe just as futile." She narrowed her eyes. "Do you recall those nightmares?"

"Not well. Terrible, hostile shapes and . . . and Chinese writing that crawled like nests of snakes. . . . But the, the thing that came at me screamed in a different language. It was like a woman, sort of, in a wide-sleeved robe, her hair blowing wild, her mouth stretched open and full of teeth—" Will shuddered. "That's about all. Hosteen Yazzie could make nothing of it."

"Maybe not quite his department. . . . Okay, what about last night?"

Will frowned. I could well-nigh feel how he picked his way through a minefield of confusion and of terrors he was trying to deny. "I told you, I'd felt wretched the whole day. Finally I crept into bed and fell asleep.

Fever dreams? I can't say. But they went on and on and on, and the same grisly woman was in them. Somehow she . . . rode me, like a horse—"

I tried to show I had some knowledge too by asking, "The way a Haitian obeah rides a worshipper?"

"No, no," Ginny said, "that's possession, not being literally saddled. And the obeah means well."

"My metaphor wasn't right anyhow," Will continued. "And as for worship, no, this wasn't benign or ecstatic or anything. It was grave-cold, and as if a wind blew and blew while I stumbled along under her lash— It becomes a kind of jagged blur."

He straightened. His tone steadied. "Enough. I do *not* feel sorry for myself. If enemy influences were on the loose last night, as they obviously were, it's no wonder they troubled me. I am associated with the project."

"In a very basic way," I murmured.

"But you suspect the involvement goes deeper than that," Ginny said.

"Well," he replied, "when at last I woke, got out of bed, went to the bathroom—besides feeling beaten down, I noticed dust on my feet. And, when I squinted closer, traces of it in the rug. I'm not that sloppy a housekeeper, Virginia. True, I'd flitted out to the desert yesterday afternoon and taken a walk in hopes of making my blood circulate better. Probably, as miserable as I was, I didn't notice what I brought back. But— Well, I simply don't know. Since we did have a disaster, I thought I'd give you what information I have. It may well be totally worthless."

"Don't you scientists say there's no such thing as too much data?" She smiled the best way she could under the circumstances. "You did completely right to bring this forward. The clues we have are so slight—"

The phone interrupted. "A confidential call for Dr. Matuchek from a person known to her," it announced.

"Oh, damn. Excuse me." Ginny got up and went to its corner. Naturally, she kept the scryer blank and held the audio disc to her ear. Will and I weren't nosy, but the matter seemed to be for her only. We sat where we were, unable to think of anything conversational.

I heard: "Yes. . . . Really? You're okay otherwise? . . . I understand, dear, believe me, I do. . . . The pestilential press, camped everywhere around your house. . . . Here's how we'll work it. You come out, telling them, 'No comment.' Of course they'll trail you, but . . . You know the Sipapu Saloon on Shoshone Street? . . . Okay. Get a taxi there. Arrive about, oh, 12:15. Order a beer or whatever, take a few sips, and go to the ladies' room. I don't expect even a female reporter will be prepared to follow you. I'll be waiting inside with Tarnkappen for both of us. We'll slip out and come here, where I should be able to take care of the problem. Afterward we'll call another cab to take you home. . . . Glad to help.

Gives me a feeling of accomplishment, in this general mess. . . . Okay, quarter past twelve in the Sipapu."

She disempathed and turned to us. "Sorry, guys, I'll have to abandon you for a bit," she said, "and trust you not to be curious or gossipy about the one who comes back with me. Now I'd better get my apparatus together."

Edgar flapped from her chair to her shoulder. She left the room. Soon she left the house. Svartalf dozed, Valeria sulked, Ben and Chryssa were occupied downstairs. I sat alone with my troubled kinsman.

5

THE SILENCE DRAGGED ON "HEY,"I SAID AFTER A MINUTE, "HOW ABOUT I BUILD US A pot of coffee? Uh, no, you prefer China tea, don't you? We've got the Lapsang Soochong you like so much."

"Thank you. That would indeed go well." He trailed me into the kitchen. His wonted, sometimes professorish humor flickered. "I'll have done best, unlike Keats, if I've 'stayed upon the green shore, and piped a silly pipe, and took tea and comfortable advice.' "

I had no idea where he found that quote, and didn't inquire. I'm a small-town boy whom a Hollywood talent scout brought to roles in such things as *The Call of the Wild* and *Silver Chief*, till the Caliph's War hit us and the Army had other uses for my talents. Afterward I studied engineering on my GI Bill, and then worked directly for Nornwell in the Midwest, and now indirectly here in the Southwest. I suppose the things that happened to me along the way made me a bit more thoughtful than would otherwise have been the case, though my wife's influence may well have been stronger toward that. Certainly she led me to read a lot of books, history and world literature and such. But I still liked coming back to my parents' home for Thanksgiving, along with the rest of the clan, and swapping small-town small talk. Ginny was always gracious and charming there, and always denied to me that she was bored like a naval gun. I kept my suspicions to myself and loved her for them.

Undeniably, the Graylocks of Stony Brook, New York had a more intellectual tradition than the Matucheks of Watsonville, California.

We entered the kitchen. "I wish this were mine," Will remarked. He occupied a little house in the older part of Gallup, adequate for a single man, aside from books overflowing it, but limited in facilities. Since he enjoyed cooking and was good at it, he'd come here several times to make dinner for the bunch of us.

His words showed me how perturbed he was, because he'd spoken them before and self-repetition wasn't a habit of his. Looking around the broad expanse of Spanish tile, polished enamel, and timber beams, I groped for something consoling or distracting to say. "Yeah, it's nice. But, you know, I kind of miss the brownie back in our old digs."

"You told me he made mischief," Will said, likewise trying to keep the tone light.

"Not much, and mainly with provocation, like before we broke Svartalf of chasing him. Sometimes he'd play with Val, and later Ben, when they were little. They were the envy of other kids whose house didn't harbor any such Being. I'm sorry Chryssa won't have the experience. Now and then, here, I start to put out a bowl of milk for the brownie before turning in, and bring myself up short."

Will smiled. "Ah, yes, I remember ours on Long Island. But don't the Indians have Good Folk?"

"Not that I've heard of. Bad Folk, yes. Ginny can tell you more. In this regard, the Europeans are lucky."

I've heard of schemes to import Little People. Lord knows they're plentiful overseas. Trouble is, hardly any are interested. Our American fays, leprechauns, nisser, domovoi, and whatnot mostly came over early in this century, shortly after the Awakening. It was a bewildering new world to them, and if a human family to which one had attached himself or herself decided to try their luck overseas, often the Being tagged along. Meanwhile, though, the majority adapted to present-day conditions in their old countries. Many of the dwarves, for instance, began making a good thing of the industrial age.

Similarly for half-world animals, or more so. The useful types such as unicorns are everywhere, of course, but what you may encounter in the Canadian woods will be a wendigo, not a leshy; the few surviving firedrakes are now banned from military use—never very practical anyway—and safely in European zoos; et cetera.

I realized I'd fallen into my bad habit of mentally rehashing the obvious. To avoid thinking about the immediate and unobvious? I got busy with pot, kettle, and canister. Behind me, I heard Will's voice bleaken: "Well, yes, the wee folk are generally cute. But not everything is that Awoke, by a long shot."

Was he remembering his and Ginny's brilliant, prosperous parents, killed on vacation abroad when a griffin, newly aroused, ravenous, and surely confused, flew up from a Balkan peak and tangled with their broomstick? I didn't know how to respond to so old a grief. But it became clear he had wider concerns on his mind: "Oh, the ferocious creatures weren't ever that much of a problem, and we put them in their place fast, the same as we'd done with tigers and wolves." Somberness stumbled over embarrassment. "Er, no offense, Steve. You know what I mean. However, malevolent intelligences—including humans, now that they have their ancient powers back—"

I set the water over the fire and turned around. Clearly, I thought, his nightmare was haunting him. It shouldn't, not a sensible, easygoing guy like this. To be sure, if he believed there might be some connection to the disaster at the Point, that would reinforce the bad feeling; and he had already spent a couple of months in the dumps.

Maybe some common sense would brighten his mood. "Look," I said, "we know the Adversary's active in every universe, or at least in every one where fallen humans live. If these days his agents, demons and such, can operate more openly than they were able to for a long time, why, then we're better able to spot them at it and outwit them. Not to mention the technologies we can bring to bear, everything from exorcism to clean thaumaturgics. As for human baddies, yeah, they've gained some capabilities they didn't used to have, but they don't have others they might have gotten. For instance, suppose those Tibetan prayer wheels turning to keep nuclear weapons from ever becoming functional—suppose they didn't work."

"Um-m, yes," he conceded.

"And what about science and industry?" I pursued. "Where'd your career have been without goetics?"

"Oh, I could have become an astronomer nevertheless." He hesitated. "But maybe I wouldn't have."

That puzzled me a mite. As far as I knew, his fascination with the heavens was lifelong. He married fairly late on account of it, and when his wife died childless he never seemed to consider remarrying, though he kept an appreciative eye for pretty women. His research claimed too much of him. He took out parental urges in being Uncle Will to our kids.

Or so I'd supposed. I'd begun to wonder some.

I didn't want to pry, but I did hope to jockey him into a better frame of mind. "And what about Ginny? Granted, she'd've gone far in any universe that didn't kill her outright, but I don't see how she could've had the meteoric career she did if witchcraft hadn't been available."

Meteoric indeed. After they were orphaned, he hired lawyers to pull wires and get him custody of her. Studying at Harvard, though, he couldn't do much more than put her in the best available boarding school. Driven by loneliness as well as creativity and ambition, she sailed through it and through college, taking her magistra's at age sixteen. Weary of academe, she had him pull more legal wires and went to work the next year for a New York advertising agency, mostly handling elementals and other paranormals in displays. The war interrupted. It determined her to become independent. Therefore, after the war, she went back to school and got her Ph.D. Marriage and kids interrupted, but I wonder how many long-established pros could have survived our raid into Hell, let alone come home victorious. Now she was herself established, solving all sorts of problems for people, her fees each year totalling more than my salary. I didn't care, I gloried. She said once, with a laugh, that male wolves have no doubts about their masculinity.

"Quite a girl," Will agreed. "If any devils cross her path, God help them."

He didn't attempt more jokes. Still, I'd lifted his spirits enough that he at least turned philosophical. "Yes, critical points," he mused. "I've often speculated. What if James Watt, say, had never lived? And there are countless Earths where he didn't."

The kettle whistled and puffed. I filled the teapot. "By then the Industrial Revolution was inevitable—under way, in fact, with primitive steam engines pumping water out of mines," said the engineer part of me. "Carnot's work on thermodynamics and Maxwell's analysis of how a governor operates made the really big difference. Though you also have to count in Faraday and Kelvin and Herz and . . . a long list."

"But you know history branches and rebranches, a quasi-infinity of coexisting, equally real universes. You've been in another one yourself."

I grimaced. "The Low Continuum isn't the same thing. The geometry, the very laws of what passes for nature, they're different from ours." Ugly. Evil.

"Yes, right; I misspoke myself. What I'm thinking of are worlds that are *almost* like this."

"Which Ginny thinks is the reason we've not been able to make contact with any. The differences are too subtle." I'd been involved in such an effort. Waste of time. We never got an answer to the telepathic messages we tried to send. Well, maybe nobody who received them could figure out how to respond.

The teapot was heated. I emptied it, put in the leaves, and added fresh boiling water.

"I've tried to imagine what they could be like," Will said.

"Lots of people have." I should encourage him to talk. "What have you thought about particularly?"

"Oh, suppose—and there must be worlds where it went this way—suppose Einstein and Planck did not get together in 1901. They could have tried to explain the paradoxical findings of late nineteenth-century physics separately. Instead of rheatics, we might have gotten distinct theories of relativity and quantum mechanics, hard to reconcile. Or suppose Moseley, a few years later, had not applied the new equations in his laboratory, had not discovered he could degauss the effects of cold iron and release the goetic forces— We'd have a world dominated by fossil fuels and electricity. The railroads might run the same as here, but personal transportation would be mostly horseless carriages and air travel by dirigibles."

"And you'd have been analyzing spectra, not specters."

"If I went into astronomy at all," he muttered. Quickly, louder: "I doubt anything would have been alive on the moon to detect. What was left of paranature would have stayed Asleep, hidden away. And witches and warlocks wouldn't be respected professionals, they'd be cranks and charlatans."

"And the biologists would be trying to figure out what a certain part of the DNA of people like me was for. Yeah." I took down a tray and set pot, cups, saucers, and a plate of almond cookies on it. He drank his tea Chinese style, no milk or sugar, even when it wasn't Chinese.

"The political, historical consequences are still more interesting to wonder about," Will said. "I guess by 1900 a general European war was inevitable, but the course it took, and what came afterward—"

"Hm, yes." I hadn't ever considered this much, and found myself intrigued. "Like, on our time line, suddenly those folk who'd maintained some tradition of, uh, magic it was called—suddenly it was really working. They had a head start, in the practical if not the theoretical areas. Africans, Australians, our own Indians, especially hereabouts—something to bargain with and wangle a better deal from the white man— It's one of those things I've always kind of taken for granted. Might have been very different." I picked up the tray. "C'mon, let's shift."

We moved back to the living room. I poured; we sipped and got into a bull session we both enjoyed. How good to see Will's heart returning to him.

Ginny interrupted when she opened the door. He and I rose to our feet, for another woman was with her: Curtice Newton.

She looked fine. No doubt her head was bandaged, but she covered that with a turban. She went straight over to me and took my hand in both hers. "I haven't had a chance to thank you properly for saving my life, Steve," she said in her direct fashion, "and never will be able to. But thank you."

"Aw, nothing heroic, not for the likes of me," I answered. "Mighty glad to've been of help."

I'd always felt a tad awkward with her—a big, comely woman, red-haired like Ginny though she kept hers bobbed short. Probably all I'd ever do about spaceflight was some of the engineering, with help from my wife on some of the artificing. Curtice Newton was among those who were going to *go*.

If we could salvage Project Selene—or maybe, just maybe, get somewhere real with Operation Luna—or whatever. If, if, if.

The four of us chatted for a few minutes, politely, carefully. I sensed a certain constraint and was not surprised when Ginny said, "If you two will pardon us, Curtice and I have business. It shouldn't take too long, and afterward we can think about lunch."

They went off to her arcanum. Will and I sat back down. His gaze followed them out of sight. "A dream walking," he breathed; I barely heard.

Oh-ho! "Well, you can try," I said, "but I understand quite a few young bucks have the same idea."

He blinked, then chuckled. "And an excellent idea it is, but not mine. I know my limitations."

He turned solemn again, though not gloomy. I realized he couldn't have rid himself this fast of the darkness in him; but it had retreated to the depths, leaving his normal personality in charge of surface thoughts and emotions. "I meant that Captain Newton can hope to meet, to experience in full, what to me has been . . . a midsummer night's dream," he said low.

"Huh? I call it hard, cutting-edge science, what you've done."

"But the beginning—" I saw him come to a resolution. His eyes met mine straight on. "Steve, I've never told this to anyone but Ginny, under pledge of secrecy. I'd like to share it now with you. Whatever the present trouble is, we seem to be in it together, and your knowing may conceivably make a difference. Besides, you . . . you're a fine fellow. My sister could not have done better."

"Oh, hey, sure she could have," I mumbled, blushing. "I was lucky, that's all. But if you want to tell me something private, I promise it'll stay private unless and until you release me."

He nodded. "I knew you'd say that, and say it truly." After a pause: "You may speak of it if, somehow, dire necessity requires, or in case of my death or permanent disability. This isn't a thing I'm ashamed of. On the contrary. It was . . . intimate, in a way nothing else has ever since been for me. It shaped my whole life. That alone makes it hard to talk about. And it was indescribable. By anybody. I'm no poet. But I don't believe Sappho or Shakespeare could have found words for it."

"Well, I've never seen a good description of lycanthropy, what it actually feels like, even by two or three fine writers who've been there. Why don't you give me the dry facts and let my imagination do what it can?"

He leaned back in his chair, crossed his legs, bridged his fingers, and spoke very quietly.

"I was fifteen years old. Interested in astronomy, yes, but equally interested in baseball, sailing, handicrafts, travel, literature—in spite of what the English teachers did to it—and still more in girls. You may remember we lived on the outskirts of Stony Brook. One summer evening a full eclipse of the moon was due. I thought I'd like to watch it from start to finish, unpestered by hoi polloi. There's no snob like an adolescent with intellectual pretensions. My mother packed me some sandwiches, I put them and my Newtonian telescope on my bicycle luggage rack, and pedaled off into the countryside—a dozen miles or so, to a meadow I knew in the Brookhaven area.

"I arrived after sunset and settled myself in tall grass where daisies glimmered and crickets chirped. Trees stood scattered, with night already underneath them but their crowns faintly aglow. One house was in sight, well away, its windows like stars fallen to earth. The earliest real stars were blinking forth in a sky that slowly went from deep blue to violet. The air lay quiet, cool but with a sort of ghost in it from the day's warmth and green smells. And then the eastern horizon lightened and the full moon rose, huge and pale gold, with marks across it the color of the dusk that had met me before deepening away. . . . I'm not trying for fancy language, Steve. I'm trying to give you an idea of a place that was suddenly no longer just an open spot but—that line from Dunsany—'beyond the fields we know.'

"The eclipse had begun, dimming an edge of the disc. My telescope showed me how sharp-edged the boundary of that shadow was, and somehow this made everything else the more mysterious, but I don't know whether I spent more time peering through the eyepiece or with my own eyes on the vision. I was utterly lost in it. I do remember how I wondered, fleetingly, why that should be—here was a commonplace astronomical phenomenon, right?—but I soon forgot everything other than the night and the moon.

"To this day I'm not sure what brought on the trance, though I can guess. What I can't guess is why it should have come over me, a kid, a prosaic, loutish beast of a boy. Older, wiser, better people must have been watching too, around this whole half of the planet. Why didn't the, the influence touch one of them? Well, maybe I simply happened to be the only human at a site that . . . they . . . wanted to seek out. It was so beautiful, after all."

A small chill tingled through me. I'm an ordinary kind of guy myself, but great Powers once gathered around me, because they foreknew that the future would turn on what my wife and I did or did not survive to do. And Will was her brother. I doubted that what he told me of had been entirely accidental. If nothing else, his latent abilities— I kept silent.

"As the shadow crept onward, I felt more and more taken out of my flesh," he went on. "A strangeness was everywhere around me, in the air, in the earth, in the starlight that strengthened as the moonlight waned, a strangeness wild and sweet, like the happiness I'd felt when a girl I was in love with smiled at me, or like—oh, I can't describe it, except that alongside was also a hint of anxiousness, even fear—

"The eclipse totalled. The moon stood dark, tarnished red, while early dew on the grass caught the glint of stars. And there *they* were, flying, whirling, dancing, through the air, over the ground, come down from the sky to their great mother, who was my mother too, and everybody's—"

Will gasped, the way a man does when memory hits hard. I left him in peace.

Soon he could go on: "I barely saw them, understand. Glimpses, hints, a highlight, a translucency, a tracing of shadow. . . . Think of starlit mists in a mild whirlwind, while somewhere, softly, something sings what could be by Bach or Mozart at their dearest and loveliest. . . . Half-seen, slender female figures, if that wasn't simply the way my imagination was bound to render them. Long, flowing hair, long flowing draperies, wings, maybe, a face that was—oh, elfin or, or I don't know—"

He stopped again. When he hadn't spoken for a minute or two, I ventured, "They sound to me like traditional—you know, medieval—ideas of the Fair Folk. Not the sort that name was a euphemism for, who lived in Elf Hill or a sidhe mound or a dolmen and could bring mortals to grief. No, innocent spirits of the woodlands and waterfalls, who came out after dark to rejoice. I recall a picture I saw as a child, in a fairy tale book—a log laid over a stone, and half a dozen of them playing teeter-totter with a nisse but not weighing enough to counterbalance him. Like airy, free-wandering nymphs, with no power to talk of, but also without sin, maybe a free gift of God to put some extra happiness and beauty into the world."

Will nodded. He grew fairly matter-of-fact: "That's what I've since thought is likeliest. It fits with the folklore I've studied and with what the specterscope has revealed, though as you know, there are nine-and-ninety contending notions about what *that* is. If they were what you and I suspect, then the implications—"

"Look." He leaned forward, his gaze searching mine. "Imagine these harmless, once gladsome Beings as they came Awake when the electro-magnetic inhibition of rheatic forces dwindled to an end. It was to a transformed world, a world of railroads, steamships, machine shops, huge cities, farmlands across hundreds of square miles, glaring lights, wilderness reduced to a few enclaves. Above all, perhaps, a world where the dominant culture was pragmatic, capitalistic, scientific-minded, where goetics was essentially a new set of technologies, where the different kinds of Awakened creatures had to seek and struggle for whatever niches they could find— What might spirits as gentle as these do? Try to become pets, playthings, tourist attractions? Or try for freedom?

"I think they fled to the moon."

The idea that the lunar population consisted of refugees wasn't altogether new to me. It'd been kicked around a little ever since Will reported his first discoveries. However, I hadn't heard it in just this form before. Also, he needed to talk. "Uh-huh," I said.

"Probably they'd always gone to and fro. The folk tales suggest as much. They're ethereal; they can fly on the changeable streams of gravity, of space-time. But if they can't endure direct sunlight, they can only take that route through shadow—that is, during a lunar or solar eclipse. I think they got together and made the great migration, oh, decades ago. They don't mind vacuum. They can take shelter from day, whether by going underground or by flitting around as the moon rotates—and a night there is two weeks long, you know. They can create their own insubstantial, invisible-to-us dwellings, gardens, pools, fountains, shrines. . . . But I think they always long back to their old haunts. Or they have unfinished business here, or contacts they want to keep up, or— Anyhow, whenever they can, some of them return, and stay on Earth till the next opportunity to cross space. One of those visitations came on me."

"And?" I asked after a while, softly.

He shrugged and half smiled. "The eclipse ended, the moon brightened. I was lost in their nearness. Toward dawn they left for woodlands or caves that would hide them from the sun. Perhaps they laid sleep on me, or perhaps I collapsed, exhausted. When I woke and crawled home, hours later, my parents gave me billy hell. I didn't want to talk about what had happened. How could I, really? The folks may or may not have believed the story I cobbled together. They were wise and didn't pursue the matter. But from then on, my course in life was set."

The faerie touch. "Could they have had that in mind when they appeared to you?" I wondered.

"Well, naturally, I've considered the possibility. If they'd spoken directly to me or anyone—assuming they are able to—we'd only have had that person's word for it, soon forgotten. But scientific evidence— Humans were bound to reach the moon someday. Given foreknowledge, maybe they wouldn't ruthlessly set about industrializing it. Maybe, having had time to think, they'd . . . show mercy. . . . I don't know. There's so much I don't know."

Will scowled. His tone harshened. "Except that the specterscope does seem to have begun giving indications of evil already up there. And lately I've had that experience in the desert that I told you about. In the light of what's happened it looked like a perverted version of my first, but merely a horrible dream—until yesterday when the moon flight program crashed—"

The telephone chose this instant to break in, as telephones are apt to. "A confidential call to Mr. and Dr. Matuchek from a person known to them, who claims urgency," it said in its tapioca-bland fashion.

"Rats! Sorry, Will." I went over to the foul thing and snugged the audio close. "Steven Matuchek here."

"Federal Bureau of Investigation," came the mandated identification, followed by a voice I hadn't heard for years. "Steve? This is Bob Shining Knife, calling from Washington."

"Hm? Oh. Hi. How are you?"

"Okay personally, wife and kids too, hope the same for you. Listen, the Bureau's taking over the investigation of what happened last night." No surprise. "When I heard, I remembered you and Ginny are involved."

"Um, we're not what I'd call involved," I said cautiously. "We're just on the scene."

"Considering the Johannine case, I'm not so sure about that. But in any event, Steve, we know each other, and I hope we still like each other. I've a notion you and Ginny—" a brief laugh "—or Ginny and you can be of real help. If you'll, uh, go more by the rule book this time. As soon as I got the news, I put in for assignment. Catching a redeye, arriving in Albuquerque tomorrow, going on to Grants, can I see you two in our office at ten A.M.?"

"I didn't know you had an office there."

"It's been arranged, and personnel are being flown in." He gave me the address.

This was his style, and certainly we could have done a lot worse. Nevertheless— But that could wait. "Why Grants?" I asked automatically. "The Federal Building's here in Gallup."

"Yes, but what with Grants being close to the NASA site, we can operate better. You'll be there?"

"I think so," I said. "Ginny's busy right now. I'll tell her, though, and call you back if we have any problem. By the way, her brother happens to be here, Dr. Graylock, who first discovered Beings on the moon. He may have useful information. Shall we bring him along, if we can?" Not that I meant Will should be pumped for more than he cared to let out.

I'd seldom heard Shining Knife hesitate. "Um-m, well, I think not. We'll want to talk with him, of course, but I've run a quick background check and . . . I don't think he can contribute at this stage."

What the devil?

We exchanged a few politenesses. I disempathed and returned to Will. "Sorry about that" was the best I could say. The mood between us had evaporated. We sipped tea and voiced banalities.

Ginny and Curtice arrived to break the dismal spell. They were radiant. "All done," Ginny told us. "I'll throw together a belated lunch. The kids will be overjoyed at the company."

"Thank you," said the celestonaut. "I hate to decline, especially when you've been so kind already. But could I take a rain check? They badly want me back at the Point, to tell them and tell them and tell them what little I can. It was plenty hard getting leave to go home and rest for a short time."

Will had risen, like me. The liveliness had drained from him; again he seemed gaunt and aged. "And I," he said. "I thank you too, for much more than this invitation, but last night is catching up with me and I'd be a pretty ramshackle skeleton at the feast. What I'd better do is go back home myself, snatch a bite of any old thing, and try for some honest sleep."

Curtice gave him a sharp glance—she'd doubtless heard rumors—but stayed by the decencies and only said, "I s'pose everybody's fairly well outgewashed. Have a thorough nap, Dr. Graylock."

Thus we bade them both good-bye and found ourselves alone. Though a disappointment, it had its advantages. Ginny made sandwiches and took them with some milk down to Ben and Chryssa, who were still absorbed in their own interests. Meanwhile I got out cold stuff, including two beers, for her and me. Val would probably sulk for a couple of hours yet, then descend on the kitchen like a devouring flame.

Ginny and I sat down to our food. Edgar croaked on the back of her chair, Svartalf ambled over and mneowrred. She gave them both their treats. I told her what had passed between Will and me, and about Bob Shining Knife's call. She nodded and said, "All right, we'll do what we can for him." After a moment: "But I'm doubtful what use it'll be. I want to meet with Balawahdiwa as soon as possible."

I figured she must be right about that, and didn't ask for details. Instead: "What was Curtice's problem, anyway? Is it confidential?"

Ginny laughed. "Yes, sort of. But I imagine you can guess, and I know you won't blab, so best you have the truth. They were to take the sanitation spell off her after the mission, of course, and somebody tried, last night at the infirmary. Given the confusion, and maybe whatever curse is lingering, he failed, as she found out this morning. Rather than make a fuss at NASA—poor girl, she has enough henhouse to cope with there as is—she came to me. I fixed her up."

"Oh. Yeah, I would've guessed."

After all, nothing about the life-support systems for spaceflight was supposed to be secret. We'd been exposed to ample, if coy publicity about hygiene in microgravity. A water elemental, a minihydro, was to float around the toilet cubicle and absorb urine. I'd seen the embodiment being reduced to steam. As for solid wastes, a cantrip recovered from ancient Egyptian papyruses was to turn them instantly into stone scarabs, the sale of which as collectibles ought to help the NASA budget.

"She's back to normal?" I said. "Okay, DNQ. You know I'm good at keeping my mouth shut."

"Unless for food or beer or— Well," Ginny murmured, "I trust we can relax now till tomorrow morning, and even manage a smidgen of fun. We have a busy time ahead."

That was the understatement of the year, if not the century.

6

THE TEMPORARY FBI STATION IN GRANTS OCCUPIED SEVERAL ROOMS ON THE GROUND floor of a commercial building in what had once passed for downtown. A window above proclaimed a dentist. The agents flown in crammed the quarters and spilled over the sidewalk. More, I knew from having called my lab, were at Cardinal Point, grilling everybody, peering everywhere after clues, and in general tangling Project Selene up worse than Coyote himself could have hoped to. These here were mostly bound for the field, therefore not wearing their usual business suits. They seemed ill at ease in broad-brimmed hats, open-necked shirts, stiff new Levi's, and stiff new boots—though some had shod themselves in canvas, which I knew they'd regret by day's end. They stood around waiting for their transportation like a tour group. Real tourists who came by gave them quizzical stares. Locals, Indians especially, cast glances sharper and colder.

They weren't stumblebums, understand. They'd simply been thrown overnight into a land and a situation foreign enough to bewilder anybody. I saw a few comfortable in well-worn outfits, faces tanned and creased by the sun that already hammered us. They'd been working hereabouts, out of Gallup, a fairly long time. Plain to see, each would guide a party around some predetermined section of the malpais. Though tenderfeet, the newcomers did have skills and equipment that might spot something significant.

Among them, posed as masterfully as each could manage under the circumstances, were half a dozen really high-powered thaumaturges. Their particular working garbs identified them as such. I saw a white beard spilling down a purple robe embroidered with stars; ostrich plumes, a

necklace of leopard's teeth, and a grass kilt over a black skin; a grand-
motherly type with a ferret peeking from her big apron pocket, who
passed the time knitting a scarf of interlocked Möbius strips; and—yes,
yonder, unmistakable, Bob Shining Knife.

He and another man kept slightly aside. The sight of his tall, rangy
form bright with painted patterns where breechclout or medicine blanket
did not cover him, the craggy features surmounted by a bonnet of eagle
feathers, brought memories of last time to me across the years like a fist.
I caught my breath. Ginny clutched my arm. She too remembered. Then
I glimpsed her smile, followed her look, and half grinned too. Though
practical for this day's work, Bob's desert boots took the edge off the
dramatic effect.

We approached. He blinked at sight of Edgar, big and glossy-black
on Ginny's left shoulder. He controlled his face immediately and trod
forward to give her and me his firm, quick handshake. "Good to see you,"
he said. The tone was as brisk as the gesture. Nevertheless, we knew he
spoke sincerely. It was just that he was so much the honor-duty-country
type. "Been a long while. Thanks for coming." He turned his head.
"Steven and Virginia Matuchek, I'd like you to meet—"

"Gruk," interrupted the raven. He ruffled his feathers in a marked
manner.

"Oh. Your new familiar?" Not wanting a scene, the agent bowed. "I'm
sorry, sir. May I present myself? Robert Shining Knife, Federal Bureau
of Investigation."

"Edgar," croaked Edgar, more or less mollified.

"How is old Svartalf?" Shining Knife inquired.

"Still with us," Ginny replied, "but, yes, old."

Shining Knife gestured to his companion. "Now let me introduce Jack
Moy, of our San Francisco office."

This was a compact young man, whose clothes and bearing suggested
he spent vacations in places like the Sierra and the Mojave. Though the
round face was Chinese, his English was straight Californian. "Glad to
meet you. I've heard a lot about you lately." He seemed amiable. Seemed.

"From the files?" Ginny asked in her most guileless fashion.

"Well, yes, mainly. Your, uh, episode was before my time." Moy whistled. "But what an episode it was."

"I take it you had Mr. Moy look it up when you co-opted him, Bob,"
Ginny said to Shining Knife with the same mildness.

He nodded, imperturbable. "Yes and yes. Let's get started. Okay?"

"Only us four—us five?" I wondered.

"Today, at least." Shining Knife strode off. We could either come
along or stand where we were and waste our sweatiness on the desert air.
Behind us, a bus carpet pulled alongside the curb to take on the first

bunch of agents. Ginny nudged me and inclined her head. I glanced that way. A pair of teenage boys—Navajo, I guessed—lounged against a wall across the street. They snickered to one another and sneered, obviously at Shining Knife. If he noticed, he ignored them.

Our destination was the parking lot of the large new Flying Horse Broomotel. He led us to a rugged twin-sprite four-seat carpet with an outsize coffer at the rear. The Landlouper's well-worn condition and New Mexico license plates showed that it doubtless belonged to the Gallup office and he'd wangled or commandeered use of it.

"Where are we bound, anyway?" I asked.

"I hope you can tell us," he answered. "We'll talk as we go."

He took the key from somewhere inside his breechclout—the gourd shoved there rattled—and made the sign that released the warder charm too deftly for me to follow. I suspect Ginny did. We boarded. Taking the driver's seat, he spelled a windfield around us and a cloudlet overhead for shade. Ginny sat beside him, Moy and I behind. Edgar hopped off her and perched ahead, one foot clasping either of the two power control globes. They flushed angry red for a moment, but regained proper crystal clarity. Shining Knife gestured. The rug lifted and wove its way south through traffic.

The town fell away beneath us. From above, you could practically read its history. It had been a thin sprawl around a railway depot till Project Selene settled nearby. The resulting inburst of people and associated industries filled every vacant space and continued the sprawl farther. It was now bigger than Gallup, without having gained any of Gallup's charm. Mount Taylor loomed in the distance like a rampart that might someday, somehow stop the onrushing tide of losangelesation.

"For a guy who's barely arrived, you sure swing mucho weight, Bob," I said. "Are you in charge of the case?"

"Oh, no." He barked a laugh. "God forbid! I report directly to Mrs. Gutierrez Padilla in Albuquerque. But what with past experience—not only with you two—I've gotten a roving commission. I can act fairly independently.

"Carry on," he ordered the sprites. They obeyed, though they clearly didn't appreciate a bird on their balls. He looked first at Ginny, then me. "The fact that you're here, and we've been involved before, helped decide that."

Tactful of him to use a neutral word, "involved." Last time around, Ginny and I hadn't exactly—what you might call—cooperated with the government. However, we didn't—exactly—oppose it either. Let's say that it and we had the same general objectives, but didn't see eye to eye on policy or procedure.

"May I ask why you've brought Mr. Moy in, evidently carrying a similar status?" Ginny inserted, tigress polite. "Amazing, how fast you've both moved." A touch of lightness: "A vigil spell, or gallons of coffee?"

"As for me," Moy said in candid California style, "I majored in Asian history, with an idea of going into the Foreign Service. When I got more interested in detective work, I went back to school, concentrating on Far Eastern talismanics and geomancy." The FBI requires every agent to have a degree in either sorcery or accounting.

"We've reason to suspect Asian complicity," Shining Knife added. "Jack came straightaway to my mind, and I called him."

Moy frowned. "Hey, easy, there. If you please, Mr. and Mrs. Matuchek, this is mighty delicate stuff. A false accusation, or a true one if it's not handled right, could upset a lot of applecarts."

"Such as those pushed by gentlemen in striped pants," Ginny said tartly.

She followed the news closer than I did, but I got her drift. The Chinese Revolution, the new Soong Dynasty a figurehead for a Taoist junta, the ruthless drives not only to put down the last bandits and warlords but to purge the country of alien influences, regain lost territories, make China once again a world power— They weren't necessarily pushing cookies in our State Department; over there, they were treading on eggshells. The situation wasn't just explosive, it was as scrambled as my metaphors.

Ginny acknowledged the fact. "All right, we'll stay discreet. But if we're to be of any service, we'll need to know what the reasons are for your suspicions."

"And for openers," I said, "the reasons for your bringing us in. Look, we're as surprised and ignorant as anybody. All I've ever done at the Point is communications R and D, straightforward scryotronics. And Ginny's an independent witch. We've consulted her a few times, but on strictly technical problems."

For instance, an experimental relay satellite that suddenly changed test messages into Breton obscenities. It turned out that when the bronze parrot was cast, the contractor had used an old, broken church bell from Quimper. That was no bad idea, lingering sanctity of St. Corentin and so forth, but the thaumaturgic tests were sloppily done and nobody spotted a korrigan trapped in the metal. Cosmic rays broke down the quantum-resonance charm that bound it, and naturally it cut loose. Having identified the trouble, Ginny recalled the Being to Earth and set it happily free in the Forest of Broceliande.

"I've a hunch you don't simply happen to be on the spot," Shining Knife replied. He kept his gaze forward. City was giving way to sage, gray-blue under the sun and the depths of heaven. The air whispered hot around our passage. Its dryness made my nostrils tingle. He lifted a hand.

"No offense, friends. I only mean that you may, entirely innocently, tend to be nexuses—uh—nexi?—"

"Nexuses," Ginny told him.

"—when major powers of darkness are afoot. Because you have unusual powers of your own. Though you use them for good, of course."

She tensed. "You don't mean the Adversary in person? Do you?"

"Can't say, at this stage. Most likely, Beings who're on his side but acting by and for themselves. That's plenty bad enough."

She scowled. "Coyote's hostile, no doubt, and not a very nice fellow anytime. But I don't believe we've a right to call him satanic."

"No judgments yet. We've barely begun collecting information. My hope is that you can help us gather more. If nothing else, you have your particular abilities, both of you. You know the territory and the people."

"Not intimately," I warned, "after two years."

"But I've gathered you, Virginia, have made friends among the Indians and learned quite a lot. That alone may make a difference. I know too damn well that the FBI isn't popular on reservations."

"Hereabouts they call you Fibbies," I stated bluntly.

He sighed. "I've heard. Unavoidable, I guess. When we, as federal agents, have to come in on certain crime scenes, we're apt to interfere with the tribal police, who often know better how the matter should be handled. Though I did think that I, being an Indian myself—"

"Sorry, Bob." Ginny patted his hand. Her voice had softened. "Locally, they look on outside Indians the way, oh, a Frenchman might look on a visiting German."

I saw his rueful grin. "And me an Oglala Sioux. Can you mediate?"

"I can try, but the connections I've developed are mainly Zuni." She paused. "Are the Hopi and Navajo shamans being stiff-necked?"

"I've been told they are. Of course, it's early in the game. Still, I've heard that those of them who've been questioned have clammed up."

Her red head nodded. "What did you expect? The shamans made an agreement with NASA. In exchange for various benefits to their people, they'd see to it that Coyote and other Beings they knew about would be kept out of Cardinal Point. Now *something* has broken or wormed past the spells. By implication, at least, they're accused of either incompetence or conspiracy. Not only their pride, but the honor of their tribes is at stake."

"Yes, well, yes, but I should think if they opened up to us—"

"That's more complex than it sounds, as well you know, Robert Shining Knife."

He bit his lip. "Um-m, yeah. Possibly our operatives were kind of hamhanded yesterday. Is that unforgivable? The situation came at them in a rush, out of nowhere. Can you help us make amends?"

Ginny shrugged. "Maybe I can refer you to someone who may be able to." Sharply: "You've something more specific in mind for Steve and me. Otherwise you wouldn't flit us off like this. What do you think we can do that your thaumaturges can't?"

He sighed again. "I'm not too sure. Put us onto a spoor they might not scent?"

"Where? Obviously you've gridded the locality, and each of your teams will go over its assigned square with magnifying glasses and dowsers."

"They could miss traces you and Steve wouldn't. That's why I was anxious to get us in the field ahead of them."

"You're talking about a lot of acreage," I put in. "No way can we cover it all. Where should we head?"

"I hoped you'd have an intuition. As a medicine man myself, I knew from the first this isn't a routine case." Shining Knife's shoulders slumped. "It was worth a try."

"Hold on, man," Moy said. "We haven't provided the Matucheks near enough information. Like, we're asking them to make straw without bricks, right?" To us: "Okay, let me fill you in a little bit, like on the Asian angle."

Ginny twisted around to look straight at him. Edgar peered from the globes. It was easier for me. He leaned back in his seat, making a relaxed, open-handed gesture. "You see," he related, "we know—Military Intelligence and everybody else concerned does—the Chinese are hot to get into space and would dearly love to be first. Prestige, seizing the high ground, et geopolitical cetera. They can't do that unless they stymie our effort, right? Also the Europeans', but it's way behind ours, and as for the Russians, with that huge religious revival of theirs they'll be content to orbit a few ikons. Now, the FBI keeps liaison with Scotland Yard, so we know Fu Ch'ing is currently in England."

"Fu who?" I blurted.

Moy gave me a capitalized Look. "You've never heard of the insidious Dr. Fu Ch'ing?"

Under the cloudlet, against the sun-glare beyond, the bones stood forth in Ginny's abruptly pale face. "I have," she said.

Moy nodded, more calm because he'd dealt with this more. "Sure, you would have, Mrs. Matuchek." To me: "It isn't publicized. The evidence has to stay confidential—protection of sources and so forth. Beside . . . hm-m . . . any journalists who've picked up some hints, either they came to bad ends, quick-like, or they've been smart and kept quiet. He's the top thaumaturge in China, and also its top secret agent."

"Not that he acts under orders," Shining Knife observed. "There are times when he *is* the Chinese government."

The small hairs rose across my body. Wolf, I'd have given a better display. "If he's that big, why isn't he under constant surveillance?" I demanded.

"Impossible," Moy explained. "It was indirectly, through their own spies, that the British Secret Service learned he's come to England. Applying their resources, they might find out where he's headquartered—maybe they have, a time or two—but what use is that? If they tried to raid the place, he'd be gone, taking everything important with him."

"Does the Yard have any idea what his purpose is?" Ginny asked.

"They and the Foreign Office can guess. Make trouble wherever he can. But mainly, insert some bad luck into the European Conference on Activity in Space. It's meeting in London this year, you may know, and has hopes of actually accomplishing something. But meanwhile, we Americans were ready for a major launch—and there Fu Ch'ing is, better connected to us across the Atlantic than across the Pacific. Wouldn't he try to take advantage of that?" Moy shrugged. "It's a thought. One of the many we need to pursue."

"My brother has Chinese connections," Ginny murmured. "Possibly that has sympathetic, sensitizing effects on me—" She stiffened. "Why didn't you invite him along today?"

As seldom before, Shining Knife sounded awkward. "He's a, a scientist, isn't he? Not a practical goeticist. I don't think this is in his area of competence."

Ginny clenched her jaw. "So you say. I thought jargon was beneath you, Robert."

I saw him wounded. He masked it fast.

She relented for the time being. "However, what we want is the truth. All right, after what you two have told us, plus whatever knowledge we two have, I can try."

She stood up on the carpet. The cloudlet hazed her head; stray locks fluttered like flame. She took her wand from her belt pouch and extended it. The star-point at the tip burst into brilliance, even in this light. It lay loosely in her right hand while the green eyes half closed. The raven jumped to her shoulder and spread his wings straight aloft, like pieces of night. When she reached behind her and touched her left fingers to my head, tiny lightnings went through me.

I heard her murmur and sensed her think.

The wand swung about of itself to point southeast. "Go yonder," she said.

7

WE LANDED IN A GAUNT PART OF THE MALPAIS, BEYOND SIGHT OF ANYTHING HUMAN, and got off.

Mostly that great volcanic basin is rather beautiful. Grass, brush, and small evergreen trees cover it more fully than you might expect in so arid a land. Sandstone cliffs, like pale gold, rim it on the east, mesas and ridges on the west, beneath the royally blue sky of high altitude. But Ginny's wand had led us to the edge of a lava outcrop. Black, ropy masses lay tumbled before us, hot and hard; sharp shards waited underfoot for us to stumble on and slash ourselves if we fell. The sun savaged them.

Even here life kept a hold, a thin growth of stuff like saltbush, snakeweed, and bunchgrass, gray spatters of lichen, now and then a tiny flower. However, this was not a friendly place.

"I think you'd better go wolf, Steve," Ginny said into the quietness. "We'll need every capability we have."

"Yeah." Having expected that, I'd prepared. I went to the rear of the rug. The G-men had opened the coffer and were taking out their apparatus. "If you'll make room for me, I'll transform," I offered. "Provide you a better nose, if nothing else."

"Uh, won't the ultraviolet be dangerous for you?" asked Moy as he buttered sunblock over his exposed skin.

Evidently he wasn't too familiar with the subject. Nobody can know everything. "Not in itself, except for inhibiting the change in either direction," I said. "In my movie days, we often shot a scene under pretty fierce edisons." To make conversation while they emptied the coffer: "The reason werecritters were traditionally believed to be nightgangers was that in nature only a full or nearly full moon gives the combination of polarizations, strong enough, necessary to trigger the hormones and such. Getting caught in animal shape by dawn could mean you were in big trouble. You might have to do desperate things, trying to stay alive through the month. It helped give our kind a bad name—which, in turn, helped sour their dispositions and make outlawry look not so bad."

"Ah, yes, it comes back to me now. The Bureau does employ a few therianthropes, you know." A few; we tend not to be organization persons, what with the wild instincts latent in us. "I never chanced to meet any till you, Mr. Matuchek, either professionally or socially." Moy smiled. "At least, that I'm aware of."

I nodded. "We're fairly scarce to start with. And there isn't a lot of demand for the ability anymore. Trite in show biz. These days Incantational Light and Technics can provide way fancier special effects. We do some police work, as you say; some military; and the Park Service would like to have more of us as rangers than it's got, but the pay's lousy. So, often, to avoid prejudice or cranks or inane questions, weres keep their nature to themselves and only change privately, for fun."

"They have semi-secret social groups," Shining Knife said. "*Not* the Lions, Elks, or Moose."

"It's hardly a Chinese thing at all," Moy observed. "Last I heard, the scientists hadn't agreed yet on how much that's due to culture, how much to genetics. Genetics mostly is my personal guess, because Japan's different."

I registered my surprise. "But aren't the Japanese and Chinese people close kin?"

"Not really. The distant ancestors of the Japanese came mainly from Southeast Asia. I'm told that weretigers are well-known down there."

I'd tangled with one once, Near Eastern. "Notorious, but rare. A man's got to be monstrous tall and heavy to have the mass of a respectable tiger. Wereleopards, now, or weredeer—" My mind wandered irresponsibly off to a silly old college song, tune of "Auld Lang Syne."

We're deer because weredeer because we're dear—

"Okay, Steve, the space is yours," Shining Knife said. Sweat blotted his blanket and shimmered across the thunderbirds, solar discs, and whatnot else painted on his body. I was pleased to see that among the objects removed were a cooler and four thermoses, plainly containing lunch. No doubt the bottles were full of lemonade or iced tea, but I imagined a few cans of beer in the box.

I took off my boots and clothes, down to the knitsuit underneath. Tossing them at a seat, I climbed into the coffer. Shining Knife closed the lid. Cramped in darkness, I fumbled after the Polaroid projector hung on my breast, aimed it, and thumbed the switch.

Transformation roiled me.

Wolf, I rapped with a paw. Shining Knife let me out. I sprang forth. Unshod, I felt the harshness of the terrain; but though I was a timber wolf, not a coyote, my pads were tough as leather. The heat was harder to take. Only my feet and black nose could sweat. I lolled my tongue. The steamoff from it sent a measure of—no proper human word available—relief down to the end of my abbreviated tail. The glare hurt worse. My eyes were nearsighted but sensitive. Ginny hurried over with a pair of dark glasses from her pouch and slipped them onto my muzzle. They were prescription, too; I saw almost as well as before.

This meant less than you might suppose. The dimwitted human aspect of me appreciated it, but I was largely lupine, my brain attuned to scents, sounds, breezelets that stirred the fine hairs in my ears and ghosted along my pelt, the *taste* of that air— Again, I haven't words. No language does. A lizard scuttered between stalks of grass. My nose told me how cool-sweet its flesh would be and I resisted the temptation to snap it up like a canapé off a tray. Somewhere nearby a rattlesnake lay coiled in the shade of a rock, a thicker, sharper smell: *touch me not.* The sun baked fragrances out of weeds and a faint memory of ancient brimstone out of the lava. . . .

"All set?" Shining Knife called. "Let's get going."

I don't remember the next few hours very clearly. As said, while in some ways I was smarter and more aware than ever in human shape, I didn't have my normal IQ by a long shot. Besides, I never was a warlock. I knew the everyday cantrips and such, plus those needed for my engineering work, plus oddments acquired here and there, but the Art of my companions went leagues beyond that, and on three separate roads.

Ginny, her own glasses on her like a mask, set Edgar aflight as she might have loosed a hawk. The wand quivered in her grasp, seeking to and fro; the star-point now blazed, now dimmed to a coal; she uttered words in tongues unknown to me.

Shining Knife danced. The eagle bonnet shivered, the blanket tossed, as if borne on unfelt winds. His voice keened high. The gourd rattled in his hand. Sometimes he'd pause and stride across yards of desolation, to hunker down and peer, take a pinch of soil and sniff, ponder on what he had found. And sometimes he'd sit cross-legged, stare straight out over immensity, lose himself altogether from us.

Moy walked around slowly, also often stopping. In his left hand, supported on the arm, he carried a clipboard holding several sheets of paper. Some were covered with Chinese characters, some were blank. A container at the top held small implements. He'd take sightings with compass, goniometer, and plumb bob. He'd consult his texts. With a calligraphic fountain brush he'd make notes, which included vivid sketches of the scenery. Other writings were calculations or spells.

Me, I coursed to and fro, snuffing the earth and the air, hunting for spoor. Beetles, ground squirrel scat, packrat burrow, stray feather, forsaken bone. . . . For a while a stand of rabbitbrush threw me off. Its smell has been variously compared to dog piss and to a blend of thyme and skunk. Pretty overwhelming.

I worked my way around it and happened to come on the first clue.

But that was when I saw Edgar descend for a close peek. Nor would either of us have found anything if the party as a whole hadn't charmed—intuited, reasoned, made—progress forward in the right general direction.

Traces, weathered but too strong to be quite gone, a reek that raised the lips off my fangs and my muzzle on high. . . . The howl rang lonesome through the noonday silence.

The others joined me as fast as the terrain allowed. I vaguely followed their excited voices: "—demonic. . . . Nothing I've ever met before. . . . Or I, unless— Mr. Moy? . . . Let me examine this more closely. If Mr. Matuchek will please outline the scented area—" My nose scuffed the dirt and got dust up it. I sneezed. That was okay; it blew out the odor.

"Shen—I think," Moy said low. "Could be something else—not clear enough to tell—but, yes, the geomantic alignment—"

We pressed our search harder. The trail, dim, repeatedly lost and regained, led toward unseen Cardinal Point. Once I heard Moy mutter, "Possibly accompanied by some kind of o-bake," and didn't understand.

What I did know, when I came on it, was the remnant of a big fat male stench not unlike what I might have left, except for overtones that made my tail-stump try to tuck itself between my hind legs. I mastered the fear but didn't quite dare make a noise. Instead, I lolloped back and tugged at Ginny's jeans.

She and the agents squatted to exercise their particular Gifts. Edgar flapped to perch on her shoulder and croak in her ear. She nodded grimly.

"Out of my department, I'm afraid," Moy said after a few minutes.

"In mine, I think," Shining Knife answered. "We've had word on the Plains—" He glanced at Ginny. "Coyote, right?"

"Yes, I'm sure." Her tone was flat. "He met the other or the others, whoever or whatever they were—he met them here. But first, in his insolent fashion, he signed the territory."

To me, at the moment, that seemed a fairly natural thing to do.

"Rendezvous arranged by Fu Ch'ing?" Shining Knife wondered.

"I can't say," Moy replied. "Let's push on."

We did. The dome of the VAB at the Point hove above the horizon, wavery in heat-shimmers. We glimpsed distance-dwarfed figures scrambling about, FBI personnel. Probably we were near the end of our own usefulness.

No. Shining Knife spotted the last indications we found—crushed stems, scuffed soil—and pointed me at them. Human smells barely lingered. A few feet away, Coyote's and his cronies' drowned them. However, the physical marks were plain. I heard Shining Knife interpret them: "Somebody landed a broomstick, and walked around in company with the Beings. A man, not a woman, to judge from the footprints, blurry though they are. Steve, do you by any chance recognize a scent?"

I shook my long head. After two days in this weather, what individually identifiable mortal odor could remain? Inwardly, I shivered, and I choked off a growl. A hint, a tinge? No. Impossible. Besides, we canines don't rat on our friends.

Our party searched a bit more but found little or nothing. Also, by then we were exhausted and starved, and had emptied our canteens. We trudged back to the carpet. Edgar flew, and sat there when we arrived. "Lunch!" he demanded hoarsely.

My companions set it out. Meanwhile I crawled into the coffer and rechanged. That takes practice when you're an animal. The confined space didn't make it easier. First I squirmed around to lie on my back, so that the flash, hung from its cord, rested flat on me. Holding it down with my right paw, I used my left to press the switch. After that I worked it around, caught it under my jaw, and let it shine over my belly, hind legs, and tail. Not a dignified procedure, but sufficient for transformation.

When I came out, Shining Knife had evoked local HQ on the annular phone and was reporting in Middle Sumerian. It's been reconstructed by tablet animation techniques, but is still obscure enough that hardly anybody knows it—not even thaumaturges wanting yet another exotic language for spellcasting—except in places like MI and the FBI, where they worry about eavesdroppers a lot.

By the time he was finished and I was dressed, the sandwiches, potato salad, and drinks had been set out. No beer, damn it. When he's on the job, Shining Knife is such a Boy Scout. Well, thirsty as I was, iced tea went down fine. We reversed the front seat of the Landlouper and sat face to face under the cloudlet, eating off our laps. Edgar stuck his beak in and nipped as he pleased. He figured he'd earned it.

Being newly human-intelligent, I needed explanations. "What did we actually find?" I asked.

"Plenty," Shining Knife said. "I doubt we could have without your help and Ginny's." The raven's beady eyes ransacked him. "And Edgar's, of course. Before the assigned search teams got this far, nature would have wiped out every helpful sign." Nature, always seeking for balance, blurring tracks to oblivion, evaporating volatiles, annulling memorials and memories. "Your country thanks you." He could say things like that without running for office. I liked him anyway. Too bad we kept clashing.

"As of now," he went on, "the teams have only gotten evidence of Coyote's nearness on the night of the disaster. Probably the, hm, the demons didn't need to approach any closer than we did today. From that distance, they could weaken the guardian spells."

"How?"

"Subtly, so that nothing visibly changed, no alarms went off, no warning was given," Moy said. "Cardinal Point was protected against Western goetics, white, Indian, and paranatural. It was not protected against influences more exotic. Nobody expected attack from that quarter. Also, to this day there's a great deal we don't know about the fine points of Far Eastern thaumaturgics. I'd guess that these Beings opened a way for Coyote to play his tricks."

Yeah, I thought, *real Asian.*

Moy brought me up short: "But I know enough about the subject that I can tell you they couldn't have done this without guidance, information, supplied by someone reasonably familiar with the layout and the goetics. Obviously, I'd say, the man who met them."

Ginny's voice leaped: "You keep saying 'they.' Who or what, besides Coyote, do you mean?"

"I'm sorry, but that's still obscure to me."

"More so to me. I trained at schools like Harvard and Trismegistus, not Berkeley. You mentioned shen, Mr. Moy. As I understand it, those are Chinese Beings, related to the elements but not really as Western ones are. Could you clarify?"

Her intensity spoiled his enjoyment of his ham sandwich. Shining Knife and I tautened likewise.

"Not in any nutshell," Moy said. " 'Shen' in Chinese is about as catch-all a word as 'spirit' is in English or 'daimon' and 'genius' were in Classical civilization. Some shen may, as you put it, be elementals of a sort, but not conjured up by humans the way we conjure up things like Hydros and salamanders. Others may be . . . not exactly ghosts, but a certain part or aspect of a human that stays around after the body dies. If that person is then paid honors and looked to for help for a long time—sort of like a medieval European saint—well, unlike the saint, the spirit's powers will grow. Some at last become very strong." He sighed. "I could spend the rest of the afternoon and not cover the nuances. Try the article in the *Encyclopaedia Sinica.*"

Ginny frowned. "Also unlike a local saint, a shen isn't necessarily benign, am I right?"

"True. Most are, some aren't. It's similar in Japan, with different names. The malignant kind feed on the fear they inspire and the sacrifices people make trying to appease them. They become roughly analogous to Western devils. But it's not a purely spiritual thing. Evil shen can do physical as well as moral harm."

"So can devils," I said, remembering. *Which means, on the plus side, they can be killed.*

"Did the shen all fall Asleep as the Iron Age advanced?" Ginny persisted.

"Apparently, except maybe for isolated localities," Moy answered.

"When finally they Awoke, the evil shen saw what arrears of mischief waited for them. The chaos after the Manchu Dynasty fell gave them a field day. After the Mandate of Heaven came to the Soong, the Taoists, above all, got organized, and have been mounting a campaign to quell them."

"I know that. Who doesn't? Please go on."

"The question hasn't been properly addressed, I think—if the wicked ones escape the mages and priests, where shall they go, what shall they do? We have a few hints. The business on hand provides more."

"M'm. You're guessing, then, that for whatever reason, perhaps inspired by Dr. Fu, they want to sabotage the space program. Somehow they got together with Coyote, who wants the same—"

As Ginny's words trailed off, Shining Knife said, "Yes, they met mainly through the man who joined them that night to see the job got done. A reasonable hypothesis, anyhow."

My belly muscles tightened. I made a mental note that our Operation Luna needed better security, insignificant though it might be.

"You mentioned another kind of Being too, when we were out hunting," Ginny said. "I got indications myself, but couldn't name them. Something—" She hesitated. "—more eerie. Did I hear you use a Japanese word?"

"I don't know a lot about Japanese spirits—kami, o-bake, whatever," Moy admitted. "There are important differences from the Chinese. The oni might correspond to Scandinavian trolls, sort of. But you're aware the Shinto authorities in Japan, same as the Taoists in China, are trying to purge all the shrines of what they call unauthorized Beings. You may not like every current policy of those two governments—I don't myself—but both countries are going to be cleaner."

"And so the . . . demons . . . look for new strongholds? It'd be logical for the Chinese and Japanese ones to make alliance. But you gentlemen think they need the help of humans. What humans?"

"Dr. Fu, maybe," Shining Knife said fast. "But, hey, we've done a good day's work here. Let's finish our meal and scoot back to where we can relax."

Ginny and I swapped a glance. Edgar joined in. We realized our leader didn't want to pursue the topic. We weren't sure why, but knew the matter was settled.

Therefore we soon flew back to Grants, making small talk when we weren't silent. The silences felt companionable. There's nothing like a worthwhile undertaking to forge bonds. Whatever our disagreements, now or in the future, I was glad to have seen Bob Shining Knife again and met Jack Moy.

We shook hands in the parking lot. "I'll be in touch," Shining Knife said, as ambiguously as we knew he must. Ginny, Edgar, and I returned to our broom.

"What do you think about this?" I asked as we flitted.

"I'd rather not, yet," she sighed.

Poor girl, she'd laid out far more effort than me, even if it showed less. I stroked her mane. "Okay, then what's your opinion of a tall, cool drink?"

"Best offer I've had all day." She laughed.

Of course it wasn't that simple. Ben had gone on a campout with the family of his best friend. Val, whom we'd persuaded to look after Chryssa, didn't mope at us. Instead, as agreed beforehand, she took off to meet a giggle of girls her age at a shishkebab parlor.

Well, Ginny and I only meant to throw something together, whatever it might be, when we felt the need. Meanwhile our youngest wanted stories and jokes and love. Svartalf graciously accepted some of the attention.

Thus an hour or more passed before I got around to the mail. Ginny came back from settling the kid down with a Wanda Witch show to hear me mumble, "Uh-oh," not precisely in those words.

"What's gone wrong now?" she asked.

"See for yourself." I handed her the letter.

The heading was federal, Inquisition for Revenue Securement. Operation Luna generally and we specifically were under income tax audit. Since we claimed part of our home costs as office expenses, the examiner wanted to meet us here. Sincerely, et cetera.

"Coincidence?" I speculated. "Or the Enemy at work?"

"I don't know." Ginny's features stood keenly against white walls and sun-yellowed blinds. "Maybe coincidence."

"You'll need time to collect our records, won't you?" God be praised, she took such horrors off my shoulders.

"That's no problem. But—" Her eyes sought mine. "Steve, the more I think about today, the more certain I feel that we must see Balawahdiwa. Soonest. Tomorrow, if possible. While I try to arrange that, suppose you check with Barney Sturlason."

She went out. I got onto the phone. It was past quitting time in the Midwest, but I caught him at the plant.

His image well-nigh filled the scryer. "*Ja*," he rumbled. The blocky, crew-cut gray head wove back and forth, like a lion's when it's set on by a pack of jackals. "They're already infesting Nornwell. I didn't want to worry you about it, especially after the blowup, but— Well, carry on, and don't forget, we keep a pretty good tax diabolist on retainer."

That eased me. Neither Ginny and I nor Nornwell had attempted any kind of fraud. Bloody nuisance, of course, but— I called the local IRS and made an appointment for day after tomorrow. Ginny returned and told me Balawahdiwa would receive us in the morning. I wondered if she'd cast a minor spell to make events mesh this efficiently. She mixed a gin and tonic, I poured a beer, and we retired to the patio, beneath the trellis and its honeysuckle. Best to take what pleasure we could while we could.

8

ZUNI LIES ABOUT THIRTY MILES SOUTH OF GALLUP. WE WENT THERE LEISURELY, START-ing while the day was still cool and skirting the eastern border of the reservation for the sake of the views. First the sunbeams turned the Wingate rock fiery for us. As we swung south, the Zuni Mountains ran along to our left, on the edge of the Continental Divide. In itself that mass wasn't too impressive, mostly a rounded ridge crowned by pines. But time and weather had done their own sorceries at the bases. Even with the sun low behind, the sandstone glowed tawny, red, white, often in bands like the stripes of Old Glory; and shadows brought out the relief of cliffs, crags, crevices, outthrusts and upthrusts, changing moment by moment as the light did, so that it was almost as if that banner rippled in a geological wind.

When we bore west, away from Ramah, we passed over valleys and low mesas begrown with piñon and juniper. Where two summer-dwindled streams flowed together to make the Zuni River, the land wrinkled upward again and we flew above the Gates of Zuni, the notch that the water had cut. Beyond, we found another valley, more broad and open, guarded on three sides by colorful steeps. Conifers and cropland greened it, though sparingly, for here was a parched country. The river always ran small; at this season the bed was nearly dry, though full of reeds.

The pueblo had in the course of time spread to both sides of it. Three miles off, Corn Mountain dominated the southeast, a giant, banded mesa rising sculptured, nearly sheer, to its own forest—Dowa Yalanne, as sacred to the people and central to their history as the Acropolis once was to Athens.

Courtesy, if not law, demanded we come down and fly in at man height above the rutted dirt road from Gallup. That wasn't much altitude. Indians in these parts are mostly short and sturdy. Shining Knife stood forth among them like a Swede in Istanbul. The languages and cultures were about as different too, or more so.

A few dwellers were out tending patches of corns, beans, squash, chilis, peach trees, and occasional sheepfolds. They mostly wore faded denims, sometimes a headband instead of a hat. More often than not, men's hair fell to the shoulders. They used hand tools, and I glimpsed a cart drawn by a burro.

This was choice rather than poverty: a ceremonious, deeply religious folk keeping to their traditions as much as possible. They weren't fanatical about it; fanaticism wasn't in their nature. There were enough brooms, truckrugs, phones, crystals, and other such stuff in the pueblo to serve their modest needs. Their children attended a good school elsewhere on the reservation. They were strict about sanitation, and had modified their ancient healing practices to accommodate medical spells, antibiotics, and I know not what else. In fact, Ginny had told me that clinical practice in the outside world had learned things from them.

Several of the workers saw us go by and waved greetings. Given their history, the Zunis nurse prejudices against Spaniards—who also managed to garble their name, Ashiwi, and throw a tilde on top of the mistaken n—as well as Mexicans and Apaches. However, their relationship these days with the Navajos was fairly cordial, and of course they'd always had fellowship with the Hopis. On the whole, they'd gotten along comparatively well with Americans, ill-treated though they often were till lately. It stirred my heart to hear one man cry, "Hello, there, Dr. Matuchek!" Ginny waved back.

Well, from the beginning of our New Mexico stay she'd taken a special interest in them. Maybe it was happenstance, her meeting Balawahdiwa in Gallup and falling into shop talk. Or maybe, once more, it was something subtler. Anyhow, she'd become popular in the pueblo—her respectful questions, her study of the unique language, her helpfulness with minor problems. And though as a woman she was debarred from some things, I don't suppose her looks did any harm, no matter how foreign.

For a passing moment, my mind going grasshopper, I wondered how the tribe would have fared—did fare—in another history. Say the one that Will had speculated about, where science didn't find rheatics and therefore goetics didn't develop, so that machines more and more dominated technology. Would this road have been paved? Would these plots exist along it, or would there have been a concentration on sheep farming for the market, or what? . . . No matter. We were here and now. But I did get a sense of strength, an idea that the Zuni soul would not easily surrender anywhere or anywhen.

We entered the town—or village, which is just as inaccurate—and landed at a parking site by the church. Lately restored, its simple squareness and the cross on top of a belfry arch loomed above a weed-begrown cemetery and a couple of *hornos*, round clay ovens. The interior was currently being decorated with vivid murals of native religious motifs. Though Catholicism had had considerable influence, the local faith was so firmly rooted that missionary efforts to replace it had, shall I say, petered out.

Otherwise little that was old remained. Homes were mostly one-family, low and small but modern, generally well apart on the dusty ground. There were a couple of stores and cafes. Aside from the mountain, sacred sites weren't in plain view, unless you counted the open areas where ceremonies took place in season. No visitors except us had yet appeared. The dwellers were going about their business, much of it indoors. School hadn't yet begun and children romped around. We'd arrived at a pause in the year's round of dances and other rites.

We picked our way beneath the sun, through the mounting warmth, to Balawahdiwa's house. Maybe because of his status, he'd chosen to renovate one of the surviving earlier buildings. It stood foursquare, dry-laid stone chinked with adobe, ceiling beams projecting below the flat roof. However, the windows were aluminum-framed and the door plywood.

I knocked. His wife admitted us: a stout woman in embroidery-trimmed blue blouse and long, sashed skirt, a necklace of silver, turquoise, and shell across her bosom. *"Keshi,"* she said, and rendered it into uncertain English: "Welcome. Welcome. Please come."

"Thank you, Mrs. Adams," I replied. I never could wrap my tongue around her Indian name.

Ginny managed it, "Waiyautitsa," in the middle of a proper Zuni phrase. We went in.

A fairly spacious room lay beyond, cool, darkish, neatly white-plastered between stone flagging and massive timbers. On the mantel of a fireplace stood a bowl of sacred cornmeal, and beside the hearth an up-to-date pair of thermostatic dolls, Eskimo and African. Elsewhere lamps, a farseer and music runer, a well-filled bookcase, and austere furniture stood on handsome rugs. In one corner an upright loom with a half-finished piece of weaving reminded us that ancientness was still very much alive.

I'd heard from Ginny that beyond the door at the rear lay a regular kitchen and bathroom, plus a pair of cubicles for beds. It was all unpretentious, not what a white man might want if he bore a name famous in the history of his people; but the Zunis didn't go in for personal display.

Balawahdiwa sat alone at the table. His children were long since in households of their own. He drank one of his countless daily mugs of coffee and watched a chessboard. Animated, the pieces fought the game out by themselves. The runer was tootling the Dixieland jazz he also liked.

Aside from a massive signatory ring, he was dressed like a farmer. He still tended the family plot, though he also occasionally made jewelry that fetched good prices.

Mainly, however, he was the chief Priest of the Bow.

He rose for us, signaling the chessmen to truce and the music to silence. "Welcome, Steven and Virginia," he said. "I wish the reason for this visit were luckier, but we are always glad to see you. Sit happy."

Unlike Waiyautitsa's, his English was fluent. When he was a boy, his Deer clan saw the promise in him and pooled its resources for him to attend the state university. When the war reached these parts, he was among the guerrillas who made life miserable for the invaders. Afterward he returned home, to become increasingly a leader in his kiva and in pueblo affairs generally. Those invaders he'd put out of their misery had qualified him for his high religious rank.

Though he stood half a head shorter than me and his hair hung grizzled, his hand clasped mine with at least equal power. The wide, strong-boned face was deeply creased around the mouth but otherwise unwrinkled. The eyes shone like polished obsidian.

His wife gave us coffee, started more brewing, and settled back down at the loom—not self-effacement, simply carrying on what she'd been doing. I'd seen the pattern of what she wove at dances and realized that this would be a ceremonial kilt. *Who might she be making it for?* I wondered.

"The Zunis were sorry to learn of your trouble at Cardinal Point," Balawahdiwa said, "but thankful that nobody came to serious harm."

Ginny spoke in his language. He thought for a second, then turned to me.

"Your lady found a polite way of asking if I wasn't just being polite," he explained. His bit of a smile faded. "In a way, yes. We may as well talk frankly. In fact, we'd better. You probably know I was not among those who blessed the NASA compound against hostile spirits. A couple of men from here joined in. I might have, if I'd known you folks at the time. But my feelings were so mixed I couldn't rightly take part. They still are, to a certain extent."

"Well, uh, some people do think the, the project will violate the, uh, sacredness of the moon," I said clumsily. "That's not the intent. With, with, uh, Beings already living there—"

He nodded. "As Virginia's brother first discovered. Yes, if we establish communion with them, that should be wonderful. Mainly, I've wished the facility were somewhere else. It's pulling in too much that's loud, garish, greedy—" He lifted a palm. "I'm not an enemy of your culture, Steven. All mankind owes it thanks for many gifts, not least the United States

Constitution and Bill of Rights. But nobody's perfect, and this overgrowth doesn't belong here."

No, I thought, *not in the peace of the desert and the harmonies of its dwellers.*

Ginny broke in on my sentimentalism. "Sir, I've said this before and I'll say it again. You're human too. Your ancestors were. The Anasazi had to leave the north, long ago, because they'd wrecked their environment, farming it barren, stripping it for firewood. Wars, witch hunts, raids for loot and slaves, torture, battues to kill more game than could be eaten before it rotted—all went on as enthusiastically in America before the white man arrived as in Europe or Asia or Africa."

Balawahdiwa shrugged. "No argument. But I suppose you see what I mean."

"Yes indeed, and no argument about *that*."

"Some of us hope spaceflight can be done a lot smaller and quieter," I ventured.

Balawahdiwa nodded. "Virginia's told me a little about your . . . Operation Luna, do you call it? How high are those hopes?"

"Not awfully," I admitted.

"This is beside the point," Ginny said. "You never wanted Coyote to run wild over Project Selene, did you?"

"No," Balawahdiwa said, almost too softly to be heard. "It could go to his head."

A giddy head at best, I thought; *but a demigod's.* Sometimes, when the mood hit him or the payoff looked right, he had helped mankind. Oftener he'd snared himself in his own mischief, even gotten killed, though after a while he came back to life. And what had he won, what knowledge had he brought back, from those journeys beyond death? Always he was the Trickster. Tricks can get out of hand. The madcap can turn really vicious.

"And when he attacked, the other night," Ginny said, "it was with the help of foreign Beings."

The priest's features congealed. "I know. They stink of evil."

"You know?" I exclaimed. "How?"

Immediately I saw the question was stupid. He answered as if it were not. "Certain of us went up on Dowa Yalanne and made medicine. I myself scouted around in the malpais. We've learned a few things."

Ginny's fingers gripped the table edge. "I expected you would. That's why I asked to see you."

"To request Zuni help?"

"Before the government clumps in on elephant feet and tries demanding it," I said.

"That would be unwise of the government. Maybe you can warn it off." Balawahdiwa looked searchingly from one to the other of us. "You, my friends, I will give any help I am able. Not that I wish anyone else hurt, either. And, as I agreed, quite aside from projects and careers, we'd damn well better head Coyote off before he goes on a total rampage—if we can. Which we certainly can't with federal agents and bureaucrats and journalists and local pompasses on our backs. Will you drop a hint to the right people?"

"We'll do our best," Ginny promised.

Waiyautitsa came over, refilled our coffee mugs, and returned to her weaving. I wondered more and more about that kilt. Everyone sat mute for a while.

Balawahdiwa's gaze went to Ginny. She met it. The silence lengthened. Clatter and voices outside reached us faintly, as if from far away. The light in the windows waxed, the shadows on the floor contracted.

"You're not appealing on general principles alone, are you?" he murmured at last.

She shook her head. "No," she answered as quietly.

A chill walked my spine.

When the priest spoke again, his matter-of-fact tone came over us like a benediction. "At least we're lucky in the time of year. The big summer Rain Dance is behind us, and there's only minor stuff till the Doll Dance in October. Of course, already before then preparations will be under way in earnest for the Shalako." I'd heard that the Zunis took that midwinter festival as seriously as devout Christians do Easter or Jews Yom Kippur, and worked making ready for it as long and hard as New Orleans krewes do for Mardi Gras. "But I'll be fairly free this next month or two." Since it wasn't like him not to mention others, I guessed that he figured most of the searching and . . . mysteries . . . would necessarily fall to him. As chief Priest of the Bow, he must command lore and powers nobody else did. "Let's start by comparing notes, and let's in the name of all that's holy be frank and honest. Later we can decide what to keep to ourselves."

The session lasted a couple of hours. Part of it went in his language. He and Ginny apologized, but English didn't have the proper words or concepts. Ah, well, when it came to describing what I'd found while wolf, they must be content with statements as bald as a basketball, no real explanation of how I knew what I knew.

In the end, grimly, Balawahdiwa summed up: "Coyote was somehow put in touch with alien Beings who want spaceflight killed, probably more than he does. Or else someone led them to him. I suspect he mainly resents the encroachment on his territory, although he rejoices at a whole new set of challenges and possibilities for havoc. The Beings could temporarily and unnoticed annul the charms that protected Cardinal Point, because those were charms against local spirits and European-tradition evildoers. Your Fibby is probably right about their being Chinese demons—most of them. We Zunis have no information there. But we do seem to know more where it comes to ghosts. Not that we can put a name to that which accompanied the . . . the shen. But the signs were clear to us, and damn scary." His fist clenched on the table. "I've never before winded cold malignancy like that."

I heard the pain in Ginny's voice and reached for her hand. She clasped mine tightly. "And the human who met them?"

"We don't know, any of us," Balawahdiwa replied, gone gentle. "The dreams we dreamt on the mountain say he *could* be someone close to you."

"And the smells I smelled— No!" I shook my head violently. "Too faint, too contaminated. Not to mention the chance of malicious witchcraft, to throw us off the scent."

Ginny locked glances with Balawahdiwa. "Probably I can best look into that angle," she said fast. "What about you, sir?"

"I believe my fellows and I have done everything we can by ourselves," he answered. "I shall have to seek further help elsewhere."

"Where?" she whispered. "From who?"

"Nebayatuma, perhaps. He ranges widely, he sees much, his flute can lure truth off of tongues." Balawahdiwa paused. "Or Water Strider? No, not yet. If ever I dare . . . I'll go out into the desert and seek, Virginia. That's all I can do right now, seek."

"We too." Hand linked to hand around the table.

"Okay." Balawahdiwa mustered a grin. "How about we put our feet up first? Care to stay for lunch?"

I wasn't sure whether lunch at home was a Zuni custom or a friendly idea of his. Ginny declined with thanks. Though she didn't say so, I knew what was too much on her mind. He didn't press us, but sent us off with a hearty good-bye and good wishes.

We took a straight path back toward Gallup. "Let's call on Will," Ginny said.

"What can we tell him?"

"Very little at this stage. Leave it to me. Mainly I want to see him, in the light of what the situation's become, and chat a while, and . . . let him sense he's not been forsaken."

I squeezed her arm. "He never will be, darling."

"You're the sort of guy who would say that, Steve."

"I mean it. Be God damned if I can believe he'd do evil."

"No, he wouldn't." She broke off. I knew when she didn't want to talk. We took what consolation we could from the views around us. Welcome white clouds were sailing out of the west.

Gallup appeared ahead, high above the valley beyond. She was one batwing flyer. Our stick went through traffic like a snake threading a picket fence, and still I felt safe. Will's place was in an oldish, tree-shaded section. We started downward.

Ginny snarled. She veered the Jaguar. I saw what stood parked outside the small house, and added coarse words. Among the brooms was a Landlouper carpet that we recognized.

The FBI was there.

"I guess it's an interview," I said inanely.

"In force like that?" she replied. "I'd say investigation."

"Well, but— Should we go in? Maybe we can give him moral support."

She slumped, ever so slightly. "No. That'd be worse than useless."

We flew on at random. She straightened and turned to me. "Steve," she said, "let's not go home right away. Not till we've put our faces straight for the kids to see."

Ben was still camping, Val again babysitting Chryssa. She'd protested too little, methought, and had accepted our wage offer without dickering. Had something happened, or been said, or whatever, down at the shishkebab parlor yesterday, to drive her back into herself? She'd certainly been glum at breakfast. But what does a father ever know?

"Okay," I agreed. "Are you ready for lunch by now? Someplace with beer."

She managed a smile. "Occasionally, my dear, you're a great man."

We headed for the city center and parked where we could. Being farther from Cardinal Point, Gallup hadn't exploded quite like Grants, but its downtown was badly congested, the sidewalks thronged. Boutiques were taking over from the original businesses. Walking along, we passed one new to us, the Cunning Cactus. Among other kitsch, the window displayed a floor lamp in the shape of a giant saguaro. Besides those upraised arms, it had enormous eyes, a pug nose, and a rosebud mouth open to register surprise. Sometimes I wished the Pueblo revolt of 1680 had succeeded permanently.

We'd decided we wanted an atmosphere loose, easy, even a touch raucous, rather than elegant. Distraction. Probably we didn't hit the same place as our daughter's gang, since this had an on-sale license. Lamb, eggplant, onion, and tomato, pulled off their skewers into pockets of pita bread, were mighty heartening. America has gotten several excellent ideas since the war from the former enemy—though some of the combos you see are pretty weird. Frosty steins of Brockenbräu went better yet.

Unfortunately, not only did a farseer infest the joint, the volume was high. We could have ignored slush serials, fashion parades, and commercials in which the announcers sounded as though they were having orgasms. This, however, happened to be a news commentary, and Serious about the space program.

Congressman Blather declared that our disaster revealed it for the boondoggle it was, consuming tax money that ought to subsidize inefficient Wisconsin dairies, mismanaged New York banks, obsolete Texas oil refineries, foreign tobacco sales, and military bases in his district. Having presidential ambitions, he cast his net wide.

The Reverend Blither did also. Besides his declaration that a landing on the moon would corrupt its pure and innocent natives, as Western civilization had corrupted everything it ever touched, the project flaunted our utter lack of compassion for panhandlers, drug dealers, muggers, burglars, prostitutes, pimps, and, above all, his admirers.

A comedian made much of al-Bunni's having served the Caliphate. "He wants to put horses in the sky. Never mind whose heads the manure lands on." A cartoon showed our chief artificer as a crazed rabbit with ears that stretched to the moon and bounced it between them like a ping-pong ball. The fact that "bunni" means "brown" in Arabic was ignored.

I could go on, but why? "The project seems to be deep in political muck," Ginny said.

"It's often been," I reminded her. "This situation is desperate. Project Selene's got to concentrate on justifying its existence, which means the real work will be stalled indefinitely. NASA may knuckle under and cancel it."

"Operation Luna, then?" she breathed through the noise.

"Maybe. Maybe. Though how we can get over the threshold— Oh, hell, love, let's concentrate on our lunch, shall we?"

"And one another." Her smile was a kind of bugle call.

So, worried and tired but somewhat refreshed, we came home. The house seemed alarmingly quiet. Edgar dozed on his perch. But where was Svartalf? Why wasn't Chryssa racketing around with her usual liveliness? Heading rearward to check, I caught a voice. Relieved but curious, I continued.

Along the way I passed Valeria's room. The door stood open. As always, it showed a total hellhole. At her age, tidiness offers no obvious rewards. She did keep herself clean, and about as neat as an adolescent's peers will allow her to be. And she did make good grades in school, no matter how uppity she got. A real teacher *likes* awkward questions. Maybe inspired by her mother, though we didn't try to force interests on our kids, she'd become fascinated by Southwestern Indian lore. I glimpsed several books on the subject from the public library, on a shelf underneath a tacked-up Bat Man and Mina poster. She was also a great science fiction reader. Svartalf, who commonly shared her bed, sprawled there next to a copy of Lyle Monroe's latest *Magister Lazarus* novel, bought with her own money. *Ah-ha*, I thought, *when she's through with that I'm going to borrow it.*

I found her in Chryssa's room, telling a story. The infant sat enthralled. Apparently this was just beginning, and neither of them had heard us.

"Once upon a time there was a girl called Moldylocks. She had that name because she hated to bathe. It didn't matter to her that she drew flies and her bellybutton was full of moss. When she first saw a copy of Rodin's famous, brooding statue 'The Thinker,' she groaned, 'That poor man, he has to take a bath.'

"One day she went for a walk in the forest. It was a long, long walk, because she wanted to get as far away as possible from any soap. At last she came on a cottage. She didn't know it belonged to Papa Bear, Mama Bear, and Little Bear. Nor did she care. They'd trustingly left the door unlocked. Moldylocks, being Moldylocks, went straight on in.

"She found a table with three chairs around it, and tried each of them. The big-sized chair was upholstered in ankylosaur skin and too knobbly. The middle-sized chair was so soft that she sank into it down to her guzzle and barely escaped with her life. The little-sized chair was just right. Moldylocks planked herself in it hard enough to splinter the cane bottom, but what the hell.

"There were three bowls of porridge on the table. She tried them each. The big bowl was too hot, and besides, it was half full of bourbon. Yuk! Moldylocks preferred single malt Scotch. The middle-sized bowl was fat-free, low-sodium, and totally organic. Yech! The little bowl was just right, and Moldylocks ate it all like a subduction zone eating a continent, only faster—"

I stole back to Ginny. Things were under control. Val was keeping her sister amused, if maybe a trifle bewildered. Still, plain to see and hear, plenty of devilment remained in her. I wondered what way it would strike next.

9

WE CALLED WILL AND INVITED HIM OVER FOR DINNER. HE ACCEPTED EAGERLY, BUT WE were shocked at how haggard he looked when he arrived. "Rough day?" I asked after we'd sat down with drinks.

We'd mentioned knowing the feds had been at his place. He sighed. "Oh, they were polite. But very, very thorough. I wouldn't have believed so many questions were askable about my whereabouts and doings these past several years—as if anyone could remember in that kind of detail— not to mention my Chinese associates and, well, it seemed like nearly everything else. They even went over my poor old broomstick, whisking dust into envelopes."

Ginny scowled. "You shouldn't have permitted that. Nor should you have talked as freely as I'll bet you did."

"Why not?" He sounded surprised. "They're investiagting a major crime."

"You needn't give them a free ride. They didn't bring a warrant, did they? You should have had an attorney on hand."

"Good Lord, why? Paying a fat fee in order to make it seem I've something to hide? I don't!"

Ginny and I exchanged a stare. She shook her head slightly. I nodded agreement and told him, "You never know how things will go when you deal with the government. Which is why no smart person does, more than he absolutely has to. Did they appear, um-m, satisfied?"

"Well, the gentleman in charge thanked me, but said they'd probably want to see me again, and requested me not to leave town."

"Requested," I muttered. "I want a talk of my own, with Shining Knife."

"You didn't plan to go anywhere soon anyway, did you, Will?" said Ginny. I knew she wanted to steer him from the idea that he might be under suspicion. Bad enough how it nagged us.

"Certainly not," replied the astronomer. "I learned from them that as far as they're concerned, the Point can resume work tomorrow. My moon studies—and I must get in touch with colleagues worldwide, to find out what they may have observed— Aren't you going back, Steve?"

"I'd like to, and they want me." I'd been on the phone to my department chief. "How communication systems were affected, or how they might even have been involved— Can't, though. Of all times in the history of the universe, an IRS auditor has chosen this one to come around and harass us."

The girls had sat quietly on the couch, Chryssa absorbed in a picture book, Val listening to the conversation while she sipped a Hepta-Up and stroked her buddy Svartalf. Now the older cried, "I didn't know that, Daddy!"

"No need for you to fret about it." I shrugged. "Like soldiering in wartime, financial management means long periods of boredom broken by moments of stark terror."

"He's joking," Ginny said. "We've nothing to fear except, true, the boredom."

"And the resentment," I added.

"Don't hang around, Val," Ginny went on. "You've accumulated good karma lately. Go enjoy yourself. Wasn't your circle planning a picnic?"

"Yeah. I won't be there." From the girl's tone, suddenly glacial after her cheerful rascality earlier, I could tell that the reminder had swung her mood back hellward. From the red that came and went across the clear face, I could guess she was still boycotting her boyfriend. Maybe he'd come to the shishkebab parlor yesterday evening, tried to mend fences, and clumsied it up. Remembering myself at that age, I felt a certain unwilling sympathy for him.

Ginny and I knew better than to inquire. "I'm sorry to hear that," she said, "but do as you want, go where you choose. Just be back by dinnertime."

"Do you expect the session will be difficult?" Will asked us.

"Well, our finances are rather complicated, you know. Steve's salary arrangement, my business, our investments, and, of course, Operation Luna."

He grunted and puffed hard on his pipe. "I'm involved in that myself." He sounded more anxious than he did about the FBI.

"Sit tight," Ginny advised, "carry on your daily life, and do not babble to anybody before you've consulted me. Let me decide what counsel you may need and see that you get it." She smiled rather bleakly. "Thank God, I am not one of His innocents like you."

I couldn't help wondering: *Like you, Will?* This nice, soft-spoken fellow with his gray beard and drawling humor—

Anger on his behalf, anger at the whole wretched mess, fueled what I already felt. "There will doubtless be a Black Plague's worth of snooping into every corner of our affairs, privacy be damned," I growled, "and tons of paper to find, and hours, days wasted that could have gone into something productive."

"Oh, it shouldn't be that bad," Ginny said. "I knew that someday the goblins would come, and prepared against them."

"Do you mean you understand the US Tax Code?" inquired Will, amazed.

"No, not really. I'm not a nigromancer."

"No mortal does," I declared. "Therefore they can always reach into their kettle and pull out an eye of newt or toe of frog you never imagined."

"Yes, I've heard of cases," Will said. "On the other hand, I've heard of taxpayers who, um-m, trumped this with a lizard's leg and howlet's wing."

"Their lawyers did, and battened off it," I grumbled, "A man is presumed guilty until he proves his innocence, at his own expense of money, energy, and lifespan. Is that what the Founding Fathers had in mind?"

Valeria had followed the talk with that intensity which could be hers. Whatever self-pity she felt got lost in youthful idealism. "If everybody hates the IRS, why do we have one?" she asked. "I thought this was a government of the people, by the people, and for the people."

"It is," I told her. "Unfortunately, these days the three classes of people aren't the same."

"Now, wait, Steve, you're too cynical," Will objected. He leaned back, regarded the girl, and smoked more like a philosopher than before. "Human affairs are always messy," he told her. "Whether that's because we're fallen angels or high-powered apes or both is a matter of opinion, but there the fact is. On the whole, our country copes with it better than most. Nearly everyone working for government agencies—" He threw me a look. "—like you, Steve—and I include tax agencies, nearly everyone is a perfectly decent person, earning an honest living by making the laws work—laws enacted by our democratically elected representatives."

I might have gotten in a few licks about regulations, interpretations, and court decisions, but Ginny was ahead of me, doubtless for the best. "This is supposed to be happy hour," she decreed. "Let's discuss something cheerful, like funerals."

So Will told a story he'd lately heard, about two nuns driving a unicorn buggy through a moonlit night, on their way back to the convent from a church-sponsored fiesta. A huge bat flew down, landed on the whiffletree, and turned into a leering vampire. "Quick, sister," gasped the driver, "show him your cross!" The other nun pointed and snapped, "Young man, you get off that whiffletree this instant! I *mean* it." He got a laugh from Val, anyhow, which made Chryssa chime in.

I segued out of my bitterness with one about a general at the Pentacle who was going fishing and passed a bait shop that offered "All the worms you can use for a dollar." He went in and said, "Give me two dollars' worth."

Ginny supplied some real wit, and conversation improved. The mood grew outright blithe over dinner, and stayed like that till the last goodnight was said, and a while afterward.

This was just as well. We wouldn't have much fun again anytime soon.

10

ALGER SNEEP ARRIVED PROMPTLY AT 1 P.M. HE WAS SHORT AND SKINNY BUT RAMROD straight, with flat dark hair, cold brown eyes, and a nose that waggled at the tip when he spoke in his high voice. He marched directly in as I opened the door for him, though he did take off his hat and transfer it to the left hand that held his briefcase. The right hand flashed his identification card. The cartouche around the Anubis emblem showed that he ranked fairly high in the area office. He returned it to his wallet and extended the hand stiffly. Well, I'd doubtless shaken worse. I made this exchange quick.

"My wife Virginia," I said. She was pure cool graciousness. "Our daughters Valeria and Chryssa."

They didn't advance. Val stared as if at something loathsome. "Excuse me," she said to us, word by stony word. "I'll go and practice my goetics. *If* I may." She turned and stalked down the hall. Svartalf gave our visitor a yellow scrutiny, jerked his tail straight aloft, and followed her. "Guch," went Edgar from his perch, as though vomiting. Chryssa wailed and burst into tears. Sneep's mouth pinched together.

"I'm sorry," said my wife, hunkering down to embrace the little one. "I'm afraid she's tired and tense. There, there, darling, don't be afraid. Mommy and Daddy are right here. I'll tuck her in for an early nap. Suppose you show Mr. Sneep to the office, Steve, and fix him a cup of coffee if he wants."

Not too auspicious a start. "This way, please," I said. The examiner and I walked off. "Uh, if you'd come in the morning, the kids wouldn't have been a problem," and I wouldn't have had to spend those hours idled and fuming. Ginny, at least, could begin to pick up the threads of her consultation work.

"I expect a long session," he replied. "Best not to interrupt it for lunch." His tone implied we might well have used the break to destroy evidence.

I gave him a sideways look. Something odd— His clothes? The gray business suit, pinstriped shirt, navy blue necktie spotted with white gammadions, pointed black shoes, were straight establishment. Weren't they? The hat, while wider-brimmed than usual back east, was conservative in this land of the desert sun. It seemed new and expensive, but even civil servants are allowed a touch of vanity. Nevertheless, I wished I could go wolf and better smell the strangeness that barely touched my senses.

No, probably a bad idea. My animal impulses might get the better of me.

We went into the office. He peered around, finding mostly a large desk with ordinary equipment like a telephone and a reckoner, a couple of swivel chairs, and several filing cabinets. On one of these stood a plaster bust of Athene. A window revealed our garden. Ginny had painted and potentiated a defensive-cautionary sigil on a wall, an ankh with an eye in the loop above the incantation PROTEGE SEMPER NATES TUAS PAPYRO.

"This isn't Dr. Matuchek's studio, is it?" Sneep demanded.

"No, nor her interview room. Here's where we keep our records and do our clerical chores."

"I may want to inspect the rest, including your office, Mr. Matuchek. But this is the place to start."

I swallowed a nasty taste. "Haven't exactly got an office, myself. I do some work in my study, now and then." Anybody who calls it my den will get thrown to the cutesypoos. "But it's more for hobbies, reading, relaxation. We don't claim it as a business part of the house."

He settled at the desk, planking down his briefcase and hat. "There may be questions regarding it. Section 783(c)4. I'll decide later. Shall we begin?" He extracted a bulging manila folder.

"The accounts are my wife's department," I said. "I wouldn't know where to find what. She'll have the youngster asleep soon. Meanwhile, would you like that cup of coffee?"

"Not yet." He gestured. "Sit down, please." Maybe my ears were prejudiced, but the last word sounded grudging. "We'll discuss the situation informally, in a preliminary way. The big picture."

I took the other chair. "You mean you haven't got it already?"

"Only what you and your associates have reported on their returns and other legally required documents." What more was he after? And why? We were *not* big game. "Certain things are unclear to us." *Yeah*, I thought, *you're tax collectors, not launch-and-dock-it scientists.* "Frankly, your public announcements have not been very forthcoming." *In other words, if we choose to play close to our vests, we're probably dealing from the bottom of the deck.* "We require further details."

Recalling Ginny's cautions to Will, I considered stalling till she arrived and decided whether to call for a lawyer. But no, that'd make the atmosphere really unpleasant. What incriminating thing could I say? I didn't know of any.

"You have Operation Luna in mind?" was my gambit.

He nodded. "In considerable part."

"Well, Mr. Sturlason tells me the IRS came at him several days ago. Hasn't it learned everything it needs to know?"

"That's back east. And the information transmitted to us here indicates Nornwell Scryotronics and Operation Luna have a tangled relationship, which even extends to NASA—and to you, your wife, and certain others. So your personal tax returns are involved too. Yes, we have heard explanations at Nornwell. We would like yours for comparison."

"It won't contradict theirs!" I flared.

"I didn't say it would, Mr. Matuchek. I only want to ask a few simple questions." Sneep gestured at his folder. "This is a substantial amount of material given me all at once. You can help me digest it."

And what will the end product be? I refrained from saying. Still, that glimpse of human limitations eased me slightly. Sneep had his job. Probably he had a wife and children. Probably he didn't beat them. I leaned back, folded my arms, and crossed my legs. "Okay, what can I tell you?"

I've seen pit bulls go less straight to the point. "Describe Operation Luna in your own words."

"Well," I said, inspecting each phrase before I turned it loose, "it's a small private corporation. Not a nonprofit, we hope, though so far it's always been in the red. Mr. Sturlason and a few old friends back there are shareholders." Old friends indeed, Ashman, Griswold, Wenzel, Nobu, Karlslund, Abrams, who'd stood by us in those long-ago terrible days when the portal opened between Earth and Hell. Except for Barney, none owned much stock. Their means were modest. It was their dream that was big. "And here in New Mexico there are Gi—Dr. Matuchek and me. As I suppose you know, we've been able to buy into a fair chunk of the outfit. Dr. Matuchek's brother, Dr. William Graylock, has taken a few shares too, but just a token, just to get in on the action. Such as it is," I finished ruefully.

"What activities do you plan?"

"We don't plan, not at this early stage."

"Early? The corporation was formed five years ago."

Oh, Christ, how can I make him see? "Look, we were interested in space. Project Selene had lately been founded. I dearly wanted to work for it myself, but it was still a sprout, with as many engineers as it could use. Besides—" I braked my tongue. Why go into purely personal matters? Then, seeing those suspicious eyes on me, I figured I'd be smart to complete the sentence. "Besides, I hated the idea of leaving Nornwell.

It's not located in my favorite part of the country, but otherwise it's a great outfit, a happy shop.

"Anyhow, our group focused on the commercial possibilities of spaceflight. If we could foresee them, organize ourselves to take advantage— among other things, by offering valuable advice—then when humans did get off Earth we'd be in on the ground floor, so to speak."

"What are those commercial possibilities?"

"Who can say? Energy's obvious—solar energy pouring onto the moon and through ambient space." I couldn't resist patronizing Sneep. "Brooms and carpets don't fly, saintelmos don't light up, industrial processes don't take place, for free, you know. Whether the energy comes from fuel or a waterfall or goetic quantum-wave transference across a potential difference, or whatever, it's conserved, same as mass is conserved in a transformation. Build collector pyramids on the moon, and we'll have power to do damn near anything. How'd you like to live in a flying house, or see a real Atlantis raised in midocean?"

Enthusiasm kept me talking. "Industry— Well, for instance, properly 'chanted moon rocks can draw water by tidal sympathy. Highly efficient pumps. You could make vitreous drops shine according to lunar phase— jewelry. What may be the medicinal value of a pinch of moondust in a glass of wine? The notions, the speculations— I could go on all day. Some doubtless won't work, but others ought to, and there're bound to be still others nobody will have thought of till we get there."

Sneep frowned. "Haven't you allowed for political opposition?"

"You mean international rivalries? I should think the gains will be ample for everybody." Given the likes of Fu Ch'ing, I didn't believe matters would be that simple, but neither did I care to get into side issues.

"First you'll have to meet objections within this country."

I grimaced. "Yeah. I'm no politician, though." For some reason I felt a need to justify my group morally. "Nor are we go-to-hell technoberserkers. Back then, hardly anything was known about the dwellers on the moon, other than that they exist. Now it seems they may be . . . vulnerable." Again I chose not to discuss the complications, the evil that might already lair yonder. "We absolutely would not hold with exploiting or distressing them. But who's to say at this point that a human presence will? They may be glad to have us. We may improve their condition."

Will thought otherwise: that they'd fled there to escape the industrial world, which we had then proposed to bring after them. I didn't want to concede Sneep anything, but I did feel bound to add: "However that may be, even if the only people we'll ever place on the moon are a few careful and considerate scientists who don't stay too long—even then, we've got the whole Solar System. What price the metals in an asteroid, or salt from a dead sea bottom on Mars to use sympathetically against floods, or a vial of Venusian atmosphere to repel insects and demons, or— No limits, once we get out yonder. Eventually, the stars."

That was what called us, I didn't say: called us, and surely millions more humans with wonder and adventure in their hearts. The Golcondas, industries, profits were really just ways to pay—by providing benefits, not extorting taxes—for the farings and discoveries. Sneep wouldn't understand.

"Operation Luna is a research organization," I ended flat-footedly.

"Your ambitions have expanded of late," he said.

"Why do you care?" I snapped, goaded. "Okay, OpLu has run at a loss till now, but it's collected enough to qualify as a business venture." That was mainly through the occasional consultation fee, selling our opinions on this and that to contractors working for NASA. There was also something Byzantine but, I was assured, legal about the arrangement whereby certain Nornwell people were lent to Project Selene. "We've reported every relevant transaction completely and accurately. If you mean to challenge that, talk with our lawyers, not me. I'm only an engineer."

Sneep made me sit while he riffled through his papers. At length he glanced up and said, "Your work on alternative vehicles is questionable."

I didn't know whether I wanted most to bare my teeth or lift my nose and howl. Having drawn three breaths, I retorted, "In what way? Look, we're not unique in thinking the government's approach is unnecessarily big, awkward, and expensive." After all, it was the government's approach. "Sure, Project Selene has done brilliant things, blazed necessary trails, but since then— Blame Congress and media pressure and whatever else you want. But read some pro-space publications; talk with physicists and paraphysicists. You'll find out things like how much less the cost of launch could be—to start with, eliminate that standing army of paperpushers— and how much simpler life support could be, and— Oh, hell, just compare the costs and risks of a space mission to an ordinary transatlantic flight. They ought to be about the same. They aren't. And now that . . . that fiasco at the Point has shown how fragile the space program really is."

I found I'd uncrossed my legs, unfolded my arms, and gestured kind of wildly. With an effort, I settled back in the chair.

"Is Operation Luna, then, trying to undermine Project Selene?"

I blew up. "*No*, God damn it! Can't you by any stretch of your mind imagine us as anything but crooks? For your information, I don't cheat on my wife either."

"I did not imply that, Mr. Matuchek. No offense intended." His tone made clear that offense had been taken.

I swallowed hard. "All right," I grated. "I'd have thought you knew this already." Maybe he did, and was out to get my goat. "If not, please listen.

"In the last year or two, a few technically qualified members of Operation Luna, along with a few others, have been seriously investigating alternative ways of spaceflight. We do it on our own time, or on Nornwell's, with our organization's money, plus what we throw in out of our own pockets. We do it with the knowledge and approval of Project Selene, Dr. al-Bunni himself, who told us he'd cleared it with the bureaucracy. He doesn't mind. On the contrary. He does like grandiose stuff, which is also what the government and the media want. But mainly his goal is to put humans in space, by any means it takes. Why not encourage an alternative? He's even arranged for us to have a small piece of moon rock, along with meteorites we've acquired ourselves, for our experiments."

I sank back, half wrung out. In a moment's blessed silence, I stared out at the flowerbeds.

"Moon rocks?" Sneep seemed genuinely curious. "How do you get them?"

To talk straight science was like a drink from a mountain spring. "Meteorites are blasted off the moon—or Mars, or oftenest asteroids, maybe also Jovian satellites—by big impacts. After wandering around for thousands or millions of years, some hit Earth, survive the atmospheric flameout, and strike ground. There are spectroscopic, alchemical, and symbolical techniques for identifying where one came from; I'm not too well up on that.

"The point is, since a piece of a heavenly body is in resonance with its source—law of contagion, you know—it gives impetus and direction to a spacecraft. I suppose we'll develop beyond the need for them," *if celestonautics doesn't die out in the near future*, "but at present they're pretty essential. Even if you don't intend to go the whole way—and so far, of course, we haven't—a chip off the ultimate goal helps like a, well, like a relic of a saint was once supposed to."

And maybe did, now and then. The original goetic power lasted well into the Iron Age, early medieval times, diminuendo. I'd seen arguments that a few creatures were around and a few minor spells effective as late as the eighteenth century. However, by then ferromagnetism was almost everywhere and had driven nearly all survivors into hiding places and the Long Sleep.

"I see. Interesting. Thank you," Sneep said, nearly like a human being. "You have given me angles to consider, Mr. Matuchek."

"While you do," I suggested, "how about I make you that cup of coffee?" A chance to be elsewhere!

"Well, yes, five or ten minutes for me to think before we attack the details. Skim milk, no sugar." Sneep returned to his papers. I rose and went out.

Along the way I heard a little *click-click*, looked behind me, and saw Edgar walking down the hall. Preoccupied, I gave it no further thought. He had the run of the house, and usually went on foot through narrowish spaces like this.

In the kitchen I started a potful, estimating we'd need that much in the course of the session, and brooded at it. The process was almost done when Ginny appeared. "I thought I heard you in here," she said. "Chryssa's lulled."

My heart rejoiced, not only because sunlight streamed through the window to make flame of her hair and caress her thinly gowned slenderness. "What a relief!" I answered. "I dreaded going back alone. In this kind of business, I'm a lamb to the slaughter."

"What exactly has happened?"

I told her. She scowled. "You shouldn't have barked at him, no matter what. One is exceedingly polite to such people. Amicable, if possible."

"Must one be? We haven't done anything wrong or failed to touch any required bases. Uh, haven't we?"

She shook her head, sighed, but gave me a smile. "My poor, dear naïf, that's entirely beside the point. Get an inquisitor personally mad at you, and he'll find ways to make you wish you'd never been born, whether or not he really hopes to make wages. We're guilty till proven innocent, remember?"

"Okay, I'll be good." I managed a grin. "And you'll be good-looking. Plus tactful, efficient, and generally irresistible." I paused. "There is something peculiar about him, though. I can only sense it vaguely, but—his clothes—"

"Oh, that. I felt it too, and ran a quick spell check after leaving Chryssa. It's simple enough. As I suspected, his outfit's been veracitized. When he hears a deliberate lie, it makes his skin tingle."

"Ugh! Is that constitutional?"

"Its evidence is not admissible in court, but—" She shrugged.

"At least he'll know we're on the level."

"Not necessarily. Any proficient witch or warlock could easily cast a counterspell."

"Why don't you, then?"

"Because he or somebody may have left a detector in range of us. If I did anything more potent than the check I mentioned, it'd register. It wouldn't reveal precisely what I did, but it'd probably turn his suspicions of us into convictions."

"Yeah, I forgot. Better we take no chances. We don't want to be convicted."

"Don't worry about it. I imagine all you have to avoid is saying how much you like and respect him."

"I'm safe, then."

"I need to be more careful."

I nodded. "A lightweight object with a rheatic charge reacts to any spell, however weak, that hits it, right? The results could be embarrassing. Though I don't expect any cantrip of yours would misfire."

"Thank you, dear. Let's proceed." Ginny arranged things on a tray. I moved to take it, but she did first. *Why, yes*, I realized, *part of the hostess image she means to project.* I stiffened my sinews, summoned up my blood, and followed her.

We came to the office. She nearly dropped the tray.

Sneep sat rigid, fingers clenched on the arms of his chair. He breathed hard as he glared at Edgar. Perched on the bust of Athene, the raven looked unblinkingly back at him.

"Good heavens," Ginny exclaimed, "what's this?"

Sneep swiveled around, white-faced. His voice trembled with indignation. "Your . . . your familiar . . . flapped in and . . . *stares.* Do you think I have to be under surveillance, Dr. Matuchek? That I'm a, a robber?"

"Of course not!" Ginny replied, adding quickly, "You're an income tax collector."

But Edgar thinks otherwise, I realized. *He knows we don't want this intrusion, and he's gotten overzealous.*

"I'm so sorry. A dreadful misunderstanding, I'm sure." Ginny set the tray on the desk and turned to the bird. "What's the matter with you?" she shrilled. *Nice acting*, I thought. Her real angers were soft-spoken, ice-cold, and dangerous. Then I remembered Sneep's clothes and wondered what they'd hint at.

Well, she must in fact be annoyed with the featherbrain. He'd spoiled the atmosphere she wanted to create. She lowered her voice. "You apologize to Mr. Sneep right now."

"Nevermore," said the raven sullenly.

"Get out of here! Scram, you—you Edgar Allan Crow!"

He raised his hackles and hissed, but spread his wings, landed on the floor, and marched off. *Poor fellow, he's hurt*, I thought. *He meant well. I'll bet Ginny's unhappy at having to be so harsh. Which doesn't make him less mad.*

"We do regret this very much, Mr. Sneep," she said. That probably passed the truth test, since she didn't specify the reasons why we regretted it. "It's no way to treat a guest." Likewise true, including unwelcome ones.

"Edgar's rather new on the job. Sometimes he behaves childishly. You do understand, don't you?"

"Yes," he clipped.

She returned a forty-kilowatt smile. "So you have children of your own?" She sat down and offered him a cup. I hung back, not to interfere with this charmcasting.

Sneep didn't actually thaw, but a few minutes of her chitchat and responses he couldn't escape making calmed him. "We'd better start work," he presently said.

"I'll fetch me a chair," I proposed.

Ginny's look mingled compassion and fortitude. "I don't think that'll be necessary," she said. "I am the family business manager. Just stay available in case we need you."

Greater love hath no woman, I thought, shaped a kiss, and retreated while the retreating was good.

It seemed wise to check on Edgar. A search of the house failed to locate him, though it was closed against the heat. The door to the auxiliary workroom also stood shut. Val was in there with Svartalf, I knew, presumably going through witchy lore and exercises as she'd announced she would. The raven must have rapped with his beak and she'd let him in. Probably all three were taking out their assorted resentments in some double-double rite. Any IRS detector ought to identify it as very mild stuff and dismiss it. Every book and instrumentality in the house was sealed against outsiders—except as, bit by bit, Val mastered the responsible use of them. She'd progressed well beyond the ninth-grade level, but not far enough to be scary.

If she was angry, I could sympathize. Spirited and born with a tremendous aptitude, she naturally chafed at the restrictions on her. It was especially galling that she wouldn't get her flyer's license till she turned sixteen, when she could already damn well handle a stick. I'd taught her the basics and let her take over, safely off in the desert; she'd wanted it so much. And I had little doubt she'd cajoled two or three older boys into the same. It wasn't easy, being her age. I remembered.

Best I not interrupt. I went to fetch a beer from the fridge and took it into my study where nobody would disturb it. There I tried to lose myself in a mystery novel. But, excellent though *The Case of the Toxic Spell Dump* was, I failed. Sitting stalled like this when real work called me was too dismal. Of course, compared to what Ginny was going through—

A shout and clatter brought me to my feet. I sallied forth and saw Ben, sunburnt and dust-smeared, burst into the office. I dashed to the rescue.

The desk was strewn with documents. Sneep sat hunched over them.

Ginny's expression told me that she'd stared out the window for an hour or worse while he wordlessly rummaged our files. "Mom, Mom!" our son yelled. "There you are! I'm back! I had a terrific time! Look!" He extended his hands. I glimpsed what they held. "I found this horny toad. Can I keep him, can I? Mr. Goldstein gave him a name. He's the IRS Monster—"

Somehow I brought the lad away, shoved him under the shower, gave him clean clothes, et cetera. Meanwhile Ginny performed what damage control she was able.

Afterward she told me that the ordeal had been harder than she expected. Mostly, as said, it amounted to waiting. Sneep maintained machinelike correctness. But when he had questions, they drilled deep. Witch or no, how the hell could she keep in mind every jot and niggle? She must trudge back through the records herself and reconstruct trivial deals made two or three years ago. It could seldom be done on such short notice.

By about six o'clock he'd assembled a large stack of papers. "I'll take these along to the office and research them," he told her. "You'll hear from me."

"I can doppelgang copies for you," she proposed.

"If you please, Dr. Matuchek, we do that ourselves. Precaution against a possible hex. If we find no irregularity, the originals will be returned to you in due course."

"I set my teeth and made allowances," she told me. "He'd taken a couple of insults himself today, after all. Nevertheless—"

I've run ahead of myself. Ginny summoned me to say good-bye to Mr. Sneep. Chryssa was elsewhere with her dolls, pouring them pretend tea. Valeria, Svartalf, and Edgar sat in the living room. The girl's grim little grin worried me. But what could I do?

I opened the front door. Sneep stepped into the late afternoon blaze. Val sprang cat-silent to her feet. Maybe only I saw her gesture and mutter.

Sneep's expensive hat flapped its brim and rose off his head.

"What?" he yelped. "Hey, wait!"

Valeria sped to the door, Edgar on her wrist. "Go get it!" she shouted gleefully. The raven soared.

"Hold! Stop!" Ginny cried. She hurried outside too and raised her arms for a revocation.

Unfortunately, Edgar had overtaken the hat. It made a clumsy attempt to dodge. Not being a falcon, he grabbed it in his beak. It struggled. He let go and bashed it on the crown. It fluttered wounded down to the sidewalk.

"Svartalf," Val purred.

That old cat could still move like a streak when he chose to. He was onto the hat in an instant. It tried to escape. He batted, clawed, and bit at this marvelous prey.

Ginny's correction took hold. The hat, what was left of it, went lifeless. Svartalf took it between his teeth and trotted proudly back to us. Edgar flew to the rain gutter. "Kah, kah, kah," he exulted, "Billy Magee Magar."

I don't wish to recall what followed. We apologized and offered restitution, but be damned if we'd bellycrawl, or give our daughter more than a reprimand in front of a stranger. Sneep was icily polite. Watching him depart, I thought he figured he'd gained a certain moral ascendancy over us.

Once we were alone, it hurt to keelhaul Valeria. "But you hate him," she protested.

"We don't," I stated, more or less sincerely. "He may not be our favorite person on earth, but he's a man, doing his duty as he sees it," more or less, "and entitled to normal courtesy."

"Also," Ginny said, "you clearly haven't learned your social lessons. Ancient wisdom: It's stupid to make an enemy of someone whom you don't intend to kill."

Valeria tried to meet her eyes and couldn't.

"Furthermore," Ginny continued, "and more important, don't kid yourself that you were defending the family or any such idiotic thing. You're loaded with personal grudges, which you took out on him simply because he was a convenient target. You'll never get your witch's license if you don't show more self-control."

Hoo, am I glad she's never had to read me the riot act. Her occasional rebuke has been plenty enough.

The upshot was that we sent Val to bed without supper—which therefore became a cheerless meal, much to Ben's and Chryssa's distress—and confined her to the house for a week. She accepted the sentence as stonily as a soldier ought. I knew we'd all end up in mutual forgiveness.

Yet the consequences of this ill-omened day would be with us for we knew not how long or heavily. It was as if we'd fallen under a curse. Maybe to keep us entangled and helpless?

||

THOUGH THE NEXT DAY WAS A SATURDAY, GINNY AND I BOTH WENT TO WORK. RATHER, she let her clients know she was again available and received a couple of them, while I flitted to Cardinal Point.

The place looked and felt forsaken. It had bustled the week around, but now little went on other than housekeeping and bookkeeping. Most staff were on leave, which they feared might turn into layoff. It certainly would if Project Selene didn't get an appropriation to pay for a second try. Congress was in adjournment, its members presumably back home taking the pulses of their constituents. They'd reconvene in September to take the purses. What news and commentary I'd followed thus far made it seem unlikely that much largesse would flow our way.

Even so, security was as tight as Torquemada. Four armed guards stood under improvised sunshelters around the three-quarters-empty parking lot. Maybe it was only a late arrival breaking their boredom that caused their gazes to stalk me, but I didn't appreciate being an instant suspect. At the gatehouse, where I'd hitherto simply picked up my badge, the man said, "I'm sorry, but we've got a new procedure. Please come in for identification."

"What?" I replied. "You know me, Gitling."

"Sure I do, Mr. Matuchek. But it's the rules. We, uh, have to make sure no Seeming or, uh, anything gets by."

"Good Lord, somebody disguised? Whatever *for?*"

"Sorry, sir. No exceptions. Orders from Washington, they tell me."

An offside room had been rigged as an inquisitory. A witch ran a dowser over me while chanting a disspell, took my thumbprint and did the same for it, had me sign my secret name and waved a doppel of it above till the paper flapped in response. (Not my real secret name, of course; the one given me when I came to work here.) "How much blood do you need?" I snorted.

"None, sir, seeing you passed the prelims."

She was young and cute, which took the edge off my annoyance, and sounded very tired, which roused my sympathy. "Rough job, huh?" I asked.

"Not too bad anymore. But when the order first went into effect—

employees, consultants, investigators, press, politicians—especially the press and the politicians."

"Yeah. Those'd scream to high heaven. At least they don't agree on which class of 'em owns the universe. But I suppose by now this bottleneck has reduced the flood a lot."

She nodded. "Essential people mainly, I guess."

"And *I* guess it hasn't helped the project's popularity one bit. Of all the officious official idiocies— What the devil is left to sabotage? I'd like to know what al-Bunni had to say about it."

Her lips twitched. "I heard tell of, er, 'grandfather of a thousand mangy camels.' "

"Which must have been in English. I understand Arabic gets more eloquent. Well, cheerio, sort of." I took my badge from her and left. She'd told me getting out was still uncomplicated.

The weather had mildened. Clouds moved stately over a sky from which spilled light that was merely radiant. A hedge of southernwood gave off a pungent scent as I brushed against it, like a friendly, hopeful message.

The next sight yanked my thoughts back and cast them down. I'd detoured to see how things were at the paddock. They were terrible. It was as if the bronze of the great proud horse was already tarnishing. Holes gaped where parts had been removed for study. Machinery, obviously brought here yesterday, hulked nearby, ready to complete the demolition on Monday. A breeze off the malpais sighed emptily past.

I zigged back to my proper goal, the building that held the communications lab. Hollowness greeted my entry. Upstairs, the lab itself was bright, equipment sparkled, something hummed, my werewolf senses caught a tingle of power, less clearly than my animal form would have but nevertheless heartening. However, nobody but Jim Franklin and a couple of assistants were on hand. The assistants nodded and continued their work. He came over to meet me and try to drive off the air of desolation with his big white smile.

"Welcome back, Steve," he said. "How've things gone?"

"Away, I hope." No such luck; but I didn't want to dump our tax woes on him, and better not to mention the co-opting of Balawahdiwa to anyone just yet. "And here?"

"Well, we had a busy time for a while, studying what the event did to the com gear. Mostly not much—it withstood impact pretty well, the way it was made to—but some effects are sure goofball. Like a Doppler tracker gone into reverse. Red shift for approach, blue for recession. What this remnant of us is working on is a voice receiver that gives only yips and howls."

"Coyote's idea of a joke," I muttered.

"Could be. I've been wondering whether an incident my father told me about was a prank of his. At the time, it was taken to be a mistake in the spell."

"When was this?"

"Back during the war. Dad was working at the Dry Gulch proving grounds. They developed nasties there to send at the enemy, you may recall. Had a giant sidewinder airborne, putting it through its paces, when suddenly it turned into a rattlesnake the same size and fell down amongst them. Luckily, the range safety officer had a hyperborean charm primed and froze it before it bit somebody. They spent a few days respelling, and the next trial went okay. But maybe Coyote had passed by—southern California wasn't built up like it's become since—and gotten playful."

"Hm. And then afterward, seeing this really big installation sprout in the middle of his stamping grounds and attract thousands of people, he got more serious. Odd, though, that I've never heard of the business, and odder that Ginny hasn't. It's possibly relevant here."

"Dad told me confidentially. It was classified till last year. No reason that I can imagine."

"I can. Government."

"Uh-huh. They finally got around to releasing the file, along with a mess of other obsolete-looking stuff, but by then it wasn't newsworthy, even within the profession. I have gathered that the Smithsonian's acquired the snake, out of the Army's cold storage vault, and may put it on exhibit. That should rouse some public interest. The thing did nearly crottle their greeps that day. *Crotalus bunyani.*" Jim was an amateur naturalist.

I looked around. "Where's Helen?" I asked, meaning Krakowski, our section chief.

"Summoned to headquarters, like nearly everybody else important. Damn if I know what NASA thinks they can do there except answer stupid questions, when they could be at something useful. Double damn if I know how al-Bunni's avoided it so far."

"Maybe he pulled wires. He does have friends high in the military. Or maybe he thundered the bureaucracy down. Or maybe he quick-like invented a religious occasion that forbids him to travel." I shrugged.

"Well, Helen told us to carry on as best we could, and when we ran out of work go home and stand by for a call . . . whenever it may come. We three are here today because I've got an experiment that won't keep. I expect in the course of next week more and more staff will phase themselves out and"—bitterly—"concentrate on angling for reassignment elsewhere, or whole new jobs."

"Ouch. What can I do?"

"I'm glad you showed. We can use your particular talents."

Jim's little team was trying to discover why the scryotronic communicator was making coyote noises. This might give a clue to the way the destructive force had operated, which would be mighty valuable knowledge at the next launch, if there was one. He knew the main crystal was somehow bollixed. He had an idea that it had gone into wave-mechanical oscillations, jumps to and fro between alternate histories, so to speak. The notion wasn't easy to test. The apparatus he'd rigged involved linked mandrake amplifiers. They're cantankerous buggers. If he left them untended longer than overnight, he might as well tear the whole thing down and start over.

Myself, I was more an engineer than an artificer. I knew just the elementary theory of rheatics. When forces transmit at infinite speed, such familiar concepts as frequency don't quite apply. But even in human form, I had a keen nose and a knack for handling wildlife. That included mandrakes, sort of.

Nobody has yet gotten any to breed true. Each is a law, or maybe I should say a caprice, unto itself. You'd better tickle it right, or it'll get into a snit and either give you no results at all or make you wish it had.

I sensed my way forward, carefully, carefully, tuning and retuning by fractional increments, through the next few hours. None of us went out for lunch. We snatched what we'd brownbagged while we worked on. The cafeteria would have been pretty depressing anyway. Here we cheered ourselves with progress.

"By God, Steve," Jim said at last. "I think we've done it. The plumbing is perking, and we ought to have our data in time to go home for dinner."

"Or first stop off for a beer." I rose, knuckled my bleary eyes, and stretched cramped muscles. "Unless you've stashed an illicit six-pack in a fridge?"

" 'Fraid not," Jim replied. "But no sense in your hanging around here. Hoist one in the Mars for us on your way back." I wondered how long our favorite local bar would keep that name or even stay in business.

To this day I don't know whether it was coincidence or if the phone had been charmed to monitor us. Whichever, it said: "Mr. Steven Matuchek, please report to Dr. al-Bunni in Room Seventy-seven of the Suleiman Elaboratory."

We four gaped at each other. "Holy hoodoo," Jim breathed, "the big cheese's personal bell jar. What *you* done, man?"

"*Lapsituri te salutamus*," I answered from the prayer to St. Ineptus, patron of klutzes, and went out.

12

THE BUILDING WAS SOME DISTANCE OFF. IT LOOMED AT ME AS I APPROACHED. THE ONION- oid cupola on top lent meaning to Jim's figure of speech. A text from the Qu'ran, flowing Arabic inset above the main entrance, added to the demonstration of how much al-Bunni was valued, how much was granted him. This had nourished not only jealousy but ethnic hatred, on which the likes of Blather and Blither were quick to batten.

President Lambert's influence and pork barrel politics countered them. Though he was now out of office, public interest, even enthusiasm, had done the same as mission after mission flew from Cardinal Point, each more spectacular than the last. But the modern American public is a fickle bitch. This gigantic failure of ours was provoking a reaction in proportion, which our opponents well knew how to make feed on itself.

I found al-Bunni alone in the workroom reserved for him and whomever he invited. After the glass eyes in the bronze door had scanned me, it swung aside and I stepped into a long chamber, greenishly lighted, handsomely but sparsely furnished except for the scientific apparatus. Sweet smoke wafted from a censer into cool air. A minor-key flute melody wove through it.

Al-Bunni advanced to meet me, which was courteous of one in his position. Usually he wore Western clothes, with a penchant for the gaudiest Hawaiian shirts he could buy in New Mexico, but today it was a white kaftan. It made him seem still bigger than before. The dark, crag-nosed face had none of its wonted joviality—and was the black beard suddenly more grizzled? His hand gripped hard, though, and his basso rumbled levelly. "How do you do, Mr. Matuchek. Thank you for coming this promptly."

"Glad to, sir," was my lame response, "though I'll be da—uh, doggoned if I know why you called." My use of "doggoned" showed me how rattled and puzzled I was. We werewolves detest that word.

"You'll find out. The reason does you credit. But come." He took my elbow and guided me to an ebony-and-ivory table. "Please sit and let's talk. Coffee?" With his own hands he filled two cups from a silver pot above a flame. They were tiny, but the brew met the traditional specs: black as midnight, strong as death, sweet as love, and hot as the Pit.

He offered me a cigarillo too, and, when I declined, lit his own. "How goes it for you and your family?" he inquired.

"We're getting along." Again I had no wish to relate some details and knew better than to touch on others. I did describe our search through the malpais with the two feds.

He nodded. "Yes, I have had some report of this, under bonds of strict secrecy. Why not release the findings?"

"Well, sir, they might alert the enemy, and they aren't conclusive yet, and they'd be bound to make NASA look worse. Some people would say this proves our incompetence, that we didn't think to take those precautions. Others would say we're trying to cover up that incompetence by blindly accusing minority and foreign Beings."

"Ah, America," he said wryly. "I hesitate to tell even the FBI what I have found out for myself."

I almost spilled my coffee. "What? Sir."

His look riveted me. "I will tell you, and you may tell your wife. Need to know. But I put you on your sacred honor not to let it go further unless and until I allow. I have trouble enough already, thank you."

"Honor, sir. Yes."

"I called in a djinni from my homeland."

To my half horrified stare he responded: "Yes, I'm aware of the wartime encounter you two had with one. But take it easy. The djinn are as different from each other as humans are." *Uh-huh,* I recalled at the back of my mind, *"djinni" is singular, "djinn" plural.* "Some are evil, yes, virtual demons. Others are pious servants of God. Most are in between, same as us. I'd had dealings with this one in the past and found him reliable. At present he's taken a post as the tutelary spirit of Jebel Kharûf in the Negev of Palestine, right near the Egyptian border. So he hears news from the Powers of Air around the world.

"He confirmed for me what your FBI only suspects, that Asian Beings are in collaboration with at least one local godling and at least one local human to wreck our space program. Later they'll try to head off the others. He knew no details, nor where to find any. It's as alien to him as it is to you. And when I asked if he and his kind could help us, he said no. They feel they'll have as much as they can handle, safeguarding their own territories."

Al-Bunni shrugged. "Hard to see how they could help, anyway, under your laws, no? In fact, if it came out that I had just consulted one, picture the conniptions at INS, NSA, ICC, FBI—"

"Yeah," I agreed. "And Congress, the White House, the Equal Opportunity League, the feminists, the American Legion, the media, and Chicken Little. As for co-opting any, forget it."

NASA wouldn't even engage native American or American-born Otherfolk. That wasn't entirely its fault. The question had come up early on, and several unions took a firm stand. If Cardinal Point hired so much as one leprechaun, the teamsters, the machinists, the electricians, and the geomancers would walk.

We sat for a while in silence. The incense curled, the music keened.

"You said, 'Need to know,' " I ventured at last. "Why Ginny and me in particular?"

"You have your Operation Luna," he answered. "You remember I have given it some trifling help."

"Yes, sir! Not that we've accomplished much. If we had more funding, more staff—" I bit my lip. "No, sorry, that sounds like whining and isn't what I meant. If *you'd* favored our approach, as a sideline, I can't help believing we'd've had people on the moon by now. And, uh, a small deal like that would be easier to guard, wouldn't it? Less vulnerable."

"Not only to sorceries, you are thinking."

"Well, uh, O'Brien's Law and— Never mind."

"I do mind. I am well aware of that law, like any other engineer or Artificer. 'Anything that can go wrong, will.' I agree. Project Selene and its constructs have inevitably been huge, complex, therefore full of the unforeseeable. Only God thinks of everything." I suspected the terminal sentence was more a sigh than a piety.

"If we are to be serious about a permanent human presence beyond Earth, we will eventually need large vessels with large, powerful boosters," he went on after a while. "But it does make sense to start small and learn as we go. True, each step would be riskier than any of NASA's. But there would also be much less to lose."

He drew heavily on his cigarillo. "I have done more than give your group what slight aid I was able to. I have checked into your concept personally. In fact, I've considered it ever since I was a boy, looking up from the desert sands to the stars and dreaming. To ride my own horse, or just my own broomstick, wild and free—

"Well, but always the pressure was on for quick, splashy results. First the Caliphate, then the United States Army. I thought a civilian agency would be more patient. But no, NASA too must forever push the envelope, as the saying goes. I've learned what sort of political pressures drive this, and resigned myself to reality. At the same time, again for political reasons, NASA has a fear that borders on hysteria, fear of losing lives. Every imaginable precaution must be built into the system and procedures, no matter how complicated and expensive this makes them."

I nodded. Enough celestonauts had grumbled to me and others. They were willing to take chances for the sake of getting on with the job, the vision. Why didn't the bureaucrats let them?

"I have done the best I could under the conditions imposed on me."
Al-Bunni's voice took on some briskness. "Nor do I complain. It is as God
wills. Besides, I *like* big beasts. To work on one, give your heart and soul
to the work, and then see it gloriously rise—ah, it's as well that such
occasions come far apart, or space artificers would have no children."

He set down his demitasse and continued more slowly: "But meanwhile, whenever I found some time and resources lying loose, I investigated alternatives as thoroughly as I could without anyone but a few
confidants knowing. I finally reached the point where I could write preliminary specifications and sketch a tentative design for a moonstick."

The blood racketed in my ears. I could barely whisper, "Sir, if you . . .
you . . . have done this, can't you make a report, write a paper, let the world
know?"

He shook his head. "Pointless. Unwise. You see, there is an element
of risk that NASA would never accept. That's why I haven't solved the
problem of life support for so bare-bones a spacecraft, among other
things. I gave up, because it had become clear that the whole thing would
be disallowed. I would merely find myself called a bad team player. That
would damage Project Selene more than it would me."

"Why?" I floundered. "That is, of course you wouldn't claim you had
a perfect solution. This would be a, a scientific paper, something published
for discussion."

He lifted a finger. "Oh, but there are so many gaps in the concept
that such a proposal would be scorned—laughed out of court, do you
Americans say? So minimal a craft must omit material reinforcement,
shielding, nearly all redundancy. My research of the literature did not
turn up any metals, spells, or other hardware and spookware that would
suffice instead. Nor did I discover any American thaumaturges or Beings
who might be able to provide it.

"Probably the Chinese have some on tap, but they will hardly tell us.
The Russians and West Europeans are taking the same approach as we
have taken in Selene. There may be some who could help us, quite likely
there are, but they are not in the registries. Disreputable individualists,
no doubt. In any event, *I* would never be authorized to engage any."

He gusted a real sigh. "I'll be entangled in hearings and infighting
and God knows what till God knows when. We won't make another attempt like the last here at the Point for years, if ever we do. And then,
as before, we'll be a conspicuous target, with more points of weakness
than we can foresee or provide against. We'll be leashed by regulations,
and everything we undertake will have to please Congress."

The old warrior resoluteness took over afresh. "But you—you and
your wife are unfettered. You're tough, ingenious, discreet, and not afraid
to break or bend a rule when necessary. It's worth a try, at least."

He surged to his feet and went to a filing cabinet. I rose too. His words trailed him: "I will give you the data I've compiled, the calculations I've done, and the designs I've drawn, for whatever your Operation Luna can make of them. You will share this with your associates, but try to make sure that my name does not go further than to those who can keep a secret. Perhaps you can accomplish something. Perhaps."

He took a stone from a drawer. It resembled a neolithic celt, as that make of lorestone generally does. Nothing but a code number in red paint indicated what kind of information the crystal structure and particle waves embedded. The numerals were the true Arabic, which don't have the same shape as ours. He laid it in my hand. It was dense, a weight that felt strong. I clutched it, dumbfounded, unable even to howl.

13

GINNY AND I WEREN'T CHURCHGOERS. WITH ALL DUE RESPECT, WE'D NEVER FIGURED OUT which of the world's countless sets of rites and dogmas lead to the best relationship with God. To tell the truth, we hadn't tried very hard. Some people have a strong religious drive, others don't. We assumed that ordinary human decency, to the extent we could maintain it, met minimum requirements. We might have sent our children to Sunday school so they could learn something about that part of their heritage. However, these days they got plenty of it in their social studies and science classes.

So ordinarily our Sunday mornings were lazy. After coffee and a look at the paper, we'd rouse whatever youngsters weren't awake yet. While they made themselves sort of presentable, either Ginny or I would fix breakfast, depending on what was wanted. She had a Cordon Bleu touch with crepes, while I was proud of my flapjacks and, lately, huevos rancheros. Having told the dirty dishes to go wash, we'd all relax some more. Formerly Valeria, afterward Ben, would be down on the floor, bottom up, reading the funnies, but now they sat, or rather sprawled in unlikely configurations; and as yet Chryssa demanded we read to her. Oftener than not, the pack of us would then go out—for a picnic, a horseback ride, a show, a visit with friends who had children too, whatever—though in the past couple of years Val was apt to take off with her own bunch. American bourgeois.

Not today.

It had begun the evening before, when I took Ginny aside into my study, closed the door, told her what had happened, and showed her the lorestone. "It may mean we can *go!*" I exulted. "As soon as we've read it ourselves—you handle the spelling and unspelling, I'll translate the engineerese—we'll get in touch with Barney Sturlason and—and—" My voice sputtered out. I saw how those green eyes regarded me.

The hand she laid on mine was cold. "In death's name, no," she whispered. "Not a word. Not a thought or a midnight dream if you can help it." She whirled, sprang to the window, and drew the shade down against the long, golden light outside, Her free hand made signs in the air.

I gaped. "Huh?"

She turned back to me. "You and al-Bunni, how could you be so careless? The enemy may be anywhere. I've warded this house, and I suppose he's arranged for some provision at his building, but you stuck that thing in your pocket, sauntered to your stick, stopped for a beer along the way, and now— Oh, yes, you're big and strong and always in full command, you two." The red head shook. "Men!"

"But, but, honey, I did stay alert, and I was never alone. Supposing somebody"—*something*, shivered through my bones—"was trying to keep a scry on me, why, all that traffic ought to've confused it hopelessly. Rheatic noise level—"

"It could still perceive an element of the unusual, and want to find out exactly what." She clenched a fist. "I don't think you appreciate the situation. You've met Powers of darkness before and you have some extrahuman abilities, but you are not a warlock. I wonder how clear the danger is to the Fibbies, in spite of the stuff they saw and took back to study. Out there in the malpais, those traces—the lingering spoor of evil— And since then I've been studying too and trying to augur, every chance I got."

She stepped closer. Her breath went quick and harsh. "We're not just up against a native godlet, angry or mischievous. Nor his demonic allies, though they're worse because we know so little about them and any friendly native Beings have no hold or influence on them. Al-Bunni said the djinn themselves are alarmed, didn't he? But there is at least one other as well, subtle, cold, like hate itself become a spirit."

Suddenly my tongue was parched, my tone hoarse. "What is it?"

"I don't know, only that it's terrifying." She paused. "I have a guess or two, but speaking aloud at this stage would disrupt the spells I'm trying to weave. Right now they're so vague, so fragile, that a clear name, whether correct or incorrect, would make them go wrong."

Like letting a molten alloy congeal too fast, and getting fatal crystalline flaws, I thought inadequately. Aloud: "I'm sorry. You're right, I didn't think. I was overjoyed at this gift and forgot what everything else might mean."

She set her fears aside and eased in the panther style I well knew. "Well, quite natural. I'm happy about it too, of course. In all probability, no harm was done. I simply want to make sure none will be. Then we'll rejoice."

Her smile flashed. "Here's a promissory note on that." She came into my arms.

After a minute, though, she disengaged, took the stone, and left for her workroom. When I knocked on the door later and inquired about dinner, she asked me to bring a couple of sandwiches and coffee. So I did, and cobbled together a meal for the rest of us. Luckily, a National Geographic special which we all wanted to see was on the farseer.

The kids were rapt, especially Val. She was still a bit stiff toward me, but not cruel as she could easily have been, nor often sulky. A week's house arrest even offered opportunities to an active mind like hers. She read a lot, practiced her goetics and piano, with a tendency to military marches and laments, played complicated reckoner games, and ran up considerable bills on the phone and the Mesh. Tonight's show could have been written for her.

It was about the Long Sleep and the Awakening. The scenes from the past were beautifully done. It was as if we saw the prehistoric world, mammoths and dragons, cave bears and centaurs, cave men and elves. One episode was funny at first, when a Cro-Magnon tried to make a spear point out of a unicorn's horn and it crumbled away. What with the effects of sunlight and other natural chemistry, even if half-world creatures or plants can endure these while alive, their remains after death can't without special treatment, which is why they have left no fossils. But the narration grew serious as it told how knowledge of such basic differences led to fear and abhorrence. That may be why Stone Age art shows little or nothing of them.

"No doubt hunters occasionally pursued the Other game, and sometimes came upon intelligent Beings," said a professor who was interviewed. "They may even have made friends—or deadly enemies. Folk tales of men or women who wandered into strange realms may well go this far back, to those eerie, evanescent elfin civilizations." A picture appeared of a rainbow-shimmering bubble village and soaring spires, more rheatic than substantial, at which a man in leather garments peered from forest cover, half lured, half frightened. "No doubt some shamans kept some regular contact. But the early warlocks and witches largely concerned themselves with trying to control the elements, the world, and fate. They groped and stumbled forward, but also sideways and backward, for they had no concept of scientific method."

Are we today so very far ahead? I wondered. Unwillingly, my mind drifted to Ginny, alone in her room waging her war against she knew not what.

"Magic, as protogoetics was called, suffered a setback in the Bronze Age. God-kings didn't like the idea of competition. Warrior aristocrats discouraged practices that might make the lower classes equal in strength to them. Magic began to get a bad name. Nevertheless, the human population was still small; there were still vast areas where paranature and its inhabitants flourished; diviners, healers, spaewives, and poets quietly carried out their arts. So too, we must admit, did evil sorcerers."

Yep, said my restless mind, *same as now. Give humans power, any kind of capability but especially power over other humans, and some will misuse it. And probably the rogues are less of a menace than the busybodies.*

"—the Iron Age, ferrous materials spreading across the planet, ferromagnetism canceling rheatic forces that natural magnetism had always kept unstable at best. . . . The withering of paranature, of its whole ecology—"

Pathetic scenes, a field of dead asphodel blowing away in dust, a dead mermaid on a beach drying to nothing faster than the jellyfish stranded beside her, vines grown over the lips of an image that once spoke oracles, a human mage desperately gesturing and chanting against the drought that seared his people's fields—"Some few held on a long while, in odd corners of the Old World or throughout the New World, the Arctic, the Pacific. But the remorseless advance of European civilization—"

Remorselessness, said my unruly mind. *Is that the inability or refusal to acquire more than one walrus?*

"Perhaps a few Beings survived on upper Earth—" Like maybe Coyote and—who were the rest? Balawahdiwa had spoken of somebody else, and there his voice held awe. . . . If they were resentful, could you blame them?

"—the European dwarves probably longest, because iron had never bothered them. In fact, they had become not only skillful smiths, but adept at infusing their works with goetic might. Stories of the things they forged, wondrous jewelry, golden steeds, enchanted weapons—"

Hey, I thought, *dwarves, sure, if anybody can make the special stuff al-Bunni says we'll need, it's the dwarves.*

"But otherwise, meanwhile, the last remnants, animal, vegetable, intelligent, had retreated. Their whole ecology destroyed, they could only withdraw far under earth and sea, cast the final spell, lie down to Sleep till a better day or till Judgment Day."

A wry scene showed a dwarf packing his blacksmith tools and climbing down into a mountain crevice. He could live in the world as it had become, except how could he keep eating? His trade with gods and Faerie was gone. How many humans would pay for his work, the more so when witchcraft and paganism were now abhorred?

Iron, steam, electricity ran rampant. . . .

All prologue. After touching on Planck, Einstein, Moseley, Maskelyne, and the discoveries following these pioneers, the show became mainly about how the Sleepers, one by one, two by two, bunch by timid little bunch, occasional wild firedrake or bumptious troll, Awoke, came forth, and found their way into the new Goetic Age. This was oftener scry than reconstruction. We got some piercingly lovely scenes, like nymphs with dew under their feet and dawnlight in their hair. Some were bleak, like the hunting down of a rusalka that murderously haunted Lake Ilmen. Some were a bit esoteric, like the synods of various churches debating whether Faerie folk could legitimately be godparents. Some were every-day, like arguments about whether or not a bowl of milk set out for a Scandinavian nisse who did housework after dark constituted minimum wage. . . . It went on. Worried, I didn't pay as much attention as it de-served.

And now came bedtime, kid after kid according to age, and finally me. I lay awake for what seemed a long while, but Ginny didn't join me till after I'd fallen into an uneasy sleep.

14

SO ON SUNDAY WE ROSE LATER THAN USUAL. WE WEREN'T DISCOURAGED OR SOMBER, BUT there was a lot to do and the need to get on with it was like rowels. Valeria came in, Svartalf at her heels. When she saw us brooding over our coffee, she stopped. The cat took the occasion to sneer at Edgar, who flicked his tailfeathers back at him.

"Good morning," said Ginny and I together.

Blue eyes regarded us for a second before the girl curtsied and replied in the manner of happier times, "Salutations, O Paterfamilias and Matri-arch. What plan you for our sabbath delectation?"

"Nothing fancy, I'm afraid," Ginny told her. "Cereal, toast— We're very busy."

"Popsy Scrunchies with *milk?*" She raised her hands and gasped. "Maybe actual toast and *jelly* on the side? *Vive la gourmetise!*" Not sarcasm, I realized; a forlorn attempt to keep some cheerfulness alive. "Well, say," she proposed hurriedly, "how about I take over? My hash brown spatoonies and cetera the other day weren't too bad, were they? If you can stand a rerun?"

Ginny was able to say gravely and graciously, "Thank you, dear. That would be a help." Me, I could only nod, gulp, and blink to unblur my vision. My daughter knew perfectly well she couldn't bribe or wheedle us into shortening her sentence. She offered love anyway.

Ben had entered, more or less kempt, and heard. "Hey," he said, "if we haven't got anything planned, can I go over to Danny Goldstein's after breakfast? I could spend the day."

Ginny's smile faded. "You don't want to wear out your welcome there," she said slowly.

I followed her thought. The Goldsteins weren't Orthodox, but they were fairly observant Conservative, which meant that ordinary goetic technology was allowable for them but not the invocation of unhumans. Our home had Ginny's two familiars for guardians, plus trigger spells to call on stronger help in emergency. Theirs didn't, nor did the streets between. Once, when we lay at strife with the Adversary, a demon had stolen Val—

"Aw, Mom, I won't," the boy said. "I'd've gone yesterday, except they had Temple and then a family dinner. Danny asked could I take along the IRS Monster. And he found a real Indian arrowhead, did I tell you?"

Ginny and I both drew breath. Teaching our children fear at so early an age and penning them in was no kindness. Besides, after the disaster that Val's kidnapping brought on the Powers of evil—without even doing her harm—they had probably put that tactic in the Terrible Mistakes file. At least, I suspect the smart ones among them are quicker studies than most generals and all politicians. While we figured our present enemies didn't come straight from the Low Continuum, word would have gotten around. The Adversary was certainly interested in this case, even if he kept himself in the background.

Ginny gave me a slight nod. "Okay," I said, "you can go, but not till after lunch, and be back here by dinnertime. We can't bum off friends too much." Though, damn, Martha Goldstein's sweet-and-sour salmon and cheese blintzes were to diet for.

Ben registered disappointment but accepted the compromise like the sensible guy he was.

"I'll rout the sprout first," Valeria volunteered, "and see to it she doesn't get her dress on backwards and her hair into elfknots like certain people I could name," which wasn't really fair to her brother. He shrugged it off with a resigned look at me that said, "Girls!"

Thus, after we were coffeed, Ginny led me to her arcanum and secured it. The room, darkened when needful, was light and airy this morning. Sigils, crystals, talismans sparkled. Scrolls on the walls glowed with the colors of hieroglyphs, archaic scripts, and illuminations. Sprigs of green-leaved oak, ash, and thorn sprang from a vase like a shout of life. The mother-of-pearl eyes of a small tiki seemed to twinkle. Even the old leather bookbindings took on a glow. She herself was the most vivid. I couldn't resist a grope and a nuzzle. Her hair smelled summery.

"Whoa, eight-limbed Sleipnir," she said, with a moment's grin. "We've got serious business here, I'm told."

"I was afraid of that." I let go and looked around. "Where's the wonderstone?"

She pointed to the safe in a corner. I knew it was warded forty ways from Wednesday; you'd need a powerful spell just to detect that there was anything remarkable inside. A chain went from its bottom through a hole in the floor, down to bedrock. The combination for the lock was a curse on any unauthorized person who twirled it out. Today I saw that she'd added a Seal of Solomon.

"Wow," I said. "But how can we use it?"

She opened a drawer in her desk. "I drew the contents forth through a translator from Arabic into English, as an imprint on this." She took a sheaf of papers and laid them on top.

"Wow to the nth. That's why you were awake half the night."

"Oh, it wouldn't have been too bad if al-Bunni had consistently used Arabic, with English loan words as necessary. But no, he kept throwing in German terms. Worse, trying to invent them. I think he wanted to show his command of the language off to himself. It's awful. You wouldn't believe what trouble things like *Besenstockstrohbindenbeschleunigungskraftwiderstehenzauberstoff* gave my sprite."

"Poor darling. We'd better suppress that detail. Germany might declare war," I muttered, my attention on the papers.

She laughed. "Stop slavering and give them a quick once-over. Don't worry. They'll crumble to ash if anybody but you or me touches them."

I flung myself into a chair, grabbed the stack, and plunged. Ginny settled too, fingers bridged, eyes closed. She wasn't dozing, I knew at the edge of awareness; she was devising.

Presently I emerged. Eagerness tingled in me. "This is True Cross, all right," I said. "I'll need to study it carefully, of course, over and over, but plain to see already, he's anticipated work OpLu couldn't have done for years, if ever. Well, he's a genius in his field, and had resources available to him that we don't."

The gaze on me grew hungry. "He has a design?"

"Um-m, not entirely. He has the basic layout and goetics for a broomstick that should be able to cruise from end to end of the Solar System.

But his calculations show that some of the materials, especially in the shaft, require properties like none we've yet developed, or have much idea how to develop. Without that, the rheatics—got to hold off hard radiation, you know, as well as supply control and boost—so much force concentrated in so small a volume would shatter the whole works. I noticed a notation, or should I say a query, about the metal of enchanted swords."

"Which may or may not be pure legend."

"Yeah, who'd try, when firearms were everywhere?" I did recall a blade I'd wielded once, and I'd heard of others, but what special strengths they had were from olden association; the steel was mundane.

Ginny's voice shivered. "Barney Sturlason could sic his artificers onto the problem."

Reality raised its ugly head. "Wait. Wait a minute, sweetheart. We can't bull forward like that. For openers, it'd be a breach of faith with al-Bunni. He kept it to himself because making it public would give too much mana to his and Project Selene's political enemies. In fact, he set it aside before he'd considered issues like life support, because he saw no possibility of anything like it being approved. All he felt he dared do was give our bunch a bit of quiet help, like releasing that chip of moon rock to us. Then NASA could tell the Republicans in Congress that it doesn't really stifle private research. But everybody looked on that as just a token."

"And now matters are desperate enough that he has passed the information on, under the rose." Ginny nodded. "Brave of him. And not only faithless, but foolish of us, if we let the world know. Our highly placed friend would be damaged, our enemies alerted. Still, he can't have meant we leave this lying idle."

"No, no. Suppose we give Barney the material, in strict confidence and without saying where we got it—though he'll doubtless guess—and then we all mull over what to do with it. If nothing else, he'll need some advance notice so he can shift money around and be ready to write OpLu a check for expenses."

"*If* we decide we can accomplish something. Yes, that makes sense." Ginny pondered. "We won't take chances with the mails or any direct transmission."

The morning felt abruptly less bright.

However, once we'd agreed on what to tell him, it was cheering to see Barney's homely phiz in the telephone. We caught him at home, a time zone east of us, shortly before he left for the golf course. After his surprised hello, Ginny said flat out, "We have an item for your eyes and no other. Can you send a trusty courier to fetch it?"

He reacted as I expected, fast and steadfast. "How trusty?"

"Ultra. Preferably inconspicuous. But, mainly, able to detect, and evade or defend against, possible attempts to waylay him. They could be subtle attempts, if you follow me."

"I believe I do. Let me think. . . . The best that comes to mind, I can't get hold of today. I'll try tomorrow, and hope he can reach you Tuesday. Will that do?"

"It will have to. Better safe than sorry. Can he come to our house?" Barney nodded. "Fine. When he's ready to take off, have him call and ask me for an appointment at his arrival hour, like anyone who'd like to consult a witch about something. He'll be a man, yes? Let him identify himself over the phone as Mr.—the gentleman you used to tell those stories about."

Barney couldn't avoid chuckling. His great-uncle had been a North Woods lumberjack, a fairly epic figure even in that era. Most of the stories were not fit for polite society. Like the one concerning him, Lena the camp cook, a gallon of moonshine, and a bear in the outhouse— Never mind.

Barney sobered. "You think you're under surveillance?"

"We don't know, nor how close it may be," Ginny answered. "We're hedging our bets."

"Right. I've had my hunches. God, I wish we could talk together at ease, like old days!"

"We will," I said. "Actually, what we've got for you is good news. We just want to keep it good."

After a little soothing gossipswap, we disempathed. "Okay," I said. "Now, what about Will?"

For an instant, I saw Ginny taken aback. That disturbed me. She recovered, but frowned. "What? When you promised al-Bunni secrecy?"

"I promised him discretion, and that we'd keep his name out of things. But in his own words, he gave the stuff to Operation Luna for whatever we can do with it. 'We' can't be you and me alone. We'll have to bring in others, carefully, but bring them in."

"Why Will, though, at this stage?"

"He knows more than anybody else we know of, about what's on the moon."

"However much that means."

I gave her a puzzled look. "And if we do start serious work, we'll certainly need an astronomer. Yes, I realize astronomers are specialists these days—uh, nights—but he's skilled in the fundamentals, and knows where to find what further information we may want, and— Well, damn it, Ginny, he's your brother. Don't you trust him?"

"Oh, yes, of course. But I am—frankly, I'm more worried about him than I've pretended. This off-and-on, undiagnosable condition of his—" She reached a decision. "I've wanted to see him again anyway, to check up as best I can. I tried to call yesterday between clients, but no answer. Let's both try today, and play by ear." She rose, leaned over me, and hurriedly kissed my cheek. "Now run along. I'd like to straighten out a few things here before breakfast."

I wandered back to the kitchen, where Valeria was busy. The smells made my stomach bay. "Want some help, punkin?" I asked.

"No, thanks. It's almost done. I made Ben set the table." Her slim figure tensed in the blue jeans and GOBLIN MARKET/HALLOWEEN SALE T-shirt. She turned to me. Her voice nearly lost itself in the sizzle and sputter on the range. "Dad, what's happening? Really-o happening?"

"Why, uh, well, a situation we can't, uh, discuss for the time being," I stammered at the big eyes and intent little face. "Your mother and I are helping where we can, investigating what went wrong at the launch. But, but don't be afraid. Things are fairly well under control."

"Nixway," she said. "And not only your troubles with that scabrous tax man. Daddy, I *know* you and Mom. And Uncle Will. Something's awfully awry. Isn't it?"

"Well, we're pretty busy, sure, and troubles do come in bunches—"

"You're woolmouthing the news people too, aren't you? They blat about whether the crash was due to sabotage or stupidity. But it wasn't either, not really, was it? You and Mom, you come and go. Where? Why?"

Over the years we'd told her, oh, how cautiously, about her snatch to Hell and rescue. To her at the time—her time—it had been a quick, hilarious whirlaway. She had scarcely any conscious memory of it. But our account afterward must have touched depths. Besides, she always was unusually watchful and given to thinking for herself.

I accepted. "Okay, soldier," I said. "It is a dark business. Stay alert, and if you're ever in the least doubt, yell for help. I honestly don't think matters will come to that. But right now I can't say more. Your part is to stand by. Savvy?"

"Aye, aye, sir," she whispered, and went back to her cooking. How long her lashes were over her cheekbones, how delicate her hands on pan and spatula. Yet she played a mean game of volleyball and could make a horse do whatever she wanted.

"Great." I allowed myself to squeeze her shoulder for a second. "And we don't let on to Ben and Chryssa, right?"

"Posolutely and absitively not." Then she chirped as if this were any Sunday, "Stuff's ready. Want to go howl the pack together?"

Thanks largely to her, that meal became fairly happy. Even Ginny and I managed a few jokes. When it was done, Ben went off to his books and games till he'd be free to visit his friend. Val winked at me and said to Chryssa, "Hey, small one, want we should put on our floppy hats and go in the garden like for an hour or so?" I'd rigged a swing, a slide, a sandbox, and a miniature merry-go-round out there. Since they hardly saw use anymore except when a playmate came around, Small One naturally squealed with delight.

After they were gone, I murmured, "Quite a girl, that first daughter of ours."

"Working on her karma," Ginny replied. "I wonder how long till she overdraws the account again."

"*I* think she's being a trouper."

"Well, we have an hour's privacy here. More would be above and beyond the call of duty, I agree. Let's use it."

15

HAVING DISCUSSED WHAT WE COULD SAY AND HOW, SAME AS FOR BARNEY, WE RESO· nated Will's phone. This time we got him. The image was pale, hollow-eyed, shockingly haggard. Beard or no, I saw the tic in his right cheek. Ginny hung onto an outward calm. "Hi," she greeted. "Where were you yesterday?"

"Business in Albuquerque." Dull-toned, he offered nothing further. I had a feeling it would be unwise to inquire.

Instead, I asked, "You free today? How about lunch or dinner? Or both, if you care to."

"No, thanks. I'm sorry, I can't."

"Busy?"

"Yes. I . . . may be onto something new in my research. Rather not talk about it till I have more data."

"Good. Listen, there's a possibility of Operation Luna making a serious start. We can't say more than that right now. We'd like to pick your brains for ideas, though. Sure you can't come over? If not today, soon."

The gray head shook. "I'm sorry," he repeated. "Later, yes, certainly, but I can't say when." The prospect I opened for him had put no life at all back into his voice.

"You've fallen sick again, haven't you?" Ginny challenged.

"Under the weather. I'll recover. Don't worry."

"I damn well do. None of those doctors and sages you've been spending money on has done you a mote of good. Have they? I want to check you over myself. If something paranatural is involved, I'll have a better chance of spotting it and doing something about it than any outsider. Kinship, DNA sympathetics—"

"No!" His cry jangled harsh and uneven. "I won't have it! You don't understand!"

What hideous shame did he carry inside him that his sister must never know about? I couldn't imagine.

He spoke more calmly, with a crooked half-grin. "You two really shouldn't be seen with me till this case is cleared up. I'm a prime suspect, you know."

"No, I don't know," Ginny snapped. "Whatever gave you that notion? Yes, you were interrogated at length a few days ago, like everybody else in sight. You cooperated fully, more than I think I would have without a lawyer standing by. What more can they want?"

"Two of them were waiting when I got home yesterday," he said. "They wanted to come in and talk. I was tired and in a bad mood, and remembered what you'd told me. We stood on the porch awhile. I declined to explain what I'd been doing out of town, except that it concerned my scientific work. They quizzed me about my Chinese connections—as if I hadn't been through hours of that earlier—and hinted heavily that I'd do best to notify their office before I left Gallup again. I'm no sleuth, but I'll wager that someone's keeping a watch over me and someone else is listening in on this conversation."

"They . . . they may only wonder if you . . . have information you don't recognize . . . that'd be a clue for them," I ventured lamely.

Ginny's lips tightened. "We'll do some investigation of our own," she said. Softly: "Carry on, old dear. And do think about letting me examine you."

After a few more words we disempathed and stared at one another. Her face wasn't simply redhead-fair, it was white. "Impossible," she breathed. "Will could no more do—any such things—than I could murder you."

"And you've had your provocations," I tried to jape.

"Some ghastly coincidence. Maybe I can 'chant forth a hint of it." She didn't sound hopeful. "I hate to pry, of course, but—"

I rallied my wits. "Meanwhile let's see what I can do with a professional pry bar."

"Hm?"

"Bob Shining Knife, who else?" As eagerness flared in her: "Wait, better I tackle this myself. Having you on hand could put him too much on his guard. I'm nothing but a big, dumb Bohunk werewolf."

A slow smile gave a glimpse of her teeth. "Ye-es. No smarter than Karel Čapek, no more of a threat to the establishment than John Huss." Me, I'd rather have been compared to Thomas Masaryk, who broke our people free of Austria-Hungary after the Kaiser's War, but I got her idea and was touched. "Also, you're his friend. You went hunting, fishing, poker playing, beer drinking together more than once, back in the Midwest. Male bonds. Go jerk them if you can."

When I called the broomotel in Grants, he'd just gotten back from a ten-mile run. "Kind of late in the day for that, wasn't it?" I asked.

"I slept late. Up half the night, working. The weather's slacked off. It wasn't too hot yet." He wiped a cloth over the sweat that polished his coppery countenance. "What can I do for you, Steve?"

"I need to talk with you. Privately."

"You know I can't discuss a case in progress." He tautened. "Unless you have something new to contribute."

"I might or might not. You be the judge. But it does involve personal matters."

He hesitated. "If it's about— You know I can't play favorites either. I meant to go around to headquarters this afternoon and see what the lab boys have made out of—what we found."

"Aw, c'mon, Bob, that can wait a few hours. Give me a break. I'll stand you lunch, if your bosses won't think it's bribery. Don Pedro's. Chili to make Lucifer flinch, and Dos Equis on tap to sanctify it."

"Um-m, thanks, I'm not sure about a heavy midday meal, but— Oh, all right, come here. We'll be alone. My roommate's already busy." He glanced at the image beside mine. "Hi, Ginny." Sympathy tinged his greeting. And maybe a touch of apprehension?

I spent the time en route arranging my thoughts and making a treaty with my conscience. Once in the past we'd defied him, his agency, the whole United States government, to go get our Valeria Victrix back. Only the spectacular outcome kept serious charges from being brought against us. But that had been an exceptional pickle. Neither Ginny nor I believed that, as a general rule, untrained, unorganized, unauthorized individuals could really fight crime, whether or not they wore silly comic-book costumes. That way lay lynch law. On the other hand, I was not about to mention our dealings with Balawahdiwa and al-Bunni, though they were certainly relevant and might contain important clues. Sometimes a person has to exercise personal judgment and take the chance of being mistaken, or stop calling himself or herself free. George Washington, for instance, or Sojourner Truth.

The unit where Shining Knife stayed was the usual, functional and characterless. His very presence, let alone his outfit hanging in the closet, overwhelmed it like a bagpipe at a tea party. "Have a seat," he said as we shook hands. I took one of the two chairs. He chose to perch on one of the twin beds. His black eyes stabbed me, not quite the way Juliet's did Romeo. "What do you have to tell?"

"Sort of abrupt, aren't you?" I parried.

"We had our sociability over the phone. This is a major affair, and the more my associates and I look into it, the nastier it seems. Don't waste your time or mine, Steve."

"All right," I said just as coldly. "What do you guys have against Will Graylock?"

He went impassive. "I've explained before, I can't speak about that. Among other reasons, at this stage it wouldn't be fair to the subject. Not everybody investigated is necessarily a suspect. He might be a material witness, for instance, maybe without realizing it. What did you come here to say?"

"That my wife and I *know* him. Her brother, after all, who saw her through to adulthood when she was orphaned. Bob, you know us. Would we cover up for a criminal, in a crime that could have cost lives and did wreck my work of the past two years? We don't want you baying on a false scent. I tell you, and this is a question of fact, not family: Will Graylock is incapable of any such act."

When Shining Knife sat silent, he forced me to end awkwardly, "To start with, he's no warlock. And he's new to this area, and hasn't taken more than an ordinary benign interest in the Indians and their cultures. How the devil could he have any ties to Coyote?"

"Nobody claims he did," Shining knife answered. "For that matter, nobody claims Coyote, or any local Power, is the mastermind behind the sabotage. Maybe so, maybe not. We do know, and that 'we' includes you, Asian Beings are involved. A human reasonably familiar with the Cardinal Point layout had to help them, advise them. Will Graylock's behaved pretty odd, hasn't he? Once alerted to that, we've, my team's begun to find how odd.

"I'm not telling tales out of school here, because you know more about this than we do, and I'd be glad to hear whatever you want to share. Meanwhile, he's had close Chinese contacts for a long time, friends, colleagues, correspondents; he's made several visits to the country, some extensive; he speaks the language and is well versed in the history, literature, and anthropology. And demonology?"

Shining Knife finished his hammerblow sentences in milder style: "I can say that much because it's obvious to you. Now, what can you say to me?"

"That, yes, he isn't well, and nobody's diagnosed the trouble, but he has been going in for tests, examinations, and treatments. Do you suppose an invalid would traipse around the malpais after dark? Or a quiet, decent, rationalistic scientist would get involved in any kind of conspiracy? Why would the conspirators *want* him? Good Lord, there must be a couple dozen people at the Point with Chinese connections of one sort or another. A few Chinese journalists and diplomatic personnel and whatnot have been given the grand tour. Why aren't you investigating them and their guides?"

"Who says we're not?" he retorted.

I wasn't to be stopped in midcareer. "And what about this mysterious Dr. Fu Ch'ing? Your buddy Moy didn't exactly give him a clean bill of health last week. Why aren't you on his trail?"

Shining Knife fell silent a few seconds. "That's easier said than done," he replied at last.

"But you think he's currently in England. Well, don't you have liaison with Scotland Yard?"

Shining Knife smiled ruefully and spoke readily. I guessed he was glad to get off a topic painful to me, if only for a moment. "Sure we do. And the Yard has first-class thaumaturges, as well as operatives of every other kind. They did get word, through their own lines into China, that Fu was bound for England, with no good intentions toward Western civilization. They were even able to establish that he had arrived, shortly after the fact. But that's all. In spite of every effort, they still have no idea of his whereabouts."

I rubbed my chin, feeling likewise relieved by the change of pace. "Funny. If he's as great a warlock as Moy claims, I should think activity, forces, spirits at that level would be hard to screen off untraceably."

"True, sort of. But you see, he keeps conjuring up false traces of his presence everywhere around the country. The Yard, MI, everybody's run ragged chasing them down and drawing blank at the end. The latest site I heard of was Buckingham Palace." Shining Knife turned grim. "It's also all too possible that Fu's got double agents inside Scotland Yard and the British military. He thinks and acts in terms of decades. Nobody knows how old he is."

"So you fellows have to be wary," I murmured. "How certain are you of your FBI?"

"We're trying. Whoever or whatever is behind the trouble at Cardinal Point, a knowledgeable human agent on the spot was clearly required. We begin by finding who he is."

"And I tell you, Will Graylock—"

"There is such a thing as demonic possession," Shining Knife interrupted very quietly.

I sat as if he'd slapped a muzzle on me.

"I've given this a lot of thought, Steve," he went on. "I'm glad you came today, even if your idea was nothing but to be a character witness. Do you suppose you could persuade him to volunteer for a psychoscopy? I'll bend the rules and tell you, if he comes through clean, that'll revive a lot of questions that right now seem like they may have an answer."

"He can't be possessed," I gabbled. "How on Earth or Below could he have been?"

"If perchance he somehow is," Shining Knife said, unrelenting, "then, assuming he didn't invite it, he's legally innocent; and an exorcism will liberate him."

"But, but it's impossible."

"The possession, or his agreeing?"

Both, I thought. The lump in my throat blocked off speech. Will was such a private man. The days-long search for a demon didn't involve merely spells, though some of them would be uncomfortable enough, or medical procedures, though some of them would be undignified enough. It included sessions with—opening himself, his life and heart to—a psychic analyst.

"Fifth Amendment," I mumbled. Nobody has never broken an occasional law.

"Yes. It works to his advantage, Steve. Didn't you know? The Supreme Court's ruled that anything revealed under psychoscopy is immune to prosecution. I knew a man once who tried very hard to convince the police he needed one. He failed. Turned out he'd committed a murder. As for anything that a demon forced someone to do, I repeat, as long as he didn't invite it in, obviously he's innocent."

But the intimacies, I thought, *his wife, other women before her and maybe after, the mystic beauty that gave his life its direction, so strange and precious that he had told none but his sister about it, of all people now living, till at last his need and his trust brought him to share it with me—*

And everything else that any man may damn well want to keep to himself. "I wouldn't submit," I stated.

"He'll be safe, Steve. Home free, I'll bet, whatever the outcome. If it turns out he is afflicted, he'll be made well. Won't you at least propose it to him? Better from you, better yet from Ginny, than an outsider."

I thought of the tortured face and dragging voice. "Not today," I said. "We need to think this over."

The rest of our conversation was short and constrained. We did not go to lunch.

Flying back, I realized the clues pointing toward Will must be stronger that Shining Knife had admitted. A hell of a lot stronger. But what could they be? Dust and other traces, closely analyzed? Goetics partially reconstructing those blurred footprints?

Hey, a really gifted villain might arrange things to frame a guiltless party—and wasn't Fu Ch'ing supposed to be the Genghis Khan of crime . . . ?

Ginny met me at our front door. She took both my hands in hers. I felt the tension, saw it on her, heard it in her. "We'd better catch a nap this afternoon, darling, if we can. We've gotten a note from Balawahdiwa. A son of his delivered it, and didn't stay. It said only, 'Come after sunset. Be ready for the mountains.' As soon as I'd read it, it became ash."

16

VALERIA, OUR BUILT-IN BABYSITTER, STRUGGLED GALLANTLY NOT TO ASK QUESTIONS. After dinner she said she wanted to call a friend. I heard strangled tears. She vanished into her room. The conversation was interminable. However, I daresay she kept it light. "Arnie's broom? That old dustmop? Now, Larry's Fiat Lux, I mean when his elders let him have it, there's a swoopersweeper! . . . Saturday? Yes, I'll be out of durance vile by then. The Gustafsons' swimming pool? Magniff!" Or something like that. I don't eavesdrop, but occasionally I'd passed by her door when it was open and she a-chatter, on the bed with legs propped high on the headboard and likely as not Svartalf on her stomach.

Ginny and I outfitted ourselves. Besides rough-country garb, I wore my skinsuit and carried my wereflash. To her outfit she added a cloak, not only for warmth but as a minor talisman; Fritz Leiber had once played Prospero in it. The owl pin on her shirt was much more potent, a badge of her order that had been to Hell and back. She'd given her best wand a magnum charge. The raven perched black on her shoulder.

Our stick bore us south. The night was windless but already I felt glad of my jacket. Once we'd gone beyond city lights, the stars gleamed brilliant around an ice-clear galaxy, so many that I could hardly make out the constellations toward which we flew, the Archer, the Eagle, and over our heads the Lyre and the Swan. We spoke little; we felt too small.

Beneath that sky, we easily found the pueblo and our way through its almost empty lanes. A yellow glow spilled from the windows of Balawahdiwa's house, but he stood outside. *Must have scryed us coming, or whatever he does*, I thought. Unlike us, he wore no hat; the grizzled hair looked ashen in the half-light. Otherwise his clothes resembled ours, except for a kilt and sash. They didn't look funny above his pants; we knew they were sacred.

"Greeting," he said without preamble. "I'm sorry not to invite you in, but we should take off at once."

"Far to go?" I asked inanely.

"Not in space," he answered. "In spirit, yes, very far."

"Shall we flit together?" Ginny suggested. It had been her idea to take our Ford. Three riders would have cramped the Jag.

Balawahdiwa nodded. We walked back to the parking space. Rather than rack the stick, we'd snapped its legs down, figuring it wouldn't stand there long.

"I sought to call on Nebayatuma," he told us. "He too has gone beyond death and returned. From him stem the Sacred Clowns. But—I don't know why, and maybe I never will—he who came to me was the other flute-player, the hunchbacked wanderer Owiwi. You're more familiar with his Hopi name, Kokopelli."

"He'll help us?" Ginny breathed.

"First he wants to know you, and of you."

Well, I thought in the cold and the silence, *that's reasonable, if reasonableness means anything where gods and spirits are concerned.*

We took our places, Ginny at the control crystal, Balawahdiwa beside her, me behind, and lifted. He pointed easterly. "We're bound for the Zuni Mountains," he said. "I'll guide you as we travel."

Air whispered around the windfield. The chill deepened. Ginny didn't cast any heat spell, and somehow I knew it wouldn't have been right. She wrapped the cloak close about her.

"I mustn't tell you much," Balawahdiwa went on after a while, in the same soft, even tone. "Sacred things, you understand?" We both nodded. "I purified myself and went out in the desert in search of a dream. The dream told me I should go to those mountains. There I made the medicine and waited." Fasting and thirsting, I expected. "He came at moonrise. We had talk. Tonight moonrise is later, but you need time to make your hearts ready."

"Gruk," said Edgar hoarsely, and stretched his cramped wings a bit.

Balawahdiwa smiled. "It is well that you have one with you who is of earth and the winds."

If he meant natural nature, I had my doubts. Edgar stole every coin and button he could, to hoard. He swiped Svartalf's kibble when he got a chance, and had to be forcibly restrained from raids on the cat's twice-weekly treat of canned fish. I'd seen him eat a cigar butt. Once when were hosting a cocktail party, he grabbed the olives out of three martinis before Ginny caged him. And we were lucky that Val didn't play much of that wretched excuse for music, sway 'n swivel. He loved it, he danced to it, he screeched right along with it.

"I know you don't lack courage, you two," Balawahdiwa said. "But you'll need all your resolution, all your honesty of purpose. Mostly Kokopelli is a friend to man. But he is ancient. He has his terrible side."

Yes, I thought, *the Anasazi knew him, and maybe peoples before them. Chiseled and painted rocks over the whole Southwest bear his image. As for terrible, what of Apollo and his deadly arrows, Odin and his Wild Hunt, Huitzilopochtli eater of hearts—what of Jehovah and his vengeances?*

We flew on over the miles. Now and then a few human lights twinkled lonely. They soon fell behind us.

"The Anasazi were not entirely peaceful farmers," Balawahdiwa said once, barely to be heard. "There were cannibals among them."

The mountains bulked ahead. I've said they aren't too impressive by day, except for the wonderful color-wild cliffs below. Still, in a few places they reach about nine thousand feet; and in this hush, starlit, the masses of them rolling downward into darknesses, I felt what mortality really means.

Balawahdiwa had been pointing the way for Ginny. His finger dipped. She made a tricky landing on a boulder-strewn slope. Bunch grass, silver-gray in the night, brushed my calves as I got off. I caught faint smells of the stunted evergreens that gloomed around the open area, but probably my companions could not.

"From here we walk," Balawahdiwa said. His breath smoked ghost white. "It's a sign of respect and a part of becoming ready."

He led the way, surefooted as a bobcat. Ginny and I followed. Often we groped and staggered. We hadn't given ourselves witch-sight; any spell cast in advance might prejudice our case. We both had good dark vision, and heaven out here was brighter than city dwellers ever know, but the murks were many.

Nonetheless we toiled on for a couple of hours or more. I didn't check my watch. This was not a place to chop time into numerals. The way led upward, now and then around a bluff or through a defile where stones rattled underfoot. Gloom lay thick in wooded stretches. Mostly, though, we were on bare mountainside, among rocks and sparse plants, outcrops and hollows. Sweat gathered under my clothes and felt clammy on exposed skin. My nostrils dried out as I snatched after the thin air.

Finally Balawahdiwa raised his hand. "Here we stop," he said. Heard through the blood thudding in my ears, his voice sounded far-off and like a prophet's. "Here we wait, keep silent, and calm our souls."

We'd reached a flat spot atop a ridge, thinly begrown, roofed with sky and the Milky Way a tremendous, upholding arch. The least of winds had begun to rustle. We sat down cross-legged in a kind of circle, to abide.

I couldn't see the others well. Balawahdiwa was motionless, expressionless. Ginny's gaze reached into light-years. I did my best to become stoic or reverent or whatever was called for. After a while the ground beneath my bottom got flinking hard and frosty, while my thighs protested the position they were in. Edgar, who'd settled at Ginny's side, shifted from foot to foot till he resignedly tucked his head under a wing and went to sleep. But we'd tried, both of us.

A waning half moon climbed from the Continental Divide. Phantoms grew more solid, darknesses less heavy. The wind strengthened. I heard how it piped through the scattered trees, over the stones—

No, it was not the wind. It was music, an eerie, hiccoughy whistling in no key known to me—

He came before us out of the night, dancing to the tune of his cedar flute. We saw him the way we saw the land, strange, starlit, moonlit. He had chosen to be man-size. His face, bent over the flute, was obscure, but some kind of feather headdress plumed upward. His arms and legs were so skinny that he well-nigh seemed a huge insect. I never quite saw whether he was really hunchbacked or only wore a big pack full of who knows what. Leather clothes closely fitted him, but his equipment stuck out, erect, for horses to envy. The gods aren't bound by human etiquette.

We rose. Ginny and I bowed and I removed my hat, not knowing what else to do. Balawahdiwa made a more complex gesture and spoke in, I think, the Zuni language.

Kokopelli lowered his flute and looked at us. I felt myself searched from the inside out.

Otherwise, from then on, I was a spectator. I didn't understand what happened, nor did Ginny afterward tell me much. Edgar, too, kept his beak shut. Ginny joined the talk to the extent she was able. It was slow and careful talk, with long pauses in between.

And yet, more and more, Kokopelli grinned, finally laughed. The moon rose higher, shrunken and pale. He edged near her and murmured like a brook through a flowerfield.

Though I was neither female nor wolf, the scent, the power flooded over me. It was like nothing I'd known since we long ago came up against a succubus-incubus down in Mexico. Stronger, maybe—here was a god-ling, at least—but then, I'm male and it wasn't meant for me. All I knew was such a rush of lust that if she and I had been alone—

And she admitted later she'd gone giddy and horny too. I can only guess how much more. Yet she held fast to herself, kept her stance, and declined Kokopelli's proposition, doubtless politely but maybe almost as calmly as I knew she'd declined others.

He appeared to take it amicably, which suggests to me the American gods are gentlemen in ways the Greek gods weren't. He made a gesture that might have corresponded to a shrug. The wildness blew away on the night wind. He addressed Balawahdiwa in straightforward fashion. After a minute or two Ginny regained enough balance to join in. Me, I stood dazed. Edgar slumped like a bag of black potatoes. I don't know what he'd experienced.

Kokopelli finished with us. He turned and danced off into the darkness. We heard his flute-song dwindle into silence.

For a span we stood unmoving. I felt wrung out. The wind poked fingers beneath my jacket.

At last Balawahdiwa said, word by word: "He likes you well enough. You are genuine. He's aware of the foreign Beings, and does not like them at all. I think they scare him too, but he'll never admit that."

He fell into bald practicality, as if in defiance: "However, they are allied with Coyote, and Kokopelli can't bad-mouth them to him without better evidence than we've offered. It'd be like somebody telling you not to trust a political ally, who's probably pleasant as well, and has buttered you up, and convinced you he's got the plan for reaching your goals. The native Powers do resent NASA's intrusion on their land and their people's lifeways."

"What can we do, then?" Ginny asked beneath the half moon and the wind.

"Prove that the aliens didn't wreck the space launch for sport, but have wider ambitions. Kokopelli frankly doesn't believe they're on the moon, and won't make a fool of himself by passing such stuff on to his fellows. You must also show you can do better for this land than you have been doing. Else, he says, they'd just as soon see your works destroyed. You wouldn't be the first who've come and gone in this old, old country."

Balawahdiwa sighed. "I think I've done as much as I can, for now, anyway," he ended. "The next move is yours."

We started back down the mountainside.

17

THE CARPET CAME OVER A HEIGHT NORTH OF US LIKE A FLAT STORMCLOUD.

Our encounter had lasted longer than we realized. Wearied, we made a slow and stumblesome return. Dawn found us with, I guessed, a couple of miles yet to go. The sky behind us whitened and wan light sneaked over the world. Above us spooked the moon, ahead of us the last stars were dying out. Ruggedness and trees still hid our broomstick. We were on a broad open stretch, though, the nearest woods several hundred yards downward on the right, darkling against sallow clumps of grass and bleached rocks. The wind had stopped, but the night's cold filled air and earth.

I think Edgar saw the carpet first. He squawked from Ginny's shoulder. We humans stopped and peered the same way. Against the ever more luminous heavens, it was a foreshortened black rectangle, featureless. Ginny's voice shivered through the stillness: "Who in Hermes' name is cruising here at this hour on that?"

A flash in me remembered that Hermes isn't only the Messenger and the Thief, he's the Psychopomp, conductor of the dead to Hades. The prosaic part of me squinted and tried to identify the thing—a large family-type carryall, for passengers and groceries and lumber and whatnot else—a Plymouth Conestoga or a Baghdadi Caravaneer, I couldn't make out which—serviceable, but not what you'd ordinarily take far off the regular traffic lanes or attempt to land on rough terrain—

Balawahdiwa sensed the aura first. "Evil!" he shouted. "Beware!"

The carpet slithered to a halt and hung some fifty feet behind us and above the slope. Light gleamed off metal abruptly thrust out in front.

The war came back to me on a tide of instinct. "That's a rifle!" I cried. "Run! Zigzag!"

The first bullet spanged off a boulder close by. Chips flew. An instant afterward I heard the *crack*.

Ginny yelled and pointed. Edgar took off. She burst into speed along with us men. We bounded, we leaped, to and fro, down toward the concealment beneath the trees.

I cast a glance over my shoulder. The sun mounted the crest. It dazzled away all sight of enemy and familiar. Its afterimage burned in my vision. I tripped over a stone, rolled, lurched to my feet and onward.

Ravens are big birds. Could Edgar get past the gunfire, reach the gunman, and peck his eyes out?

The bullets whanged, right, left, ahead, behind. That bastard must have a surplus military weapon with an outsize clip, like an M-7 or a Swiss Schraubenzieher. They're legal, at least in this part of the country. He wasn't much of a marksman, but by sheer volume— Were those stupid trees an inch nearer?

Edgar flapped back out of the sun-glare. He staggered on his wings. A powerful warding spell must have smacked him off.

Spells!

I veered to catch Ginny. She'd lost her hat. Her locks rippled like flame. The cloak fluttered wildly behind her. "Give me that," I said. She caught on at once, undid it, passed it to me, and sped on. The bullets pursued her.

"Help her!" I shrieked to Balawahdiwa. "Shield her!"

I threw myself to the ground and pulled the cloak over me. In the sudden darkness I heard him: "You're too easy a target—"

"Run, God damn it!" One hand unzipped my jacket and ripped my shirt open, popping buttons, to get at the wereflash and uncover enough skin. The other fumbled around my drawn-up knees, undoing belt and fly, hauling my pants down in the darkness where I lay.

Yes, said a passionless voice at the back of my head, *he may very well guess what I'm at and concentrate on me. If he nails me before I've transformed, that's it. But I'll have bought time for Ginny to get to safety.*

The Polaroid glowed. Change writhed and churned.

Agony struck. For an instant I whirled away from myself.

I awoke. No more than a few seconds could have passed. The pain was gone. Another slug hit, and another, but like heavy blows with a soft hammer. I was wolf. My wounds, including the first one, healed nearly as fast as I took them.

I threw off the cloak and snarled at the sky.

My outer garments hampered me. Three more bullets smote. The impacts knocked me around. I tore off clothes with my teeth, except the skinsuit, stepped from the boots, and dodged away, unhumanly swift. My howl railed at the enemy.

Unless he got me right in the skull and spattered my brains—not bloody likely—I was safe from him. Unless his ammo included some silvernosed rounds. But those *are* illegal for civilians.

Wolf, I savagely exulted. I wanted his throat between my jaws. Canine, I wanted to dash downhill and catch up with my beloved. Human, partly, I knew I should keep springing about in the area where he was and draw his fire.

He did keep trying for me, forlorn though the chance was. Whether or not he killed my companions, I'd make my way home, turn into a man again, and bear witness. The bullets sleeted. I danced with them and jeered.

He got smart. The carpet slid forward, downhill, after the others. It dropped lower, too. Myopic though my lupine vision was, across this distance I spied an ordinary broomstick secured on top. The sight wasn't clear, barely a clue to what the thing was. Just as vaguely, I spied the one who lay prone on the leading edge, rifle to shoulder. Did he wear a ski mask? I couldn't tell.

I bayed and gave futile chase.

But now Ginny and Balawahdiwa were under the trees. The woodlet engulfed them in branches, needles, shadows. The carpet veered, hung for a moment, and began to withdraw.

Ginny trod forth. She had taken her wand from the sheath. Its star flared scarlet. Beside her, Balawahdiwa raised his arms. I heard him chant, a sound that raised every hair on my hide.

They could duck back under cover if they had to. They didn't. The forces they flung cast blue fire around the carpet. Suddenly the air reeked of lightning.

The carpet wavered. Smoke trailed its unsteady flight. It disappeared behind the summit over which it had attacked, wobbling more and more.

I reached Ginny and dropped on my haunches, tongue unreeled, lungs pumping. Her wand had faded to normal. She went on her knees. "Oh, Steve, Steve!" She threw her arms around my shaggy neck and kissed me right on my wet black nose. Then Edgar arrived and demanded his share of attention. He'd done his best, hadn't he?

Later I retransformed under the cloak. Balawahdiwa surveyed the holes and bloodstains and shook his head. "This was historic, wasn't it?" he said. "Too bad. I hope you can get it repaired. If not, you'll give it honorable burning, won't you?"

The trace of wolf lingering in me exclaimed, "How about we take our stick and track that torpedo down? He can't get far."

"No," Ginny replied. "You told us he has auxiliary transportation. He'd scarcely hang around his grounded rug."

"Besides," Balawahdiwa pointed out, "he remains armed and dangerous. Best we go home. You'll have breakfast at my place, I hope? Later you can report this to the authorities." He paused. "We had better decide how much you should report."

18

WE RETURNED VIA GRANTS. SHINING KNIFE'S INVESTIGATIONS HAD TAKEN HIM ELSEWHERE for the nonce, but we had the luck to catch Jack Moy. While not auld acquaintance, he was intelligent, and as *simpático* as his job allowed him to be. He found a tiny room among the crowded offices where we could talk by ourselves.

I let Ginny handle most of that and worked at maintaining my poker face. She told no lies, not really. She being friends with Balawahdiwa, we'd asked if his wisdom could help. He'd led us into the mountains for some night hours of meditation and communion. Indian medicine didn't take the headlong, linearly logical, impersonal course of

Western goetics. It was indirect and patient. You began by preparing your own spirit.

Moy nodded. "Yes, I've heard something about that since I came here," he said. "I think a Taoist would understand."

"Are you of that faith, if I may ask?"

"Well, a civil servant with a wife, two children, and a mortgage gets to be more of a Confucianist, I guess. Go on, please."

The rest of the account was straightforward. His questions went to the point, a few of them at me. Once he said, "That was heroic of you, Mr. Matuchek."

"Naw," I said, "desperate," and meant it. Ginny's look and the brief touch of her hand on mine were worth more than medals.

At the end, Moy formed a soundless whistle. "A wicked business for certain. Have you any idea who it may have been or why he assaulted you?"

"None," Ginny answered, "except that I suppose he fears what we might accomplish. That implies he knows the situation well."

Moy's almond eyes drew into slits. "Someone close to you, then?" he said very quietly.

Ginny sat straighter. Her words crackled. "Not necessarily, sir, not necessarily at all. Project Selene could have been infiltrated years ago. As for my husband and me, we were public figures once. Anyone could look up the stories about us. Since then I have become well-known in my profession." And formidable, she needn't add. "We have not spoken to anybody else of what we found in the malpais with you and Shining Knife, but this kind of opponent could readily learn that the four of us were out there together. Meanwhile the findings have been disseminated widely through the Bureau, correct? Let me suggest you check up on some of your own personnel."

"No offense, Dr. Matuchek," Moy said hastily.

"You might also set diplomatic pussyfooting aside and look into the possibility of foreign agents more thoroughly than I suspect you have. But I can't run your shop for you. We have told you as much as we can," whether or not that was precisely as much as we knew, "for whatever use it may be to you. You have our address and phone glyphs. Now, if you will excuse us, we're tired and had better go home to rest."

And *that* was the absolute truth. I didn't see how Ginny managed it, poised there as if her begrimed outdoor garb were a freshly cleaned business suit and speaking the way an old-time schoolteacher would have to a slightly difficult pupil. Me, I ached and prickled, my eyeballs smoldered, and my head was full of sand. It's only comic-book heroes and their ilk who bounce directly from one brush with death to the next, wisecracking along the way. Real humans react to such things.

"Certainly," Moy agreed. I can't say whether he, like Britannia, waived the rules. "You've given us something enormously valuable, I'm sure—" He could not altogether quell a grin. "—even if it wasn't quite your intention. On behalf of the Bureau and the nation, I thank you. Do you want an escort back to Gallup and a guard for a few days? . . . No? . . . Well, then, good-bye, and do get a good rest."

We shook hands and left.

Westbound, I said once, "My brain's dragging in the dirt behind me. I wonder if we shouldn't've accepted that offer of protection. The kids—"

Ginny bit her lip. "No. The danger's not likely any worse than before, and probably less, since the enemy showed his hand."

"And had to fold it. Yeah. But there'll be a new deal soon."

"Scarcely the same. We, the Fibbies, the Zunis, we've been fully alerted. And he's left a trail for our sleuth hounds to follow." Her laugh rattled. "Oh, my, I'm worn out myself, scrambling metaphors like this. But all in all, I wouldn't expect fresh violence, at least in the near future. As for goetic attempts, our house is well warded. Let's not have any more government agents around than we can avoid."

"Always a good idea in principle. In this case, you also think they'd cramp our style?"

"They could." I hadn't the energy to ask further.

Somehow we made it home. I called in sick at the lab, not that that made any real difference. Meanwhile Ginny gave Valeria furlough if she'd take Chryssa over to a neighbor who had a contemporary little girl. Val had already seen Ben off, lunch packed, to play softball with some other boys. Edgar lumbered to his perch and slept. Svartalf lay cat-flat in the sunlight. Ginny and I fumbled our way to bed.

I've gathered that most people who've been through mortal danger are apt to have nightmares afterward. I don't claim to be any tougher. In the lycanthrope strain it may be nature's way of healing the trauma; or maybe I'm just lucky. My dreams go erotic.

However, it was hunger that roused us about four hours later. We still had the house to ourselves. Having showered and changed clothes, we went into the kitchen. "The nap helped," I mumbled, "but I sure hope to turn in early tonight," and yawned.

"Fenris would be proud of that gape," Ginny said. "Yes, me too." She had her own way of taking off the psychological effects of stress. It involved mentally reciting a mantra while visualizing a fractal mandala. Beyond my abilities.

Fenris couldn't have tackled my roast beef sandwich, piled high with horseradish, onion, and tomato, more gluttonously. Coffee worked its fragrant miracle. I gave her a suggestive leer across the table. The smile I got back, through a mouthful of her tuna salad, was responsive but wry.

"The younger generation will start returning any minute," she reminded me when she'd swallowed.

The phone called. "And that stinkful nuisance always does," I growled.

Yet we'd told the sprite to repel subscription pitchmen, self-styled worthy causes, and other such infestations. They usually pick dinnertime anyway. "Come on in," Ginny cried. I gollopped my food, an electric chill forcing itself into my skin past every skepticism, while the instrument floated to us and settled down.

Shining Knife's image looked out of it. "How're you doing?" he asked.

"Fairly well," Ginny replied. "What are you up to?"

"I thought you'd like to hear. I reached the office shortly after you'd left and helped organize an immediate set of searches."

"Set," I thought. *He takes—they take—this matter tombstone-seriously. I doubt he'll describe what every one of those parties is in search of.*

"I'm all ears," Ginny said. I guess she calculated the cliché would lighten the atmosphere a trifle, because she had features more prominent.

Indeed, his expression became a tad less official. He stayed with his account, though, like a hunter on a spoor. "We found the carpet in the general area you told about. We don't know whether the flyer brought it down on its last gasp or abandoned it for the broomstick Steve saw. Either way, he and the stick are gone, no footprints or other traces in the vicinity. No sign of that rifle, either. But where you were we collected plenty of spent rounds and may be able to trace them."

I'd come entirely wakeful. "If I were the gunman," I suggested, "I'd've taken that weapon someplace else in the desert and buried it."

"Yeah, we've got hoardfinders going back and forth within a large perimeter," Shining Knife answered. "Meanwhile, the registry on the carpet has identified it for us. It belongs to a family in the older part of Gallup. They'd reported it as stolen this morning. They have a broomport, not a garage, and left it rolled up there and locked as usual yesterday evening. That's a peaceful neighborhood. Somebody hotspelled the talisman during the night and made off."

"Hm," Ginny said. "Have you any idea who?"

"No, except that the thief is obviously at least a fairly competent thaumaturge, or possesses equivalent powers. He, she, or it needn't be identical with your would-be murderer. I'd guess so, but they could be in cahoots." Shining Knife inserted a pause. "We'd really like a talk with your friend, the Zuni gentleman. I haven't got the hang of his name yet."

"Matthew Adams, more properly called Balawahdiwa." He and Ginny had agreed she couldn't evade naming him to the FBI.

"We sent a team there, but he seems to have walked out."

"He has a right."

"Material witness."

"He was being shot at too!" Ginny flared. "Get your damn warrant if you must, but I assure you nobody in the pueblo will betray him, and Steve and I certainly don't know where he's chosen to seek."

Shining Knife raised a palm. "Hey, wait a minute, Ginny—"

"If anyone has a chance of getting at the root of this evil, it's Bala-wahdiwa. If you bureaucrats will *give* him the chance."

"All right, all right! Look, we don't want to arrest him or anything. We'd simply like to know what he may have discovered or deduced, and work together with him."

"Yeah, sure," I said under my breath, although I did believe my quon-dam pal was sincere, sort of.

"That will be for him, a Priest of the Bow, to decide," Ginny said more clearly and a lot more coldly.

Before Shining Knife had time to resent this, I put in: "If nothing else, Will Graylock should now be off the hook."

A few clock ticks passed. "Oh?" he said neutrally.

"Think, man. Never mind anything else, like his having nothing against him unless it was overstaying a parking meter or two. Look at his whole life. He's never been involved with firearms in any way, shape, or form. Served during the war as a civilian intelligence analyst. Hasn't been a hunter, a target shooter, hell, even a fan of Western movies." I'd been slightly hurt when he admitted he hadn't seen me as Tom Spurr's faithful companion. He made it up by complimenting me on my role in *The Hound of the Baskervilles*.

"As for wizardry," I plodded on, "yes, he's had to be good in some lines, like what it's taken to invent and use his specterscope. But I tell you as an engineer what you ought to know better than I do, that sort of work is no more related to unbinding locks and stealing vehicles than a minestrone is to a manticore."

Shining Knife was silent for a longer while than before. I refilled our coffee cups. Through no fault of its own, the taste had gone bitter.

"Well," he said at last, slowly, "that's as may be. You have a point. I did mention the possibility of possession."

"And do you imagine I, his sister, a five-star witch, would have caught no hint of that?" Ginny interrupted like a pouncing lioness. "I've been more concerned than you are, going further back. He's not well, that's true, but suppose you leave him alone to recover!"

I'd rarely seen Shining Knife flounder. "Well, but, but if he'd consent to an examination—get rid of loose ends—"

"Would you kindly tell me what those may be?"

He couldn't, of course. Regulations bound him. They weren't unrea-sonable. If somebody is a suspect, in any degree, you don't tell his nearest and dearest what tracks he should cover. The knowledge made a hard lump in my throat.

"No accusations," Shining Knife finished. "No accusations whatever, yet. We have to look at every conceivable angle. You understand, don't you? You two've been through a rough go. Relax, don't worry, we'll keep in touch," et cetera, until finally: "So long."

Ginny and I stared at one another.

19

TIME STRETCHED AND SNAPPED. "IF ONLY I DIDN'T FEEL SO GODDAMN HELPLESS!" broke from me.

She reached to squeeze my hand. "You were anything but, this morning."

"Thanks, sweetheart. You and Balawahdiwa weren't exactly freeloading. But that was when the enemy came out in the open—at last, after all these days when— Oh, hell, it's still like groping around in a fog. Can't see anything, can't tell north from south, can't even grab hold of the clammy faceless gray," to slash and bite and feel blood spurt hot.

"Why, we helped the agents learn that foreign devils are involved, we brought Balawahdiwa into partnership, al-Bunni gave you his spacecraft plans, last night we met none less than Kokopelli—and if you don't know how extraordinary that was for a white person, how many mages and anthropologists would give half their teeth and a left kidney for the experience, you haven't really learned anything about this country—and then we frustrated a direct attack and have undoubtedly provided the FBI with a number of important clues."

Ginny had spoken fast, but somehow her tone rang leaden.

"Yeah," I said. "Except we've been barely on the fringe of the investigation, and I've a notion that from here on we'll be eased out. We aren't official, and we are related to Will Graylock, and in the past we didn't stick meekly to our assigned parts as passive civilians. We've got those plans, but unless we can find some way to make hardware from them, plans is all they'll be for a long while—maybe forever. Kokopelli doesn't take us seriously enough to speak for us to his higher-ups, and I wonder if Balawahdiwa can approach them directly. We escaped alive, but the enemy's not going to underestimate us again. No, he'll keep on with his dirty work, but quietly, while you and I sit idle and the G-men— Oh, they aren't fools, but I've got a hunch the enemy took their measure beforehand and made provision against their methods."

My witch laid fingers around chin and gazed out the window. "Yes, that may well be," she murmured. "Coyote could act on impulse, but those behind him, who urged him on and opened the way and then doubtless helped—yes, I believe they're thinking far ahead."

She looked back at me. It was as if a green fire flickered in her eyes. Now her voice took on a shivery kind of life. "If this is a plot by Fu Ch'ing, to wreck the American space program as part of gnawing away at the foundations of all the West— Perhaps it isn't. But our ignorance itself is a heavy handicap. I can imagine him snickering in his hideaway, at the middle of his web. One way or another, we need to know."

I couldn't respond in kind, not at once. "The British have been trying hard, and they aren't fools either."

"No, but— Steve, I've been thinking. The fact that they've failed thus far seems to show that he's taken their measure, in your words. And surely also of every thaumaturge they might reasonably consult, whether from other government agencies or independent operators. Nevertheless, Fu Ch'ing is mortal. And demons too have their limitations—in some ways narrower than the limits on humans. Nobody can think of everything."

Excitement rammed into me. It felt cold and smelled of thunderstorm. "Hey, you don't mean—"

"Cardinal Point was—is again, by now—well warded against every plausible kind of hostile spell and Power, whether American, European, or Indian. Nobody thought of Far Eastern forces. They aren't too well understood in the West anyway. Well, I've acquired some small amount of Zuni lore and skill. Would the enemy be prepared for that?"

"My God!" I leaped to my feet, shaking. "And you and I together, we'd be unexpected in ourselves, if we manage it right— The old firm!" I whooped. "Matuchek and Matuchek, confounders of the ungodly, rescuers of the afflicted, we also walk dogs! Yahoo!"

"Easy, wolf, easy," she cautioned. "So far it's just an idea. It may be worthless. We'd certainly need to plan and prepare, and we'd need somebody over there to help us, somebody strong who has never occurred to anyone, and—" She broke off. "And that's enough for the time being. Put on your cheerful mask. We have company."

I calmed myself, sort of. Ben came dustily into the kitchen, where he'd heard us, and stopped at the breakfast nook. His feet plodded, his head drooped. "Hi, scout," I greeted. "How was the game?"

"All right," he mumbled.

"Your team lost, huh?"

"Naw. We won."

"Well, good for you."

"Not me. I struck out every time at bat. In the outfield I missed two balls I should've got."

"Too bad. Well, everybody has an occasional off day," I said desperately. "I don't imagine your teammates hold it against you."

He looked up. "I wasn't thinking," he blurted. "I was scared. About you and Mom."

"What?" said Ginny. "Oh, my dear. We told you yesterday evening we had to go out and might not get back till this morning." She reached up to stroke the rumpled hair. "And here we are. What is there to be scared of?"

"N-nothin'. If you say so." His lip quivered. "I, uh, I better go wash and change." He hurried off.

"What the devil?" I muttered, dismayed. "Has Val been telling tales? And why? What about?"

"She hasn't, I'm certain. Children are more observant and smarter than their parents are apt to know," Ginny replied bleakly. "Ours have heard something of what happened in the past. It's natural for them to wonder if it could happen again. The Selene fiasco was bad enough. Now we come and go on mysterious errands, and we and Uncle Will are obviously worried, and we won't tell them what it's all about."

"Um-m, yeah. . . . But how can we?"

"We can *think*."

Seizing after anything, I said, "You know, I'd guess Ben's more frightened on our account than on his own."

"I expect so. He's your son." *And yours*, I thought. Ginny's voice lost its momentary softness. "That is a horrible fear. I know."

Finishing our meal in an automatic way, we repaired to the living room. We hadn't long to brood till Val returned too, leading Chryssa by the hand. The little one ran straight to Ginny and buried her curly head in her mother's lap. She didn't cry, but she clung. Ginny hugged her and murmured.

Val regarded me. "How was your outing?" she asked. She didn't smile. "You look like the ants came at the picnic with machine guns and freight cars."

"Oh, it wasn't a picnic," I said. "You heard us explain we needed to do some nighttime research. It took all night, it was tiring, and afterward we had to be at a conference about it. How was your day?"

She shrugged. "It was a day. If you don't want me for anything, I'd like to relax a while." She stalked off to her room. There was no reason for her to slam the door. I know when I've been rebuffed.

Because she felt we'd rebuffed her. That hurt worse than fire ants.

Ginny got Chryssa more or less comforted and settled down in the game room. Ben was on hand there. She came back to me and said, "I told them we're going to call on Will, if he's receiving, but we'll soon be home again."

"We are?" I asked vaguely.

"If possible." She resonated the phone. To my surprise, her brother seemed much better, even at ease. "Sure," he said. "Come on over. Be happy to see you."

Ginny took her wand and summoned Edgar from his perch. I wondered why. We got on our Jag and skimmed the streets. Passersby gave us fleeting glances. Some waved. We'd become an ordinary sight hereabouts. It was as well they didn't see us closely. My emotions were a hash, glad, angry, fierce, eager, sad. Ginny, who steered, had taken on the look of a Valkyrie canvassing for candidates.

After a while she spoke, knifelike through the murmur of traffic and cleft warm air. "This trouble in the children settles the matter, doesn't it? We won't let things writhe on and on, not if we can do anything at all by ourselves."

My heart bumped. "Go after that highbinder in England?"

"I'll have to study the situation. It may not be feasible. But we can dare hope."

"Uh, this involves Will?"

"Inevitably, if we'll be away for any length of time. Of course, we'll make no mention of what we really have in mind."

I must force: "You don't trust him—entirely?"

Her fingers tightened around her knees. "That's beside the point. The idea is to take Fu Ch'ing by surprise. What Will, or anybody, doesn't know can't be . . . tricked . . . out of him." She was silent for a bit. "We can tell him about the al-Bunni plans in nonspecific terms. If something comes of that, it won't stay secret long."

We entered his neighborhood of old houses, old trees, old memories. She lifted us into the top traffic lane, which nobody else was using, and unsheathed her wand. "Edgar," she said to the bird on her shoulder, "seek out any spy who lurks hereabouts," added several arcane words, and touched the star to his beak.

"Gruk," he croaked, "yoicks," and took off. We circled around several blocks while he disappeared beneath the sunlit green crowns.

He was soon back, flapped alongside, and pointed with his beak. We followed. When he landed on her shoulder again, she aimed the wand straight earthward. It flashed. She smiled as sweetly as any cat at a mouse, brought us to street level, and cruised past the spot. Two vehicles stood on their unfolded legs a couple of blocks diagonally from the rear of Will's house, barely in sight of it. Neither was noteworthy, a broom and a small carpet with its pavilion up and curtains drawn.

We passed on by. Ginny nodded. "Two men inside," she said, "doubtless Fibbies. They're employing a scryer and a spell checker. Whenever Will leaves, I daresay one trails him, on foot or on the stick."

"They'll note our arrival," I said unnecessarily.

"And why should we not visit my brother?"

"Hey," I cried, "if he's been under surveillance, then after that encounter we had, he's got to be in the clear!"

"A great enough, alien enough Power could deceive their eyes and blind their apparatus."

Her starkness shriveled my timbre. "You don't mean you really believe—"

"No. I don't. But it is a possibility that will have occurred to the agency. We need facts—positive, not negative evidence—who and what the enemy is, what he's been doing and why."

We settled in front of the little house. Sun-speckled shade cooled an outsize, not too well mowed lawn. A goldfinch chirped energetically, somewhere among leaves. Will met us at the door. His clothes were sloppy and comfortable, his handshake firm, his voice hearty. "Welcome. What's the occasion?"

"Oh, to say hello and, well, see how you're doing," I replied. "You're looking pretty good."

"Feeling it, too. Sorry I was such a moomph yesterday." *Was it only yesterday? Judas priest!* "In rotten shape. But now— Come in, come in."

Ginny had kept her wand loosely in her hand and stayed a bit aside. From the corner of an eye I saw her give the rod a casual half twirl that swept the star-point over his breast before she collapsed and sheathed it. Edgar leaned forward at the same instant, wings partly spread, beak aimed.

"Why, is anything wrong?" she said to the raven, quite lightly, and once more spoke a phrase unknown to me. He buzzed into her ear. She laughed. "Just fidgety." We went inside.

Crammed bookshelves fairly well lined the living room. Volumes spilled over onto worn carpet and shabby chairs. They included an *I Ching* and *Book of Songs* in the original—he'd identified them for us earlier— through scientific and historical tomes to literature from Shakespeare to Sherlock Holmes, with plenty of modern paperbacks in various languages. Some of the covers on those were gaudy. Two fine old Chinese scrolls found space on the walls. Something in the background, I guessed by Vivaldi, turned the tobacco-tainted air lyrical.

Will cleared seats for us. "Beer?" he offered. "I've made a discovery, a Dutch brew, worth sailing far for."

We said yes, please, and settled ourselves, Edgar on the mantel amidst a souvenir collection of Japanese figurines, dogs and badgers and whatnot.

Will went off to the kitchen. Ginny leaned close to me. Her whole being glowed. "Steve," she whispered, "he's at peace."

"He does seem okay." It wasn't easy to keep my reply as low, the way her relief washed over me.

"Nothing bad registered. Nothing. Oh, it was a superficial scan, like the others I was able to make before. I couldn't be sure then and I can't be absolutely certain now. But there *is* a difference, not merely in his appearance and behavior."

"Uh-huh. Extracting information even when your data points are below noise level—"

"And I know him. He's himself again, completely himself."

Let's hope he stays that way, I thought, and kicked the thought downstairs.

Will returned carrying a tray loaded with crackers, cheese, glasses, and three frosty bottles of Vanderdecken. Having set it before us, he put a saucerful of the snacks on the mantel for Edgar. "What a change in you," his sister said frankly. "I'm so glad."

He chuckled. "Me too."

"How did it happen?"

He extracted pipe and pouch from assorted pockets. "Well, after we talked on the phone I heated some soup. Afterward I couldn't stay on my feet and went to bed. Slept the clock around and more; must've been ten A.M. at least when I woke. Ravenous, if your familiar will pardon the expression. Did horrid things to a steak and appurtenances, soon felt marvelous, got an idea, worked on it, and was relaxing for a bit when you called."

"But the cause?"

He shrugged. "Who knows? What caused the malaise in the first place?"

"Unless we learn that," said Ginny slowly, "we can't tell whether it will recur."

"Or, if it does, how to fix it," I added.

Will nodded. "I've been thinking about that." He stayed calm. "Off and on throughout, when I had a chance and was in shape to. Who wouldn't? Likewise today, till my idea seized me." He filled the pipe and tamped it with a thumb. "You're the expert, of course, Ginny. In this field, my notions are inevitably vague. But I wonder if my trouble hasn't been a simple matter of resonance."

"Hm." She frowned. "Naturally, that occurred to me, but since you wouldn't agree to a thorough examination—"

He darkened for a minute. "You know why. I told you. Privacy. I have not told you how much turmoil this has brought to my conscious-

ness. Imagine, though. Would you have let me probe you, however lovingly, however confidentially, unless you'd become more desperate than
I was?"

I, at least, could imagine; and Ginny was my wife, for Heaven's sake.
After all, Will hadn't been continuously miserable. Those were episodes.
In between them he was more or less okay.

"Resonances?" I asked.

He snapped fire from his ring. Ginny explained for him: "Goetic
forces were surely striking at the project, like waves against a seawall, long
before they broke through. Will was a large part of its original and continuing inspiration. By the law of sympathy, he may have responded to—
shall I say backwashes of those thwarted tides. They could have produced
depression, confusion, and psychosomatic illness."

"Why didn't it happen to anybody else?"

"His innate personality may make him unusually vulnerable. And then
his early experience with the Fair Folk may have made him hypersensitive
to such influences, almost like getting an allergy. In any event, now the
wall has been breached, the damage has been done, the assault is in
abeyance, the whole situation has changed."

She did not say it was less dangerous.

"I'd guess the aftereffects took this past week to wear off," Will proposed. "An optimistic diagnosis, perhaps, but why not accept it till further
notice?" His cheer had revived. He sat down across the coffee table from
us, filled pilsner glasses, and raised his. "To a better future. *Kan bei.* Or
proost, I believe, is the Dutch word. What's the Czech toast, Steve?"

"I dunno. I've heard my family doesn't even spell the name right any
longer." We clinked rims. The drink was cool and tingly. "How about
dinner with us again this evening?" I invited.

"Thanks, but sorry," he replied. "I told you I had a great idea today.
I want to develop it further, turn in as early as possible, get up before
moonrise, and take my portable specterscope into the desert."

With the FBI tippytoeing behind, I thought. *Oh well.* I wished them
joy of it. Me, I find few things more exquisitely boring than standing by
while somebody else tinkers with a piece of apparatus. "What is this idea?"

"Um-m, on the technical side, I'm afraid. A test of the hypothesis that
the Fair Folk are indeed there. That implies that some are always moving
away from the morning terminator, the sunrise line, to avoid direct sunlight. Since by the laws of thermodynamics they are at a temperature not
identical with that of their immediate surroundings, a minuscule Doppler
effect on the infrared radiation that their presence polarizes slightly but
measurably—"

Ginny laughed. "Never mind. You *are* back to your own self."

"Well, fine," I said. "However, I expect you'll agree the real test is for somebody to land and meet them."

Will was not an unworldly academic. On Long Island he'd been a keen sailboat racer; here he went camping and backpacking; he'd taken more money from me in poker games than I had from him. He caught my drift, lowered his beer, and clamped his gaze upon me. "You have hopes beyond another Selene," he breathed.

We told him that we'd obtained certain calculations and preliminary plans that looked promising. He didn't inquire further. Nor did he jump up and dance, though we saw it in his eyes. "A possibility, you say? But to realize it—" He sighed. "That, the how of it, is out of my department."

"Not absolutely," Ginny said.

He jerked to attention. "What do you mean, please?"

"Steve and I may have to go back east in this connection." I sat in awe of her steadiness. "Back east" implied the Midwest, Nornwell; it did not actually say so. "A week, perhaps more. We aren't free to discuss details yet, and if we do leave we shall have to word our calls home carefully. The hostiles are still loose, you know."

He smoked like a steam locomotive. "Are you that worried about Coyote or whoever? Parochial and unsophisticated Beings, I should think."

"Coyote—or whoever—apparently has allies." She could admit this because the press had already speculated about it, along with much wilder stories. My favorite rumor had to do with the moon inciting free love, which led to a plot against a lunar landing by the Pope and the Ku Klux Klan. "Let's play cautiously."

He nodded. "I see."

She caught me also by surprise: "If we do have to take off, would you come over and stay with the children?"

He barely grabbed his pipe before it dropped and ignited his pants. "What? Are you joking?"

"Some adult must. You're our best bet."

The FBI surveillance will come along, I thought. *Which in the present case is not a bad thing.*

"But," he protested, "but I don't know anything about—about child care."

"You know more than you think," she pursued. "Not that there would likely be much call on you. Valeria is quite mature for her age. Ben is a sensible and well-behaved boy. Between them they can mostly do for Chryssa whatever she can't do herself—except be the father stand-in and tell her bedtime stories and other such roles I know you enjoy. We'd arrange for our housecleaner and her mother to give extra help. They're kind and reliable people. As for your work, I'm hoping you can take it over there, and sleep there, and know where to call for help in any unlikely emergencies."

He bit his lip. "It's a considerable responsibility," he stalled.

She looked straight at him. "We trust you, Will."

20

ON OUR WAY HOME, GINNY AND I REACHED ANOTHER AGREEMENT. WHEN WE ARRIVED, I knocked on Valeria's door. She opened it and glowered. "We need to talk by ourselves," I said. "There's something important for you to know."

Her face came alive. "Yako," she replied, whatever that meant in her argot, and followed me to my study. Her mother felt that her father could best handle this, preferably in a masculine atmosphere. Well-worn leather chairs; a couple of ship models on shelves and a half-built one on the desk along with other clutter; a bookshelf whose contents ran to Mark Twain, Jack London, mystery novels, and stacked-up *Arizona Flyways* as well as engineering references; a bowling trophy; pictures on the walls that included me with my high school football team and me canoeing in the North Woods; also on the wall, a cutlass that sailed with Decatur and afterward went on a journey more long and strange; my pistol, which I still used for target shooting, locked away, but a faint fragrance of Hoppe's No. 9 in the air—

We took our seats, she on the edge of hers. My swivel chair creaked as I leaned back, crossed my legs, and bridged my fingers. Otherwise we kept silent maybe half a minute. The blue eyes were enormous. For the first time in years, I missed my pipe.

"Val," I said at last, "you probably think we owe you an apology and an explanation. In a way we do. Trouble is, right now it's impossible, and will be for some while to come. Back in the war, men got told to do this or not do that. Period. Usually the reason seemed plain. Like clearing the enemy off a hill that gave him too good a position for his artillery. Sometimes, though, we didn't know sh—diddly about why. And we never were briefed on the overall tactics. That'd have been bound to leak to the enemy, and he'd know what to prepare for and where'd be the place to strike back at us. Nor were those tactics fair. Some units got thrown into a meat grinder, and their officers knew beforehand that would happen.

Others stayed in reserve and mainly were bored to death. It was how things worked out.

"I know this is ancient history to you, buried in the books with Waterloo and Gettysburg. But plenty of guys are above ground yet to whom it was grunt reality. And it's still in the nature of conflict, of life itself. If you haven't read the Book of Job let me recommend it to you."

Val gulped and shivered.

"All right," I continued after another stillness, "that affair at the Point was, is, more than a malicious prank. It turns out to involve truly dark Powers. What they are, what they want, and how powerful they are, we can only guess. Your mother and I have taken part in trying to find out more and do something about it. We wanted to spare our children fear and nightmares. So we evaded questions. Maybe now and then we lied. It was well intentioned. But to suppose that you, at your age, with your intelligence, would not soon realize we weren't leveling with you—too late, I see that was an insult. For this we do must humbly apologize."

"Oh, Dad!" She half reached toward me. The hand dropped. But sudden tears glimmered on her lashes.

"We still can't tell you much," I said. "This *is* a sort of war situation. Not that we're high brass with any clear understanding. But we do need to keep certain things secret."

"Yes, it's a gitzy business," she whispered. "Scabrous, too."

I smiled. "What we can do, if you're willing, is enlist you."

She leaped to her feet. "What? Me? Yes, sir!" she whooped. "Molly O'Kay!"

"Whoa, pony, whoa down." I waved her back to her chair. "It'll be Home Guard duty, keeping alert, standing by, a lot of KP. Which is vital stuff. Your Uncle Will did as much toward winning the Caliph's War as most front-line soldiers. Likewise for military mechanics, quartermasters, and, yes, clerks. We'll *depend* on you."

Her lip quivered, the rest of her shuddered, then she sat quietly and replied, "Yes, I, I understand. If I can just have an idea of what it's all for."

"It seems the bad guys mean to sabotage the American space program—permanently," I said. "The FBI and other agencies are working on that. Your mother and I were able to contribute a little, and we've called on the wisdom of her friend, the Zuni priest." This much I could tell her. Part of it was no more than common sense could deduce from available facts; part was by now known to both the Feds and the foe. "I can't go into detail. That'd endanger us. However, I can share something special, if you'll keep it to your absolute self."

Her forefinger drew a cross over her lips. "On my soul's honor." How utterly solemn she could be!

But when I spoke of the spacecraft plans we'd gotten from a source I must not name, of the possibility of Operation Luna making an end run around both the politicians and the enemy, she shouted and laughed and sprang into my lap to hug me. "Magniff! Like—like stars in the mashed potatoes! Oh, Daddy-man, you are a sly old woof!"

"Easy, there," I urged after she'd calmed slightly. "This is at the earliest stage, remember. Don't count your chickens when the rooster's barely been introduced to the hen. Probably your mother and I will have to go back east for a week or two and investigate further." That misdirection hadn't hurt me when we used it before. It did this time. "If so, Uncle Will will move in here, but most of the housekeeping responsibility will fall on you. He knows as much as you do about our new prospects, so you and he can discuss them if you want, but only when you're strictly alone. Mainly, though, what we need you for, starting this day, is to create a better atmosphere at home. Join with us in lifting Ben and, especially, Chryssa out of their fears. If they see you relaxed and cheerful—savvy?"

After she had swallowed hard, her answer came bravely. "*Sí, señor.* I feel a lot better already."

"Good. We can maybe figure out tactics, like jokes and games. But first— Well, no denying there'll be a load on you, and it may from time to time get heavy. Are you prepared to shoulder it?"

"I am."

"Okay. In return, your sentence of confinement to quarters is commuted as of tomorrow morning. Go out and have fun while you can, punkin."

"Th-th-thanks." The youthful earnestness remained. "I'll always be on call, sir. And if anything really bad happens while you're gone—" Fire blazed up. "God help the baddies!"

That alarmed me a bit as I recalled Sneep's visit, plus various earlier incidents. Feeling it would be unwise to spoil the present mood, I contented myself with a mild warning. Thereafter we plunged into plans for things to do.

The upshot was that dinner became a happy meal and the youngsters quickly got back their merriment. Soon they looked forward to the change of pace while their parents were gone.

As for me, I returned to the lab. Thus Ginny, not I, received Barney's courier and gave him a copy of the documents. She told me that, as promised, he bore no resemblance to the colorful woodsman whose name he borrowed. He didn't even wear the winged Federal Express cap. Rather, he showed just enough individuality that he wasn't too conspicuously drab and anonymous. "Yeah," I said, recalling an incident once at Nornwell, "from a private detective firm. Watson and Goodwin, I'll bet. Their operatives are expert at self-effacement."

Otherwise Ginny was occupied most of her waking hours. That wasn't with her practice. Again she'd phased it out, canceling or postponing appointments, referring urgent cases elsewhere. I'd have worried about her future career if I didn't know her reputation had become proof against moth, rust, and disgruntlement.

In fact, this was part of her problem. Word would fly around that Dr. Matuchek must be up to something. The enemy's spies would scarcely buy the idea that it was a much-needed vacation. Well, let them share the impression that we planned a huddle with our partners at Nornwell. So far, we hoped, they wouldn't suspect why, but they could make several different plausible guesses, and if one of them happened to be the "real" reason, Operation Luna, it was a blind anyway.

Barney gave it substance when he called on Friday. That resonance was encrypted, but we couldn't be dead certain of security and he kept his language well guarded, like us. Still, that big, easygoing man had gotten as enthusiastic as a supernova. "It looks great," he boomed. "You'll want funds. Suppose I transfer fifty thousand dollars for startup expenses—to your personal account, to keep things simple. We'll worry about the bookkeeping later."

"First we'd better worry about the feasibility of the whole thing," I said, hedging the way any engineer had better.

"Sure, sure, but that's what you're going to investigate, isn't it?" The letter we sent along with the plans had made clear that he shouldn't confide in anyone else till further notice. "You can call on our facilities anytime, like a superreckoner to solve some complicated question. Its operators don't have to know what the calculation is for. And so forth. But mainly, I'll bet, you'll be working by yourselves, on the spot. R and D costs money. I don't mind this much risk. Looks to me like we've been dealt three of a kind. We might draw for a full house or a four."

"*Might,*" I said. "Oh, well, we'll keep reasonably good records here, and if the effort fails, it's deductible, isn't it?"

"We'll want a conference with you, *viva voce*, soon," Ginny added.

The letter had given a slight but sufficient hint that we didn't really. "Sure. Anytime. I'll see to it that you aren't pestered while you're hereabouts. Only give me a little advance notice, please. You remember the code message for that."

There wasn't any. Ginny caught on at once, I a second later. "We do," she said. "Meanwhile, carry on. Give everybody our best," by which she meant his family and our small gang of dreamers.

This was among the few interruptions in her labors. Mostly those were too esoteric to seem like the hard work they were. She ransacked arcane files, learning what she could about Fu Ch'ing, his cohorts, and possible allies for us in England. The last of these searches drew her into long comunications over channels known to few. She studied the goetics of our local Indians and, besides the books, passed considerable time down on the Zuni reservation, occasionally at peculiar hours. I gathered that Balawahdiwa wasn't the only adept she inquired of, learned from, and practiced with, but she didn't encourage questions about it. Having decided in due course that, yes, we should go, she slipped off to Albuquerque and made the travel arrangements. I didn't ask what precautions she took.

I myself had far less of a role. Three days passed at the Point, in the lab, more and more frustrated. We simply hadn't anything worthwhile to do. Then Helen Krakowski, newly back from Washington, sighed that I might as well take indefinite leave of absence. Project Selene appeared to have been decanted into a Klein bottle.

The next several days were *good*. Barney's call Friday morning began them. After that I didn't spend, I gained, many hours with the kids. Their mother being busy, I took them to shows and on excursions—not always all three, because Val had her own pleasures to pursue while she could, but generally she did come along—and once Ben and I went fishing, just the two us— Never mind. In between, I worked on my ship model, played a little poker, finally read *War and Peace* . . . No matter.

"I've found the man we want," Ginny whispered at last in our bed. The window stood open to a night not yet gone cold. A breeze lulled. She lay close beside me. I put a hand on her thigh and through the silky nightgown felt how the muscles stirred.

Nevertheless the news jarred me to hunter's attention. "You have? Who?"

"Nobody you ever heard of, though he knew my parents and once had a scientific collaboration with my father. Tobias Frogmorton of Cambridge University."

"Huh?"

"Professor emeritus of archaeology, Fellow of Trinity College. He's lived sedately, lifelong bachelor, except for field work in younger days. During the Kaiser's War he was a cryptographer. After taking a thaumaturgic degree with honors, he put that knowledge to use, notably in deciphering Mayan and Aztec inscriptions—animating copies, observing responses to experimental readings and enactments. It's become a standard technique, which has lately cracked Minoan Linear A. His skills were invaluable in the Caliph's War, reconstructing intelligence from fragments of information. But he's been retired and obscure for years—a large plus for our purposes. And he is willing to help."

"Well, if you say so," I muttered dubiously.

Her lecturer's tone livened. "Among other things, he may be able to provide us with a familiar."

"What? You're not taking Edgar along?"

"No. British quarantine regulations. I suppose we could get an exemption for him, I being a licensed witch, but that would mean the kind of attention-drawing paperwork we want to avoid."

"Good work, sweetheart." I pulled her to me.

Thus, two weeks and three days after the disaster, we kissed our kids goodbye very early in the morning. Will flitted us to Albuquerque flyport. We shook hands with him, ignored the tickets to the Midwest that we'd openly bought—maybe we could get a refund later—and used those Ginny had arranged.

The flight to New York was uneventful. We'd have liked to break the journey there, as sensible people do, but didn't really dare. Instead, we changed carpets at Idlewild for London. The transatlantic crossing wasn't bad. A Boeing 666 gives room to walk around in the pavilion, have a drink at the bar as well as a couple of meals in your seat, and try for a snooze. Just the same, six or seven hours aloft can get long, particularly after a hop across the continent, and half a hundred fellow travelers don't make for restful surroundings. We reached Heathrow pretty well wiped out and, having gone through passport control and customs, wanted nothing more than the nearest available hotel room.

Some hours of sleep and a big, fat English brunch restored us. Still trying not leave a trail, we didn't rent a broom but boarded a train for Cambridge. I like those puffy little locomotives, the genial conductors, the compartments where people mind their own business and read their own newspapers unless perchance you fall into an interesting conversation, the beautiful countryside through which you steam, even the meat pies you can buy at the stops. Ginny does too, I think. In any case, we felt rather jolly as we chugged north to our meeting.

21

CAMBRIDGE GAVE US A PROPER ENGLISH WELCOME, RAIN. OUR GLIMPSES OF SEVERAL lovely ancient buildings were blurred as we cabbed from the station to a hotel and, after unpacking and phoning, on to Frogmorton's house. The weather was soft, though, cool and silver-gray. When we stepped off the taxi and out of its field, Ginny stopped a moment. "After New Mexico," she sighed, "I have an impulse to stand here, staring up, with my mouth open."

"Like a turkey?" I answered.

"Have you no poetry in you?"

"Oh, sure. 'Rain, rain, go away. Come again another day.' " It's apt to give me a phantom ache in the tailtip I no longer have. Even so, I might have enjoyed it if we'd thought to buy an umbrella. Or if she'd spelled it off us; but that was more effort than it was worth.

We opened a garden gate and strode fast along a path lined with zinnias. Their colors flew gallant as battle flags. Everything else was green, vivid, intense, nearly arrogant when we remembered our Southwest. Through a line of willows behind the house, I spied the river. Our errand felt unreal amidst this peacefulness.

The Lindens probably took its name from trees long gone; an elm companioned it now. It was old enough—older than Albuquerque, not much younger than Santa Fe. Beneath a steep, tiled roof, most windows in the whitewashed walls had eighteenth-century casements with nine-teenth-century glass, but the oaken, iron-bound front door must be orig-inal. I felt shy about wielding the knocker till I saw what a drunken brass face leered at me, right out of the Restoration.

A formidable-looking housekeeper let us in. When we explained who we were, she rustled ahead of us through a vestibule to the—sitting room, is that the right word? It was rather dim today in spite of an edison shining inside a beaded lampshade. Furniture was antique, unmarked by children or cats. Books were as thick as Will's, but all neatly shelved. Between the cases, forebears stared from their sepia photographs. I couldn't help won-dering if we'd come to the right place.

Frogmorton left an armchair to greet us. He was short, skinny, round-shouldered, in baggy tweeds with a drab tie. White thin hair, white tooth-brush mustache, and horn-rimmed spectacles ornamented a beaky face as wrinkled as a washday bundle. "Ah, Mr. and Mrs. Matuchek!" His voice was high, almost squeaky. "No, I beg your pardon. Dr. and Mr. Matuchek, eh? How good to meet you." He shook my hand briefly—his felt bird-like—but clung to Ginny's. "I well remember your father, that great scholar, and your dear mother. Our acquaintance was before they were blessed with offspring. We lost touch, as one does. One intends to resume a relationship, but somehow time slips past until suddenly it is too late. *Fugaces labuntur anni.*"

"They do indeed," Giny murmured while I, fumbling with the rem-nants of my Latin, decided this was probably not obscene.

"Mrs. Turner, bring in the tea, if you please," Frogmorton said. "A bit early for tea, perhaps, but we should fortify ourselves for the work ahead, don't you agree? Do please be seated. Smoke if you wish. Until we are positioned for action, will you permit me a few inquiries as to how you have fared over the years? I have been aware of your past exploits, of course, and have examined the detailed record of them since you first called. However, I shall be grateful if you care to bring me up to date on the Graylock family. And the, ah, Matuchek family, needless to say."

Ginny talked for both of us. Frogmorton chattered and chattered. I didn't want to appear surly, but a word had to be honed mighty thin to slip in edgewise, so I concentrated on the tea, cucumber sandwiches, and seedcake, suppressing wistful thoughts about a pub.

It got more interesting after Ginny steered him onto his own subject. *Hey*, I thought, *if Ben does go into paleontology, he ought to hear about these techniques. I'll bet they can be adapted.* Unfortunately, however, Frogmorton tried to spice the conversation with jokes. They ran to stories like that of a medieval monk who had a pot of wine at his side as he copied a chronicle. The penmanship got wobblier and wobblier. At the end he wrote *"Male scripsi, bene bipsi."* Frogmorton laughed and laughed. Ginny and I did our best.

The housekeeper cleared away the clutter. "We shall be in my closet, Mrs. Turner," he informed her. *Huh?* I thought. "Do not allow us to be disturbed by anyone on any account. If perchance the Last Trump sounds, I daresay we shall hear it ourselves. Otherwise dinner for three will be at eight o'clock."

"Have no fears," he added as he led us off through a series of rooms. "For evening meals I rely on my cook. He does an excellent leg of mutton, if I may say so. Your father, Dr. Matuchek, used to complain to me about the difficulty of obtaining mutton in America. And we shall have something a little choice in the way of claret."

To my relief, "closet" turned out to mean a large chamber at the back of the house. He unlocked the door and bowed us in. Floorboards creaked underfoot; wormholes peppered murky oak wainscot. Three windows had been left unchanged: small, leaded, with glass like the bottoms of beer bottles. We were in dusk till Frogmorton barred the door and touched an object. It was a bronze statue, Greek or Roman, of a torchbearer whose branch flared with sudden cold corposant fire. More light streamed from the eyes of a grinning Mayan jaguar or feathered serpent or whatever it was. More books lined the walls. Papers filled pigeonholes above a desk long enough to double as a workbench. A few pieces of goetic equipment rested on it. Otherwise a cabinet, a couch, and three Victorian office chairs were the only furniture. A fine layer of dust grayed everything and a spider had set up shop under the ceiling.

"Pray pardon the untidiness," said Frogmorton. He found a feather duster and scuttled about making random motions. "I am seldom here, now in my *otium*, and cannot entrust its maintenance to anyone else, not even Mrs. Turner. An honest, conscientious woman, granted, but if, for example, she took volumes off the shelves for cleaning, she might refile them alphabetically!" Horror shook his voice. "And, to be sure, certain articles should not be so much as touched by laymen." Again he attempted levity. "The wrong laying on of hands, heh, heh."

Ginny looked around. She had unfolded a wand from her purse. The star-point flickered, ice blue, bloodred. "You do have some powerful things here," she agreed. "Don't you worry about accidents, intruders, fire, whatever could happen in your absence?"

"I have spelled in an alarm." He nodded at the Mayan figure. "If untoward circumstances arise, it will call for assistance, loudly as well as goetically."

I decided that if it did cry, "Help! Help!" it must be a jaguar.

But why, why had Ginny settled on this old dodderer for our ally?

Then all at once he stood straight, looked squarely at us, and said in a voice no longer thin but blade-keen: "Very well, shall we to work? We can speak freely. The house was warded during the war against espial human and nonhuman. I have kept its defenses active and up-to-date, for I always hoped they would never be needed again, and I always suspected they would."

We sat down and commenced. He and Ginny spoke, or queried, directly to the point. I put in what I was able, not much; but I wasn't bored, Lord, no.

More than an hour went to exchanging information. They'd have been unwise to communicate other than minimally before now, no matter how secure the channels seemed to be. She filled him in on the space project situation, the native Beings, the spoor of Asian demons, the potentials of Zuni lore, and the unpleasantness out in the mountains. For his part, he knew considerable about Fu Ch'ing, and since she contacted him had managed to learn more.

"Largely through professional connections, you know. He is enigmatic but not totally isolated. Published several brilliant papers in the past, *exempli gratia*, on modifications of Feng Shui, geomancy, required by the theory of plate tectonics. Poems too, esteemed by connoisseurs, also for their calligraphy. Various colleagues told me this or that about his actions, his movements, yes, a few of his idiosyncrasies. And I still have acquaintances in the Secret Service, who were willing to pass along in confidence what little they knew. . . ."

"Yes, you are quite right, it would be futile for you to approach the Service, Scotland Yard, or any other official agency. They could only listen to you, and must needs forbid you to act. Moreover, while they have not been subverted, it is far too possible that they have been infiltrated to some unknown degree. Witness the failure of every attempt to track him down."

"I think a version of a Zuni finding spell that I've learned might do the trick," Ginny said. "He wouldn't have safeguarded against that, would he?"

Frogmorton raised his brows. "Eh, what? Surely useless in this clime, this cultural setting. If it functioned at all, it might well merely warn him."

"I know. But I said a version. An adaptation, which you and I will work out between us. Look, Southwestern procedures of that kind are basically shamanistic, musical. That's not in the English tradition, therefore it'll be unexpected. Yes, I realize it occurs in China and through-out Central Asia. But this will employ a different scale, plus British ele-ments you will supply to create a unique hybrid. And the *use* of it, the methods by which we bring the cantrip to bear, everything we'll employ will surely be unknown to Dr. Fu."

"By God, we blindside him!" I exclaimed.

That was about all I got to say for another hour. Ginny and Frog-morton were off into technicalities, nearly as incomprehensible to me as modern literary criticism. Yet they kept my attention, ransacking musty books, uttering strange words, and operating peculiar instrumentalities. I shared the excitement that grew in them. The air fairly crackled with it.

And finally my love turned to me, aglow, and said, "I think we've got our basic spell, Steve. You'll take part too."

I realized I'd grabbed at the lens under my shirt. "How?" I admit I barked.

She laughed. "For starters, any suggestions you can make about the principal song. It's the core of the spell, you see. Fu Ch'ing hides his whereabouts by generating false indications of other places while screen-ing his own. We need a counterconfusion to annul this while a concurrent Finding exposes the reality."

I throttled back my emotions and nodded. "I think I see. Kind of like light waves interfering. They black each other out at some points and reinforce elsewhere."

"The analogy to particle wave interference in the famous two-slit ex-periment is perhaps closer," Frogmorton said. "By preventing ourselves from making observations, we establish—"

"Never mind," Ginny interrupted. He took it like a good sport. "The point is, we must tailor that song for the problem. It has to be British, using words powerful in their proper contexts, put together in such a way that they almost but not quite make sense. While you sing it, Steve, Pro-fessor Frogmorton and I will carry out the rest of the rite."

"An Irish melody, as old as possible," he urged. "The Druids em-ployed music in their Art, and a little persisted until recent times among the peasantry of the remoter counties. Some force should remain."

"Irish, hm?" Ginny pondered. "O'Carolan? No, it would take time to look up a piece of his and longer for Steve to learn. . . . Wait. Everybody knows this one, and nobody knows how old it is, though apparently it goes well back." She hummed a few bars.

"Oh, no!" I groaned.

Don't get me wrong. My wife is half Irish and we're both proud of it. We've visited Eire twice on vacations and been delighted with the country and the people. We know that throughout their history the Irish have contributed more than their share to world civilization. Nevertheless, when one of those fileted tenors launches into "Danny Boy" the devil in me mutters, "Oliver Cromwell, where are you now when we need you?"

Ginny caught my drift. "As a matter of fact, earlier words exist for the 'Londonderry Air.' A love song beginning, 'Would God I were the tender apple blossom—' "

"That will do for a first line," Frogmorton said eagerly. "Anchors text to music, don't you know. Thereafter the sense must drift free, while continuing to be poetic."

"Lines of great literature, you mean."

"Precisely. Blank verse until the last, which the melody requires be an Alexandrine."

Poetry and goetics are everywhere and forever intertwined. Besides, Frogmorton was the sort of chap who likes few things better than to relax with a refreshing verse play or sonnet sequence. The library in here was well stocked with stuff of that kind. I could help. We attacked the collection, riffling pages, strewing volumes, gabbling our discoveries.

"We want some Shakespeare for certain. *Macbeth*, the witchy one."

"Uh, this from Ben Jonson—"

"—a touch of earthy vigor. I remember during the last war, a song British soldiers often sang, rather vulgar—"

"Frankly, to me Pope is Dryden as dust, but now and then he does come up with a rock-solid line."

"—sensuality, opposing Fu's cold calculation. The *Rubaiyat*—"

"Hey, did Rupert Brooke himself write this? We've got to work it in somehow."

"Shelley, *The Revolt of Islam*. An added dimension for the continuum of cultural conflict. And it has the necessary scansion."

I'm being impressionistic. Actually we hopped to and fro among the texts like fleas on a griddle, we proposed and argued and struggled to fit pieces together and trashcanned most, for another hour or more. Eventually we had a scrawled thing that ought to serve.

Ginny made a fair copy, using an eagle quill pen on a sheet of wyvern-wing parchment. Frogmorton thrice dripped wax from the bees of Delphi on it, to stamp with the sigils of Thoth, Solomon, and St. George. Meanwhile I rehearsed. My partners didn't visibly wince. They only made me keep still while they readied the rest of the proceedings.

Outside, the rain had gone heavy, filling the windows with murk. We heard it hammer on walls and roofs. Wind piped. Inside, lights dimmed to embers and dusk laid hold of us. Ginny and Frogmorton enacted their gestures, chanted their words. At their signal I took the parchment, though I couldn't read it in the gloom, cleared my throat, and strove to stay on key.

> "Would God I were the tender apple blossom
> That struts and frets his hour upon the stage.
> To be made honest by an act of Parliament
> Call up the bloody Territorials.
> Worth makes the man, and want of it the fellow
> Beside me singing in the wilderness.
> Now there's a choice—heartache or tortured liver!
> A sweeter draught than ye will ever taste, I ween."

I concluded with a wolf-howl and bowed off. Nobody applauded. Well, they were still busy. I barely saw them as deeper shadows, dancing and gesticulating. Sparks spat blue in midair. I caught a brimstone whiff.

A crystal globe on the desk came alight. Writing appeared in it.

No, nothing alien, nothing ominous. Simply:

3, UPPER SWANDAM LANE
LONDON—

The globe blanked too fast for me to catch the postal zone.

Corposants brightened to normal. Ginny and Frogmorton let out shuddery breaths. Sweat glistened on their faces. They'd been through a mill.

"Did you get all of that?" I cried.

"Oh, yes," Ginny whispered. "How could I not?"

"And I," Frogmorton said, no louder.

He shook himself. Amazingly for an old geezer, he went directly back to the shelves, took down a huge atlas, spread it on the desk, consulted the index, and turned to a map of a city section. His finger traced over the page. Ginny bent close.

"Here," he said. "A sideway, virtually an alley, in Limehouse."

Her laugh rattled. "Limehouse? Isn't that ridiculously obvious?"

"Which may be why he chose it, Dr. Matuchek. I don't know what the building is like, although I would guess an abandoned warehouse or a dubious commercial establishment in that rather decayed district. One can readily learn. At any rate, there he sits motionless, like a spider in the center of its web, but that web has a thousand radiations, and he knows well every quiver of each of them.

"Enough for the nonce." Frogmorton turned away. "I decree that we have earned a bit of ease."

From the cabinet he took glasses and a bottle of Ragganmore, bless his tasteful heart. His alembic furnished Highland spring water. We sat for a while in companionable silence. The weather wildened.

"Perhaps we should inform the authorities," Frogmorton ventured at length.

"No," Ginny answered. "You know perfectly well Fu would be gone before they got there. Later, okay, *pro forma*, we can if you like. But first Steve and I have to go."

"The dangers are incalculable."

Her tone went steely. "Sir, my brother's reputation and liberty are at stake."

And possibly all our hopes and ambitions, or Western civilization, or humanity's future in the cosmos, or something else that I didn't feel like windbagging about. Mainly, I was goddamn mad. Whoever or whatever the jackals were behind our troubles, I wanted at them.

"I know," Frogmorton said softly. "I raised the question from a sense of duty." His glance dropped. "I regret that age and infirmity make me useless in anything but an advisory capacity. *Morbi tristisque senectus.*"

Ginny reached over and patted his hand. "Do you really imagine we can manage without your counsel?"

"Yeah," I chimed in. "Unlike the young gaucho named Bruno, I say as a werewolf I do know that muscles are fine, sharp senses divine, but brains, they are *número uno*."

Resolution rose afresh in him. "What do you mean to attempt?" he asked.

"That depends," I replied. "Basically, I guess, break in, confront him, and demand to know what the hell is going on."

Frogmorton frowned. "He is well guarded."

"Unless they keep silver bullets loaded, I've a notion I can handle his, uh, dacoits or whatever you call 'em."

Now Frogmorton winced. "We don't want violence, Mr. Matuchek, do we?" His tone steadied. "Indeed, I suspect Dr. Fu employs it—the physical kind—only as a last resort. You will be in much greater peril from things much more recondite."

"That's why I'll need a familiar," Ginny said.

There's a lot of misinformation around about familiars. They don't just run errands and such. They lend their thaumaturges psychic strength and, through whatever degree of rapport is possible, their nonhuman viewpoints, insights. They can serve as vessels of power or of spirit—they can be comrades in battle—how well we knew!

"Plus a weapon against Fu's critters," I added. "Can you help us with that too, sir?"

Frogmorton nodded. "Conceivably I can point you toward both, in a single embodiment," he said. "Conceivably. It may prove infeasible. I cannot promise more."

The wind skirled.

"Go on, please," Ginny begged.

He looked past us into the darknesses that, despite the lamps, laired in the corners under the ceiling. "I know of a sword."

Presently he went on, still staring elsewhere, speaking like one in a dream: "Long ago, as humans reckon time, a young man, during the Kaiser's War, I had occasion to visit York. That was the heart of the Danelaw, you may recall. I served as a cryptographer. Someone in the War Office got the idea that if we could turn up an inscription in an obscure runic alphabet—there were several, you know—it might be spelled into the basis of an unbreakable code. Balderdash, but orders were orders, and so I went sniffing with my goetic instruments all about the region.

"Exploring in the city itself, I came upon an object preserved in a minor church, a sword. It had been donated centuries before to the Abbey of St. Oswald's by a nobleman who had no further use for it. The type had gone out of style, you see. Besides, he meant to take vows and end his days as a monk. It has never drawn much notice. Apart from being in good condition, it does not appear unusual for its era, and any historical associations were already more or less forgotten. It was simply a curiosum, among numerous others.

"The abbey was razed after the Dissolution. Most of its treasures had been confiscated by the agents of Henry VIII. However, some had been ignored as being of no particular worth. There is a fugitive tradition that the monks hid certain especially valued and sacred objects behind brickwork. Be that as it may, pious hands did lay the pathetic remnants of movable property in the ancient undercroft.

"In the eighteenth century the buildings that had sprung up on the site were torn down and a new St. Oswald's erected, merely a parish church to help accommodate the rapidly growing city population. The known relics were brought forth for display, albeit down in the vaults, since the Georgian era had little interest in them. Nor did the antiquarianism of the Romantic movement change this. The building was too recent and architecturally uninspired. Its medieval objects had lain too long alone to have any reputation left such as might attract the curious.

"A Victorian gentleman did impulsively pay for the sword's restoration. His diary records surprise that it had not rusted, but what with chemistry being then an infant science, he does not seem to have wondered why. Only the organic parts, grip and scabbard, had rotted away and needed replacement. Shortly thereafter he died, before he could publicize the matter.

"Thus the undercroft and its contents continued to have few visitors. Vergers, of course, occasional clergy, tourists more active than most, and chiefly, the guest book shows, military men. But their interest was in the small souvenirs that soldiers back from the Napoleonic and colonial wars had donated, as was not uncustomary. These too were mostly downstairs. Among them, the sword was only an archaeological token."

Frogmorton paused for a sip. Ginny leaned forward. Light slid flamelike across her mane. "And?" she prompted.

"And I discovered a tremendous latent power in that blade," Frogmorton told us. "I established that it was dwarf-forged and given a spirit, far back in heathen Norway. It came to England with the Vikings. It can think, it can speak, it can hew through stone, steel, and spells. But all this became as nothing. The sword fell into the Great Sleep generations before it ceased to be carried into battle. It was still dormant when it received its new scabbard, and its powers remain bound until it is unsheathed."

"You didn't?"

"Good heavens, no. I detected the potential, but why loose it? I could imagine no use for it in the ongoing affray—or, for that matter, afterward in the Caliph's War—considering how limited its range of action must be. Rather, I visualized impetuous young men seizing on it and causing nothing but mischief within our own ranks. I take my Hermetic Oath seriously. Ergo, I maintained discretion.

"But as for you—what slight and uncertain auguries I was able to obtain after hearing from you suggest that here may be a weapon proper to your hands."

Lightning flared. Thunder crashed.

22

WE SLEPT LATE THE NEXT MORNING, AND THEN HAD THINGS TO DO. AMONG THEM WAS AR- ranging accommodations in York. With August Bank Holiday approaching, that wasn't the easiest job in the world. We waved money at a travel agent and got a suite in a posh hotel. Besides the expense, this was showier than we wanted. On the other hand, we might well need more privacy than a single room in a B&B offered. We shopped for several items we'd need—better here than close to the scene of the crime—and caught a train that brought us there by midafternoon.

We'd seen it before on our travels. One time isn't enough. The world has some towns that compare with it for beauty and charm—not many—but none that surpass. Mellow gold-hued sandstone of ancient walls and towers, crooked narrow streets with names like Whip-Ma-Whop-Ma Gate, half-timbered houses whose arcades line them and galleries lean over them, pubs where the beer and the friendliness are as genuine as you'll ever find and you can still hear the broad dialect of yeomen come in to market, history reaching back beyond the Romans and not embalmed but alive, here all around you— As we passed by the Merchants' Guildhall after we'd checked in at our lodging, we swore we'd come back when this miserable business of ours was behind us, and bring the kids, and take a week or more.

We found St. Oswald's on Oglethorpe Street. For a while we stood and stared, letting pedestrians surge around us. Though I strained my senses, nothing came to me but voices, shoe-clack, odors of man and smoke faint in the sunny air. Ginny couldn't very well unlimber a wand and check for peculiarities. The building did for sure look unpromising, brick, squarish. "Failed neoclassical," she muttered. Maybe the dull appearance wasn't entirely its fault. It lay almost in the shadow of the Minster. That most glorious of churches rose above roofs like God's personal benediction.

"Well," I said, "let's do it."

She nodded. We mounted the steps and entered. The interior was cool and somewhat dark. I don't know whether that was merciful to the altarpiece or made it still more rococo. Memorial tablets were sparse on the walls, under nineteenth-century stained glass that hadn't benefited from the Burne-Jones influence. A couple of bewigged busts in niches seemed to disapprove of us.

Nobody else was here but a little gray verger. We hadn't the heart not to let him show us around and tell us about the two gentlemen represented. Since one of them had fought in the American War of Independence and we were Americans, we heard about him at length. Finally we could drop some money in a collection box and ask to see the crypt.

"Certainly, certainly. Tickets are a shilling, if you please. Goes toward upkeep . . . Thank you very much. This way, if you please." He pottered to a door, unlocked it, switched on an edison, and led us down a flight of stairs. The first few were brick, evidently part of the rebuilding, but beyond that they were stone, deeply worn, hewn out in early Norman times. "The undercroft is quite small, you see. Undoubtedly it was much larger beneath the abbey, but earth and rubble have buried most. We believe proper excavation would uncover parts of the twelfth-century walls and foundation, as well as—who knows?—treasures the monks hid away from King Henry's expropriators. That would also mean a modern metal stair-well—do watch your step, please—but I am afraid our humble house of worship lacks glamour."

A lightbulb hung in a cramped vault. Flagstones lay damp underfoot. The walls were masonry. "Observe the herringbone pattern," the verger said with pride. "The work is timber grillage, but otherwise the materials are largely Roman." He gestured toward a flat brick wall at the far end. "Except for that, of course. The Georgian builders put it in to keep this remnant clear. Who knows what lies behind?"

Glass-topped exhibition cases filled most of what floor space there was. They looked kind of time-worn themselves: nineteenth century, if not older. Ginny's jaw clenched for a moment and a chill along my nerves stirred every hair on me. We had glimpsed the sword. It was all we could do not to barge straight over and peer.

Instead, we smoothed our faces and made interested noises while our guide pointed out this and that. "—medal bequeathed by Colonel Horatio Bullivant, who distinguished himself in the Peninsular Campaign. . . . Ghazi musket from the fatal battle of Maiwand. . . . Rather more antique, this rosary, said to have belonged to the last Catholic bishop but one—"

—and so on, until I could say, "What about this sword?" and hope I just sounded inquisitive.

It rested in a case together with a handsome earthenware bowl, a corroded bronze crucifix, a couple of bone chessmen, and a few more objects from the Middle Ages. The weapon dominated. About three feet long, blade broad on top and not tapering much to a bluntish point, it had a short, straight iron guard and a wide, flat-bottomed pommel rounded like a scoop of ice cream. Both were inset with gold curlicues. The haft between was wrapped in shagreen, doubtless part of the resto-ration. The scabbard was leather-covered wood, set with polished garnets. Was I fooling myself, or did I catch a sense of ferocity ready to spring, like a lynx in a cage? The jewels glared under the light. . . .

"Ah, yes." The verger was less than fascinated. "A venerable piece, dating back to the Danish period. Perhaps it properly belongs in a mu-seum, but here it has been for some seven hundred years. It is remarkable chiefly for its excellent state of preservation. Now the bowl you see, that is a rather fine example of local thirteenth-century pottery. It was a gift from Ulfrida, the wife of a prosperous dealer in salted fish. She acquired a posthumous reputation as a saint, although it never reached Rome—"

A card in the case read: *Sword donated about 1225 by Sir Ranulph Daunay of Thurshaw Manor as a sign of contrition for past bloodthirsti-ness before he took monastic vows. Style and workmanship date it to Scandinavia, approximately ninth century. Presumably it came to England with a Dane whose descendants married into the Norman house. Although the design grew obsolete, fragmentary chronicles suggest that scions of the family carried it into battle as late as Sir Ranulph's time, possibly under the impression that it was lucky. The reconstruction of hilt and sheath, the latter emplacing the stones that had been on its predecessor, was the gift of Mr. Humphrey Sedgworth, banker, in 1846.*

Real romantic.

Ginny and I had roughed out our plans beforehand. The conditions we found told us how to improvise. We made much of other relics, explaining that I was a military history buff and Ginny a fan of Regency romances. We fussed around till the verger gave up, pleaded that he must return to his duties elsewhere, and tottered upstairs.

At once we were at the sword. Ginny's wand came forth. When she'd whispered the right words, its star flared, blue-tinged white. She traced the latent powerfields like a hummingbird tracing flower scents; I remembered that the hummingbird was an incarnation of the Aztec war god. Me, I snapped any number of Polaroid photos and measured the dimensions of the sword as exactly as possible.

We dared not take too long. After about half an hour we tucked away our gear and left. The verger bade us a wistful good-bye. He didn't get many visitors who cared this much.

We returned in silence to our rooms. I slumped into a chair. Ginny began unpacking the stuff she'd require. "I don't feel right about this," I mumbled.

She frowned. "It is technically a theft. Of course, we'll return the thing when we're done with it."

"If we can. In any case, it's a violation of trust."

"Necessity knows no law. You didn't hesitate before."

"Not till I'd met that nice little guy."

"Whatever happens, shall we make a substantial donation to the church? I mean substantial. Anonymous, probably, but it's obvious their building fund or poor fund can use it."

Unless the whatever that happens involves our getting killed or worse, I thought.

But no, this approached self-pity. I think the British call it whinging. I myself had preached to my daughter that sometimes we humans have to break the rules, certain moral rules maybe included, and take the consequences—the blame, if our judgment turns out to have been wrong. I rallied my spirit, got up, and lent a hand.

I won't describe the work of the next hour or so. Some details are public knowledge, others are restricted to licensed operators, still others were proprietary, unique to Ginny. Goetics remains as much Art as technology. (Well, that's fairly true of mundane engineering too.) Basically, we used the data we'd acquired and my calculations from them to draw up specs for the sword and sheath—the material objects, that is. Then Ginny laid out the stock we'd brought from Cambridge according to Frogmorton's description. Mainly this was an iron bar, a couple of laths, a piece of leather, and a few pebbles. She put a Seeming on them. To every unaided sense they became identical with the exhibit. You'd have needed a vernier and a pretty accurate scale to tell the differences, short of a chemical analysis which nobody had ever done anyway. Oh, someone who cast a minor spell or simply had a Gift would realize something was funny, but it was a safe bet that no such person would visit the crypt anytime soon.

Afterward we went downstairs. The hour was early for dinner. We had a high tea instead, to which I added a stiff drink. Returning to our suite, we drew the shades and tried to sleep. That took me a while, but there was ample time. Night comes late in the English summer.

Also, it's short. Our clock owlhooted us awake at 2 A.M. We scrambled into our clothes. Besides my skinsuit underneath the street garb, I wore a topcoat and Ginny a cloak, cover for what we carried along and hoped to carry back. A distinct advantage of staying at a first-class hotel was that we didn't have to ring anybody out of bed at odd hours. That annoyance could have stuck in the memory.

Ginny smiled at the drowsy porter. "We thought we'd enjoy a starlit stroll on the walls," she explained in a voice that would have turned Scrooge's heart to warm mush.

"Be careful of your steps," he cautioned like a benign uncle. "You have a torch, ma'am? Good. Have a nice walk." He stood sentimentally looking after us.

I laid an arm around Ginny's waist. "Too bad we aren't really going to," I sighed. "Saving the world sure does get in the way of enjoying it."

She leaned briefly against me. "That's another matter we'll have to make amends for." Then her stride turned brisk.

The air was cool, damp, very quiet. Larger streets were lighted but the old "gates" lay full of shadows and old dreams. Once a policeman passed. He gave us a quick, close look, nodded affably, and continued on his beat. Somehow that deepened our loneliness.

St. Oswald's had too damn much illumination on it. We'd expected this, however. After scanning the sidewalks right and left, we went fast up the stairs to the portico. Ginny drew a Hand of Glory from her purse. It was only a monkey's paw, a tiny withered thing that glowed faint blue when she touched it to a door. (The monkey had died at an advanced age of a surfeit of bananas.) Its powers were equally slight. But ordinary locks clicked open under those black fingers, and closed again behind us.

No candles burned inside. St. Oswald's wasn't High Church. We used our flashlight—no, here in England, torch—to make our way through the nave to the inner door and down to the crypt.

Those innocents had installed no alarm for us to nullify. The Hand undid the case. I swung the glass lid back and grasped the sword. It felt massive, though not heavy. Unlike too many heroes of fantasy fiction, our forefathers were practical men who didn't wear themselves out swinging unnecessary mass. Even a battle ax ran to only about five pounds. Nevertheless, it seemed as if I gripped something *alive*.

Ginny freed me of my left coat sleeve and unslung the fake beneath. She laid it in the case, taking great care about its position, hung the real one from my shoulder, and dressed me again. She lowered the lid. I heard its lock, too long unoiled, grate back to closure. We retraced our thievish steps.

The street still stretched empty. I realized I was shivering a bit, the smell of my sweat sharp in my nostrils. "This was almost too easy," Ginny said.

"Y-you mean the enemy knows and—helped us along?"

"No, I mean if we went back to the hotel right away, the porter would wonder why." She laughed and tucked her arm under mine. "Guess we'll have to take that walk after all."

Unreasonable gladness jumped in me. Fears and tension fled. "By God, I get my wish!"

A staircase led onto the city wall. Most of the medieval circuit remains. The top has been paved for easy footing. We wandered hand in hand between the battlements. Beneath us slept the town. Opposite gleamed the river, and outlying homes gave way to broad countryside. Steeples, portals, the strong delicate towers of the Minster reached for the stars that glimmered overhead. Now, when traffic was hushed, we breathed stillness and ghostly fragrances from gardens. Often we stopped. The east had gone pale before we turned back.

The porter smiled as we came in. "I hope you enjoyed yourselves," he said, wearily amiable.

Suddenly noticing how rumpled my best girl's hair had gotten, I felt sheepish. She, though, returned his grin. "Oh, my, yes," she purred.

"You'll be having your breakfast late? Perhaps lunch?"

"No, likelier at the usual time," Ginny replied. "We aren't sleepy yet."

He tried not to grin wider. Reality, the weight beneath my coat, jabbed into me. Yes, we had something in mind that we just weren't able to put off. No, it wasn't what he thought. Damn! And yet, and yet—

In our suite, the door latched and the DO NOT DISTURB on its knob, I slipped my coat off, removed my burden, and shakily set it on a table. Ginny joined me. For a time that we didn't reckon, we looked. Day waxed beyond the shades. My nerves once more strung close to the snapping point, I caught sounds of people coming astir.

"All right, let's," she said very softly. She unshipped her wand and made other precautionary preparations. Standing back, alert, she nodded to me. "Draw it, Steve."

And see what happens.

I took the scabbard in my left hand and lifted the weapon. My right went around the haft. It could barely squeeze between guard and pommel. The idea was to provide a tight, secure fit, and men averaged smaller in the past than now. Slowly, I pulled.

The iron sheened darkly. A line in *Beowulf* came back to me, "the brown blade." But this one had a bluish overtone with a damascene ripple. Dwarf-forged to cut through steel and stone, monsters and magics—what alloy, what heating and quenching, hammering and grinding, runecraft and songcraft had gone into it? I swung it through an arc. In spite of my awkward grip, a beautiful balance made it move like my own arm. A feeling of savage life flowed into my marrow.

A sound like throat-clearing rasped across our silence. "Ahem!" The scabbard dropped from me and thudded on the carpet.

"Har d'je do, m'lady, m'lord," said a raspy, vigorous baritone. "Gad, how good to be free again! Deuced bore, lying there, unable to do a bloody thing—if you'll pardon the language, m'lady—nothing but listen, ever since I Awoke. Fifty years? A hundred? Felt like a thousand, I can tell you. Outrage. Calls for a letter to the *Times*. Yes, and questions in Parliament, egad. Heads will roll for this, or there's no discipline and justice left in England, by Jove!"

Repartee failed me. The blade wobbled in my clutch. "Uh, I, uh, p-pleased to meet you," I stammered. How did you shake hands with a sword? That edge could take my fingers right off.

Ginny recovered faster. She's more used to dealing with the eldritch. I'm only a werewolf. "We are honored, sir," she said. "Excuse me, but before we go further, how would you like to be positioned?" Obviously I couldn't keep hold of it indefinitely, and it might think that simply laying it down was undignified.

Obviously, too, the spirit 'chanted into it had an equivalent of vision as well as of voice box—and who knew what more senses? I imagined cold blue eyes under shaggy brows darting to and fro. "Over yonder," it said. "That thingummy in the corner, ha? Best place I see. Where are we, some petty nobleman's manor or what? Demmed sparse furnishings, I must say. Any tapestries on any wall in here?"

"An inn, sir," I explained as I parked the terrible Viking weapon in the umbrella stand. "Things have changed a lot since you, uh, since you were last active."

"Last Awake, you mean, young fella. I dozed off, um-m, let me see . . . last engagement I'm sure of was, um-m, Tenchebrai, yes, Tenchebrai. Reign of Henry, y' know. Not long after I'd come back from Constantinople. Tenchebrai, yes, we gave that scoundrel Robert a proper thrashing, we did, him and his Frogs. There we stood, a thin red line— No, I'm mixing my epochs, damme. Hard to keep sorted out, when all I could bloody well do after I Awoke was lie there and hear whatever happened to be in bloody earshot. Unbelievably boring, most of it. Clergy, demmed heretics, the lot of 'em, and la-de-da pilgrims. Now and then a proper milit'ry man, true, or better yet two or three together, who'd talk about something worthwhile like battles."

"Henry," Ginny whispered to me. "Must be Henry I. Early twelfth century, I think."

The sword had gone dormant with the waning of rheatic energy everywhere, I realized. For generations before then, no doubt Christian owners had kept its nature secret and persuaded it to talk to nobody but themselves. Afterward that knowledge was suppressed and died out. Nonetheless a tradition went on in the family, that here was a brand more often victorious than not. So, antiquated though it was, it continued in use for another hundred years. But by then it was just another chunk of shaped metal, remarkable in some ways such as the keen, enduring edge and the immunity to rust, otherwise obsolete. Finally it was handed over to the Church, along with its last wielder. . . .

"Ahem!" the sword interrupted itself. "Beg pardon. We've not been properly introduced. Nor is anyone about who can do the honors, what? Needs must. Soldierly straightforwardness. Allow me. Decent lineage, never fear. Forged by the dwarf Fjalar in Norway, the Dofra Fell, mountains, y'know. That was on commission from Egil Asmundsson, jarl in Raumsdal. Independent kingdom then, y'know, though already rather under the sway of Halfdan the Swart southwards. Not unlike a native state in India during the British Raj. Good warrior, Egil. The first man he killed with me—But later, later. He called me Brynjubítr. Meant 'Byrnie Biter' in the language. I've since borne a hodgepodge of different names, or none. No respect, those younger generations. You may call me Fotherwick-Botts."

"Huh?" I croaked.

"Adopted from Major-General Sir Steelman Fotherwick-Botts, O.B.E. After his retirement he came down to the crypt rather often. I'd hear him discuss the milit'ry relics, battles past, the arts of war, and other good stuff with young officers he'd brought along or else with whomever was there." *And who couldn't escape*, I thought. "Admirable chap. Solid. If only I'd been with him at Bloemfontein—"

So that's how this Being's picked up what he knows of the modern

English language and style. No, Edwardian at best. And there's a lot of frustration here to work off.

"Allow us to introduce ourselves," Ginny inserted into the monologue. She even managed a sketchy account of what we needed.

"Jolly good!" exulted the sword. "A Chinaman, eh? Crafty, they are. Not that I've encountered 'em m'self, y'know, but I've heard stories. As long ago as down in Byzantium— I'd better describe my career for you, what?"

Its voice shifted into recitation gear. "Briefly put, except for Viking expeditions I was in Norway until the battle of Hafrsfjord. There we stood, a thin mail-clad line— But that ruddy Harald Fairhair had the vict'ry. Not wishing to live under him, my then warrior—Trygvi Sveinsson, good man of his hands, they called him the Fierce, tell you about him later— joined a crew in Denmark and won a homestead in England. A generation or two afterward we were converted—fine white robes they gave the newly baptized; quality declined deplorably as time went by—and what is this bloody heresy these days?—but I kept up the side, ruthlessness and so forth, best's I could. Was at Stamford Bridge. Accounts of it absurd, dead wrong, near's I can gather. There we stood, a thin Anglo-Danish line—Ahem. A while after the Norman Conquest, my then wielder left the country, like many Englishmen, to join the Varangian Guard down in Constantinople. Jolly good engagements we had there, I can tell you. And I shall. He came back with quite a decent sum of money and reconciled himself with the Normans. His son—"

Fotherwick-Botts paused, as if to catch the breath he didn't need, before going relentlessly on: "But enough outline. You'll want the details. To go back to the beginning, when the dwarf delivered me to Egil Asmundsson and he went off to take vengeance—no, damme, justice it was, justice—on Herjolf the Pugnosed, they met in a meadow—"

"Oh, my God," I muttered to Ginny. "What've we let ourselves in for?"

She shuddered. "I'm afraid this is one of those ancient enchanted swords that, when they're drawn, tell of every battle they ever fought," she whispered back. "At least, *he* will, poor devil, after lying so long silenced. And before then, in the Christian period, he could only talk a little bit, secretly, to such of them as wouldn't be horrified and throw him into the sea for a piece of pagan witchcraft. Suddenly, now, he can cut loose—I mean speak freely to us."

"—I hewed into Herjolf's shield," Fotherwick-Botts told us, "but Egil did not let him twist me aside in the cleft. Common trick back then—"

"Judas priest," I gasped, "three centuries' worth, or whatever it is? How'll we get any sleep?"

"We can sheathe him," Ginny replied. "With proper apologies, of course. He'll start where he left off when we draw him again. I hope we can persuade him to glide over most of it, but I'm afraid we'll hear a great deal before he'll give us any real help. We'd better keep this suite through tonight, at least, and not take the train but rent a broom to go to London. Slowly."

"I say, are you paying attention?" barked the sword.

I'd have groaned louder if I'd known of the more important disaster hitting us meanwhile at home.

23

AND YET IT WAS ONLY AN OVERTURE, A FEW PIPS AND TWEEDLES BEFORE THE DEVIL'S band started to play for us in earnest. We heard of it together with what was much worse, when it barely registered on our awareness. Later we sorted out the facts as best we could, because this too we must deal with, but at the time it seemed almost incidental. Nobody imagined the eventual consequences. If we had—well, that's useless. If an elephant were little and round and white it would be an aspirin.

My reconstruction of events is partly guesswork. No matter. This whole account isn't for publication. Too explosive, as well as being often too personal. It's going under hundred-year seal. Maybe after that it can give some kind of unforeseeable help to somebody in the unforeseeable future. A warning, if nothing else.

Things began when Alger Sneep of the IRS called on Thursday and demanded to speak with us. Will, who'd established himself in our house, explained that we'd gone away. No, he didn't know where or for how long. "Ha," said Sneep. "This makes investigation urgent. Please prepare to receive me tomorrow morning at ten A.M."

"But I don't know anything," Will protested. "I'm merely here for the sake of the children. I expect Gin—Dr. and Mr. Matuchek will be back in a week or two."

"We may well have some questions for you too, Professor Graylock. Last time I met with mischievous obstructionism. You will find cooperation with us to your advantage, Professor Graylock."

Ginny or I would have stiffened our voices and replied that first we'd speak with Mr. Sneep's supervisor, whose name and phone glyphs he would provide at once. Soon we'd have checked with Barney, and he'd doubtless have called one of the lawyers he kept on tap. American tax-payers do retain some rights. Not many, but some. Federal tax collectors seldom feel obliged to list those rights. Will was caught entirely off guard.

Just the same, he should have shown a bit of firmness. Later he ad-mitted not quite knowing why he didn't, unless the fault lay in a combi-nation of his troublesome health and a notion that we had nothing to fear because we'd done nothing wrong. Anyhow, he accepted the ap-pointment.

When he told the kids at dinnertime, Valeria lifted hands and eyes dramatically ceilingward, looked back down, and curled her lip. Yes, she did, actually and literally. "What?" she shrilled. "That nastard again? Why can't we just have black plague?"

"We, er, we must be polite to him," Will said. "He does represent our government."

She nodded. "Dad agrees."

"No, er, tricks or anything. Do you hear me? Your parents were very displeased last time. Let us have no repetitions."

"No, we won't." She squinted into space. "I'll make the necessary arrangements." Catching his expression, she gave him a grim smile. "Not salt in the coffee or any such silly thing. I'll behave, and do my best to keep him out of trouble."

After the meal and cleanup she retired to her room with Svartalf. Will worried. However, he could not think of any objection when she explained she wanted to practice her spellcraft. Though precociously skilled, she was still capable only of minor, reasonably safe conjurations. The old black cat had by now become more her familiar than her mother's, but a stabilizer as much as an energizer.

It was she who admitted Sneep next morning when he rang. "How do you do," she said. Her cold graciousness, which would have done credit to Elizabeth Báthory, was not marred by pony tail, bare feet, faded blue jeans, and a T-shirt reading KILL THE FANATICS!

His lips compressed. "How do you do, Miss Matuchek," he said, clutching his briefcase tightly.

"Everything's in order, Mr. Sneep. I've left the younger children with a neighbor, where they'll be safe."

He gave her his gimlet look. "Do you mean there will be danger?"

She went totally bland. "Not from us. Please come in." As he did, she stepped aside, out of arm's reach.

They entered the living room. Edgar flapped his wings on his perch. "O villany!" he screamed. "Ho! Let the door be lock'd."

Will had risen from the chair where he'd sat attempting to read a scientific journal. "That's rude," he protested. "I'm sorry."

"I've been teaching him lines from Shakespeare," Val said, smiling. "Don't you think households should be cultured, Mr. Sneep?"

"Unfortunate," Will sputtered. "Indiscreet. We owe you an apology, sir."

"Bad bird." Val's tone wasn't even half-hearted.

"Well, uh, please sit down, Mr. Sneep," Will gulped. "Would you care for coffee? Valeria, will you fetch it?"

"Thank you, I believe I had better go straight to work," clipped the agent. "There's a great deal requiring explanation and substantiation. Perhaps you can help, Professor Graylock."

"That, er, that isn't my proper title. Never mind. I don't know what I can do in the absence of my sister and her husband."

"Can you tell me why they suddenly left—" Sneep paused, then pounced. "—right after a large sum of money had been transferred to their bank account?"

"Well, no, not really. That is, I understand it has to do with the Operation Luna enterprise. . . ."

Val widened her eyes. "How did you learn right away, Mr. Sneep?" she marveled. "You're real efficient, aren't you?"

He clenched a fist. "Banks are required to report such transactions, Miss Matuchek."

"I see. And I'm awful sorry. I *think* I paid $1.98 for these panties I'm wearing, but I could be wrong, I've lost the receipt. They'd know at the store, the Old Ranger Trading Post, and—"

"That will do, young lady!" her uncle yelled. In haste: "We all want to resolve this problem, whatever it is. Frankly, I should think it could wait till the Matucheks return, or that your Midwestern office can get a perfectly satisfactory accounting from the people at Nornwell. Meanwhile, I'm told you have taken a large selection of the Matucheks' records to study."

"Some questions call for immediate answers, here on the spot." Sneep's manner implied that otherwise we'd pull a fast one. "To start with, I need to see Mrs., ah, Dr. Matuchek's studio."

"Her arcanum?" Val cried. "You can't!"

"I beg your pardon?"

"Not while she's away—" At this point, if not before, Ginny or I would have been quoting the Fourth Amendment, possibly to good effect. Will was sort of numbed, though, and Val naive, as well as being only a young girl. (Maybe "only" isn't the word I want.) She blurted, "Nobody can. It's warded. Against robbers and priers and—" She caught Will's eye. "And l-layfolk who might endanger themselves if they got in. You'll *have* to wait till my mother gets home and undoes the spell."

"Several official forms are missing from the documents we have seen,"

Sneep told her. "Perhaps they are in there. Certainly I must get the dimensions of this house to verify whether the office space claimed as deductible is correct."

Val bridled. "Are you calling my mother a liar?"

Will tried to intervene. "This is unfortunate, but, but surely understandable. Isn't it? I haven't had cause to visit the studio myself lately, but believe me, if my sister has warded it, any attempt—well, I warn you, I sincerely warn you."

"If the spell is hazardous to life or limb, it's highly illegal," Sneep reminded him. "I trust Dr. Matuchek knows better. We'll see. I too have resources available to me."

He reached into his briefcase and took out a box. Stooping to one knee, he released a tape worm. The creature inched along the baseboard, measuring and recording. Sneep rose. "Now, that studio. Down the hall yonder, isn't it?"

"No, don't, please don't," Valeria begged. He ignored her. She followed at a yard's distance.

As they advanced, the corridor went gloomy, and more gloomy, until it was coalsack dark. And it reached on, and on, and on. Echoes rang hollowly off unseen walls. Air turned freezingly cold. Will-o'-the wisps darted here and there, ghastly corpse blue. Something afar howled, something closer snickered.

"Illusions." Sneep lifted his ring finger. A beam of light sprang from the bezel. He trudged forward. "Ah, yes," he said after a while. "An asymptotic warp. Intruders would take an eternity to reach the end."

"It's easy going back," Val said from behind. Though Ginny had briefed her and would never set up anything that could harm her, the words wavered. This was an environment straight out of nightmare.

Sneep halted. "The spell is within the limits of the law," he acknowledged.

A glowing, blobby image appeared ahead of him, opened a fangful mouth, and gibbered.

"Accordingly," Sneep said, "it is annullable by the powers vested in me."

He fished a book out of his briefcase. As he held it in one hand, it opened to the page he wanted, which shone bleak white. He read aloud:

"If the taxpayer's passive gross income from significant participation passive activities (within the meaning of section 1.469-2T (f) (2) (ii) for the taxable year (determined without regard to section 1.469-2T (f) (2) through (3)) exceeds the taxpayer's passive activity deductions from such activities for the taxable year, such activities shall be treated solely for purposes of applying this paragraph (f) (2) (i) for the taxable year, as a single activity that does not have a loss for such taxable year."

Before this fearsome cantrip, the phantoms quailed and dissolved, the blackness fled, space shrank back to normal, and Sneep stood triumphant in our ordinary home. The lock on Ginny's door opened of itself for him.

He peered around. His gaze fell on the studio couch. "Ha, a bed," he almost chortled. "Claimed office space must be used exclusively for business purposes."

Val had entered too. "Mom—my mother—sometimes she thinks best when she's lying down," she said. "Or I've seen her spread papers out on it for referring to."

"Can you swear that no one ever sleeps here? A guest, perhaps?"

"We've *got* a guest room." Val settled into a chair. "Go ahead. Do what you claim you have to."

Sneep frowned. "We don't appreciate interference with our duties, Miss Matuchek."

"Oh, I'll sit quiet, 'n case you need me." Will himself, when he arrived, couldn't move her. She sat. She said never a word, but she glowered. Teenagers are good at glowering. Our Valeria holds the championship.

Sneep was—I won't say vengeful—stalwart in his way. He scouted doggedly around the room, though he left cabinets and drawers alone. He took many notes, including about pictures and books and decorations. Do no other workplaces contain anything personal?

A raucous and rattling noise interrupted. Will came back in. "Oh, dear," he said, "I'm afraid the cat found your worm inching around and couldn't resist. I, er, I took it away from him, but the raven had already snatched a piece that was bitten off and flown out the window."

Sneep departed shortly afterward. He left ominous words behind him, to the effect that Ginny and I had better report in soon. We were out of touch, though, and hadn't gotten around to calling home.

Maybe that was just as well. Fotherwick-Botts droned on at us unceasingly except when he demanded, "What d'ye think of that, eh?" or when we mumbled with elaborate deference that we really must sheathe him and hide him away for a while. It lasted through Saturday in York and all the way to London on Sunday and in our hotel room there till nearly midnight.

Then finally he harrumphed and said, "And that was Tenchebrai. Jolly good scrap. Stout lads. Pity there's nothing more recent to tell you. I fell Asleep, y'know. Of course, I've passed over any number of lesser fights. You'll want to hear about those. But now we've work ahead of us, don't we?"

Eagerness rang in his voice. "Action again! Have at 'em! Thor help us—ahem!— Ha, ha among the trumpets, and all that sort of thing."

24

FOG SMOKED CHILL AND WET, STREET LAMPS GLOWED BLURRILY THROUGH IT, LIKE SKELE-ton trees from whose tops watched yellow-eyed goblins. Farther off they vanished into formlessness. My wolf nose drew in tides of smells, oily, chemical, rusty, rotted, sometimes a breath of something unknown to me. My pads and Ginny's sneakers whispered on pavement that stretched empty, gray where light fell, murkful elsewhere. Dreary brick walls hemmed it in on either side. Fresno, California, prosaic market town, felt a long ways from Fresno Street through Limehouse—on another world, maybe in another universe.

The district had been rehabilitated some since Victorian times, we'd learned. Businesses such as the Aberdeen Shipping Company were no longer islands of respectability in a swamp of squalor, vice, and crime. Others had moved into the old buildings that formerly housed slop shops, gin mills, cribs, and worse; the city had policed the area in both senses of the word. Still, at best it remained seedy, and reform hadn't taken any firm hold on this particular neighborhood along the docks east of London Bridge. When we'd walked through by day, we'd felt no urge to enter any pub.

For sure we wouldn't after dark, when the locals and the sailors had gotten thoroughly drunk—though a cafe would maybe pose deeper-going dangers. It would have been still more foolish for a woman to venture where everything was shut up and deserted for the night, even with a male escort. Unless, of course, he looked like a gigantic hound and was actually a timber wolf.

I'd better keep that shape till we got back to the railway station where she'd lockered my clothes for me after I changed in a gent's. Since my skinsuit might give my nature away to somebody who'd pass the word on ahead of us, I wore only a collar with a leash that passed beneath her cloak. There also she kept my lens, just in case, her own gear, and Fotherwick-Botts.

We'd needed fewer precautions earlier, when I was human and we made like tourists seeking a quick, cheap thrill. Yet in a way we had had to take special care, because that was our scouting expedition. Who knew what watch-spells Dr. Fu had set?

We simply strolled by daylight through Upper Swandam Lane, past his hideout, and onto the high wharf beyond. Luckily, no ship was tied up there at this time. Ginny's looks had drawn attention enough elsewhere, leers and an occasional low whistle. I could imagine dock wallopers finding ways to keep her in sight. As it was, we took cover around the corner of a shed while she used her wand and skill to work what Art she dared. Carefully, carefully, feeling her way, alert to pull back at the slightest quiver of reaction— But the Sensitivities weren't primed against her hybrid Anglo-Zuni approach; and she didn't really try to probe, she simply skimmed off impressions of the layout and the general situation. Nor did we linger after she was done.

On the way back to our modest Whitechapel hotel, she walked like one in a dream. I didn't interrupt. She was in self-communion, evaluating what she'd discovered. Once we'd come to our room, she roused, took the sword from the suitcase where he'd lain wrapped in my bathrobe, and told us crisply:

"Two doors flank number 3, leading to what must have been small, probably disreputable shops but now stand empty except for some dusty stored things. The buildings on the opposite side have been converted to a warehouse, which turns a blank rear wall onto the alley and doesn't seem to be much used. The entrance to number 3 itself goes underground, into a long, low room and a couple of lesser ones behind. It contains the dingy remains of a low-class hotel lobby, a hotel which must have gone broke years ago and which Fu's agents could easily rent from the present owners. I caught ghostly traces—wasted lives leave residua that can hang on for a long time. They suggest that before it became a hotel this was an opium den. But no matter, I suppose. Number 3 includes the floors above the shops. Several rooms there have been refurnished in what seems to be high style, but I didn't check details."

"Any boltholes?" inquired Fotherwick-Botts. "Wouldn't be a proper Oriental lair without secret escape hatches, eh?"

"No, apparently not. The back of the house fronts on a narrow strip of ground between it and the wharf, mud at low tide, submerged at high. Not suitable for a tunnel. I suppose you could jump out a window and flounder or swim away. Also at the back, where the top story projects a little, is a trapdoor, but I suspect that was for disposing of corpses and other inconvenient objects in old days. No, Fu Ch'ing must rely on secrecy, and on forewarning from his agents or guardian spells if the authorities do find where he is."

"And on fighting-type guardians if somebody unexpected breaks in?" Keeping my voice level was tough.

Ginny nodded. "Armed men and . . . potentials. It'd have been reck-

less of me to try counting or identifying them. But my Finding is pretty
clear, they aren't a terribly strong force. One like that could too easily
betray its presence, whether by numbers of foreigners suddenly in the
area or by emanations from the Beings and the latencies. Scotland Yard
will have scouted around, after all. I think the idea is merely to fight a
delaying action while Fu and any top lieutenants of his make their escape."

"Fly out a window?"

"Hardly that simple. Raiders would be prepared for it. Plain Tarnkappen wouldn't work either, against modern police equipment. Something really powerful in the way of a transformation or a Seeming, maybe;
but it would take time to prepare. We hope to surprise them, moving too
fast for their getaway measures."

"Tally-ho!" the sword whooped. "Sweep 'em off their feet! St. George
for merrie England, by Thor!"

"Sh, not so loud, please," Ginny hissed.

"Uh, maybe we should notify the police," I said. "You've done one
hell of a job of tracking, sweetheart, but now—well, it's only the two of
us, I mean the three of us, and—"

The red head shook. "You forget that Fu probably has spies in those
forces. British lawmen aren't incompetent by any means, but they'd naturally need time to verify our rather peculiar story, get their warrants,
and everything else. Ample time for Fu to be warned. Nothing useful to
them would be left."

"Okay. Still, I don't think we should depend entirely on ourselves. If
something does go badly wrong, we'll crap out knowing our efforts were
worthless."

"Aye, hold cavalry in reserve behind the hill," agreed Fotherwick-
Botts. "Besides, it lends tone to a battle."

Ginny went along with that. We worked out a scheme, which she
implemented from our room. Remarkable what you can do these days if
you know exactly what resonances to send where through the phones.

Thereafter we discussed our personal tactics. Not that that became
elaborate or went on very long. We knew too little.

Besides, Ginny and I were aware of the military maxim that in any
engagement the first casualty will be your own battle plan; while the sword
harked back to eras when you might occasionally pull a smart trick like a
feigned retreat, but mainly you just charged.

I always hated the idea of exposing Ginny to danger. And my personal
hide counted for something too. Nevertheless I admit to a certain thrill
rising in me. We had a hunt ahead of us.

First, once again, we gulped an early meal and went back to our room for a few hours' rest. This time, oddly enough, I dropped off almost at once, and enjoyed pleasant dreams. I loped on a slope in flowery Arcadia . . .

We went out before the last of the management had gone to bed. If later we rang somebody up in the small hours, what the hell. We'd either have succeeded or failed—or come to grief—in any case, blown our cover and have no further need of it.

And so we found ourselves walking down deserted Fresno Street to where Upper Swandam Lane ran off.

It opened before us like a gut, and nearly as black. Ginny had laid witch-sight on us both. Through fog-swirl, we made out the wharf as a block of blackness at the far end, and a sullen gleam off the river beyond. Mainly, though, I smelled, and felt every hair of my pelt stir to the slowly shifty airs. The alley slept. . . . No, not the thaumaturgic forces that barely rustled along my werewolf nerves. I glanced up at Ginny. Light from the nearest lamp touched the fog-drops in her hair. I tugged at my leash. She followed me.

Sometimes, in the gloom, we kicked aside litter, a bit of glass that clinked, crumpled paper that rustled, a bone that stank. Nothing awoke. We came to the entrance we wanted.

Even enhanced eyes could barely make out the flight of steps that plunged down to a door. The stairwell concentrated stenches—reptilian— at which I snarled and bristled. Ginny unclipped my leash. She knotted it about her waist. Throwing back her cloak, she took the scabbard from its awkward position beneath her left arm. Expanding the belt it hung from, she fastened it slantwise across her shoulders, where it wouldn't get in the way and might give a little protection. She reached into the pouch at her hip, snugged a silver and amethyst ring engraved with an Osiris eye against her wedding band, took forth her wand and extended it. Her right hand drew the sword. It sheened moon-wan in the scanty light from the street. I heard her whisper to it: "For God's sake, *keep quiet.*"

She went down the stairs, I at her heels, to the landing.

One degree at a time, pauses between, during which the river flowed louder than our breaths, she turned the doorknob. Nothing happened. Well, we hadn't expected otherwise, simply felt obliged to try. Probably no Glory Hand, monkey or human, could open that lock. Probably the attempt would set off goetic alarms. Stealth had become pointless. She lifted the sword and swung.

A woman hasn't the upper-body strength of a man, but she was athletic and had deep resources to call on. Her weapon was dwarf-forged, enchanted, a sunderer of all things. I believe I heard "Yoicks!" ring from the blade. Then it crashed and clove.

Wood splintered. Sparks flew where metal sheared. The cut went nearly the length of the door, as though splitting a man from helmet to midriff. Any latches and deadbolts gave with the lock. Ginny pulled the sword free. That impetus dragged the door ajar. I slipped past her, wedged my snout in the crack, swung the barrier aside, and bounded in.

The old hotel lobby had been refurbished the way a landlord would expect a group to do who rented this El Cheapo for a co-op residence. A few second-hand armchairs sagged on a threadbare carpet. A discouraged aspidistra stood in a tarnished brass pot near the unused counter. A color print depicted a clipper ship in high seas under full sail, the way depicted square-riggers always seem to be in all weathers. An edison glowed dully from a dusty globe overhead. A flight of stairs curved aloft from the rear between two inner doors. Protective drabness for the dragon.

It didn't last. Half a dozen men swarmed from behind those doors. Two were white, two maybe Chinese, two smaller and darker, from southern Asia somewhere. All wore dingy street clothes. The night watch, no doubt. All were armed, long knives, a hatchet, a pistol. They didn't yell or anything. They ran directly at us.

I leaped for them. They couldn't hurt me, but Ginny— Behind me, she pointed her wand. The electric bulb exploded and darkness clapped down.

I hit the nearest of the thugs, dacoits, whatchacallems full tilt and bowled him over. Witch-sight gave shadowy vision. Mostly I went by my ears and nose—and, after a moment, my tongue. Snap, slash, hot blood, live bodies, and now they did cry out. It could have been a mixup back during the war. The wolf of me wildly rejoiced. The man of me remembered, far back in my head, that I'd better not kill if I could avoid it. The modern English are stuffy about such things.

The modern English. Ginny had started up the stairs. Her wand cast fire-bright, frost-cold light before her. More men advanced downward, these in assorted sleeping garments but also armed. *"Yuk-hai-saa-saa!"* roared Fotherwick-Botts. "Haro! Have at 'em! Your widows will remember this night, you scurvy scoundrels!"

My playmates had scattered, such of them as were in shape to. I sprang to join my comrades—and on past them, before the gang could make the mistake of encountering that sword. Ginny got the idea straight off and doused her wand. Again it was strike and rip in the dark, foreign curses, screams of pain the same from any human throat, and a salt drunk-making taste of blood over my teeth.

A gong boomed. A pipe whistled on an eerie scale. Suddenly I panted and growled alone on the stairs. The opposition had fled. At a command?

Ginny joined me, a shadow, a touch, a oneness of woman-scents that poured through the reek and heat to call me back to sanity. The sword glimmered vague in her hand. "That was deuced selfish of you,

Matuchek," he grumbled. "Not sporting at all. Not playing the game. When I haven't cloven a skull or even lopped off a leg in eight hundred years—"

The stairway shivered beneath us. I heard a dry rustle. The rank reptile stench flowed over me and into me. A deeper blackness unrolled. It hissed, geyserishly loud.

Ginny rekindled her star. Light glistened off the scales of a cobra. It poured down the steps, thick as two men, tail reaching behind the curve of the well, head well-nigh lost in the dark above us. Yet I saw the hood outspread, like monstrous blunt wings, the glitter of eyes, gleam of fangs, forked tongue that flickered in and out.

No therianthrope, I knew. A conjure. For an instant I cringed. From someplace unknown I rallied the will for a hopeless attack.

"No, Steve!" Ginny cried. "Back! This one is ours!"

I crouched stiff. "Down, Matuchek," Fotherwick-Botts ordered gleefully.

The nerve of him— Sheer resentment held me paralyzed while Ginny swept past.

The cobra struck. The sword whistled and thudded. The witch's wand flew back and forth in her left hand. Drops of venom bounced off it. Where they hit the steps, they left small pits.

Blood coursed from a wound in the cobra's nose. It gaped, as if astounded. Again the sword bit, and again and again. A chunk fell off the hood. A gash opened in the belly scutes and gushed.

I howled my joy.

Abruptly the snake was gone, along with body parts and fluids. It had been plenty real. Air popped, rushing into the vacuum its mass left. Ginny and I stood alone in the star-glare of her wand.

"Well smitten, shield maiden," the sword said. "I must confess I didn't care for the notion of a woman wielding me, but you were a bally Brynhild, damme. My compliments."

"Thanks," she gasped. Sweat sheened on her face and darkened spots in her blouse. Both her weapons trembled slightly. Yet she stood fast, and added with a crooked grin, "I don't carry a shield, though, and as for the maiden part— Let's proceed."

We advanced to a corridor lined with doors. Abruptly it lay aglow in a mother-of-pearl softness which seemed to radiate from the air. The silence had become so absolute that we might have been the last creatures alive.

A tall, thin, stoop-shouldered man stood awaiting us. He had donned slippers, an embroidered robe, and a mandarin cap topped by a large spherical button. His hands were delicate, his fingernails very long, trimmed to points and polished. His head was bald or shaven. Despite the golden-hued skin and wispy white beard, the features beneath a brow like Shakespeare's, agelessly smooth, seemed almost too sharp to be Chinese. I know eyes don't really pierce, but damn if I didn't feel his.

"Good evening," he said, as quietly as a tiger might. His Oxford English bore the least, musical hint of another accent. "My apologies for this regrettable rowdiness. Had you notified me what caliber of opponents you are, your reception would have been properly dignified." *Yeah*, I thought, *and deadly. Unless you just decamped.* "However, as the learned Sun Tzu wrote, and later your Machiavelli, a test of strength is often the necessary prelude to meaningful negotiations. Shall we here call a truce?"

25

DR. FU CH'ING'S PRIVATE QUARTERS WERE—WELL, IT WAS AS IF THE ROOM WHERE WE talked reached impossibly vast, with lacquered pillars, gilt carvings, ivory-inlaid ebony furniture, silken hangings, scrolls of beautiful art inscribed with poems, and yet was a secret niche for gods and sorcerers to whisper in. He and Ginny sat in straight-backed chairs, a small table between them. The sword rested upright against a sculptured temple lion. I sprawled on a carpet whose rich hues my wolf eyes could not appreciate but whose texture caressed me. Incense wafted as faint and sweet as the twanging music, we knew not from whence.

After Ginny declined wine, mute servants brought tea and small cakes. She checked them with her wand, as unobtrusively as she could, before she took any; Fu smiled a tiny smile. I got mine in two bowls and lapped them up fast. Mainly I had a Sahara thirst, but the sugar took the blood taste out of my mouth and made me better able to listen to the conversation.

Elsewhere, no doubt, the highbinders were attending to each other's wounds. How many were they, anyway? No big number, surely; just enough to fight a holding action. Fu's operations extended across continents, but mostly they were subtle, a theft here, a spot of blackmail there, an occasional selective murder, a spell cast unbeknownst to the victim. We'd come this far by sheer bulling through.

He admitted as much. "I did not anticipate such a concentration of physical force in so small a band," he said impersonally, "and the goetics you employed is to a considerable extent, unfamiliar to me." He finished his tea and signaled for a refill. The barest pulsation went through his voice. "Fascinating. Might you possibly contemplate an alliance, or at least an exchange of information, honored colleague?"

"Sorry, I'm afraid not," Ginny replied.

"I should say not!" blustered Fotherwick-Botts. "With a Chinaman?"

"Down, boy," snapped Ginny. The sword gasped and gobbled but was too outraged to find words. "My apologies, Dr. Fu. What manners he didn't learn in the Middle Ages he acquired from leftover colonialists."

Fu sounded momentarily amused. "That is obvious, Dr. Matuchek." He went grim. "They are what I strive against, the hyenas and vultures preying on my poor China."

"Gad!" sputtered Fotherwick-Botts. "What's the world come to? Once upon a time, if anyone, let alone a native, used such language about Her Majesty's Empire, he'd've been horsewhipped on the steps of his club. Even nowadays—" He hesitated. "Er, do natives have clubs?"

"*Please* let me handle this," Ginny said. She made a small gesture at the sheath she'd removed, along with her cloak, which hung from a hook in the wall. It conveyed: If you don't, I'll shut you up good. He snorted but yielded. A sword can't turn purple and bulge the veins in its temples.

"Isn't your hostility a little obsolete, Dr. Fu?" she asked. "The Opium War and the Boxer Rebellion are long behind us. You have a native— um—all right, yes, a native dynasty back on the Imperial throne. Extraterritoriality has ended. The matter of treaty ports is being renegotiated. Why are you making such an effort?"

"China is still impoverished. Warlords, bandits, still run free in the hinterlands, aided by foreign adventurers and foreign gold. Trade with the outside is still through foreign ships, merchants, monopolies. Her voice still goes unheard in the councils of the world. My country, her ancient civilization, must become at least equal to the other great powers, Dr. Matuchek. At least equal."

My human part recalled vaguely that in its heyday the Middle Kingdom had regarded everybody else as barbarians, useless for anything except tribute. The Chinese were really no different from the rest of us.

"Can she only do this by undermining the West, Dr. Fu?" Ginny argued. "Frankly, I should think you'd better set your own house in order."

"The Emperor's government is going about that. But it is not enough." Fu's underplayed vehemence dropped down to a purr. "Did such rising nations as France in the Baroque period, Germany in the modern era, or your United States in its expansion think in purely domestic terms? One cannot meaningfully bargain with a power greater than oneself; and no one willingly relinquishes power."

Ginny sighed. "As you like. Shall we leave the cosmic concerns and get down to business?"

He raised his brows and sipped his tea. "That is reasonable. I have only slight intimations of why you have broken in on us so unofficially."

She described the launch disaster and the traces of Asian demons at work. About Will she said nothing; that would have been to expose a hole card, not to mention a point of pain and vulnerability. "My husband and I learned you were in England, and thought we might find you when the regular forces couldn't. With the help of persons I won't name, other than our friend here—"

"Hrrumph," said Fotherwick-Botts.

"—we've come this far. What we'd like to know, Dr. Fu," said Ginny in a tone suggestive of a knife held to a throat, "is what you've been doing around Cardinal Point and what you propose to do in future. *If* you please."

Did that aristocratic face and mild voice faintly register surprise? "I regret that I cannot help you," he replied after a moment.

"Cannot, sir, or will not?"

Fotherwick-Botts made an ominous noise. I exposed a fang or two. "Like you, we would deplore any further violence," added Ginny butter-blandly. "Nor do we wish to take up more of your valuable time than we must."

Fu nodded. "I understand, Dr. Matuchek and gentlemen. But the fact is that I know nothing of this matter beyond what has appeared in the press. Indeed, since those discoveries that seem to indicate Eastern Beings have not been made public, you have given me my first news of them. Hence I am in no position to judge the validity of your inferences."

"Truly not?" Ginny persisted.

He shrugged. "I concede that doing your space program a mischief strikes me as an excellent idea. It is proper that China take leadership on the moon. But her own work will require several years more to reach fruition."

"You have a space program too?" she blurted. It had been a total secret.

"We propose to ride dragons. I would not reveal this now, save that the clues you deem you possess must have aroused suspicions and your Centrum for Illicit Arcana will doubtless mount an intensive espionage operation, which will probably soon succeed. Clever, these Americans. But, no, my present venture into the Western world has had other purposes."

I saw and sensed the conflict within her. She didn't want to challenge his word outright. That would be useless, or worse. And yet—

He caught us off guard when he frowned, looked beyond her, ran fingernails through his beard, and whispered something. The implications of what she'd told him seemed to go further than he'd said.

However, he wouldn't readily yield. The razor gaze swung back to her. "Yes," he hissed, "you suspect me of a terminological inexactitude. How shall I persuade you otherwise? For my part, may I ask why I should make the attempt, why I should give you any cooperation whatsoever?"

Ginny tensed. "It will be to your advantage, Dr. Fu, very much to your advantage."

"Do you threaten my life, you three? I thought better of your intelligences." He glanced from her to me but, pointedly, not at Fotherwick-Botts. The sword harrumphed.

"No, sir," Ginny answered. "Your entire mission is spoiled. We offer you a chance to salvage what you can. But you've got to be quick."

"Ahhhh." He leaned back and stared impassively.

"I spelled a backup for us," Ginny explained. "If anything serious happens to me, phones will immediately scream at Scotland Yard, Military Intelligence, and the nearer police stations. They will anyway at a certain hour, which isn't far off now. With no advance warning, you and your gang might escape, barely, or might not. But I imagine it would be such a scramble that you'd leave the house loaded with leads to your whole organization. By speaking a certain word, I can postpone the moment."

That he showed no emotion was to be expected. Odd, though, how I could smell none of it from him. "My compliments, Dr. Matuchek," he murmured after a while, during which the music had only deepened the silence around us. "As the saying goes, you are a foe worthy of my steel."

Fotherwick-Botts harrumphed louder.

"Thank you," Ginny said. "You will understand, we can't in good conscience let you continue your subversions here. We shall have to bring in the authorities, and do so in time for them to find enough clues here to doom your mission."

The technicalities were beyond me, especially in my present form. But it should be obvious to any layman that removing every telltale object, smudge, and fluff of dust from the place, let alone every goetic trace, would take days.

"But I will give you a chance to escape with your men in an orderly way, taking along a few vital papers or whatever, and start for home, *if* you cooperate," Ginny finished.

I admired how quickly and calmly he came to decision. "Well done, madame. You have me in check. Best I resign before it is mate. There will be other games."

No American girl could forever match an unflappability that three thousand years of history had polished smooth. "You don't get out of this one unless you pay the fee," she snapped. "I want some proof that you aren't behind the Cardinal Point sabotage and, if you aren't, information about who or what is."

Again he sat silent. The music wailed low; the incense ghosted.

"Since time is limited, you must to a certain extent rely on my honor," he said at length. "I shall show you a synoptic record of my activities in England. It will argue that I and my followers were fully occupied. As for other knowledge—" Did I catch a hint of goodwill, however temporary? "It may be that, despite disagreements, we have a common interest, even a common cause."

I pricked up my ears. Ginny narrowed her eyes. "I had a hunch about that," she murmured. "If you've seen right away what it is, Dr. Fu, you're as brilliant as they say."

"They speak far too well of my humble abilities."

"They wish that were so." Ginny's slight smile faded. Her tone sharpened. "Your government is trying to expel the evil shen from your country."

" 'Kuei' is more correct, madame. The shen and kuei elements permeate the Wan Wu, or All. From the Jên part of the Wan Wu—one may say, very approximately, the human or conscious part—are derived, on the Yang side through the Three Spiritual Energies, the benign shen; on the Yin side, through the Seven Emotions, the kuei. The distinction resembles that between, on the one hand, fays, genii, angels, gods, and the like; on the other hand, devils, ghouls, goblins, vampires, and the like. I speak loosely, of course."

"I trust you do," said Ginny rather stiffly. In Chinese philosophy the Yang principle is male, the Yin female.

"Overlaps and interchanges occur. Is this not also true in your theology? Are not your devils angels who fell from grace, and do you not speak of a person's evil genius? In like manner, sometimes 'shen' is used of all Beings derived from the Jên. But this is perhaps misleading."

"Thank you." Now Ginny sounded impatient. "Okay, your Taoist masters are exorcising or expelling—or whatever—the kuei throughout China. It's a long and difficult job—just hunting them down must be, and then overpowering them. But things can be made too uncomfortable and frustrating for them in their old haunts. Something similar is happening in Japan, right?"

"Well, what are they to do? Where shall they go? No place else on Earth can they stay for long. They can't fit into the local paranature, which is as alien to them as a jungle and its animals would be to a polar bear. Modern, rationalistic, high-tech civilization is worse yet. What have you people expected would happen?"

"That those who were not soon destroyed by native Beings would seek wastelands, and gradually dwindle away to naught," Fu said. "What you have told me suggests that the masters have not thought these questions through to the end."

"Or else don't give a damn, as long as the demons are out of their hair," Ginny retorted. "In fact, some extra trouble wished onto to us foreigners could give your government opportunities."

"It would not be altogether undesirable," admitted Fu.

"But it isn't working that way," Ginny said. "The shen—I mean the kuei, and the evil kami from Japan, and whatever else—they don't propose to perish slowly and piecemeal as your cat's-paws. If the Fair Folk can establish themselves on the moon, why not these too? That means keeping humans off it, out of space. In America the exiles have made a temporary alliance with some resident Beings who have it in for the white man. I suggest you look to your own space program. More may be going on in the background than you know."

"Oh, I shall," he replied most softly. "I shall."

"Doesn't this hypothesis fit the data?"

"Yes. It occurred to me when you had related your experiences."

"Then imagine the long-range consequences of the moon becoming a home, stronghold, and operating base of demons," Ginny hammered at him. "We want humans there, in strength, to head them off before they get well established. Does it really matter much which humans arrive first?"

"From a geopolitical viewpoint, it does."

I snarled. If we, the British, and the French had stood up to the Caliph at the outset, united, we could have squelched him then and there. But no, we were each of us anxious to keep our particular trade concessions in the Near East, and to hell with anybody else's; while the Germans enjoyed seeing the bunch of us discomfited; and then suddenly it was too late, and people started getting killed.

"Yet some considerations are larger," Fu went on. "In what do you wish assistance, Dr. Matuchek?"

Ginny let out a breath. I lowered my head. This brought it near enough to the sword that he could mutter to me, "Bully for him. An Oriental, but a gentleman. I mind once in the Varangian Guard at Constantinople—" I raised a paw to shush him.

"You can tell me about the kuei," Ginny said.

"My dear lady," Fu protested, "you request the learning of half a lifetime's discipleship."

"You know what I mean. Practical, pertinent knowledge. I've been to the books. Now I need the kind of details that don't get into the books— everyday or everynight customs, habits, strengths, weaknesses, how to *fight* them."

Fu rose to his feet. "That is not really possible in completion. How-ever, perhaps I can convey a few hints and ideas. This begins with proof of my bona fides." He nodded at me. "Will you . . . gentlemen excuse us for the nonce?"

They walked off together. Somehow, though I could not see an open-ing to any other room, they gradually vanished from sight and hearing.

"I say, aren't you going along?" asked the sword. I shook my head. They hadn't invited me.

"Well, I daresay milady can take care of herself," Fotherwick-Botts rumbled. "Still, I'd feel happier if you changed skin again. Old Norse term. Go human, d'you see? That Fu chap may or may not be trustwor-thy—mostly not—but what if his bloody henchmen take it into their dashed heads to set on us, eh? Can't very well wield me with paws and jaws."

I bared my teeth to indicate that I'd give an adequate account of myself.

"And leave me aside?" complained the sword. "Hogging all the sport, same's on the demmed ground floor? Not British, I must say. But then, you're a colonial, aren't you?

"Not your fault," he added after a minute. "Don't think I'm preju-diced. I mean, you didn't ask to be born overseas, did you? And what I hear about the American schools—never a caning— Well, I don't imag-ine the blighters will attack. Haven't the nerve. Reminds me of when my then man, Thorgest Thorkelsson—Thorgest Mouth they called him, or sometimes Thorgest the Sleepmaker, because he would talk on and on—nevertheless a good man of his hands; once he and I made meat of ten Scots who thought they'd ambushed us; tell you about that later—he was off on a spot of raiding along the Irish coast, his ship and two others—"

I settled down. Listening was better than emptily waiting. A little bit better.

Afterward Ginny told me how Fu Ch'ing did indeed level with her, sort of. He didn't let her in on his schemes, of course, but the recording crystal that he activated for her showed enough rascalities that he could scarcely have had time for anything else. He went on to a hard, intense briefing on Far Eastern demonology. She would never become a Taoist or Shinto priest, with the associated knowledge and powers, but she ac-quired a lot of what she'd hoped for.

The time felt interminable, in spite of Fotherwick-Botts or because of him, before they returned. There was a remoteness in her expression; she had encountered a great deal of strangeness. Yet she spoke steadily: "You have done your share, Dr. Fu. Now I'll do mine." She waved her wand and uttered a word I didn't know. "I have postponed the message. You have three hours. I'm sorry to rush you, but I'm sure you understand."

He nodded, evidently recognizing the spell as valid. "It is sufficient. You are in the highest tradition of Machiavelli. Sun Tzu would also approve. Both men taught that one should always leave one's enemy a line of retreat."

She bowed. "You have been very helpful, learned sir."

He bowed back. "It has been a privilege and an honor, madame."

I thought of offering a paw to shake, but decided to sit on my haunches and dip my muzzle. "Pleased to've met you," rumbled Fotherwick-Botts. Ginny sheathed him and we departed. My final sight of Dr. Fu Ch'ing was as a silhouette, an outline of night, tall at the head of the stairs. Did *"Au revoir"* whisper around us as we descended?

The lobby lay deserted aside from bloodstains, tumbled furniture, and other signs of a fracas. We went forth into cold, dank air. Day was barely breaking, a paleness through the fog that dimmed the glimmer of the street lamps. We walked mute, Ginny lost in all that had been disclosed to her.

I turned human and got dressed at the railway station. The hotel porter whom we rang up to let us in gave us a surly glance. Bloody Yank toffs, carousing till dawn, he probably thought. But being English, he reminded us of the hours when breakfast was served. We climbed the stairs to our room.

"Whoof!" gusted from me. I jerked open the drawer where we kept a bottle of Scotch. "To hell with breakfast. I'll settle for a stiff drink and sleeping till lunch."

Ginny had roused from her thoughts. "First we'll call home," she said. "We've been remiss about that."

I fetched two glasses, poured a hefty slug into each, and handed her one. "And then what?"

"Whatever moves fastest." She took a sip before she doffed her cloak and unslung the sword. "I'll tell you in detail later, as well as I can. Essentially, what I learned tonight shows that we can't put humans on the moon too soon."

"To croon a tune in June," I couldn't help throwing in. Seriously: "It won't happen through NASA."

"No. Especially since the . . . kuei and their allies aren't done with NASA by any means. Operation Luna— It wouldn't hurt to consult our friend." She drew the sword and laid him down on the bed.

"God's wounds and Satan's ballocks, what're you shilly-shallying about?" he rasped, going medieval again. "You want a simple broomstick that can make the crossing, what, what, what? I've gathered you're worried about wha'd'you-call-ems, Roentgen rays or something?"

"And stresses and a lot else," I said.

"Well, what you want is proper steel, by Jove, yes, proper steel, alloyed right and with the right spells on it, damme. Get the dwarves to forge it for you. Handy little beggars. Nobody does it like the dwarves. Made Sigurd's dragon-killer, they did, and Skofnung and Tyrfing—beastly ruffian, Tyrfing, but formidable—and others, including, ahem, m'self. Dwarves, yes, dwarves."

"We thought of that," I sighed. "Barney Sturlason, the big man behind Operation Luna—"

"*Hersir*, eh? Or baron, I s'pose. Damn these anachronisms! Too many centuries to keep track of."

"He made inquiries in Germany," I continued patiently. "It turns out that Nibelung Wunderwerke A/G has all the work it can handle. We'd have to wait a couple of years. Besides, there'd be no confidentiality with so large a company, and—"

"Yes, yes, yes! Do listen, will you? In my day, a subaltern who quacked such bally rot— Well. Hrrumph," said Fotherwick-Botts. "I forget you're colonials, and flinkin' civilians to boot. Also, I did misspeak myself. Admit it like a man. I did. 'Dwarves' was wrong. I meant *a* dwarf, the dwarf who forged me, Fjalar. Excellent workman, as you can see."

My spine tingled. "He's . . . around? Available?"

"He Awoke some decades ago. Not doing much business. Doesn't want much. Independent chap. Select clientele. But I expect he'd be int'rested in your problem. I'll recommend it to him. Worth a try, anyhow, eh?"

Ginny's voice throbbed. "How do you know?"

"Why, he's my maker, m'lady. How could I not?"

"Ah, yes," she breathed. "Sympathetic connection. You know, intuitively but surely—"

"I bloody *well* know. Same's I know that Gladstone scoundrel will be the ruin of England unless— No, he's been gone a while, hasn't he? I've only heard mention of him. But he seems to've inspired this upstart Labour Party—"

"Thank you," interrupted Ginny. "You've given us something important to think about. Now we'd better call home and let them know we're all right, before they go to bed there."

"And we likewise here," I said through a mighty yawn.

Ginny resonated the phone. It came to life with Valeria's dear face. For an instant, she stared. Then tears burst forth. "Daddy, Mom, where've you been?" she cried. "Are you okay?"

My heart thuttered. "Sure, sweetheart. You see us, don't you? What's the trouble?"

"Th-they've arrested Uncle Will—they say he's behind th-the awful things—tried to *kill* you—and, and that grismal little Sneep, he— But Uncle Will! You've got to come back. Please!"

26

AT THIS FRANTIC END OF THE HIGH SEASON, EVERY TRANSATLANTIC FLIGHT WAS BOOKED solid for days ahead. Ginny took a cab to Hampstead Heath, found a spot screened by bushes, and made heap big medicine. I don't know what it was, though since we'd packed light she remarked before leaving the hotel that it'd have to involve her owl pin, the sigil of Athene. When she came back to me and phoned the travel agency, there had been a last-minute cancellation—on Pan American, of course—and she got the seat. First class, expensive, but no matter. From New York it wouldn't be hard to reach Albuquerque and thence Gallup.

Two would have been a really tall order. Besides, I'd be more use overseas. I kissed her good-bye at the flyport that evening and returned to our quarters. On the way I read in a newspaper how an anonymous tip had sent the police to what seemed to have been the headquarters of a notorious international crime ring. The birds had flown, but left abundant clues and other evidence, including signs of a violent struggle. Chief Inspector MacDonald had told reporters only that the tip was of a nature to spur immediate action. He didn't know how much more he would become able to pass on; the government had quickly invoked the Official Secrets Act.

So far, so good. Lonely though the bed in the room felt, I damn near slept the clock around. When I unsheathed him to say good morning, Fotherwick-Botts declared he hadn't heard snoring like that since he fared with Eyvind Night-Thunder. One time in the Orkney Islands—

I headed off another war story: "We need to see this Fjalar guy pronto. How soon can you locate him?"

"Hard to tell. Sympathetic connection deuced vague, y'know. Don't feel it at all unless I concentrate. Then, ha, hum, sense that he is alive, up and about, got a smithy somewhere in—in the high north, mountains, well offside. Beyond Nidaros, I'd say at a venture. Prob'ly Norway, unless they've tampered with the borders. Can't trust those shifty-eyed politicians, what? Not that those parts did much more than pay tribute to Harald Fairhair, when I left. Haven't been back since. Not up to date. Cruising to and fro on a silly broomstick, no, I'd never find him. On foot, come close enough, yes, I'll know. Wind him ten miles off at least. What we need to do, Matuchek, is get up a safari. Native bearers, beaters, guides, a shikari who knows the country. And gifts to hand out along the way. They used to like amber. Ivory not bad either, mostly walrus, some narwhal—"

"We haven't got a year!"

"No, we don't, do we? Snow falls early thereabouts, near's I recall. Hungry wolves a hazard and nuisance too— Ahem. Forgot you're a wolf. Sorry, old fella."

I was indeed a hungry wolf. "Let's let our brains do the walking," I said, suppressing the temptation to add: *Ahem. Forgot you haven't any. Sorry, old fella.* Yesterday, trying to be helpful while Ginny was out, I'd visited one of London's wonderful shops for such things and acquired a set of maps. She had laid a sensitizing spell on them. I unrolled a topographic of the upper Scandinavian peninsula and spread it on the floor, standing the sword against the wall nearby. "Suppose you study this while I eat breakfast. Work your, um, wits hard. See if any particular locale gives you a feeling." Before I babbled more or my stomach growled louder, I hurried off.

Bacon and eggs swimming in grease, cold dry toast with butter and marmalade, and a pot of coffee wrought their own miracle. The degree of optimism that arose in me strengthened as I reentered the room and Fotherwick-Botts bellowed, "I have it! Clear as a bell, by Jove! No, more like a hammer on a whacking great anvil. Haven't had so keen a Sense since the battle of—"

"Pianissimo, please." I shut the door. Excitement tingled through me. I squatted down by the map. As my finger tracked over it the sword directed me: "A bit to the right. . . . Up a quarter inch. . . . No, you bloody fool, too far."

As closely as we could identify it, Fjalar's workshop was in the Nordland of Norway north of Nidaros, which is Trondheim nowadays, somewhere in the unpeopled heights east of a village called Mo i Rana. *What and Frog?* I wondered fleetingly, then realized that the Spanish tags I'd collected in New Mexico had confused me.

The next several hours I spent making travel arrangements and shopping. I'd want suitable clothes and boots for a highland hike; to arrive as a wolf didn't seem practical. Besides, I couldn't carry a sword with me aboard a carpet, or even a ferry. Fotherwick-Botts must go as checked luggage, so I might as well pack him with the outdoor gear. A late flight to Oslo and a room there proved obtainable. I forfeited the day's rent in London and bused to Heathrow.

Seen from the air, the North Sea shimmered silver in a dusk that became night. Ships' running lights blinked forth against darkness like the stars overhead. The gibbous moon drew my thoughts to whatever unknown things were happening in yonder scarred badlands. I abandoned that for worry about my dear ones at home. It seemed nearly as distant.

But it still lay beneath daylight. I put a call through from the small, neat Norwegian hotel and got Ginny.

She looked worn-down, the cheekbones sharp in her face, eyes pale and shadowed. Regardless, she spoke crisply: "Will was arrested Monday morning. Val appealed to the Beckers and Hannah was kind enough to come stay here," our cleaning lady's mother, a fine person aside from spoiling the kids rotten whenever they got together. "I've just been through a sawtooth session with Bob Shining Knife. He doesn't like the situation either, but the evidence forced his hand. They checked gun dealers and learned Will bought a military rifle in Albuquerque the Saturday before the attack on us. The stolen carpet had been parked not far from his house, and analysis has identified spoor of him on it. They found the rifle shallowly buried in the desert—ballistic tests match it to the spent cartridges—and verified it was the one he'd bought. A mask and gloves were there too."

"Judas priest," I groaned. "What does he say?"

"Denies everything, Shining Knife tells me. I haven't seen him yet. Claims to have no recollection except that at those times he was on harmless errands or working with his lunar data or asleep. Feeling poorly, he slept a lot."

"How in the multiple names of God do they think he got past their surveillance or gimmicked that rug or shot so well or—the whole unholy mess? He's no wizard, mechanic, or marksman. And he wouldn't, for Christ's sake! You've known him all your life. I've known him for nigh on twenty years. This flat-out isn't *him*."

"Of course not," Ginny said slowly.

The notion I'd been evading these past three weeks circled behind me and slipped its cold knife into my spine. "Possession?"

"A demon could confer the abilities, falsify the memories, and . . . operate the machinery of him. He's agreed to a psychoscopy. Had to, under the circumstances. Otherwise they would have gotten a court order." Ginny's lips drew tight. "I don't know why I never caught so much as a hint of it when I tried. But anyhow, the process has started. It may take days."

Days of indignity, humiliation, sacrifice of privacy— Well, I'd been drafted into the Army during the war. "If he can be freed, cured, it's worth it," I said. "What more have you heard?"

"Barney's rallying his lawyers and whoever else might be useful."

"His Congressman?" I suggested.

"Not till we're desperate. We still have some hopes of keeping this from the media." She smiled starkly. "Although it is nice to know he's Barney's Congressman. At least, Barney owns about fifty percent of him."

That struck me as a little unfair to say of one of the few politicians whom I considered to be occasionally right-thinking. But underneath that armor of hers, Ginny needed every consolation possible. How I wanted to climb through the phone, crawl forth into our house, and hold her close!

I must settle for giving my love to the kids—Val and Ben were out at the moment, Chryssa still busy with her nap—and a progress report, such as it was. "We're off to Nordland in the morning," I finished. "I'll call again when I can, but if that isn't tomorrow, don't be afraid for me."

"I seldom am, Steve," Ginny said low. "Thank you for being what you are."

"Same to you in spades." Never mind the rest. In spite of everything, that night also I slept well.

Thursday's breakfast was infinitely superior to Wednesday's. None of your stingy Continental plates, either: a full smorgasbord, which would have filled Thor himself. Afterward, in the room, I called about a flight to Trondheim.

"I say," Fotherwick-Botts protested, "aren't we going to the museums here? Heard about 'em, I have. Not much for museums, unless milit'ry," as if he'd ever been in one, "but they've stuff from the old days before the Fairhair Raj, eh? Heard mention of a Gokstad ship. Think I may have known the very fella buried in her. Petty native king, Olaf, his name was. I'd be sure if I saw. Bring back memories, ha, jolly good battle at—"

"No time now," I interrupted hastily. "We're bound on safari, you know."

"Yes, yes. Track down old Fjalar. Won't we two have things to tell each other! Don't dawdle about like that, Matuchek. Get cracking."

A few hours later we were in Trondheim. It's a handsome provincial town on a large bay, surrounded by gently rolling countryside. The girl-watching is great, as it generally is in that part of the world. I only enjoyed those features incidentally, while buying more maps and renting a broom. Enough people knew English.

The land steepened fast as I flitted north. The way was long. The weather didn't help, low gray skies, chill headwinds, harsh rain showers. I got a bite to eat somewhere and arrived at Mo i Rana too exhausted to do more than register at the inn where I had a reservation and tumble into bed.

And when I woke, early though that was, the children were asleep at home. Very likely Ginny was too, after everything that yesterday had done to her. I had nothing to tell worth the risk of breaking her rest. Maybe by evening I would.

It shivered through me that today was the day of the hunt. I swung from underneath my comforter onto the wooden floor. Light streamed level through a window, bleak, broken by scudding clouds, but sunlight. Trees tossed their fading leaves in the wind. I heard the surflike rustle. It called me to be off, away, out of this vale and into those mountains.

27

THE INNKEEPER SPOKE ENGLISH AFTER A FASHION, BUT WAS OF SCANT HELP. AT FIRST HE didn't understand my inquiry, or pretended not to. When I pressed it, he mumbled, "Oh, yes. *Dvergen.*" My pocket dictionary had already told me this meant "the dwarf." Scandinavians tack the definite article onto the end of a noun. "Not Christian. Better keep avay." I pressed harder, until he waved a hand vaguely eastward. "Somevere t'at vay. *Hedensk troll,*" which I supposed meant "heathen troll."

He couldn't tell me of any actual harm Fjalar had done. Probably not everybody in town was as prejudiced. However, wandering the streets for a while, I saw nothing that looked like dwarf work, even in the tourist shops, just the usual cutesypoo wooden figures. To find a person willing and able to guide me might well take longer than my partner and I searching by ourselves. I loaded my luggage and the sword, well swaddled, onto the broom, hopped aboard, and took off for the general area.

It was rugged and steep, grass growing mostly in pale tufts and tussocks between lichenous rocks, dwarf birch and willow scattered around. Cloud shadows and sunlight raced over it on a chilly wind that smelled of moss and animal spoor. We were about twenty miles below the Arctic Circle. Footpaths twisted and hikers had left their traces, but I saw no one else. Vehicles were required to land only at designated spots. I obeyed, parking on the highest, because I had no wish to draw the attention of any ranger or whoever patrolled. A map in my pocket and compass in my left hand were plausible, but Fotherwick-Botts unsheathed in my right would have taken some explaining.

Clear to see, Fjalar didn't want casual visitors. I zigzagged for most of the long day, peering and sniffing, and still wouldn't have found him without the sword's help. At first his intuition was pretty vague. We cast to and fro, trending aloft. I gasped and sweated and was damn glad to stop a while and eat the sandwich I'd brought. On the plus side, the effort and the pulse thudding in my ears muffled Fotherwick-Botts' reminiscences. Now and then he broke off to exclaim, "Ha, caught something there!" I'd relax my arm and let him be a dowsing rod. In this wise, we slowly narrowed down the direction—until he whooped, "Tally-ho!" and guided me along a faint and narrow trail. Presently I caught a whiff of sulfury smoke and the sound of iron clanging on iron.

Light streamed level from the west. The wind had stiffened and the chill deepened. I climbed onto a small, flat patch of grass and boulders. A spring bubbled. Ahead of us loomed a stony bluff. A cave gaped at the bottom. Above that mouth was chiseled a runic inscription. Not noticeably weathered, it couldn't be more than a few decades old. Pieces of slag, rusty scrap, and other junk littered the ground beneath. The smoke blew from over the top.

"Whe-ew!" I gusted. "At God damn last." My legs ached, my lungs heaved, my heart thuttered, visions of armchairs and fireplaces and hot toddies danced through my head.

"Hullo in there!" Fotherwick-Botts shouted. "I say!" He switched to Norwegian—no, not exactly Norwegian—*oh, sure,* I thought, *the Viking Age version.* He'd mentioned having learned Norman French between the Conquest and the time when he fell Asleep, but that wouldn't be any use here. Nor, apparently, was the English he'd acquired after he Awoke and lay sheathed with nothing to do but listen, year after year after year. It crossed my mind—I'd been too busy to think of it earlier—how cruel and ungrateful it would be to return him to that cabinet.

A figure appeared in the cave entrance and stepped forth. "Haa, Fjalar," my companion boomed.

The other halted warily. He was a dwarf, all right. I'd seen plenty of pictures of the German ones, who were getting rich and zipping around on their Mercedes and whooping it up on the Riviera in between jobs. This guy seemed more Nordic. He stood maybe four feet tall, but wider and thicker than me, sheer muscle and massive bone under the hairy hide. Below an unkempt blond mane and untrimmed hedgerow of brows squinted little blue eyes and jutted a majestic red cucumber of a nose. His ears were almost as big. Beard spilled down to his bellybutton. He wore a leather apron over coarse gray woolen tunic and britches, cross-garters on the stumpy calves, and wooden shoes. Everything was sooty, spark-scorched in places. My own nose doubted that he ever bathed.

Old-fashioned, yeah. He didn't come outdoors unarmed. But not a stick-in-the-mud. Instead of a spear, he carried a sawed-off shotgun.

He lowered it. His voice rolled hoarse, deep as a bear's. Yet I heard surprise, and saw it on him. "Haa-hei. Brynjubítr?" The sword's original name, I recalled.

Suddenly those two were jabbering away in that archaic language. Wind whistled and bit, shadows lengthened, I visualized the hot toddy as being followed by a hot buttered rum.

In the end, Fjalar gestured with a powerful hand. "We're invited for tea," Fotherwick-Botts told me. "Rather an honor. He's not a very sociable bloke. Never was. But I am his handiwork, y'know. Old tool tie. Besides, you int'rest him. He wants to know more."

Weariness washed from me on a tide of hope.

I must hunch over to get through the cave entrance. A downward passage led to a big room. A fire leaped and crackled on a hearthstone at the middle, coals glowed near a forge at the far end, but the air, though warm and odorous, and the hewn-out stone walls were clean. Somehow smoke found its way straight up to exits overhead. Sand covered the floor. I couldn't see very well in the uneasy red light, but made out a table and several chests, beautifully carpentered and intricately carved. Slabs of dried meat, salt fish, and flatbread hung from hooks in the ceiling. More stuff filled the rear half of the room. Besides the forge, I recognized three large kettles, an upright loom, a stack of metal ingots, and a pile of fire-wood. Most, though, was lost to me among the unrestful shadows.

Fjalar pointed to a chest by the table, which obviously doubled as a bench. I sat down, my knees not far beneath my chin. He took Fotherwick-Botts—or Byrnie-biter, or whatever name suited best here—and drove his point into a chopping block, which he set on the table opposite me. "Positions for well-born guests," the sword explained. "A rough chap, Fjalar, but a pukka sahib at heart."

The dwarf brought refreshments. "Tea" turned out to be mead, poured from a clay jug into silver-rimmed horns. He raised his, sketched a T above it with his free forefinger, rumbled, "Skaal," and tossed it off.

"Drink up," Fotherwick-Botts urged. "Mustn't insult his hospitality, y'know. I can't drink, but you will for both of us like a good fella, what?"

Dubiously, I swallowed, then wished I could have gone more slowly. This was excellent, not the sticky-sweet muck I'd known under the name of mead but dry and pungently herb-flavored. Maybe the Vikings weren't quite such raving barbarians as I'd been taught. While Fjalar dragged another chest across for himself, I asked, "What was that sign he made over his glass—his horn?"

"The Hammer." Fotherwick-Botts sounded slightly embarrassed. "For Thor, y'know. His notion of saying grace. Always was a stubborn sort. Doubt he'll ever convert. But a heart of stout gold."

Seated, Fjalar refilled. This time gulping wasn't obligatory, which was a vast relief. The first draught had set the bees that made the honey buzzing through my brain in search of more clover. I was afraid they'd find some.

It didn't help much that I could catch hardly a word of the conversation. Those voices roared happily on while my glance went oftener and oftener toward the hanging meat. Its smell wafted strong, wild, delicious. I had my lens along, of course, and in this low illumination could easily become wolf, jump, and—

No, that'd probably seem ill-bred. As Fjalar was wetting his whistle for the sixth or seventh time I broke in: "Look, this is all very well and I realize you two have a lot to catch up on, but could we talk business for a while? Like maybe over a bite to eat?"

"Eh? Oh—oh, yes. Sorry," replied Fotherwick-Botts. "Got a bit carried away, I fear. Didn't even properly introduce you. These surroundings— Too easy to go native when one can't dress for dinner, what?"

He spoke to Fjalar, who nodded vigorously, belched a laugh, and smote the table so that the horns leaped and the jug nearly toppled. The dwarf tossed a sentence at me, which the sword rendered as: "Yes, he meant you no dishonor, and trusts you won't call him to *holmgang.*"

"To what?" I asked.

"Quaint custom in his day. Duel, y'know. Pref'rably fought on an islet, to get away from the hoi polloi. Ground's staked off with willow wands and the two chaps chop at each other by turns. If you're forced outside the bounds, you've lost. Or if you're killed, of course. Much better killed. Terrible disgrace, being forced out. But if you die with a quip on your lips, like, er, um—like 'Ax me no questions'—haw, pretty good, that, for a version in modern English, and no advance notice—may have a touch of skaldic talent m'self, who knows?—if you die well, you've not really lost, because men will remember you and quote you. Fjalar would be sorry to do you in. He's curious about what you have to say."

I considered those wide shoulders and long arms. "Oh, no," I answered. "No offense taken. None whatsoever. Especially from such a, uh, gracious host. And I really do want to talk with him."

The sword translated. I think the dwarf smiled, though it was hard to tell through that shrubbery. He spoke again, rose, and went off. "To fetch dinner," Fotherwick-Botts told me. "No wife, no servants. Crusty old bachelor sort. And a confirmed pagan. But a gentleman at heart."

Tableware proved to be wooden troughs. Dinner was meat hacked off and seared in the fire, together with plenty of hardtack and a fresh jug of mead. Fjalar cut his ration with a horn-handled knife. I unfolded my Swiss Army and went to work. It fascinated him. We spent minutes going over its features. I sensed him warming to me. When at the meal's end I gave it to him, he definitely beamed. By way of napkins, one licked one's fingers. By way of entertainment, the sword described a battle or two he'd seen. In Old Norse.

That became a long night, short though it still might be at this latitude. Yet I lost any wish for sleep. Detailing the discussion as it went through our interpreter would take a book by itself. Ignoring the asides, that-reminds-mes, crude jokes, and fumbles at understanding what a speaker had meant—and taking what I told for granted—here's the gist.

When Fjalar had first Woken it was tough for a while. He didn't know what to make of steamboats on the fjords, railroads down the valleys, broomsticks overhead, towns grown huge and built of peculiar materials, lights shining brilliantly at any hour, the whole country. However, you recall that the dwarves were better off than most Beings. Cold iron never bothered them, which means that electromagnetic fields never did. They went to Sleep simply because the paranatural ecology and dwellers were gone and contemporary humans seldom wanted their skills—rather, shunned them. Besides, having cold iron everywhere did interfere with those skills, for instance, the making of enchanted swords. The dwarves laid in supplies against the day when their dreams would inform them they once more had a chance of employment.

Earlier, they'd worked alone or in small groups, generally of brothers. Their wives stayed in the background, when they had any, and their children were few. That's usual among creatures that don't age beyond maturity but will live till they suffer a fatal accident, deadly violence, lethal sorcery, or the end of the world, whichever comes first. Now the German dwarves saw the situation was different. Being German, they studied it, incorporated, and were soon negotiating lucrative contracts. Most of their Scandinavian kin moved south to join them. A handful of individualists hung on at home. Fjalar was one.

His wants were modest, whether or not he was. Mainly he liked practicing his craftsmanship in his own way at his own pace. The runes above the cave mouth translated, roughly, as

Weapons and Wonders to Order
(If I Feel Like It)
Make Me an Offer

His trade was therefore mostly with other Beings, who'd all Awakened to a need of things—fays; nisser; actual, roughneck trolls; an occasional *femme fatale* (not to him) huldre; the Wild Hunt, stopping by to get its horses reshod or a fresh stock of arrowheads—all one to him. None of them were menaces nowadays, not really, and the majority meant well. They paid him in kind or in gold or in services of their own.

Just the same, I could see why his reputation among local humans wasn't the best. They didn't advertise his presence, and they put on social pressure against visiting him. Some people did anyway. Since few of them knew Old Norse and he was apt to grump at those too, little business resulted. Oh, a certain amount; that was how he'd come by things like his shotgun, his hacksaw, his calipers, the tobacco pipe he lit after dinner, and a taste for Scotch whisky.

But he preferred to stay obscure. It helped that another dwarf, farther south, had set himself up to draw the tourist trade with demonstrations, a gift shop, a restaurant, and attractive young ladies who gave lectures on folklore.

Nevertheless Fjalar listened to me, ever more intently. The mead that gurgled down meanwhile blurs my memory a little. I do recollect him saying, earthquake-deep, and Fotherwick-Botts for once giving me a straightforward rendition: "Moon, you will not be seen from here tonight. But Garm shall not devour you, not yet."

The idea of space travel grabbed him like a lustful lover. *"To ride where Sleipnir runs—"* Also, it behooved any man of spirit to take arms against the hosts of Loki, unless he was on Loki's side. Stave off Ragnarok. . . . The theological technicalities escaped me. I could, though, describe the engineering difficulties. After that he was mine.

Yes, by Thor, he'd come to my homeland and work for me! I was a proper hero, I was, right out of the good old saga days, when many of the top warriors had been werewolves or werebears or wereseals or whatever; and my wife, she sounded like a real Valkyrie, she did; and what I'd told about the worlds beyond Midgard, well, he realized he had much to learn, but he'd enjoy that—evidently the *Edda* hadn't gone into enough detail about what the gods fashioned from Ymir's body; and as for the broomstick we needed, yes, he'd have to think and tinker, but belike an alloy such as had gone into Brynjubítur, with maybe a pinch more dragon-bone charcoal and eagle dung, plus a spell such as had powered the spear Gungnir—

He hugged me. My ribs ached for three days.

Practicality reared its ugly head. "How're we going to bring him there without endless bureaucratic paperwork that's bound to alert the enemy?" I worried aloud.

"Fly him over the bally pond, what else?" Fotherwick-Botts replied.

"Not that simple. Since the war, the U.S. has maintained strict border controls. Watch-spells everywhere. Any transport approaching, air, water, or ground, gets challenged and has to identify itself and its passengers at a checkpoint. Fjalar's status, I guess you can't call it out-and-out treyf, but it's not strictly kosher either."

Since the matter doesn't often come to public attention, maybe I should explain that the Beings play billy hell with immigration laws. The ethereal types flit to and fro across frontiers as they please, seldom even aware of them. Besides, what is their legal standing? They're not human. Governments want them under a degree of control, including protection for them from evildoers. In the U.S., Congress settled on declaring them endangered species; and lawyers may file class action suits on their behalf, which lawyers have been doing with an enthusiasm that increases as they see how much money can be involved.

Dwarves, however, are as corporeal as you and me. Do they count as human? They have the same basic shape and psychology. It isn't their fault if they can't interbreed with us and don't grow old. The German dwarves quickly arranged to become subjects of the Kaiser, later citizens of the Republic, and our State Department perforce recognizes this. But Fjalar had never bothered to do anything similar. He wanted no part of the modern state.

"And we'd have to get him a green card before he could work for us," I muttered into the dregs of my last mead. Which one that was, I don't know. I'd lost count.

"Ridiculous," Fotherwick-Botts snorted. "No such thing in good King Edward VII's glorious days. Can't we smuggle him in? Good cause, after all, trying to save the bloody colonials in spite of themselves."

"How? Oh, we can probably catch a flight from Oslo to New York or Los Angeles in a few days if we phone ahead, but—"

Fjalar interrupted, wanting to know what was going on. The sword explained. Fjalar sneered through his beard and said this was no problem. He'd built a ship that, frictionless, sailed as fast as the wind. She lay hidden in a cove of the nearest fjord.

"I'm afraid that to cross the Atlantic in acceptable time, we'd need a wind of more than hurricane force," I sighed. "And no ordinary broom can make that long a trip without recharge. Also too slow. And in either case we'd run into the border ward. No, we've got to put you on a regular flight, Fjalar. But the paperwork—"

"What is this paper?" the dwarf asked. "Let me see."

The best I could do was haul forth my passport. "This admits me to my homeland without question." He took several minutes to examine it, while the fires sank low and exhaustion overtook me.

At length he grinned and said, through the sword, "Why, this is only paper and a picture with marks on them. Show me what they must be— the Christian writing—and I will try what I can do."

I scrawled on a sheet off a notepad I carried. Fjalar took pity and led me to a bed of heaped sheepskins. He seemed tireless. Well, I'd worked twice or thrice around the clock myself on this or that technical puzzle. At the moment I was happy to collapse. I never felt the vermin.

I woke itchy from their bites, ravenous again, when a booklet flapped under my nose. And coffee was brewing, coffee! Bleary-eyed, I turned the pages. It was a perfectly valid-looking blue-bound United States passport, complete with photograph and the name *Dvergen Fjalar*, born in Norway at a plausible date, naturalized, et cetera, et cetera. "D'you see?" Fotherwick-Botts crowed. "Told you, didn't I? Splendid workmen, these dwarves. They can forge absolutely anything."

28

WE DISCUSSED PLANS OVER BREAKFAST, WHICH CONSISTED OF STOCKFISH, FLATBREAD, and that brown soap the Norwegians call goat cheese. Fjalar said he'd need the rest of today and tomorrow to make his arrangements. That was reasonable. He must pass out word to his assorted patrons that he'd be gone an indefinite while. Likewise it was reasonable that he take along the essential tools of his trade. However, when he wasn't content with hammer, tongs, runic whetstone, and such, but went on to anvils and cauldrons, we began a long wrangling session. I finally convinced him that if he required stuff so big and heavy, Barney Sturlason could have it fetched.

Leaving the sword with him for company, I found my way back to our broom, flitted to the hotel, had a late dinner, and turned in.

When the innkeeper next morning asked disapprovingly whether I'd located the dwarf, I said no, but I'd had a nice hike and campout. This was Sunday, but in tourist season enough shops were open for me to buy various items I figured we might want. Back in the room I used the phone to make travel reservations and call home with a very guarded account of what I'd accomplished.

Ginny said things were looking more hopeful for Will. The kids chattered about what we could do together in the all too few days between my return and the start of school. That was kind of heartbreaking, as busy as I expected to be. I vowed to myself I'd find some free time somehow.

After we'd signed off I took a side trip to Svartisen, the glacier that's the main local attraction. The name means "The Black Ice" and it is in fact pretty grimy, but the hollows and crevices are a lovely blue.

Early on Monday I met Fjalar and Fotherwick-Botts at the high parking lot as agreed. His luggage not only crammed the coffer, some must be lashed on top. I slipped the sword into a carrier bag and took out one of the things I'd gotten yesterday, the most adorable child-size fake-medieval costume. Fjalar made a noise of nausea. I made gestures and growled. At last I got him into it. His muscular build split the jacket up the back and the pants up the seat, but the mantle more or less hid this.

My thought was that an unreconstructed old-type dwarf would draw too much notice, too many questions. Now, I hoped people would assume he was bound for a pageant. Norwegians love pageants. They might even assume the nose and shag were fake and he a midget. Having shown him to his seat and buckled his safety belt, I climbed aboard. The overloaded broom lurched into the air.

He enjoyed the flight to Trondheim, bouncing and bellowing at the sights. If he'd made this sort of trip before, it would have been at night, maybe riding pillion with the Wild Huntsman. Not being stupid, he did keep quiet at the flyport while I turned in the rental and got us onto a domestic carpet for Oslo. After we took off, he was glued to a pavilion window till I hauled him back for landing. I'd reserved at a big hotel nearby, where the staff would have seen everything and be blasé. Nevertheless I must fend off several well-intentioned remarks and glimpsed a number of raised eyebrows. We went to our room and stayed there, ordering dinner sent up. Fotherwick-Botts told me the dwarf didn't like the food—not enough meat, too much green garbage—and complained the beer was thin. He demanded Scotch. I shuddered at the Norwegian price of a bottle, but it quieted him.

Mostly I was occupied with scissors, needle, and thread. Fjalar's costume had worked so far, but it'd make U.S. passport control wonder. I'd bought an outfit for a full-grown man with shoulders, waist, and thighs like his, as well as I could gauge. Now it had to be cut down to length. That including making the sleeves short, or his arms would pop them and stick out three inches past the cuffs. I'm no tailor, but I'd perforce learned a little sewmanship in bachelorhood and the Army; and nobody expects much of blue jeans and a khaki shirt. Fjalar griped that the socks itched and the shoes pinched. I told Fotherwick-Botts to give him a lecture on the stiff upper lip and biting the bullet.

Our flight to Los Angeles left Tuesday afternoon. I could have gotten an earlier one, but it would have been on SAS. Scandinavian attendants would soon have realized I was traveling with a sho'-nuff dwarf, and might have felt obliged to report this to the U.S. authorities. Americans probably wouldn't. So we lay low till departure time. Well, in Hollywood I'd grown used to hanging around idle between takes or in producers' offices, while "Hurry up and wait" is the motto of the Army. As for Fjalar, he scribbled runes and diagrams on a sketchpad I'd obtained at his request, when he wasn't staring into space. The engineering of our moonboat—I knew the syndrome well.

The transatlantic flight was cattle-car crowded but endurable. Fjalar received no more than slightly puzzled looks. He was indignant that he hadn't been allowed to carry his bottle of Scotch with him and that I'd only spring for so much en route. More would have gotten conspicuous. But then the movie they showed enthralled him. Fortunately, he didn't understand the sappy dialogue. Me, I'd found a paperback about the Irish revolution and how de Valera raised pookas against the British. We both broke off to watch Greenland pass beneath us, austere and majestic.

Given the mob debarking at Los Angeles, Fjalar's passport got him by with no worse than a quizzical glance. I'd counted on that. Customs gave us a bit of trouble. With all his baggage, I couldn't well have checked "Nothing to declare" on his form. However, here too they were over-worked. It was easiest to accept my explanation that the ironmongery was heirlooms and that my poor friend, besides being stunted, was deaf-mute. We'd practiced a few convincing-looking sign language gestures. Pity played its part in letting us through.

Again we must struggle with luggage and clerks, and then wait for our flight to Albuquerque. How I envied the Vikings. All they had to do was board ship, sail off, loot, and kill. Fjalar tugged my arm and pointed to his open mouth. I yielded, took him to a bar, and paid flyport prices for uncounted Scotches while I nursed a beer. They didn't seem to affect him much, though doubtless excitement had something to do with that. Nor do dwarves get hangovers, as far as I know. Lucky little bastards.

Dog-tired, malodorous, and unshaven, that evening I stumbled into Albuquerque International and Ginny's arms. The kids were there too. "Will is free," she whispered on my ear. "For the time being, at least." Happiness soared in me. For the time being, at least.

Fjalar and Fotherwick-Botts kept the children noisily occupied throughout the flit to Gallup. That is, the dwarf was silent but a sight to marvel at, while the sword told of battles, answered questions in excru-ciating detail, and harrumped avuncularly at exclamations. Meanwhile, in front, Ginny soft-voiced filled me in on events.

"Will would have joined us to welcome you, but he's utterly wrung out," she said. "They released him only yesterday. Besides, no doubt a skulk of Fibbies would have tailed him. I'm as glad not to have them underfoot, aren't you?"

"More than glad." I gulped at the thought of what grief we might well have had on Fjalar's account. "We've got to keep the dwarf as close to invisible as inconspicuous will go, till we've made our arrangements and secured them." Against ghosties and ghoulies and long-nosed governments and things that go boomp at inconvenient times.

She nodded. "I rather expected that, from your hints on the phone, and encouraged Will to stay behind. Poor old dear."

"He, uh, he tested clean?"

"Absolutely, through every probe and exorcism they brought to bear. Oh, a certain faint aura of something undefined—I've caught it myself— but that's to be expected, considering his relationship to the Fair Folk."

"The inquisitors admit he's innocent?"

"No." Light from the nearly full moon showed her face gone as bleak as her voice did. "I heard babble about some kind of possessing spirit unknown to science, able to lie so deep, so dead, that none of our tests can touch it. Asian? But their references give them no information. I suggested a judicious application of common sense. Probably what won them over was judicious application of Nornwell's lawyers. In the end, it wasn't quite necessary to get a writ of habeas corpus."

"Uh, um, the physical evidence?"

Now she sighed. "Aye, there's the rub. Ordinarily, pretty damning. But in a case like this, where cunning, powerful Beings about whom we know very little are at work, the clues may well be a red herring."

"A frame-up?"

She chuckled harshly. "Framing a herring? To hang on the wall? Well, seriously, we do know the saboteurs have had *some* human ally. Implicating somebody else would protect his identity and prolong his usefulness, plus destroying the victim's. The gun dealer recognized Will's picture but would have had no way of knowing whether what he dealt with was a Seeming. Et cetera, et cetera. I put it to Bob Shining Knife: Wouldn't he and his people do better to set Will aside and go actively in search of the other parties involved, who remain on the loose?"

"How much did you tell him about our English expedition?"

"Barely enough. That we'd tracked Fu Ch'ing by proprietary methods, and Bob didn't really want to try for a court order that we reveal Guild secrets I'm sworn to keep, and we decided the trouble hereabouts has not been Fu's doing. The FBI knows about the anonymous tip and the raid on those quarters, of course. What was found there doubtless tends to bear me out. I'm pretty sure Bob put in a word of his own on behalf of my brother.

"The upshot is that Will's free under bond and under surveillance. He must have permission to go anywhere more than fifty miles from Gallup. In other words, he's still a suspect—as an accomplice, if nothing else—and we still have to prove his innocence."

I glanced over my shoulder at the cold orb behind us. "For that," I muttered, "we probably need to land somebody on the moon, fast."

Fotherwick-Botts supposed I'd looked his way. "Ah, Matuchek," he blared, "want to hear, eh? As I was telling the children, there we were at Brunanburh, a thin hairy line—"

Eventually the lights of Gallup twinkled ahead of us. We landed at our house, unloaded the baggage, and went in. Fjalar promptly kicked off his shoes, ripped off his socks, and left tracks of ingrained soot across the carpet. Short, shaggy, redwood-burly, he fitted in that Southwestern American room about as well as an orangutan would. Edgar squawked. Svartalf bottled his tail.

The dwarf rumbled something. Ginny had drawn Fotherwick-Botts and stood him against the sofa. "He expects food and drink," the sword explained. "Chieftainly hospitality, y'know. And a gift worthy of him. Haven't got a gold arm-ring or some such thing lying about, have you?"

I went to the kitchen for a salami and a couple of beers. The drink poured straight down. Fjalar gave me a meaningful look. I resigned myself and fetched a bottle of Scotch. Glenlivet, it was, for appreciative small sips on special occasions. He glugged it much the same as the beer.

Afterward he belched, beamed, and made a remark to Valeria, who stood as hypnotized as Ben. (Chryssa was nodding off and Ginny preparing to tuck her belatedly in.) "Before we retire," Fotherwick-Botts interpreted, "Fjalar asks if your charming daughter would like to do him the honor of picking the lice out of his hair."

I'd failed to warn Ginny to lay in bug powder. "That, that's not the custom these days," I stammered, while Val giggled and said, "I'd better not tell any of the boys at school. They might get ideas."

The sword must have been tactful, whatever tact meant between those two—a four-letter word, I think—because the dwarf accepted the refusal cheerfully enough but stood expectant. I remembered about the gift. Thinking fast, I trotted to my study and brought back a carved meerschaum pipe, the last souvenir of my smoking days. My father had given it to me and I'd miss it, but Fjalar obviously saw it as a kingly treasure. Okay, we needed all the goodwill we could collect.

I showed him to the guest room. Light switches were easy to demonstrate, but the adjoining bathroom took a while. Not that he didn't quickly get the hang of it. He wanted to know all about the engineering.

Around midnight I was able to join Ginny in our own bed. Neither of us slept well from then till morning. Several of the lice had accompanied me.

29

THINGS CAN MOVE FAST WHEN MONEY AND DETERMINATION LIKE BARNEY STURLASON'S push them. The next month or so stands in my memory like a string of sun-flashes, events, on a rapidly flowing river. The stream has its eddies, currents, and cataracts—no two days the same—but those brilliances blur the sight of it.

Will came around the afternoon following our return. He was gaunt and pale, he spoke barely above a whisper, his hands trembled slightly. "Rough go, huh?" was the best I could find to say as I let him in the door.

"Nothing abusive," he answered. His look evaded mine. "No torture, no bullying. But it went on and on, and in and in . . . and, and always I was afraid they'd find something—"

"Then they'd've freed you of it, wouldn't they? As for your personal secrets, I can't imagine you having any they'd think odd—barring your moon experiences, which weren't personally personal, if you follow me— and, though I don't like giving the government any credit, my understanding is that those guys keep confessions under seal same as priests or doctors. Now come in, man, have a drink, meet a couple of really odd characters, and hear about our gallivantings."

Fjalar and Fotherwick-Botts were guaranteed to take anybody's mind off his troubles, though doubtless it was a kind of shock therapy. "I'm setting up the spells to cram modern English into him," Ginny explained. "It's tricky when he's not Homo sapiens."

Will frowned slightly. Already his morale and strength were on the rise. He and the dwarf had lit their pipes and were companionably smogging the room. "Is that method ever satisfactory?" he asked.

"With humans, as a rule, no," Ginny replied. "They acquire a mere jumble of verbal reflexes, like parrots."

Edgar bristled on his perch. "Gruk, gruk," he objected. "Nevermore."

"I wasn't referring to ravens," Ginny told him. "Although they, like people, do have to grow into a language, experience it, to reach understanding. That's why instruction in the schools makes little or no use of goetics. Fjalar, however, is of paranatural stock, and has been involved with goetics all his long life. Once I've established the proper system, he should acquire English fast—his version, at any rate, whatever it proves to be."

As he listened to our story, of which he'd so far heard only the barest outline, Will revived more and more. "Then you have learned something about the nature of the ultimate enemy?" His voice shivered.

"Something." She spoke slowly. "I'm not certain what most of it implies. Fu Ch'ing was right, it takes a lifetime of study, asceticism, spiritual dedication, to gain mastery. Not common Western virtues nowadays, especially in me. I'll want to confer with you often."

"We'll want you for more than that," I added. "If we're to keep this project guardable—against demons, politicians, bureaucrats, and the news media—we have to keep it small, minimum personnel and everybody trustworthy. We can sure use your scientific skills. Not just your 'scope, though I daresay it's got important discoveries yet to make. Your knowledge of astronomy, physics, instrumentation— Are you willing?"

He stared at me the way Dante must have stared at Beatrice, Beatrice in Heaven. "Oh, yes. Oh, yes."

The doorbell rang next morning. Ginny was shut away in session with Fjalar. Val answered it. From my study, where I was trying to relate al-Bunni's design sketches to what the dwarf had seemed to propose, I heard her soft cry, "You, sir? P-please come in." Respectfulness like that, out of her, had *meaning.* I made haste to the living room.

Balawahdiwa waited there, dressed in plain shirt and Levi's, grizzled hair falling from a headband past the strong-boned face, an Indian such as you might see anywhere. But Val stood practically at attention before him, Svartalf very quietly a little behind, while Edgar had lowered his head and spread his wings. Maybe I felt what they felt even more. It was like wide skies and ancient lands and the silence that lies beneath all sound.

"Welcome." A snatch of Zuni came back to me. "*Keshi.* This is a, uh, a wonderful surprise."

He smiled and shook hands in ordinary style, but graveness tolled in his words. "*Elahkwa.*" I knew that meant "Thank you" and figured he wasn't showing off but had excellent reason to start with it. He continued in English: "Glad to see you home again. Your wife visited me while you were gone and told me as much as she knew then, but plain to see, much more has happened since."

"And you'd like to hear? Certainly. Do have a seat. Let me call Ginny and start coffee and, uh—"

"And introduce me to your friends, I hope," he said, taking a chair.

"Sure. Of course. Come to think of it, Val, you handle the coffee, okay? Just a minute, please." Collecting my wits as best I could, I went to knock on Ginny's studio door and tell her. She replied that she and Fjalar would be out as soon as possible. You can't safely break off in midspell.

On the way back, I fetched Fotherwick-Botts. We kept him sheathed in my study closet, having explained that if visitors saw him and marveled word would soon get around. For entertainment we left a book, which Ginny had 'chanted to read itself aloud in a low voice—Kipling's verse. He was happy.

I felt a tad anxious as I bared him in the living room, but needn't have been. He knew warriors, wizards, and wise men when he met them. "My salute, sir!" he barked in lieu of actually giving one; and after I introduced him he said, "I am honored, sir," with never a word about battles or natives.

The priest quickly drew us into talk. He could put people at their ease when he wanted to, no matter how serious the business. I'd answered a few questions about our doings in England and begun on my Norwegian travels when Val came in with a tray of coffee and cookies. Ben trailed her, bug-eyed. He'd been playing a reckoner game in his room, but unlike too many kids these days, he preferred reality. Chryssa was at the nursery center where twice a week she played with children her age.

"Thank you," said Balawahdiwa as the girl set his refreshments before him. His gaze captured her. I had a feeling it went deep and deeper. She stepped back, breathing harder, half scared but shoulders braced. Ordinarily Svartalf would have attacked any man who disturbed her. Now he stood motionless, back level and tail up.

"I'm sorry," Balawahdiwa said after several mute seconds. "I didn't mean to be rude. There is future in you, my young lady. I know not what, but already I sense it, like the sharp smell of wind in front of a thunderstorm." He glanced from her to me and back again. "Do not be afraid. That future may well become glorious. We will watch over you closely and lovingly."

He could say that without going pompous or mawkish. I rose and laid an arm around my daughter. She smiled at me, snuggled close for an instant, then stood aside. The blood mounted in her cheeks. Ben looked jealous but kept his mouth shut. A good, solid boy.

"Bloody hell, yes!" Fotherwick-Botts blustered. "Thor hammer me if I let any whoreson knave touch a hair of your head. I'll cleave him from his filthy skull to his unwiped arse! If you will pardon an old soldier's language, miss."

"I had other guardians in mind," Balawahdiwa said.

"Bluff. True, though, true as the steel, straight as the blade."

"Of course. We value your help."

"None of those crooked, sneaky Oriental weapons, scimitars and yataghans and what the devil they call 'em. When I campaigned with the Varangians—"

"I am eager to learn about your background," Balawahdiwa slipped in smoothly. "Let's begin with the spells cast when you were forged and what they made of you. Rustproof, I expect? Unbreakable? How well do you keep your edge, if you don't mind my asking?"

"Not at all, sir, not at all. Happy to explain. Hr-rumph! Quite correct, what you say. Wasn't named Byrnie-biter for nothing. Cut right through chain. And plate if it's not too thick. Might need two or three strokes for heavy plate. Edge scarcely feels it. Must admit, when at last I've needed sharpening it's been the deuce of a job. If they hadn't turned Christian by then, they'd've known to send me back to the shop for it. As was, a month or more of grinding, whetting, and polishing—"

I admired how Balawahdiwa got the technical information he wanted out of the old gasbag. By the time he'd done so, Ginny and Fjalar appeared.

The dwarf was presentable. He hadn't refused to take a bath—in fact, he'd wallowed in the tub till the floor lay awash—and she had summoned forth a household-type Being to make neat new versions of his former garments. He too recognized the power in the priest, bowed till his beard brushed the carpet, and said in what English he'd acquired to date, "Ay ban glad to meet you."

In the course of the next several days he became fluent, but never got rid of that accent. He did get the two *th*'s right. They've dropped out of modern Scandinavian but exist in Old Norse.

"And to what do we owe the pleasure of this visit?" asked Ginny when everyone was settled down.

"We have thought about the work you mean to do," replied Balawahdiwa. I guessed he meant himself and his fellow leaders in Zuni. Were Others involved too? I still don't know. "We've prayed special prayers, gone on added retreats, made medicine." That last term was not properly Indian. He was showing the *Melika* a courtesy, a gesture of oneness with us. "We've confirmed it—great evil is loose, terrible Powers, and the trouble centers on the moon. I suspect you know more about those creatures than we do, while we know more about how they've misled the Beings of our land. We and you must come together."

Ben astonished me. "Maybe Val and me had better leave," he said in a small voice.

Balawahdiwa gave them a smile. "Later, yes, if and when we come to secret things. But we can't hide what I am about to suggest. We can only try to keep it quiet. I'm sure you won't blab. And—" His eyes sought Valeria. "—it's best you know this much."

The youngsters huddled on the floor and listened. From time to time one or the other stroked Svartalf, who'd crowded between them. Ginny said afterward that an experience of awe at an early age is healthy. I was too caught up to think about it just then.

"You need a site where you can work on your moonboat," Balawah-diwa said. "It ought to stand where it won't be generally noticed and casual pests can be shooed off. It should also be where we can bring our utmost strength to protect it

"The Zunis offer you a place on our reservation, near Dowa Yalanne."

Corn Mountain, Thunder Mountain, their holy mountain.

Saving the world be damned, we wanted to get away and spend this long weekend, the last before school, with our children. Ginny decided she couldn't. Not only was she helping Fjalar with his English, somebody must look after him. In spite of his robustness and the cunning in his hands, the dwarf was pretty helpless here beyond his olden territory. If nothing else, he could too easily blunder into a mess that would bring publicity crashing around our ears. Besides, the sooner she started serious exchange of information and ideas with Balawahdiwa and his colleagues, the more our chances of outwitting the demons improved. Those chances were none too many at best.

We didn't know the nature of our foe, except vaguely and fragmentarily, nor their numbers, their methods, their operations on Earth and in space, how organized they were, even their long-range objectives. Yes, they wanted to keep humans groundbound and take over the moon for themselves, but what then? Given such a base, plus its goetic potentials, they could make life nasty for us mortals. And they would, they would. But beyond that, what? Had they thought it through?

Surely the Adversary had, I realized with a shudder. He was probably not directly involved in this—yet—but he must be watching. I could easily imagine the demons creating a situation he could take advantage of.

Not that I wanted to imagine it. His aim is always to lead us into evil, and we've fallen for it too bloody often. Think of what went on in the Belgian Congo in this very century. Or think of the persecution of Jews right up till the last century, and how readily it could revive—say in a strong, modern country that'd lost a major war and proposed to take its grudges out on the whole world, beginning with them. Or maybe a big but backward country, captured by an ideology that claimed human nature itself could be changed, setting out to do this with secret police, concentration camps, mass slaughters . . . Such things can happen. Demons with a lunar stronghold, striking out of it with tricks, temptations, lies, illusions, disruptions, despair, to set man against man, could make them happen.

Well, but we live day by day, taking whatever joys come by. Ginny, bless her, told me to go with Val and Ben. She'd stay home, looking after Chryssa besides the other stuff. Once in a while, I supposed, she'd sleep.

I took the kids to a little canyon we'd heard about, tucked in the highlands well off the usual routes. It's nothing spectacular, merely beautiful, ruddy walls above grass, piñon, juniper, and sweet herbs. A stream gurgles through, offering fly fishing as well as water. At one point it widens into a swimming hole, if your ancestors don't include any brass monkeys. Birds fly around. At night the sky is cramful of stars. There's a tiny, primitive campground. That's all I'll record, hundred-year seal or no. We three came back with memories that stood me in good stead afterward when I badly needed consolation.

Meanwhile I missed out on a fair amount of excitement. Right after Ginny briefed him, Barney Sturlason swung into action. Holiday weekend or no, money gushed, warehouses opened, carriers flew, and workers gleefully drew double-time pay. When I returned, a prefab workshop and living quarters were ready to erect for Fjalar on the appointed spot and everything else he wanted was on its way from Norway, himself along to supervise.

He wasn't there for the actual start. No white person was. The Zunis performed their rites of purification and set their prayer sticks around the site. I saw those wands later, carved with faces, dressed in feathers bound on with cotton.

More securities were then added. Ginny handled the Western goetics, the Zunis their own spells religiously oriented rather than technologically. In the end we felt pretty sure that no Beings could make mischief around there. As for renegade humans, Fjalar had not only a phone but a siren to bring fast, well-equipped help. He loved making it scream. We must hope he'd control his impulses.

What could happen after our spacecraft left the protected area was less certain.

Construction, assembly, and installation proceeded in everyday fashion. Again for the sake of discretion, locals did the work. I pitched in alongside Indian laborers, carpenters, electricians, and whatnot. After years spent mainly at drawing boards and in laboratories, hammer, saw, and screwdriver felt mighty good in my hands. I was soon also enjoying the companionship—jokes, stories, lunch eaten together, maybe a beer after hours—of men with a common purpose.

Fjalar oversaw everything and bitched about most of it. Amazing, the amount of English profanity and obscenity now at his command. He didn't learn it from my wife. She's no prude, but she doesn't need that kind of language to put somebody in his place. She figured out that, considering the dwarf's character, the law of contagion had operated.

We hardly ever saw a Zuni priest anymore, and Balawahdiwa not at all. We wondered why, but were too busy to fret about it.

When completed, the smithy was a low building of cinderblock, sheetrock, corrugated metal, and so on, plunked down in the middle of sage, paintbrush, Apache plume, and so on. Fjalar's living space was tucked in one end. He didn't want a lot beyond a bed and privy; his work was his life. Nevertheless he appreciated the fridge that kept beer cold, the running water from a tank, the stove that made cooking easy, and the self-washing tableware. He'd also acquired a taste for a few modern foods, notably lutefisk and Limburger cheese, to say nothing of Scotch and tobacco. We kept him well supplied.

I doubt if he noticed how majestic the setting was. Around him reached the land, ruddy soil, bush, occasional tree, scarcely a trace of habitation other than a dirt road; Zuni lay beneath the northwest horizon. Overhead arched the sky, deep blue by day, starful by night, its winds and its stillness. Nearby the enormous mesa, Dowa Yalanne, upheaved itself, two thousand feet high, more than two miles in length, sculptured red rock nearly sheer, white-banded through the middle, up and up to a thin woodland. Twin pillars were visible from here, in Zuni legend a brother and sister who had given their lives to save their people when a flood engulfed the world. Certainly those people had taken refuge on those heights in historic times. It was a hard day's climb to the top. I'd been told that only a few ruins remained—and an overwhelming sacredness. None but the purified were welcome, and they rarely.

Fjalar settled in. We left Fotherwick-Botts with him for company. The phone connection, which we hoped was secure, would keep them in touch with us. Of course, we and a few others would often come around in person: we especially, Ginny as a witch, I as an engineer. We thought that otherwise we could maybe, for a short while, get on with our own lives.

No such luck.

30

FJALAR HARKED BACK TO AN ERA LONG BEFORE BLUEPRINTS. A JOB DID CALL FOR forethought, and he'd make charcoal drawings on bark or hides—in recent times, pencil on paper. But after that he went ahead and let things happen under his skillful hands. Always he had to improvise, for instance judging the state of the metal by its color as it glowed hot; and there were bound to be surprises along the way. So when I brought him the plans I'd developed on the basis of al-Bunni's preliminaries, I found him already at his anvil.

Stepping in from daylight to the gloom of the smithy, at first I was nearly blind. Heat and smoke rolled over me. The crash of hammer on steel went like gunfire. Coals in a rude stone furnace glowed white, fanned by a huge old dragonskin bellows that pumped itself. Metal rods above them had reached incandescence. Dressed again in wadmal, leather gloves, leather apron, and wooden shoes, beard and mane full of the soot that blackened his skin, the dwarf gripped a piece with tongs and banged it into shape.

We'd discussed technique, once he had English and I'd done some studying. I'd learned enough about wootz, case-hardening, pattern-welding, tempering, and the rest to understand that this was high crafts-manship and to appreciate how much I didn't know. Add the lore of 'chantment—songs, runes, special materials ranging from blood and snake venom to—what? bear fat and lingonberries, maybe?—anyhow, that shaggy little guy amongst the jumping shadows became pretty impressive. The sword had spoken well in advising that we engage him.

Nevertheless, he could sure be a royal pain in the rear.

"Halloa, Matuchek!" Fotherwick-Botts shouted from the wall where he hung unsheathed. "Got something for us, have you?" Fjalar's eyeballs, red-lit white against the smudge, rolled toward me. He spat. The forge sizzled. He kept hammering. "He can't stop till he's done, y'know," his roommate continued unnecessarily. "Like fu—" He broke off. I gathered he was trying to refine his language for the ladies. "Like carnal congress, as I've noticed. Daft, you humans."

Remembering the latest scandals in Washington, I thought that that was where we Americans had our carnal Congress. I didn't say it. A reform movement was under way, as hysterical as the antispace movement, and many an errant legislator was now turning over a new page.

"At ease," Fotherwick-Botts invited hospitably. "Crack yourself a beer if you like. I'll keep you amused. Never did fill you in on that skirmish shortly before the battle of Buttington, did I?"

I fetched the brew, settled myself on sacks of charcoal, and made the best of things.

Eventually Fjalar laid the iron aside. I saw it was in fact three rods, twisted together and beaten into fusion. He went back for a bottle of his own. Rather, in proper Norse style, he carried several on a platter, plus a kippered herring between his teeth, which he let fall on the dish when he'd set that down. He hunkered on the floor. For a moment the only sound was the hoarse breath of the bellows.

"*Skaal*," he toasted, lifting his drink.

"Wassail," I said.

"First, gentlemen, first the Queen, God bless her," Fotherwick-Botts reminded us.

"Sorry." I rose to my feet. "The Queen."

"Vich kveen?" inquired Fjalar. "Sigrid the Haughty in Sveden? She vas a great lady, she vas. Didn't like those little kings who came courting her, so she put them up in vun house and burned it. Married King Harald Bluetooth of Denmark. She made him vaylay King Olaf Tryggvason of Norway at sea. *Ja*, there's a kveen vorth drinking to, by damn!"

Before Fotherwick-Botts could raise an argument, I said hastily, "I've brought you the plans."

We unrolled them on a workbench littered with wood and metal shavings. My eyes had adjusted to the murk and to Fjalar's it came naturally. For the most part, the design pleased me. I'm a scryotronic, not a mechanical engineer, but I'm fairly good at building things, and I'd gotten some help from a couple of close-mouthed fellows at the Point. Besides, this was basically just a broomstick. What was different was the tremendous forces we meant to invoke, plus the capability of cruising through space and landing on places like the moon. For so small a vehicle to do this without being torn apart, we wanted the dwarf's metallurgy.

Straight off, he dashed my pride to the ground. "Vat the bloody blue blazes you mean by this silly box you got wrapped around the shaft?" he roared, in words more pungent.

"The cabin," I said. "For the crew."

"Cabin?" He bristled in all directions. An influence from the later years before he fell Asleep broke through. "Yesus Christ All-Father, ve send two men and you vant to sit them like in a king's hall? And vimmin bring mead and hop in bed with them? Hole in the head! Sailors don't need no stinking cabins. Your men, they don't even got to row. By Freyja's yugs, you ban yust plain crazy!"

I lifted my hands. "Calm down, will you? I don't like this feature myself. It'll play billy hell with the aerodynamics, and I hate to think how we'll gasket it around the shaft, but luxury accommodations it ain't. Look, would you send an unarmored man into combat?"

"Berserkers, *ja*."

"Uncivilized thugs, the Vikings called 'em," Fotherwick-Botts reminisced. "No discipline. No tone. But what fighters! Absolutely fearless. The Fuzzy-Wuzzies of their day."

"Celestonauts are not berserkers," I tried to put in.

"Ah, if they could've been properly organized," Fotherwick-Botts sighed. "Sweep everything before 'em, they would have, a regiment of Norse berserkers. With white officers, of course."

"We're talking survival," I groaned. "I thought you knew, Fjalar. Lord knows we tried explaining. Between here and the moon, the air thins out to nothing. Our men couldn't breathe."

"*Ja*, Ay heard about likvid oxy-yen," the dwarf said. "They drink air from horns, okay?"

"Not okay! And with no outside pressure on them, their blood would boil. And the ultravi—its sunburn would fry them." Not to mention X rays, particle radiation, temperature extremes, the works. The Fair Folk themselves had to flee the sun. For us humans, raw space is a hell. The alien demons felt right at home. . . . "They've got to have metal around them."

"So they vear helmets and mail like Ay seen pictures of," Fjalar retorted. "The vay Ay vill make this *himinfar*—this sky boat, she can reach the moon in two-three hours."

I realized that. Accclcration and its pressure weren't a problem. Thanks to al-Bunni's insight, the vessel ought to be in sympathetic relationship with the curvature of space itself. Everything and everybody aboard should be accelerated equally, except that we'd provide enough "downward" component to keep riders in their seats.

"The men can ride saddles," Fjalar continued. "This big, clumsy mass-mess you vant to stick on, it vill make the crossing ten times as long, and Ay think it vill make steering too hard."

"But spacesuits alone won't do," I maintained. "Can't you see what the whole mission is about?" *You stupid stump*, I did not add. It would've been unfair. If I'd had as much history and science to catch up on as he did, I might not have done as well. "They'll be gone for an unknown time. They're bound for unknown territory, with unknown hostiles there. Even a quick scouting flight calls for weapons, instruments, goetic equipment, and a refuge—a place where they can take shelter, rest, eat, drink, relieve themselves, for God's sake!"

"But Ay tell you, this cabin you vant is like putting an outhouse on a longship. The vind catches it, and down under the vater goes the lee rail. . . . The lee rail, *ja*, that's vere real seamen get their relief. That's how ve made it to Iceland and Greenland and Vinland, by yiminy."

"A point," Fotherwick-Botts agreed. "Austerity, y'know. Make do. Once, harrying along the Dutch coast, I think it was—Low Countries, at any rate, Frisia or thereabouts, my man Hog-Einar—"

"God damn it," I yelled, "I've been through the math on this and I can prove—"

The door opened on a dazzling rectangle of sunlight, broken by a silhouette. All but the bellows and the fire fell suddenly silent.

Balawahdiwa walked in. "How do you do, gentlemen," he said, as mildly as usual. "Am I intruding?"

"N-not in the least," I stammered. "We, uh, we haven't seen you for a while."

"Velcome," Fjalar greeted, ripped the cap off a beer bottle with his teeth, and reached it forth. "Please to sit down."

"Salute. Attention," Fotherwick-Botts said symbolically on his own behalf.

Balawahdiwa smiled. "At ease, General." He accepted the bottle and took a place beside me on the charcoal supply. I've never met another man who carried so much presence so lightly. "Thank you." He took a piece of kipper. I remembered that one should not scorn one's host and did likewise. A long swig of beer helped.

Fjalar went, shall I say, bluntly to the point. "Vy are you here, after this long time?"

"It's only been a couple of weeks, more or less," Balawahdiwa replied.

"It's felt longer," I said.

"Yes, you've been busy and in suspense, haven't you? I'm sorry. It was necessary. But I do seem to have appeared at a lucky moment. I heard you arguing, and believe I have an answer to your problem."

"Huh?" I exclaimed, and "*Haa?*" Fjalar grunted, and "Jolly good, by Jove!" Fotherwick-Botts declared.

The priest turned grave. It was as if the shadows deepened, the fire drew into its white-hot self, and the bellows shushed like a low surf.

"The story goes far back," he said slowly. "I may only tell you a little of it. We among the Zunis, and some in other pueblos, sensed evil afoot many months ago, more and more as time passed, but we could not discover what it was or what it intended. Though the moon was weak at midsummer, which should have aided us, my medicine society learned almost nothing when we made retreat. Nor did the others in their turns."

I knew almost nothing about that seasonal rite. The initiate men went into their kivas—heat, steam, sacred smoke—

"Then the disaster hit Cardinal Point, and everything else followed," he went on. "You know what my fellows and I have tried to do. It wasn't enough. The gods gave no dreams, no omens, nothing. You remember what Kokopelli told us, Steven. The other gods cannot have been ignorant of it, but they have not spoken to us. Now I have made a novena to Our Lady of Guadalupe."

The patron of the mission church. It had been restored, with murals that show something of Zuni life and faith. These people saw the gods, or God, in many shining forms.

"I did it on the heights of Dowa Yalanne," Balawahdiwa said very softly. "Then I was granted a vision, and there I found an eagle's egg, newly hatched, at this time of year when it should not be, a sign and a talisman.

"I returned to my fellows. After what the vision had shown me, we could make a new and stronger medicine."

We sat for a span in stillness.

Balawahdiwa relaxed and smiled. His tone became everyday: "Speaking practically, we here at Zuni understand that protecting the scouts is critical. We think we've worked out a better way to do the job." He'd been carrying a manila envelope, which he handed me. "Take this home to your wife, Steven." Once more solemn: "Part of it is holy. But she will help you understand."

31

I'D TOLD GINNY I'D PROBABLY BE HOME FOR LUNCH, MAYBE A LITTLE LATE. BURSTING IN, I hollered, "Hey, have I got a surprise for you—" and stopped short. Not one but two redheads sat in the living room. "Why, uh, hello."

"I thought Curtice would like to join us and hear your progress report," my wife explained. The pair of them had become better friends than ever since she fixed the celestonaut's fundamental difficulty. I suppose that sort of experience forges a bond.

I hesitated. "Well, um—"

The big young woman stood to shake my hand. "Please don't worry," she said. "I know you have to keep the lowest profile possible. As far as the staff in general at the Point are concerned, what's left of them, they're under the same vague impression as the public is, what part of it gives a hoot anymore. Some privately funded, small-scale experiments going on at some offside location. Yawn. But Dr. al-Bunni decided a few of us ought to know the truth from the start."

"I see." Needless to say, we kept the chief himself posted, and he'd paid the smithy a clandestine visit. He had to be aware of what we were doing if he was to have any chance of covering up for us or even slipping us a little help. More important, he deserved to. Already he'd arranged for that pair of close-mouthed engineers to advise me on my plans for the vehicle.

"All are trustworthy," Ginny added. "They feel they have a personal stake in this."

Curtice Newton grinned. "Yeah, that stick of yours will want a couple of crew, I'm told. I hope to be one of them."

My doubts eased. "Couldn't ask for a better," I said.

"I'm touting myself for pilot. I'm not sure yet whom else to recommend."

"She's the only flyer let in on the secret so far," Ginny explained, "and I'm the one who did. We want to be sure we don't pick either a stickler for regulations or a glory hound who can't keep a secret."

I waved the envelope at her. "What's here may change everything," I blurted. "Fjalar dug in his heels against a life-support capsule, but Balawahdiwa showed up and gave me this."

The green eyes kindled. "I knew he was Seeking." Louder, firmly: "Lunch first. I'll have it on the table in a minute or three. You two entertain one another, please." Ginny left.

Curtice and I couldn't easily follow her suggestion. Neither of us was a glib talker. "How's life been treating you?" I attempted.

"Not often enough." The joke fell flat. She grimaced. "Terrible, frankly. I don't want to whine, but I can't help envying you and Ginny. You've been in action."

"And you've been idled."

"While my life's dream crumbles." She struck fist on knee. "No, I *won't* whine. I'm not alone in this fix, not by a long shot. . . . But oh, Steve, if only, if only."

Her burst of emotion embarrassed her, which embarrassed me. My mind cast about for something to say. My eyes hunted for inspiration. They spied a couple of books on an end table next to where Ginny had sat. "Hey, what're those?" I asked inanely.

"I don't know," Curtice said, equally anxious to fill the empty air. "She had one in her hand when she let me in."

"Must've been reading it, then. From the public library, I see, both of 'em." I reached over while my tongue clacked away on automatic pilot. "I didn't notice before. Been too busy with my design work, except Saturday afternoon when I took Ben to a ball game. She's been busy too, her consultations and— Anyway, we haven't had much conversation these past two-three days. I guess she checked these out meanwhile." Not to seem a total babbling idiot, I opened the books to their title pages. "Hm, a collection of Japanese folk tales by, um, Lafcadio Hearn. What kind of a name is that? And the fat one, uh, *The Tale of Genji*, translated by—"

Edgar had rested quietly on his perch. All at once he raised his hackles and spread his wings. "G-r-ruk," he croaked.

"What's the matter, bird?" I called. "Something spooky?"

"Haa, damn, hell, hell, hell! *Gr-r-ruk!*"

Ginny reentered before I could start seriously wondering. "Come and get it," she invited. Relieved, Curtice and I trooped after her.

A garbanzo and pasta salad with garlic toast and white wine broke the ice to flinders. My account of smuggling Fjalar from Norway gave Curtice a laugh. She couldn't wait to meet him. We must needs confess that he seldom received visitors gladly. Also, the less he was distracted, the sooner he'd finish. Better make the introduction part of a special event. She understood. "I've had to drop whatever I was doing and talk to this or that VIP too damn often. Pose for a picture with him too, likelier than not."

"What did you say?" I inquired.

She shrugged. "Polite noises. Some of them were human."

We left the table and repaired to Ginny's arcanum in a mood tense but hopeful. She spread the half-dozen sheets of paper on her desk and sat down. We brought chairs to either side of her. Our vision strained, our pulses fluttered.

The text was neatly hand-printed in English, with scattered Zuni words and a couple of diagrams. Yet after a while Curtice shook her head and leaned back. I surrendered a minute later. "It almost makes sense," I complained, "but as soon as I try to get the gist, everything dissolves, like in a dream."

"It is quite like a dream," Ginny answered low. "A vision. Call it highly technical or deeply theological, whichever you want. But Balawahdiwa wouldn't have sent it to me if he didn't expect I could . . . find out how to . . . comprehend it."

She pored and pondered. Sometimes her lips moved, or she stared off at the wall, or beyond the wall. Sometimes she consulted a reference work or her own notebooks from the pueblo. Sometimes her fingers traced a gesture. Curtice and I waited. This silence was not awkward, nor was it wearisome. It quivered.

Finally the witch crossed herself, laid the papers back in the envelope, and rose to stretch cramped muscles. We others bounced up as if a coiled spring had let go. "Whoo-oo," gusted from me. Curtice whistled.

Ginny's look gleamed from one to the other of us. "I've got it," she said. Triumph rang beneath the spare words. "The Zuni holy men have learned how to make medicine bundles—I may as well call them that— which provide complete life support, aside from food and water. No need for spacesuits or a capsule."

"What?" Curtice cried. "Are you sure?"

"If Balawahdiwa is, I am. The principles are valid, and of course everything will be carefully tested beforehand. Won't it?"

Curtice gulped. "Of course."

"How the—how in God's name does it work?" I faltered.

"From your viewpoint, dear, partly it draws on the same paranatural laws as the wind and weather screenfields for an ordinary broom. But this spell is far stronger and subtler. The field contains pressure, maintains temperature, and fends off harmful radiation, even excessive visible light." The engineer in me imagined the energy to do that as being copped from those very photons and charged particles. While still within the atmosphere, you might use its thermodynamic differentials. . . . "Air is recycled, renewed, by interaction with a stock of water and limestone, through a chemical conversion cantrip, though a unique one." *Ah, yes,* I thought, *a CCC.* "I doubt that NASA's scientists, no matter how brilliant some of them are, could ever have created anything like this."

"I do too," Curtice whispered.

"There's sacredness in it, you see," Ginny told us gravely. "The Zuni achieved it not only by thinking, but with prayer, fasting, rites, and sacrifice. They did it less for our sake than for land and folk, their children and grandchildren. Their native gods may not yet have responded to their appeals, but in native belief, humans aren't passive supplicants. They're integral with the world. They help maintain the balance of the universe.

"*We* have work to do."

Again, stillness. Afternoon light and heat blazed at drawn blinds.

"What?" I managed to ask.

Ginny smiled a bit. "Well, not too much immediately. The medicine bundles require certain things. Some the Zunis will supply. But we're to furnish water from each of the Four Oceans."

"The which?" said Curtice.

"These days they're interpreted as the Atlantic, the Pacific, the Arctic, and the Gulf of Mexico. We can sic Barney's men onto that. I'll write a manual of how they should collect and transport it. The Zunis will contribute aspects of the totem animals for five of the Six Directions, including eagle for Up. But we are to give several mole skins, for Down, because we are the people who mean to leave Earth . . . and return. I think you can take care of that, Steve. I'll brief you later. Then we stand by for further instructions, preparing our souls as best we can."

"Stand by," Curtice said woodenly.

Ginny patted her hand. "I know, that can be the hardest duty of all."

She took her leave soon after, telling us she didn't want to be underfoot. I suspect she was more wrung out than she let on. A session like today's was uncanny if you weren't used to such things. Or if you were. I felt it myself, and even Ginny seemed kind of subdued.

Having closed the door behind our guest, we passed to the coolness of the living room. My glance fell on the books. "Hey," I said to make conversation, "why this sudden interest in Japan?"

"What?" She hesitated, which wasn't like her. When she spoke again, the words dragged. "Oh, those. Just interested."

"Never heard of 'em."

We weren't ashamed to admit ignorance in the privacy of our own home. She'd had more formal education than me; I'd knocked around in places and situations foreign to her, and once in a while read something good that she hadn't. Being married to a dullard must get awful boring.

"Well," she replied—did I hear the slightest reluctance? "Lafcadio Hearn was an American journalist who fell in love with Japan in the late nineteenth century, settled there, became naturalized—practically unheard of—and wrote about the country and the culture, trying to show them to the Western reader."

" 'Unheard of' is right, from what *I've* heard. What about the other book? Japanese original?"

"Yes. The author, Murasaki, was a lady of the Heian court in the eleventh century. Her *Genji Monogatori* may be the first novel ever written, depending on how you define 'novel.' "

"So it tells about a world very different from any we know, I suppose."

"Absolutely. And yet some things have persisted—" Ginny broke off.

I clasped her elbow. "What got you hooked on this subject, with everything else that's piling onto you?"

She looked away. Her hands clenched. "Call it a hunch. Worthless, no doubt. I don't care to talk about it now. Anyway, the material is fascinating in its own right."

At that point Valeria and Ben arrived home from school and rescued her. Me too, maybe.

Wolf after dark, I sniffed around and located my spot. Next day, having given Fjalar the news and discussed it with him, I stopped by a bait shop and bought a can of night crawlers, which I emptied on the chosen ground. Rising well before dawn, I made my way back there.

Ginny had told me that for this I must be in human form. The town slept around the park I went into. Trees hulked black, shading out what lights shone along streets, and stars glistened in the west. Eastward the moonless sky had gone bleak white. Air lay soundless and cold.

Witch-sighted, my eyes caught the faint tremors under the soil. I plied my trenching tool. A mole flew up with the clods. I grabbed it in midair. The soft, warm body struggled in my grasp. "I'm sorry, little brother," I murmured as I had been taught, "and I thank you for what you give." Bringing my nose close to its snout, I wrung its neck with a single quick motion, breathed in its last breath, and felt it go limp.

I laid it aside and waited. Others, momentarily alarmed, should soon come back to the feast. I needed seven.

Valeria's fifteenth birthday fell in midweek. We made her favorite breakfast before she left for school, and planned a modest family celebration that evening. Come Saturday, we'd throw a party for her and her friends, and keep strictly in the background.

How young she was, slim, demurely dressed and almost shyly soft-spoken—for a change—and how beautiful. Memories rushed over me. Svartalf must have gotten sentimental too. He jumped onto her lap and purred till she had to go. Ginny and I stood in the door and waved. Edgar squawked, "Cheers!" Ben took the matter good-naturedly. Chryssa crowed.

Then business claimed us. For my part, I flitted to Zuni and gave Balawahdiwa the moles. He blessed them and took them elsewhere. Afterward we had a long conversation over coffee. Parts of it touched on our situation, though barely. He said he did not know the future. Nor, he believed, did the gods. (Well, the branching universes are so many, and each so strange, that probably none but the One God can keep track of them.) They could not have been unaware of evil Beings in their country, but Kokopelli's skepticism about us had maybe misled them as to the nature and danger of it. They might look on it as white men's business, and they were not white men's gods. We humans of every race must do our utmost; my wife had spoken truth, we have our vital part to play in the cosmos. Then they might come to our aid, as Balawahdiwa knew a Christian saint had once done. Even so, the outcome was not sure and would not be. There had been planetary catastrophes in the past.

I nodded. There had also been times when evil simply bestrode Earth for centuries.

However, most of our talk ranged elsewhere, into war stories and other reminiscences, man talk, favoring anecdotes that were funny. No matter what happened, we had our past to cling to, and this shared moment.

Having said goodbye, I headed for the smithy to check on developments. A fair-sized tent a hundred yards west of it caught my notice, glaring white amidst gray-green brush and yellow flowers. Will Graylock had obtained permission to set up shop here. He'd been almighty withdrawn since last we saw him. I landed in front of his pitch.

He came forth dressed for desert and shook my hand beneath the sun-flap. I glimpsed portable instruments and rudimentary camping arrangements inside. "Hello, Steve, glad to see you. I was hoping you or Ginny or both would stop by soon."

I glanced around and didn't spot any Fibbies. Well, their surveillance no longer claimed top priority. They might well be carrying it out from Gallup, through a scryer attuned to his broom. He had to have a broom. Nobody but an Indian or a local-bred American would get far through this country on foot.

His tone had been listless, his handclasp loose. The skin, sallow in spite of the sun, stretched tight over the skull, the eyes were sunken and dark-rimmed. *Oh, hell and damnation*, I thought, *another downturn.* "How're you doing?" I asked mechanically.

He shrugged. "Surviving. Making ready to keep the moon under close observation away from city lights."

I thought about devils yonder and what they might intend. "You figure you might catch new, better indications?"

"Who knows?"

I glanced at the wan, waxing orb, almost lost in blue heaven. "What can you do before dark?"

"That's limited, yes. But I'll have another matter to keep me busy. The meteorites."

"Hm?"

"The pieces of them rather, that NASA—al-Bunni—gave us. In my opinion, they haven't been sufficiently studied. What goes into the moon-boat is crucial, after all."

I nodded, recalling.

Most people never think about the pinch of sand embedded in a broom. It's there, it keeps the go-force from lofting you unsafely high, and so what? Racers use a stone from the destination area, to hurry them along contagionally. This is only for persons competent to handle it. Still more would be required for spaceflight.

"I want to ascertain beyond doubt that the alleged chip of moon rock did come from there," Will said. "Yes, I know about the chemical and goetic analyses, but I have finer tests in mind. Imagine that the identification is mistaken. Some of those specimens are purely terrestrial, some are from original orbits we don't know, the asteroid belt, the outer comet cloud, who can tell? Given the power that will drive the boat, what if the pilot stone should be wrong for the goal?"

I winced. Certain accidents in the early days of broomflight came to me. "Well, you're better qualified to double-check than anybody else I can think of."

"Can you arrange for the specimens to be brought here to me?" Will urged.

"Yeah, I guess so, aside from the moon rock itself. That is, uh, I expect you can look at it too—"

"Under supervision. I understand. Actually, I'm confident I'll confirm that it is lunar. But examination of the rest may help in future missions."

"Why not do it back at your place in Gallup? More comfortable."

"Too much interference. I need a low noise level."

"As you like. I'll speak to 'em at the Point. It shouldn't be any big deal." I paused. "Meanwhile, this is Valeria's birthday. You're her Number One uncle. How about dinner, with ice cream and cake and candles? No present necessary." Cliché: "Just your presence."

His hands lifted, as though in defense. "I'm sorry. I'd like to, but this is the autumnal equinox. The observations I make tonight, they, they may prove important."

I couldn't argue with that. The turnings of the year do matter. I promised to convey his regrets and proceeded to the smithy. There I was delighted to see how far along the work was.

Well, Fjalar forged tirelessly, with more than human strength. Besides, he didn't have to do everything. For instance, NASA was, under the counter, providing the titanium-alloy straws for him to weld to the shaft. A specialist would quietly come around to install the spirit crystal. Et cetera.

"Ay vill be done vith the main part before the full moon," the dwarf told me. "Ay had better be, for that is ven ve can make sure she vill fly and Moon-Garm vill not shase her or any sush dumb stuff. This ban yust bare bones, you know. Later Ay add the fancy things." He rubbed his horny hands. "Haa, but you vill pay for your fancy things!"

I jumped through a quick calculation. Werewolves are naturally always conscious of lunar phases. "The full moon. That'll be Thursday next week, won't it? How about we schedule the first flight test the following Saturday?"

Fjalar hunched his shoulders. The fire behind him leaped and shadows through the gloom went wild. "No cackle-hens," he growled.

"News media? Positively not. A few of us, people who've helped make this happen and their immediate families."

What a birthday gift to promise Valeria today!

I didn't, then, think beyond it.

32

IF NASA OR SOME BIG CORPORATION HAD BEEN RUNNING OPERATION LUNA, THE FIRST flight of our spacecraft would have been an Event. Farseers, newspapers, magazines, night club comedy routines would have been choked with it for months on end, everything from Our Destiny Among the Stars versus

Our Arrogance and Neglect of the World's Real Problems to renewed impertinences about Curtice Newton's love life and taste in lingerie. On this Saturday, press and spectators would have packed the site from horizon to horizon, a site chosen to accommodate their numbers and what they'd buy. There would have been speeches. And interviews. And speeches. And a band. And speeches.

As it was, the group numbered a dozen. We weren't exactly being secretive, but we weren't handing out announcements either. Since we were a small, private outfit, we bore down on the "private" and the "small." Any more conspicuous, and we'd be entangled in politics and public relations. Any larger, and our defenses against demons would be spread dangerously thin. Surely *they* kept the closest watch on us that those defenses allowed.

Also, we'd decided our best strategy was to present what Ginny called a *fait accompli*. If we unveiled a broom that had repeatedly worked, nobody would have had a chance to hogtie us with regulations or pass a law forbidding the project. We could hope to keep a pretty influential voice in future developments. Yes, that included profits—royalties, licensing fees, shares in enterprises—for everybody in the partnership. The Zunis, above all, could find plenty of good uses for some megabucks.

But the greatest gains were not material. To al-Bunni, for one: vindication, the space program popular again, revived and strengthened. And to humans in general. They'd be alerted to the menace on the moon, which so far had just been hinted at and met with scorn from most intellectuals—paranoid, racist, intolerant, absurd, same as prewar allegations about what the Caliph intended.

Okay, maybe we'd exaggerated the threat in our own minds, though if it worried people like Balawahdiwa and Fu Ch'ing it worried me. The point was, an expedition should determine the truth. Then the world could make ready to cope. Might that bring the nations together in a lasting alliance? Daydream, probably.

For sure, way too big a load to lay on this little trial jaunt. I told myself to relax and enjoy.

My glance traveled around the bunch who waited outside the smithy. The morning was bright, still cool. A breeze whittered, bearing touches of sage and, alas, rabbitbrush. Dowa Yalanne reared into utter blue, itself white-streaked ruddy, light and shadow at play across its carvenness. Ginny stood beside me, a fiery lock aflutter beneath her cap. On my other side quivered Val, and beside her Ben. We'd left Chryssa home—you never quite knew what could happen—with Hannah Becker to indulge her so she wouldn't care what she was missing here.

Will stayed a yard or two off, alone. He'd said hardly anything. A week spent mostly in the desert had tanned him, and it was as if the sun and the high stars had worked their peace; but how reserved he was, how unsmiling.

Likewise a disappointment was that Barney Sturlason and his wife weren't on hand. He was snarled in tax troubles like a dolphin caught in a tuna net. Meanwhile he must hold Nornwell on course, doing things of actual use to people. He couldn't spare even a weekend.

Nor was al-Bunni here. He'd been called back to Washington for more infighting. NASA's representatives were Curtice, who'd pilot today, and my friend and coworker Jim Franklin, who'd installed the control and communication systems on our broom. They too stood aside, a striking and handsome pair, his chocolate skin setting off her fair complexion. The cheery way they chattered made me wonder if something was developing between them. That'd be nice.

Balawahdiwa and two dignified old men, fellow priests, also held apart. They weren't being unsociable. I realized they were busy, though it scarcely showed on them. They didn't make a production of their— prayers?—and like us they wore plain outdoor garb.

The whole atmosphere was as informal as the lavender asters nodding in the breeze. Nevertheless, I felt more than the excitement usual to a launch. Way down, underneath the fun and games, I had a sense of sacredness.

Ben's voice plucked my attention away. "Dad, how high's the spacecraft going to fly? How far?"

"They'll decide that as they see how she performs," I told him.

"If she works right, can we get a ride too?"

"Don't be a mudhead." Val sounded less superior than wistful. "This is a *test*."

"But she's really only a broom, huh?" her brother argued. "She handles like any Ford or Volksbesen, doesn't she?"

"More like a souped-up Maserati." Val had swallowed every drop of information that came in range of her, and remained thirsty. This vehicle was meant for the regions where Magister Lazarus roved!

"And that's in low atmosphere, close to the ground," Ginny reminded them. "Crewed spaceflight has never been tried, you know. We'll have to feel our way forward."

"We," Val whispered. Her gaze went to Curtice, in envy and adoration.

"Hey, man, here she comes!" Jim Franklin hollered. Except for the Zunis—and maybe Will, who stood motionless and poker-faced—we all forgot about everything else.

Fjalar lugged his creation forth by himself. The weight wasn't too much for strength like his, and no thiefproofing spell resisted. Nevertheless, sweat runneled through the soot on him and breath tossed his whiskers to and fro. Sheathed at his waist, Fotherwick-Botts bump-bump-bumped over the ground.

At Fjalar's grunted word, the parking legs snapped down. They pulled the broom from his grasp and held it horizontally. A cheer lifted from us, small under the sky, big in our hearts.

There she posed, our craft, beautiful as clean design and fine work-manship always are. The shaft shone bluish white, with a damascene ripple that made me remember how bards once likened swords to serpents and fire. The single control crystal forward was not the standard globe but faceted, shattering light into rainbow fragments. Tucked under its eigh-teen-inch span, the communication relay glinted gilt. A subtlety of sha-dowings aft outlined the bundle of polished alloy straws.

But she was indeed not meant for Earth. The parking gear wasn't a mere quartet of rods, it was four slender machines made to adjust their own lengths and grip fast with claws; for the ground where they landed could well be rough, might well be strange, and would certainly offer no rack to stand the broom upright. There were no seats, only two saddles, with stirrups and pouches; riders might have to get on or off in a hurry, and while flying could better shift body mass for close maneuvers. Beyond the single headlight the tip of the shaft ended in a safety-latched screw cap on which was etched a cross of four eagle feathers.

Fjalar had said it. As yet the vessel was bare bones. Aft, ahead of the straws, brackets waited for the coffer; we hadn't settled on the ideal shape. Somewhere along the line we must arrange for a license plate and what-ever else would satisfy the law. First and foremost—

Ginny's thoughts had paralleled mine. "Defense," I heard her mutter.

What kind? A regular military machine gun, every tenth round argent? I imagined the laugh that the shen—kuei—evil Beings might get out of that. A 'chanted sword was a possibility. I'd wielded steel myself to good effect, long ago when we raided the Low Continuum. But a witch or warlock could do better than that, couldn't she or he? Have to be one who understood the demons and how to deal with them. Fu Ch'ing, riding behind Curtice, his wispy beard flapping in the cosmic winds. . . . Hardly.

Yes, our pilot needed a partner on her expedition to a moon where worse dangers waited than vacuum and radiation. A sorcerer or priest, who was also a qualified celestonaut and fit for any unforeseeable kind of combat. . . . No candidates were in view. Give us two or three years, maybe we'd find someone who could train for the mission.

I'd thought about myself and decided I didn't meet the specs, unless worst came to worst. Ginny— No, God damn it! If nothing else, we were trying to right an imbalance in the order of things. For that it was way preferable to have complementarity, Yang and Yin, male and female.

The world yanked me back to its immediate self. Fjalar had drawn the sword. He swung him past the bow of the broomstick and boomed something in Old Norse. "Ay name you *Skyfarer*, by yiminy," he added in English.

"I say," sputtered Fotherwick-Botts, "what d'you mean by that? *St. George*, by George. Bound off to slay dragons and devils and such-like troublemakers, what, what, what?"

Fjalar grumped but didn't insist. Nobody else cared. Having no flacks, Operation Luna had never officially considered names for spacecraft. I doubt the question even occurred to the Zunis. In pillow talk with me, Ginny had once suggested *Owl*, honoring the totem of her order. That's what I'll use.

Curtice stepped forward. "Never mind," she almost sang. Her hand stroked the sleek metal. "This bird is what she is, which is wonderful. Thank you, Mr. Fjalar."

The dwarf blushed, especially his nose. Crusty old bachelor or no, he appreciated the appreciation of an attractive woman. "You ban velcome." Grandly, he gave the key. "Ride her to Heaven and tell Thor hello from me."

"Um, well, not today, I'm afraid," said Curtice.

Balawahdiwa got her off the hook by advancing too. "Shall we make ready for the task?" he proposed. "Dr. Graylock, if you please."

Will started. It was as if his mind had been elsewhere, someplace far away and dark. "What? Oh, yes. Excuse me." He ducked into the building. A file cabinet had been brought there to keep the meteorite specimens and the notes on them. Already most of those notes were his. A couple of times, having had business here or in Zuni that kept us till after dark, Ginny or I had seen yellow lantern-glow or blue witchlight through the canvas of his tent. That was a lonely sight, but neither of us interrupted. She believed the work was healing for him.

Besides, it was valuable, if not right away then later on. We hoped for eventual voyages to the planets. That'd require stones from former orbits in their neighborhoods; and those stones had better be well researched beforehand.

While his colleagues chanted a prayer, Balawahdiwa unfastened and unscrewed the nose cap. I knew the cavity inside was lined with stabilized sea-foam. Carefully he packed into it the two halves of the newly hatched eagle's egg he'd found unseasonally on top of Dowa Yalanne. There they'd stay. My spine tingled; the hair stood up.

Will returned with a yellowish lump in his hand. He gave it to Balawahdiwa, who examined it closely before he and his fellows blessed it. He tucked it into the cavity and resecured the cap.

Just a chunk of local sandstone. If the charm on it was extra strong, that was because the go-forces driving the broom would be. It channeled and controlled them. As we gained experience and felt ready for longer tests, rocks from farther off would replace it, till the broom circled Earth carrying a tektite—terrestrial, but fused and scattered by meteorite impact.

And so at last the moon rock would go in, though of course the first ventures beyond atmosphere wouldn't try for the whole distance. That piece lay in its own drawer behind a special lock with an encrypted alarm spell on it. This must have hurt Will, though he said nothing.

Today we forgot all unhappy things.

"Now, if you please, Captain Newton," Balawahdiwa said.

His companions brought over a box and laid it in his hands. He nodded to her to open the lid. Trembling very slightly at first, she took out an object. It wasn't pretentious: a furry brown cylinder made from the entire skin of a jackrabbit. Beadwork depicted a figure masked and winged, surrounded by feathers sewn to the hide. I didn't know whether the pattern was traditional or created for our use.

Packed inside were a container of mingled sea waters, the skin of a mole, and objects I knew less about, sanctified by what they stood for and by what had been sung over them. Here was a medicine bundle for a flyer bound high and far.

"Take this and bear it in reverence," Balawahdiwa said. "The favor of the Beloved Spirits lies within. It will give you clean air, comfort, health and strength wherever you travel. It is a shield against the deadlinesses beyond the sky. It shall bring you home to your loves."

"Thank you, sir." What other reply was possible? A belt with a buckle dangled from the fetish. Curtice slung it behind her left shoulder and made it fast.

Balawahdiwa took the box over to Ginny. "You get the rest," he said, his tone abruptly everyday. Or was it that to him the sacred and the ordinary were one and the same? "You'll know best how to keep them safe."

The bunch of us Matucheks crowded around and peered in at the half dozen bundles. Val reached deferentially to pat them. "Well, I expect right here, where the spacecraft and the rocks and everything else are, is as guarded a place as any," replied her mother.

"This'n's little," Val piped up. "You made it from a baby jack, didn't you?"

Balawahdiwa gave her a long look. "A thought came to us that somebody small might sometime have need of protection," he answered slowly.

"Oh." She didn't pursue the matter. I closed the box and carried it inside.

When I returned, solemnity and ceremony had given way to plain

American excitement. The Zunis too were grinning and, I suspect, cracking jokes in their language. Fjalar and Fotherwick-Botts were singing some Viking song. Their voices were worse than Edgar's. The kids bounced.

Curtice had clamped earphones on her head and positioned an empathic pickup on her chest. She made an inquiring gesture at the control globe. Jim gave her a thumbs-up and a blown kiss. She reciprocated, swung into the forward saddle, and snapped her safety harness together.

Will stayed expressionless but tense as a strung bow. Ginny moved across to him. I heard her ask, "Aren't you glad too?"

"Naturally," he said. "But I'm saving my huzzahs for her successful landing."

"She'll make it," his sister declared. "We've checked for the presence of hostiles anywhere nearby, we've warded against them, this is simply not a day when things will go wrong for us."

Nobody can foreknow everything.

Curtice inserted the key and switched on the main spell. "Off we go!" she cried. Her fingertips passed over the crystal. Its facets flashed brighter. The broomstick quivered.

She rose. The parking gear snapped down alongside the shaft. *Owl* arrowed aloft.

Jim carried a communication receiver with an amplifying speaker. "Hello," he called. "You all right?"

Curtice's words danced back to us. "Molly O'Kay. She handles like a dream. Screenfields perfect. Let's try a few maneuvers."

Already the craft was tiny in our sight. Those who had binoculars raised them. The broom soared, plunged, surged back, rolled and tumbled, frolicking in sheer bliss.

Balawahdiwa approached Jim. "Fly around the holy mountain and low above, if you please," he said into the phone.

"Really?" Curtice was surprised. "I didn't mean to."

"You will give no offense, Captain Newton. Think your thanks and your respects to the gods. They will know."

For a short while the great mesa eclipsed our little flyer. We fell silent.

A glint reappeared in the blue. It climbed and climbed. "Something spoke to me," the pilot called softly. "Not in words. But I learned I should go high, as high as I'm able today." Exultation blew away awe. "That's into the stratosphere, boys. Yippee!"

The glint vanished from us. I thought about those altitudes. Already she was beyond the point where she could breathe unaided. Jim's voice wavered. "You still there?"

His question reached her as he uttered it. Not that they'd have noticed any difference if it had gone by radio. But this was an empathic system, meant for interplanetary distances. Although I've been taught that "infinite velocity" is a meaningless noise, nobody's yet measured how fast that kind moves; and, being keyed only to certain terminals, it isn't bothered by the inverse-square law. Before long, this would matter a hell of a lot to Ginny and me.

"Yes, oh, yes," rang Curtice's answer. "I could almost be astraddle a horse down where you are. Except the stick's *flying*, rising, alive. The sky's going deep purple. The sun-glare doesn't hurt my eyes. Thank you, Mr. Adams—uh, Ba-la-*wah*-diwa. When I look away from it I see a few stars. Earth's beginning to show curvature. Like a breast— Let me fly a while longer. Please!"

"Magniff," Valeria breathed. Her fists doubled. "But oh, cracky, how I wish I could."

I laid a hand briefly on her shoulder. "Someday, pony, if you want, you shall," I said.

"Hey, I just thought of something," Ben exclaimed.

"What, dear?" asked Ginny.

"This right now, sure, it's hyper. But what about when they go to the moon? What'll they do for supplies?"

"They'll have food and water along. If you're wearing a medicine bundle like Captain Newton's, you can eat and drink as easily as at home."

"Yeah, but there's no toilet."

Ginny smiled. "That's much easier than before. The celestonauts can—hm—void directly into the void."

Val giggled. "Tiny shooting stars?"

After a time that felt long but actually wasn't, Curtice descended. Besides taking pity on us, she was a pro and this was a test flight, not a joyride. She couldn't resist a few more power loops and such on the way down. They might have buckled an ordinary stick, but the dwarf-forged steel held firm. Or they might have broken her neck, but al-Bunni's design compensated. The only acceleration she felt was one steady gravity holding her to her saddle.

In fact, she told us this caused a minor problem. Feeling no tugs of motion, she had to rely entirely on visual cues. However, they included images and readings provided by the sprite in the control crystal, according to her mental orders—ample for a skilled flygirl.

"Coming in!" she yelled at last. Dust flew from the Valkyrie landing.

She leaped off. Most of us scrambled around to hug her. The Zunis, less demonstrative, offered handshakes. So did Will. "Jolly good show," said Fotherwick-Botts where he stood planted in the ground. Fjalar must tiptoe to embrace her. His hands started roving. Jim tapped his head pretty strongly and he let go. Myself, after enfolding Curtice I laid a big, wet kiss on Ginny. She responded as enthusiastically as propriety allowed.

We all helped bring *Owl* and whatever else back into the smithy. Nobody spoke of debriefing. Curtice would write a report at her leisure. It would give us a basis for planning the next stage. Meanwhile we'd earned a celebration.

I said it first. "All right, ladies and gentlemen, let's go to Buffalo Bull's and open a keg of nails." Agreement whooped around me. It was a good thing we didn't know how the day would later blow up in our faces.

33

THE ZUNIS DECLINED IN FRIENDLY FASHION. THEY'D RATHER PARTY AMONG THEIR OWN people, who rated a share in the merrymaking anyway. I guessed that'd be quite a wingding. Pueblo Indians are only solemn when they need to be.

"I'm sorry, I'd better beg off too," Will said.

"Too bad," I replied sincerely, in spite of his flat affect. "Feeling punk again, are you?"

"Exhausted." His tone stayed machinelike, a machine that wanted oil. "My fault. I've been pushing myself hard in spite of this damned undiagnosed medical problem. Let me go home and rest."

"Yes, do," Ginny agreed. "Take a week at least. And then let's try to find a specialist in Albuquerque, a neurologist or some such."

He shrugged jerkily. "We'll see. I'll go pack my gear and strike my tent."

"Lemme help," Jim said, and "Me too," Curtice added. They were that kind of folks.

I made a move but Jim shook his head. "Thanks," he told me. "Any more, though, we'd get in each other's way." True, stowing things on Will's Völve was no contract job. However, I had a notion Jim would as soon be the only man there with our celestonaut. Poor Will hardly counted. The three of them walked off.

"Hoy, Ay come to town at last!" Fjalar roared. "Ban too damn long Ay had no feasting, by Freyja's rosy rump! They got visky there? And beer to vash it down?"

"Um, uh, wait a minute," I said, dismayed. "We're keeping this operation quiet. If you suddenly show up—"

Indignation flared. "You think Ay not ban nice? Ay ban good enough to vork for you, but not sit in your hall?" Fjalar waved his outsize fists. "Loki fart me if Ay ban not a perfect yentleman! You vant me to prove it? Okay. *Einvigi?*"

"Hey, look, I didn't mean any—I mean—What're you talking about? Some kind of legal action?"

"*Ja.* Not like *holmgang.* In *einvigi* ve fight any old vay. Shoose your veapon. Ay vill take my hammer and, *ja,* my tongs too, for to pull your nose out before Ay smash your head."

The kids stared, appalled. "No, you won't!" Val cried. Before she could leap between us, Ginny glided in.

"Fjalar, dear, please," the witch purred. "You misunderstood Steve. Of course we realize how well and hard you've worked and how much you deserve to relax. We look forward to the day when we—when our whole kingdom can heap you with gifts and honors. It's simply that we'd best not draw attention to ourselves right now."

Fjalar's wrath collapsed. Instead, he felt wounded. "Ay ban funny-looking, ha?" he mumbled. My heart went out to him. He rallied. "Don't vorry, sveet lady. Anybody makes laugh of me, Ay skvash him like a bug."

Clearly, he was bound and determined to join the party. "Nothing of the kind," she told him. "Do come along. What Steve was trying to say is that your splendid work has left you grimy and sweaty. Honorable signs of honest toil, but you should sit in the . . . the mead hall as fine to behold as any of your peers. Why don't you dash inside, wash, and change clothes? Then the girls in town can see how handsome you really are."

Her smile bowled him over. "*Ja, ja!* Ay ban sorry Ay got mad, Steve. But you should have spoke more clear, like me. Yust a minute, and Ay vill be ready." He stumped into the building.

"Jolly good," exclaimed Fotherwick-Botts. "A feast, eh? Daresay you've no entertainment planned, on short notice like this. Never fear. I'll have stories to tell. And songs to sing, by Jove. Blood-and-guts stuff, fit for heroes. Or for the march. Boots, boots, boots, sloggin' over Normandy, whippin' along the pack animals. Troll the ancient muleside carol."

I staggered where I stood. "Hold on!" I gasped. "Buffalo Bull's is a cowboy sort of place, b-but they don't allow weapons in there, and—and—" With luck, Fjalar would pass. The class of people we'd be among generally mind their own business and practically never squeal to the cops. But a sword—and one that talks and talks and talks and then tries to sing—"No, sorry, impossible. The law forbids."

"Eh? No steel allowed in? What kind of fleshism is this? God's death! I'll not stand for it, I'll have you know. When Fjalar comes back, we'll see what my maker has to say about this bloody outrage."

"Lord help us," I whispered to Ginny. "Fjalar's still edgy. If he gets really mad he'll quit, if not worse."

"We beg your pardon, sir," she attempted. "No disputing, it is a foolish law. But if nothing else, valiant Byrnie-biter, we need you to stand guard. Nobody else will be here, and the enemy always watches for his chance."

Unfortunately, Balawahdiwa overheard. He stepped close and said, "That would be a good idea if the place were left alone for any length of time. But you're just bound for Gallup, aren't you? I imagine the dwarf will return tomorrow. The protective spells won't weaken overnight enough to matter. As for human intruders, lock the door. I'll arrange for boys in shifts to keep an eye on it. Anything questionable, and our men will arrive in minutes."

"Wait, wait," I muttered desperately. "You don't understand the situation."

His look reproached me. "I do, and it is ticklish. But the Beloved Spirits turn their backs on him who lies to a friend."

He and his fellows bade us a formal good-bye, mounted their battered Buick, and flitted off to Zuni.

"All right," Ginny sighed to me and the kids, "we'll have the party at our house and pray it doesn't get so noisy the neighbors call the police. Sending out for shishkebab will be a comedown, but I suppose a keg should smooth the disappointment."

Nevertheless we had the devil's own time getting Fotherwick-Botts to accept the compromise. He was still grumbling when Jim and Curtice returned. Though his own broom stood heavily loaded at his campsite, Will tagged along. At our quizzical glance, he told us, "I thought I should tell you, all at once I feel better. Yes, I'll stay home for a few days, but no reason why I can't conduct further research there at a less frantic pace. I have a few of those stones left to examine, and I also want to sit down and think about what the data imply."

"Why, that's great," I said. Hopefulness lightened my family's faces.

Yet now we had the awkward job of explaining the change in plans to the others without ruffling the sword's feathers more than they already had been. The figure of speech gives an idea of the general mess. As we began, Fjalar appeared. He'd showered and put on a clean pair of the jeans we'd had tailored to his measurements. His hairy toes stuck out of leather sandals he'd doubtless made for himself in the past and taken along. Somewhere, maybe in a flyport, he'd seen a Hawaiian shirt and added several of those to his list of demands. This one was purple, with shocking pink hibiscus blossoms. On his shaggy head he'd crammed a Mexican sombrero. From his trip back to the old country, along with assorted tools and materials he'd brought a Norwegian flag as big as himself. It hung from a footed pole across his shoulder. True, it displayed the cross, but it was Norwegian.

"Yippee-yi-yay!" he thundered cheerfully. "Let's go, boys! The girls in the mead hall ban vaiting!"

"Uh, we've decided on our place instead," I made known, and actually felt relieved.

He bristled. "Vat you mean? You shame yourselves of me, ha? Vant you not to be seen vith me? You think Ay ban a lousy *dverg*, even ven you ban clad like thralls and Ay like a king."

"No, no, no, dear," Ginny said. "The house is more relaxed. You've worked so hard, you've earned a rest."

"A rest?" he bellowed. "You think Ay ban sush a veakling Ay need to sit and sip tea? No, by all the fleas on Fenris! After banging iron half a month, vat Ay vant to bang now is—"

"Well, uh, well," I stuttered, "you see, the trouble is, uh, Fotherwick-Botts—"

"Will bloody well not be left behind like a blasted ostler," the sword interrupted.

"Vat's this?" Fjalar snarled. I braced myself for the eruption.

Will moved in as quickly and softly as he spoke. He smiled. "Perhaps I can mediate. Certainly discrimination against either of our gallant friends is intolerable. But really, General Fotherwick-Botts, you wouldn't care for the taven originally intended. I've been there, sir, and believe me, you wouldn't. Lower classes, rowdy, no respect for their betters. All very well for colonials who feel like a bit of slumming, but for you, a ranking officer and a gentleman, definitely infra dig."

"Who you calling a colonial?" Fjalar demanded.

"He means the rest of us," I said in a stage whisper.

"As for the Matuchek home," Will went on, "you have seen it. You know how quiet and refined it is." *Huh?* I thought. "You will find the conversation today elevated and stimulating, devoted to science, literature, and the arts. If I'm not mistaken, the Santa Fe Ballet performs this afternoon. Perhaps everybody will watch it on the farseer."

Before the sword could notice us gaping, Will sighed. "Yes, General, enjoy yourself. I'd hoped to invite you to visit me. Perhaps some other day. Everything I've heard about you has made me look forward to closer acquaintanceship."

"Eh?" barked Fotherwick-Botts. "Int'rested in me? You? I've been informed you're a lifelong civilian. I use the word in its kindliest sense, of course."

"But I am an amateur student of history. I gather you're full of . . . of the most fascinating eyewitness details. Things that never got into the chronicles and have escaped the archaeologists. I was hoping to ask you about them."

"Hey? What, what? D'you mean—*battles?*"

"The opportunity! Someone on the scene who partook, and who knows the real military significance. I could listen for hours. Days, if you might sometime honor me, sir, by being a guest at my humble abode."

"I will this very day, by Jove," said Fotherwick-Botts with ill-concealed eagerness.

"Gosh," breathed Ben. Valeria squealed and hopped. Fjalar beamed, as happy for the child of his hands as for himself. Curtice and Jim contained themselves, more or less. Ginny and I swapped a look. Mine wondered how we could repay her brother. Tears glimmered in hers. He was becoming his old, real, unselfish self again.

Will turned to the dwarf. "I do want to carry on my research at home," he said. I assumed he'd let the sword drone on meanwhile; he had powers of concentration. "Two meteor stones in particular. May I fetch them?"

"*Ja*, you betcha." All amicability, Fjalar accompanied him inside and watched while he opened the cabinet and dropped them in pockets of his field jacket. Regulations required that. "Thor-hated stupid Fibbies," the dwarf growled as they emerged. "They don't trust a man so smart like you? Henhouse!"

Well, I thought, *it's true that our wardings keep them from scrying him or anything in this immediate area*, and felt ashamed of myself.

Will sheathed Fotherwick-Botts as courteously as it is possible to stuff somebody down a long, narrow hole. Fjalar closed the single door of the smithy and locked it. The windows were barred. He moved with me and mine to our family broom, which he'd share. Jim, Curtice, and Will started for theirs.

Suddenly my brother-in-law galloped back. "Wait," he called. "Wait, please!"

We stopped. "I'm sorry," he apologized. "Like a fool, I quite forgot I'll want the notes I filed earlier. Could I pop in and fetch them?"

"*Ja*, sure." Fjalar gave him the key. Regulations didn't mention documents. Will left the sword with us. As though embarrassed, he opened the door barely wide enough to slip through. We hung around, chatting. He reappeared in maybe five minutes, a folder in his hand, relocked the door, and brought the key over.

"Took me a while," he said. "I found I had to sort out the papers I'll need. I *am* an idiot today. Left you standing here in the desert sun like this."

Fjalar chuckled. "*Aa*, ve grow a bigger thirst for beer." He gave the key to Ginny. The uneasy idea crossed my mind that he didn't want to be committed to any responsibility for the rest of today.

Will left with the sword. "There goes one swell guy," I said. "Come on, let's go have the fun he's bought for us."

And so our party flitted to Gallup.

34

WE LANDED IN A TINY PARKING LOT ON THE FRINGES OF THE PREBOOM DOWNTOWN, BE-
hind Buffalo Bull's. The hour was past noon and hot. We were glad to
take shelter.

The joint was large and low, darkish, an old-style bar near the entrance, tables and booths beyond. Red-checked cloths, cheap and sturdy
tableware, sawdust on the floor, just two farseers and their audio kept
well down unless a major game or something was going on. A couple of
big-game heads behind the bar, photos of ranch scenes on the walls,
hundreds of yellowing business cards thumbtacked to the ceiling. The
lunch crowd included families as well as singletons taking a break; the
food was good and came in generous servings. A working-class place,
which people from Cardinal Point had discovered. We spied none of
them here today, in this bad time. Our seven pulled a couple of tables
together.

Conversation around us dropped down to a beehive buzz when Fjalar
planted his flagstaff on its base at the head of the board. Maybe folks in
Minneapolis or Seattle would have taken it for granted, but the ethnology
of New Mexico is different. I exchanged another glance with Ginny before
I put myself on the dwarf's left, she on his right. Possibly between us we
could keep him under some control. Ben settled by me, Val by her, Jim
and Curtice opposite one another.

While a busboy established water, plates, etc., the sensation faded
away. I began to feel optimistic. Probably we wouldn't touch off talk that'd
reach official ears. Though the main tourist season was past, this state gets
them the year around and locals are used to the occasional weirdo.

True, Fjalar roared, "Yust vater? Vat kind of *bondir* think they ve
ban?"

Ginny shushed him: "It's to quench your first thirst. Wait a few
minutes. Aren't your race as agelessly patient as the mountains where they
dwell?" Though this was obviously on a par with the notion that every
Hindu is a holy man and every Italian an incomparable lover, it worked
on him. Not to let down the side, as Fotherwick-Botts would say.

A good-looking, dark-haired waitress arrived with menus. "Hi," she
greeted. "Anything to drink before you order?"

"Hi, Conchita—" I began. We knew her from previous visits. This was a friendly place.

Fjalar broke though: "*Ja*, Scotch. Two doubles. Tightfist ban the innkeepers these days."

"He's from northern Minnesota," I murmured hastily. "Kind of, uh, rough-hewn. But an honest hombre." Before the dwarf could demand to know what that meant, I addressed the others. "Beer?" They nodded. "Okay, a pitcher of Cochise. And for the kids—"

"Vatever they vant," Fjalar said regally. "I give. Mead, rum, vat you like, my young lady and atheling?"

"Coke, please," they said together.

"*Haa?* That I have not heard of. Vell, don't drink too mush and start a fight."

We picked up our menus. "Vat's this?" Fjalar snapped. "Ay thought you said no spellcasting in here." We described the purpose and translated for him. Pork chops he understood. "Good, good. Like vat they have in Valhalla." Beef was more difficult, not in itself but the concept of such quantities. Wide-open range is scarce in Norway and cattle have always been dairy, eating them incidental until modern transportation brought imports. "Who has made so great a raid he slaughtered whole herds? Vy have you not told of this deed?" Some items, like fritos, salsa, and corn on the cob, we could not make clear. We ended by suggesting he watch and experiment.

Conchita arrived, balancing a tray. She set down Fjalar's whiskies first, with a smile. "Welcome to the West," she said.

He beamed. "Thank you. Freyja's brisket, you ban a toothsome piece!" Giving him the benefit of the doubt, I suppose he intended simply to pat her fanny; but the smack resounded across the room and she lurched.

Ginny sprang to steady the tray before it strewed its load across the table. "Judas priest!" I yelled. "I ought to call you out for that, you oaf!" Curtice and Jim added their reproaches in softer language and their apologies to mine.

"All right, Ay ban sorry," the dwarf grumbled. He tossed off a jigger. "Ay should have asked your lord first, *ja*. It vas yust that maybe you vould sit in the seat vith me, and maybe later—"

Now I roared. "Pipe down, for Christ's sake!"

Fjalar nodded. "*Ja*, this is Hvita-Krist land, no? Ay do not vant to anger any god. As soon as Ay get paid, Ay buy a goat and kill it on his altar."

"I'm awfully sorry, Conchita," I babbled, standing before her. "We never expected— Won't happen again, I swear— We, uh, we want to make it up to you—"

That implied a substantial tip. Besides, she was a good sport. "Okay, Steve, we'll overlook it. A compliment of sorts, maybe." She lowered her voice. "I can't help feeling kind of sorry for him, you know? He must get pretty lonesome. And little guys like him don't live too long, do they?"

"You are forgiven," Ginny told Fjalar in her frostiest tone. "Be glad this is a Christian country."

"Ban it really? Ay have not seen any monks. *Ja*, vell, Ay forgive everybody too. Ay ban an easygoing fellow."

We sat back down. Conchita distributed glasses and put the beer on the table. "A-a-ah," Fjalar gusted. "A shaser ban yust vat Ay need." He reached forth a chimp-long arm, grabbed the pitcher, tilted it to his mouth, and glugged. When it was half empty, which took about thirty seconds, he lowered it and asked, "But don't the rest of you vant any?"

"Bring us another," I said resignedly to the waitress. "No, you may as well make it two."

She'd also given us a couple bowls of nachos. Fjalar made havoc of the nearest. Alarmed, the kids sped their hands to collect a share from the other. He smiled benignly at them. "You like those drinks you got?" he inquired.

"Oh, yes," Ben replied. On an impulse, he offered his. "Want to try a taste?"

"Thank you. You ban a high-born lad for sure." Fjalar gripped the glass. It nearly vanished in that knobbly hand.

Maybe the Old Norse never heard of sipping. Fjalar threw the Coke, ice and all, down his gullet in one swig. It spewed back across the table. "Poo-oo-oo! By every frog in Helheim, vat have the Americans done that they must drink this?"

We mopped things as dry as we could, refrained from commentary, and discussed the menu. Conchita brought Ben a replacement along with the fresh pitchers. They helped improve the mood. After all, we were holding a small gala. Fjalar mellowed. His joke about Odin and the giantess was pretty gross, but when he started reminiscing about early times it was very interesting—an utterly different world—and rather touching—an utterly lost world.

Lunch arrived. Not expecting anything from him in the way of table manners, Ginny had shrewdly steered him onto spare ribs, French fries, and tacos, finger food. Conversation grew lively. The kids took a polite but intelligent part. Too bad that nobody, first and foremost himself, kept track of how often the dwarf crooked a finger to order more beer, with a whisky now and then for variety.

At length Conchita cleared away the dirty dishes and asked if we wanted dessert. Adults felt full, but Val and Ben were ready for ice cream and Fjalar said he'd try some.

"—folk tell how the jotuns, the yiants, ban the oldest race there is," he declaimed, "but ve dvarves, by yiminy—"

The waitress set his bowl before him. He dipped a finger in and licked. "Ho, good," he exulted. "Vat do those cows feed on? But Ay make it better." He emptied a jigger of Scotch over it. "Ve vas the underpinning of the vorld, us dvarves. And the biggest smiths and vizards, too. The gods themselves vas customers of ours. Ve vere famous. The *Edda* got a list of us. It don't list no jotuns, no, nor even all the damn gods, but the *dvergar*—"

He dipped a spoon into his ice cream and swung it toward his mouth. Naturally, the alcohol had liquefied it. A thick brown fluid spattered his beard. "Vat troll trick ban this?" he bellowed. "Who makes spells at me? Ay vill hammer him in the ground like a tent peg! Ay vill—"

"Easy, easy." Once more people were staring. I grabbed his arm. When he didn't notice, I grabbed his whiskers. "No witchcraft, no harm done, you blockhead," I said into his glare. "You've seen ice melt, haven't you, and drunk the water?"

His wrath turned directly to sentiment. I should have recognized the danger signal. "Ice melts in spring," he crooned. "All things vept for Baldr's death. The ice cream too? How sveet. Ay drink its tears." He lifted the bowl and slurped. "Delicious soup!" he bawled. "More!"

To quiet him, I signaled Conchita. She approached cautiously.

"The list of the dvarves. Hark." Fjalar raised his forefinger. "First Motsognir and Durinn. Then Nyi, Nidi, Nordri, Sudri, Austri, Vestri, Althjofur, Dvalinn—"

"Another ice cream," I rasped. "And could you bring the check?"

"—Veigur, Gandalfur, Vindalfur, Thrainn—"

"*Ay de mí*, you do have a problem, don't you?" the waitress sympathized. "The bartender's muttering about bouncing him. I hope it won't come to that."

I shuddered. "Me likewise, for the bartender's sake. Do move things along, okay? We are sorry. I promise this won't happen again." *Not in here, anyway.*

"—Fili, Kili, Fundinn, Nali—" Fjalar squinted cross-eyed from one of us to the next. "Ay not ban boring you? Ay don't vant to bore you. Friends don't let friends bore friends. Real kvick Ay vill finish. Hefti-Vili-Hannar-Sviur-Frar-Hornbori—"

Curtice leaned toward me. "Well, he did build our spacecraft," she murmured graciously.

"And we need him for the rest of the job," Jim added. "I reckon."

"—Alfur, Yngvi, Eikinskjaldi, Fjalar—Fjalar, that's me, Ay vas there, Ay vas—"

Conchita presented the last dessert and the bill.

"Frosti, Finnur, Ginnur!" The dwarf snatched the dish from her. "Now have Ay told the tale."

Overcome by emotion, he sprang onto the tabletop. An empty pitcher crashed. "Here's to the dvarves!" he trumpeted. "A *blót*, an offering, on our behalf, to good old Thor!" He hurled the dish at the wall. A fat spatter exploded. "Not blood, but you vill like it, thunder-lord."

I'd been shoving money at Conchita. I shoved more.

"Mush can I tell!" Fjalar shouted. He started a chant: "*Geyr nu Garm*— No," he broke off. "You do not know. You do not understand. Nobody understands." Tears ran into the ice cream and Scotch on his beard. "Gone, all gone," he sobbed. Mustering heart: "But men still fight! Men need veapons! In Noreg—in Norvay they still ban mighty varriors!"

Last I heard, a committee of the Norwegian parliament chooses the winner of the Nobel Peace Prize.

"The steel shall clang, the volves shall gorge," Fjalar cried. *"Fram, fram, Norrmen!"* He grabbed his flag and waved it on high. Dust puffed off the tacked-up business cards.

"Let's clear out before somebody calls the cops," I said to Jim. He nodded. We each laid arms around Fjalar's knees—he weighed more than you'd guess—and carried him away. Evidently he took this for a triumphal parade. He flapped his banner and howled violent verses.

Sunlight outside dazzled our vision. "Vat?" hiccoughed Fjalar. "The vorld on fire? Ragnarok already? Oh, vell." He crumpled into a heap. Jim and I almost dropped him.

Curtice retrieved his flag, respectful of the honorable nation for which it stood. "What'll we do now?" she asked.

"Steve and I will take him home," Ginny replied. "We'll put him in the guest room to sleep it off."

"You do know more about . . . Beings." Curtice was frankly relieved. "But if you need any help, give me a call."

"Uh, I thought maybe you and I might take in a show or something this afternoon," Jim said to her. "If that won't be, uh, an anticlimax."

She smiled. "On the contrary, I could do with some relaxation. Thanks, let's."

"Yeah, we'll manage," I told them. "We mainly need to have beer on hand for when he wakes up. Or, hm, maybe not."

We secured him on the rear seat of our broom, bade our companions good-bye, and started off. "I hope you weren't too shocked," I said to the kids. "He's a good guy at heart, and a great craftsman."

"Yah, sure," answered Ben with youthful loftiness. "I know. He just can't hold his liquor."

"The hell he can't," Val retorted. "Did you *see* how much he put down? And never went to the men's room once."

Uh-oh! I thought. *Better rouse him to take care of that before we tuck him in.*

What with one thing and another, an hour or so passed before Ginny and I sat down in the cool of our living room and drew a breath. The babysitter had left. Chryssa napped, more quietly than Fjalar. Since Ben was pledged to secrecy about what he'd witnessed and doubtless needed time to prepare himself not to share it with Danny Goldstein, he'd withdrawn to his own room and a book. Val went out to our mailbox by the street.

She returned thumbing through the stack. "Gas bill," she announced. "Something from the, hmm, Corn and Bunion Foundation—bulk rate— a pitch, right? And here's another worthy cause, Adolescent Council for Neatness and Elegance. And this envelope says you may have won five million dollars. And this—hey, for me." She flushed red and tucked it down her shirt front. From Larry, I guessed, with the muddle of worry and wistfulness that I suppose comes to every father of a young girl.

"What else, dear?" asked Ginny, lightly and smiling.

"Oh? Oh. Yes. A . . . a postcard from the vet, says Svartalf's due for his shots . . . More junk mail. . . . Hey, this'n's from the Insertion of the Royal Shaft."

"What?"

"IRS."

"That isn't nice."

Val grinned. "I'm quoting Daddy. I've heard worse from him."

"Well, let's have it, for God's sake," I said. My pulse jumped. Maybe it was a notice that we were in the clear. I ripped it open and read.

Edgar broke the silence with a doomful croak.

Ginny kept her tone level. "What's the bad news?"

I gave her the letter. "They claim we owe upwards of thirty thousand dollars plus penalties." Val was old enough and tough enough to hear. "They hint at criminal charges, conspiracy with Nornwell. It's signed Alger Sneep."

35

"YEAH," SAID BARNEY WHEN WE GOT HIM ON HIS PHONE AT HOME. "I'M NOT TOO SUR- prised." His face was haggard, his eyes were sunken and dark-rimmed, a tic jerked in his right cheek, and his voice plodded.

"Then why didn't you warn us, for God's sake?" I sputtered.

"I didn't know exactly what to expect, or I would have. Steve, it gets hard to think after a couple of weeks when they've had your most precious parts in a meat grinder."

"That bad, huh?"

"Agents everywhere, poking into everything, grilling everybody, demanding records and receipts from ten or fifteen years ago. No statute of limitations on some of the things they talk about. I haven't said a lot to you folks because I didn't want to dump on you. Now it seems they've undertaken that job themselves."

"But what in Satan's name are they talking *about*? You always griped at taxes, but you paid in full and on time, like us. Didn't you?"

"So I thought. The company and myself came clean through every audit. But this one— Well, for instance, you know how we've done a fair amount of business overseas, including some with organizations or regimes that have since gone belly-up, like Panchatantrics, Ltd. in India or the Pious Democratic Republic of Korea. We can't always now find somebody to corroborate that the deals were legitimate and the cash flows precisely what we reported. And then, there's no end to the labyrinth—maze— jungle—nightmare's nest of regulations. We may or may not have touched certain bases we're supposed to. Our own lawyers and diabolists admit they don't comprehend more than a fraction of it. They doubt the IRS does either. But the taxpayer is guilty unless proven innocent, remember."

"Any idea what they're after Ginny and me for? They claim the money you transferred to our account in August is income we haven't reported. But it's not!"

Barney sighed. "Of course not. It was to Operation Luna. Putting it in your name was just for convenience. You've kept records of outlays, haven't you?"

"Certainly," Ginny replied. "The whole matter would have been explained when we file next year. But we're accused of failure to file an amended return in September, plus some subparagraph—I forget which, though I called it up and tried to make sense of it—seems to have something to do with prevention of money laundering. Well, the bank was already required to report the transaction."

"I'll check with our legal staff." Barney's tone took on a little life. "Whatever happens, Nornwell will stand by you. Come worst to worst, you needn't go down with the ship."

Tears touched her eyes. Mine blurred for a moment. "Thank you, old dear," she whispered.

Then I remembered the threat of prosecution for us, too. Anger lifted afresh in me. "This is out-and-out harassment," I snapped. "Can't your Congressman do anything?" Ours was a freshman. The only weight he swung was his belly.

"He's trying," Barney said, "but he tells me he's up against something as slippery as it is powerful."

"Something that's out to get us, no matter what. Right?"

"Well," Barney said carefully, "I haven't gone paranoid yet. My guess is, this started as a routine, maybe even random checkup, and snowballed." *But who might have nudged the random factors?* I wondered. "They thought they smelled big game. The more heads a tax agent takes, the better for his career." He paused. "But, yeah, some interests would like to see Nornwell ruined. Certain competitors. Certain politicians, whose opponents I've given strong support. The assorted types who hate the space program. One or two of them, or a coalition, could be cheering the IRS on from behind the scenes."

Ginny nodded. "And as for us here, I suspect that little Sneep creep has seen a chance to make our lives miserable."

"Personal malice does often enter in," Barney agreed. "A big reason why the framers of the US Constitution tried to put strict limits on the powers of government." He sighed again. "Enough for now. We'll slog on, okay? At least you've told me how well the test went today. Keep up the good work."

If we're allowed to, I refrained from saying. We three spoke a few more words that meant nothing objectively and a great deal emotionally before we signed off.

Though Ginny and I did our best to assure the kids that everything was under control, dinner became a fairly cheerless meal. Afterward Val comforted Chryssa with a lighthearted bedtime story about how Moldylocks overcame a wicked wizard, Soapy Wilberforce, who'd been making people feel bad by convincing them they were made from nothing better than dirt.

Neither Ginny nor I slept well that night. The children did, to judge by how bright-eyed and bushy-tailed they were in the morning. Well, youth bounces back fast, and although Fjalar's snores had reached every eardrum, they were deep and steady, like geological forces.

He too was energetic and cheerful when at last he woke. "Good morning, good morning, good morning," he boomed, bursting in on us and the Sunday paper. "And how ban everybody this lovely morning?" I suppressed an urge to kill him. "Ah, Ay sniff hungry-making grease." We'd finished our bacon and pancakes. "My belly yawns like Ginnungagap and rumbles like Thor's car wheels. First a shot of Scotch, no?"

Ginny started to rise. "Never mind," I said. "I'll feed him." He wouldn't recognize her gourmet touch, and I needed something to do. I led him into the kitchen, gave him his eye-opener, and busied myself at the stove.

He aimed his nose at me and sighted down it from under his brows. "You got a face on you as long as the Midgard Vorm. Vat ban wrong? A foeman of yours ban happy?"

I didn't want to discuss our troubles and spoil the breakfast taste in my mouth. However, sooner or later I must, so I might as well get it over with. "Trouble with our taxes."

"*Haa*, ban its yeomen rebelling? Ay didn't know it ban yours, Steve. Ay thought it ban a *len* of this kingdom."

I stared from the frying pan to him. "What're you talking about?"

"The Taxes folk. East of here, no? They raiding you?"

The English vocabulary laid on him had holes. "No, I mean the, the tribute we have to pay."

"Ah, the scot. *Ja.* You pay the king every year so he can feed his household varriors and make gifts to other kings and to skalds that praise him. If you don't, the household varriors come vith fire and sword."

"Worse than that hereabouts. But you've got the general idea."

"Vat kind of payment he vant? Not fur or amber, Ay bet, not from this land. Maybe hides? Ay've seen herds of kine."

"Money. You know about money, I'm sure."

Fjalar nodded. "Gold, silver, *ja*. Vat's the matter? You can't skveeze enough from your underlings to glut the king? Maybe you should rise against him."

Ever tried to explain income tax to a complete outsider? Especially while cooking? Smoke soon hazed the kitchen, fans whirred, alarms beeped, Ginny came in to see and retreated after one glance. Luckily, the dwarf didn't mind if his food was scorched. Or maybe he was polite in his way—in olden times, the obligations between host and guest were sacred—or maybe he was too hungry to care. Anyhow, he wolfed the result down, say I who have knowledge of that subject. Meanwhile he listened to me and asked questions. Though naive, they were not stupid.

Having cleaned his plate, he poured another whisky, sat back, and unloosed a philosophical belch. "*Ja*, Ay see," he ruminated. "Foul men have done trollcraft on the law till they can tvist the vords around to make it say anything they vant it to."

"I don't think it was on purpose," I replied slightly reluctantly. "It just happened. Congress—the, uh, the Thing—" I had a brief vision of a mindless, insatiable Thing rising from the grassroots. "—it keeps changing who has to pay what and why. This forces the, uh, the scot gatherers to make their own rules more and more complicated . . . though, true, doing that comes natural to such people."

Fjalar shrugged his massive shoulders. "No difference. Vat you vant is the exact vord of the law on your side. Like vun time in Iceland, a man who had done wrong got the doom that for vun year he must stay in bowshot of his house. His foes lured him farther. This made him outlaw and they could lawfully kill him. But his son vent on a kvest for a stronger bow, and in the outlands he found vun. He came home and shot it from the house. The arrow flew longer than his father had gone. So the killers vas now in the wrong, and they themselves became outlaw, and the son took his revenge."

"Great, if only it were that simple," I said. "As is, though, we, Ginny and I, we're not the main targets. Operation Luna is, and its backer, Nornwell. I'm very much afraid our moon flight will be derailed."

I didn't bother to correct myself. Besides the dashing of a lifetime's dreams, I was thinking of demons unhindered on the moon.

"Vat?" Fjalar roared. "All for nothing? The boldest faring ever made, stopped before it leaves the dock?" His fist crashed on the table. The plate jumped. I looked at him anew. Yes, he'd been interested in the job for its own sake, a challenge. I hadn't realized how the dream had caught him too.

I struggled to explain the ins and outs, to the extent I grasped them myself. He brushed this aside. "Vat ve vant is the strong bow," he growled. "Not to shoot nobody. Too bad. But the vord, the . . . reading of the law that shows you are right, and none can gainsay."

"Barney Sturlason's retained some of the highest-paid tax experts in the country, and so far they aren't getting anywhere," I said dully. "Oh, they may win out in the end, or reach a compromise or something. But that could take years and cost our side a fortune, when the IRS has unlimited tax money to draw on. We might end up in the clear, but Operation Luna will have died on the vine, and as for whether Project Selene can be revived—I doubt it, without us to demonstrate a success."

"Then—" Fjalar brooded for a minute. Sunlight seeped though the window and the air grew less acrid as the smoke thinned away.

"Mimir!" the dwarf shouted.

"What?" I asked through the ringing in my ears.

"The head of Mimir. The vise jotun, who can answer all kvestions. Come on!" Fjalar hopped to the floor. "Ve go tell your vife the vitch. She vill know vat you don't, you anvilhead."

I felt too battered to resent that and followed him out. Presently we were in the arcanum with Ginny.

I saw her come alight from within. "Mimir," she breathed.

Both the *Elder* and *Younger Edda* were on her reference shelves, along with the *Heimskringla* and other such stuff. She leafed through them. Fjalar and I stood still in the shaded room among the curious objects and waited.

"Mimir—or Mim—he kept the well of wisdom beneath Yggdrasil. . . . Sent as a hostage to the Vanir. They cut his head off and returned it to the Aesir, which almost renewed the war between the two tribes of gods. . . . Odin embalmed it and cast spells that brought it alive again. Thereafter he often consulted it. . . . The sybil foretold how as the end of the world draws nigh, 'Odin takes counsel with the head of Mimir.' As well he might, seeing that Mimir at the beginning of the world had allowed him a drink of that water. . . ."

She laid the last of the books down and turned to us. "Yes," she murmured, "I have a feeling—call it a hunch, at this stage—I'll have to research much deeper—but I have a feeling we may find help there."

My spine chilled. I'd known Ginny's hunches in the past.

"Another universe, right?" she put to Fjalar. "A continuum coexistent with ours, but different, distant in hyperreality, where your gods and Mimir exist."

"Vell, Ay dunno," replied the dwarf, bewildered. "You talk too fancy for me. All Ay know is, Ay have gone there and seen the roots of Yggdrasil. Other dvarves told me how Mimir's head still lies at the vell, and Ay think a vise voman like you can find the vay. Me, Ay have seen the Tree rise up and up like forever." He gulped.

Ginny nodded. Half to herself, half to us, she said low and slow: "That cosmos was once closely entwined with ours, and surely with others. Or, rather, the crossing was easy from Northern lands. The belief factors . . . Christianity changed things. In a way, Beings like you, Fjalar, were left stranded here, like their counterparts in related universes."

And meanwhile the Low Continuum, Hell, became more accessible, I thought with a shudder. But no, like every faith, the Old Norse religion had its own hells and horrors. Its gods were in fact only Beings, however powerful. They'd withdrawn before the One God, though what His real nature is, I do not pretend to know.

The point was—my spirit surged upward—Mimir still lived, in at least one universe. Ginny could figure out how to reach him, probably with less difficulty than we'd had going to the Inferno. If he was the chief advisor to the chief of those gods, he must be a genius at unraveling the word games of skaldic poetry and Icelandic law—

And maybe, even, the United States tax code?

Ginny seemed to think it was possible. Her voice rang. "I'll look into this. Steve, can you take care of the household for the rest of today?" And keep Fjalar out from underfoot, she did not add. "Perhaps I'll know by evening. Meanwhile, do not, repeat not, disturb me."

The doorbell sounded. Already obedient, I went to see who was there. The dwarf trotted behind me. Val and Ben were ahead of us. They'd admitted Balawahdiwa.

36

"WELCOME, SIR," I GREETED WHEN MY SURPRISE HAD SETTLED DOWN. FOR SUCH A guest, of course Ginny postponed her research. We led him to a chair and started fresh coffee brewing. Edgar dipped his beak, then perched at attention. Svartalf strolled in, stopped, raised his tail for a moment, and took a seat on his haunches to look as Egyptian as possible. Fjalar hunkered on the rug beside him, Val, and Ben, who sat there in very respectful silence. But Chryssa ran over to the priest and hugged his knees. He smiled and ruffled the yellow curls. She put herself at his feet with a proprietary air, though she also refrained from prattling.

I groped for words. *To what do we owe the honor of this visit?* seemed too damn highfalutin. There he was, grizzled and leathery, dressed in a denim shirt, faded Levi's, and shoes worn into comfortable shapelessness. The Ford he'd parked outside stood aged and dusty. But he wouldn't have come unannounced like this on a social call.

"I hope everything's okay at the pueblo," was the best I could think of.

Balawahdiwa nodded. "Yes. For now. But you're troubled here."

"Well, we shouldn't cry on your shoulder."

"You needn't," he answered softly. "Trouble is overtaking us all." He glanced at the children. "I don't want to frighten you," he told them. "But not knowing is often worse. Your parents will decide."

Valeria doubled her fists. "I'd rather know." Can someone speak both stoutly and thinly? "Sir."

"Yeah, I can take it," Ben declared. "Sir."

"Me too, me too," said Chryssa. I doubted she'd understand, but figured that being with us would give more comfort than exile to her toys. Or did she already have an inkling? She closed a hand on Balawahdiwa's ankle.

"We'll wait for your mother," said the priest. Drawling: "Did you have fun at your party yesterday?"

Val couldn't suppress a giggle. "Mr. Fjalar got drunk," Ben blurted. "That was funny."

"Ay did not," protested the dwarf. "Yust yolly. Drunk is ven you make vows like you vill sail to Italy, take the Pope for ransom, kill the other men, loot, burn, take the vimmin and—"

"Never mind," I interrupted. "We'll stipulate that we had a long and lively lunch. How'd it go at Zuni?"

"Enjoyable." Balawahdiwa launched into an account, concentrating on polite but colorful details. I saw the children forget their fears while he talked.

True to pueblo ideas of courtesy, Ginny had gone to the kitchen to prepare refreshments. She returned, put them on the coffee table, and took a chair next to mine. At once she became the professional, her husband's and visitor's equal.

Balawahdiwa cut his story short without making it obvious that he did. He turned grave. His gaze locked with ours. "Then as I slept, a dream came to me," he said slowly. "That's what's brought me here."

He must have detected my flicker of doubt, because he added, "There are dreams and dreams. Most are nonsense. This one was what you call a medicine dream."

"You'd know it when it came," Ginny agreed low.

Balawahdiwa sat still for half a minute. The brightness and warmth seemed to drain from the sunshine in our windows.

"I can't tell you much about it," he went on. "That is, I mustn't. Not yet. But I can say it warned me that time grows short for us. The enemy know what we intend and they're marshaling their forces. Already they've begun to strike."

"*Ja*, they have, by Hel's blue boobs!" Fjalar exploded.

For an instant I wondered how he acquired his vulgar American slang. Maybe by some slight rapport with the vulgar American mind? "At least, we're suddenly in deep, uh, sheep dip," I said fast. "Though I wouldn't accuse anybody of being in conscious conspiracy with demons."

"Nor I, on the basis of evidence to date," Ginny rejoined, "but that doesn't mean the enemy have had nothing to do with it."

"Tell me about it later, please," Balawahdiwa said. "What I can tell you right away is that any strike at you must be only a beginning. The demons have their agents on Earth, but the moon's become where their real strength is. They're gathering, organizing, to hit all of us, all humans who could give them serious resistance, while the hitting's good."

Through horror, I looked from Val to Ben to Chryssa. The older two sat huge-eyed, breathing quickly and shallowly. We, their parents, would have plenty of explaining to do, not in detail but not mendaciously either, and plenty of reassurance to give, to Ben still more than Val.

Chryssa scrambled over to me. I gathered her onto my lap and held her close. "Do you mean an actual attack?" I rasped.

"Not a material war like the Caliph's, I'm sure," Ginny declared. "Demons are subtler than that. They have to be. But overwhelming our goetic, even our religious defenses and subverting our souls—"

"There, there, honey, you hear?" I crooned to the little one. "No boogies are coming to bite you."

"After they've gotten a strong foothold in us, we'll take care of physical destruction ourselves," Ginny said in as bleak a voice as I've ever heard.

Balawahdiwa nodded. "That's about the size of it, I reckon. We need the help of Powers that can match them, we need it bad, and we need it soon. So my dream made clear." His eyes swung back to me. "You and I have to seek it, Steven."

"What?" I nearly dumped my child on the floor.

Sitting back again, I heard him explain: "We're to go on retreat. I'll initiate you in certain things. Then together we'll call certain Ones."

"But-but-but," I protested like an old-time outboard motor, "I'm not any kind of adept or— My wife—"

"You are the man of this household and the male chief of Operation Luna. We have to follow the Ancient Way."

"But Ginny—her and me—we may be bound for another universe. I can't let her go alone." My will stiffened. "God damn it, I won't."

"Huh?" Val piped up. "Another universe? Like Magister Lazarus— like you did once yourselves?" Fox-quick, her mind grabbed the idea and ran with it. "Why can't Mom wait here till you get back, Dad?"

I eased a trifle. "Well, yes. How long will this . . . this retreat take?"

"A few days." Balawahdiwa frowned. "However, that may be as much time as we'll have. Right now, when the first full moon after the fall equinox is waning toward the half, is best for a Seeking like ours. I don't guarantee the Ones I'm thinking of will come to us, but the medicine for calling them is stronger than it can be again for months." He hesitated. On him that was a scary thing to behold. "Nor do I guarantee they and their kind can defend us and clean away the evil by themselves. But the enemy will be ready soon, soon. We need every help we can get. Pray to your Christian God."

Chryssa's voice wavered from the circle of my arms. "Jesus loves us."

I didn't doubt that, nor doubt that the Almighty could end our woes with a word. But He wouldn't. Bismarck said once that the Lord looks after fools, drunks, and the United States of America. That, though, was just a joking remark about luck. Sooner or later luck runs out. Always we mortals have to do the best we can with whatever we've got. And each of us must wage the fight for his or her soul alone.

"We have to take every possible action," Ginny said crisply. "Very likely, if I stay idle till you return, whatever I can do will be too late to save Operation Luna. Then what are our chances of prevailing? We'd never get clear information about the enemy, or get at them. But if Mimir's head really can advise us, perhaps we'll forestall that part of the attack."

"You don't know if you can reach him, let alone make it back alive!" I cried.

"That's the question I intend to study today," she answered.

"It ban not too dreadful," Fjalar maintained. "Ay don't think ve vill meet vith any trolls, and unless ve get lost among the roots, ve von't come too near the dragon Nidhöggur."

"Hey, wait just a damn minute—" I began.

Balawahdiwa's quiet words cut across mine and killed them. "In my dream, you traveled a long and strange way, Virginia. More than that I don't know. Would you care to explain?"

For a while the talk grew pretty chaotic, as might be expected when three cultures meet head-on. I don't remember enough to record, and it doesn't matter. The upshot was that Balawahdiwa received a thumbnail education in Eddic lore, and I promised to be at his place the next morning.

He declined our invitation to lunch. "Thanks, and I'm sorry, but you'll be busy making ready, Steven, and you learning, Virginia. Me, I'd better go home, think, and speak with a few others. Maybe their spells and prayers can help you."

If she went. Inwardly I hoped to blazes she'd discover the scheme was as hairy-brained as it looked. Bloody idiot dwarf!

No, that wasn't fair. I'd snatched at the idea myself, before it turned out I couldn't be at her side.

Balawahdiwa paused in the open doorway, looked past me at the children, and said gently, "It's for them. It always is. . . . See you tomorrow, Steven. Fare you well, Virginia." He took both her hands in his and breathed on them, then mine. The gesture held enormous meaning and love. Turning, he walked to his stick and flew off.

Ginny told me she'd skip lunch, and disappeared into her studio. There was no big hurry about my packing, which wouldn't amount to a lot. The kids stood by watching: how silently. I suggested a picnic excursion. Rather to my relief, Fjalar said, "No, Ay think Ay stay here. Yinny may vant my redes."

"Won't you get bored waiting?" asked Ben, maybe recalling what beer and whisky had done.

"No, Ay vatch your—farseer, you call it?" Fjalar stroked his beard. "But first, because you may come back from your trip before Ay from mine, Steve, Ay should make extra keys to the smithy and moonboat for you."

I conducted him to my workshop in a corner of the garage. His skillful, powerful hands required no jig or grinder, simply a hacksaw and file, to turn out the duplicates from an L-brace of the right thickness that was lying there. Naturally, he also needed to 'chant them properly, but those were simple spells, though none that I could follow as he sang in his rusty basso—on which account no intruder could likely circumvent them. I took the keys to my study and left them in a desk drawer.

The kids trailed us everywhere. Then they helped me prepare the picnic lunch. Chryssa made the job take twice as long as necessary, but nobody complained. We were together.

Red Rock State Park was the right place to talk reality. The air was mild and sweet, sunlight dappled the shade under the tree where we sat, sandstone cliffs sheered ruddy behind it, and everything bespoke enduring strength and peace. First renewing pledges of secrecy, I told them as much about the basic situation as it seemed I must. I left out the nastier features and emphatically downplayed the danger. Balawahdiwa was a good man but too pessimistic, I said. Though the aid of the Zunis was invaluable, none of them fully realized what resources we Americans had to call on. Never forget how we'd defeated Kaiser and Caliph and thwarted the Adversary himself. As for the immediate future, I was simply bound off on an interesting field trip. If their mother did go to Yggdrasil— if—why, that wasn't anything to worry about. Not at all like going to Hell. Merely seeking advice. Like visiting a doctor's office—no, I meant a lawyer's—no, I meant like dropping in on Uncle Will to ask him something about the stars.

I got Val and Ben kind of soothed. They could be trusted to keep quiet. Chryssa might forget to, but who'd take her seriously or even know what she was babbling about? In fact, she didn't really understand what I related, only that it wasn't happy. She still fretted. Her sister heartened her with an impromptu story about Moldylocks and the Pig Baby.

After that we could eat and play games and sing songs and look in on the museum and hike around some. Those hours were good. I wished there could have been more. But if nothing else, the kids were too tired to be overly worried when at last we flew homeward through the long light of a westering sun.

We entered into a thunderstorm of hoarse laughter. "Haw, haw, haw!" Fjalar rolled on the floor, slapped his thigh, kicked his legs aloft. The farseer was concluding an English-language performance of Gounod's *Faust*. Since that's a favorite opera of mine, I asked what was funny.

"That man, he got run through, he ban dying, and he sang!" whooped the dwarf. He wiped his streaming eyes. "He sang and sang. He fell down, he stood back up, he fell down, he stood up, he fell down, he flopped like a landed fish, and alvays he sang! Now they ban going to burn that poor girl alive, and she *sings!*"

Different folk, different tastes.

"Has my lady called on you?" I finally managed to inquire.

"*Ja*, yust vunce, a few kvestions. She vill come out soon and tell us Ay vas right. You got any more humorous shows?"

Our music library contained some audiovisuals. I wondered about Wagner's *Ring*. No, Fjalar might rupture himself guffawing. Ginny saved me from making a decision when she appeared.

She was exhausted, white-faced, her hands trembling slightly, but fire burned green behind her eyes. "I'm done," she said, her voice not quite level. "We'll go, Fjalar."

"Ay knew it," replied the dwarf smugly.

She took my hands. Hers were cold. I told myself that was from weariness. "It's all right, darling," she whispered. "I verified the crossover is possible. Ordinarily it's hard. There's no body of belief here anymore, and the time lines have branched far apart. But given Fjalar's presence, his affinity, I can make it more easily than . . . the one we made before. And we'll meet with no hostility."

Oh, yeah? my mind groaned. *What about trolls and dragons and giants and drows and the rest of that merry crew? I wouldn't trust old One-Eye much, either.* For the sake of the youngsters I kept it to myself. Nothing was ever certain anyway. Maybe here at home drunks on brooms were a worse hazard.

Dusk was filling the room. The glare and noise of the farseer deepened it in every other corner. Ginny squared her shoulders. "We should start making arrangements," she continued. "First about the children. Let's see if Will can take over again."

Action is the best medicine for anxiety. We phoned her brother and he said we'd be welcome. Leaving Valeria in charge, we flitted with Fjalar to his house. The sky was turning purple and windows had come aglow among shadows beneath. The lights on other vehicles bobbed past like fireflies. The air was as cool as a stranger's kiss.

Will guided us into his cluttered quarters, fussed about with cups and a pot of tea, finally sat down opposite us. He seemed frazzled, his smiles mostly mechanical. However, when we asked he said that, sure, he could move back to our house anytime and stay as long as we wished, "if you don't mind the FBI making eye tracks all over it. But what's the occasion?"

That I was bound off with Balawahdiwa couldn't be hidden. I told him about seeking native help against the demons. Maybe he'd have a suggestion or two. Instead, he lost what cordiality he'd shown. "That doesn't strike me as a very hopeful idea, or even a wise one," he snapped.

"Why not?" I replied, surprised. "You know something you haven't told us?"

"No. But remember what happened when last you invoked one of those Beings."

"It wasn't any of them that tried to kill us!" At once I regretted my outburst. Did he flinch? "Sorry, Will. I shouldn't have said that." I fumbled for better words. "Seeing as how you've been falsely accused, why shouldn't you cheer us on in anything that might clear you?"

"I feel dubious. Call it an intuition."

"I'm afraid we engineers haven't much training in intuition," I argued, trying for lightness. "I'm going, regardless. Nothing to lose."

Maybe.

He looked at his sister. "You too?" It sounded almost like *"Et tu?"* Why?

She shook her head. "No, I'll be working on the tax mess That'll take me . . . out of town."

"Where, please?"

Fjalar opened his mouth. Ginny's tap on the shoulder warned him and his teeth thumped together. "I'd better not speak about it yet, except that the prospect seems good." Pain was in her voice too. Deciding to keep this from him had not come easy. It was like admitting to Will that our trust in him was not quite a hundred percent. Oh, close enough, or we'd never have requested his services. But he could just possibly, unknowingly, act as some kind of information conduit. . . .

In fact, this was in a way the case. "Yes, I am under surveillance," he said with a shrug. "Possibly the stakeouts hear everything uttered in this house. I wish them joy of it."

"We've nothing illegal in mind," I declared hastily.

Fjalar broke the embarrassed silence that followed. "Vere ban Brynjubítr?"

"Ah, Fotherwick-Botts? It—he's back in the room I use for a laboratory." Will's withholdingness broke. He brightened as the sea does when a sunbeam strikes through a fog bank. "Do you want him along on your venture?"

"No, better not," Fjalar opined. "He don't know his vay around yonder, and maybe he says the wrong thing. He's not tactful like me. And if ve meet real trouble, no veapon vill help mush."

That was great news for my ears. Will's smile died. His eyes narrowed.

Before I could introduce a motion to cancel the whole crazy junket, Ginny cried, "Nonsense, Fjalar!"

Her relief was plain to see when the dwarf proceeded: "But ve should hang the sword in the smithy to keep vatch and call an alarm if need be vile ve ban gone."

Will's gladness revived for a moment. "Absolutely! Why don't you take him out there tonight, to make sure?"

"He talks a lot?" I asked redundantly.

Will winced. "I didn't realize how much. It has eroded my powers of concentration. He's gotten as far as some tenth-century affray in Yorkshire."

Ginny smiled compassionately. "Poor dear. Yes, we'll release you, with many thanks."

"Ve shouldn't bring him avay tonight," Fjalar cautioned. "He'd think you didn't like his tales, and be hurt. He's sensitive, you know."

"Tell him you're worn out and have to turn in early," Ginny suggested. Her glance at Will said that he certainly looked it. "Fjalar and I will fetch him in the morning. You get your stuff together, and as soon as I'm ready to leave you can move over."

Will's face locked into the mask we knew too well. "Ah, yes. You may rely on me."

I worried a smidgen, and Ginny admitted to me later that she did too. But whatever his problem was, it hadn't caused him to do anything really erratic. The psychoscopy had proved that the evidence against him must be a frame-up. The FBI monitored him as much in hopes of getting a clue to the somebody or something responsible as because of lingering suspicion.

The kids loved their Uncle Will, he'd done fine by them the last time around, and . . . in the event of an emergency, Val was mature enough to call for the right kind of help. Ginny told me privately she'd brief her in more detail, just in case.

What with all this, my renewed objections to the Mimir expedition were brushed aside.

Before then, Will had declined our invitation to dinner, saying that he was in truth fatigued. We returned home and actually had a rather pleasant family evening. If the cheer was a tad forced, it wasn't fake. Eventually Ginny and I were alone together and made our own farewell.

37

NOW THE STORY SPLITS AGAIN, THREE WAYS THIS TIME. I'LL HAVE TO RECONSTRUCT TWO of them from what information came to me later, most of it brokenly, and the best guesses I can make. Nor may I say much about my own experiences. They're branded on my memory, but I gave my word of honor I'd keep certain things secret.

Ginny had been awake and active for hours while I still slept. At the earliest decent time she flew back to Will's. He let her in, himself also fully clad. "I hope I haven't disturbed you," she said for politeness' sake.

"Oh, no." He spoke dully. "I've been up for two or three hours."

She looked at the wan face. "You sleep very little these nights, don't you?"

"I manage. I thought the dwarf would come with you."

"Why pummel him out of bed and coffee him? I've a great deal to do in the shortest possible time."

"Such as?"

"Just now, taking the sword to the workshop. Frankly, I'd as soon not have Fjalar along. Those two can get into dialogues so long and rambling you wouldn't believe it. And he would doubtless criticize my work, as if it weren't perfectly simple and straightforward."

Did Will stiffen? "What work, if I may ask?"

"Well, you remember the idea is to leave Fotherwick-Botts there on watch, to notify the Zunis if anything untoward happens. But I'm not entirely satisfied with the alarm system. This is a busy time of year for them. They may not be able to respond at once. Or if the 'something untoward' is more subtle than a burglar or a vandal, they may feel confused, unsure how to react. That's especially true while Balawahdiwa, the man among them who's worked most closely with us, is absent the next several days. It occurred to me that I can provide a direct line of communication to Steve. Whether or not he can come immediately in person, he can give advice. I have to have it ready for him before he goes."

Will seemed to turn the idea over in his mind, weighing and peering, before he nodded. "Yes, a reasonable precaution. I'll fetch the garrulous glaive." Sometimes his academic humor still flickered.

The blade had been sheathed. Ginny left it so, said good-bye—with the slightest catch in her voice—and went out into the chill, hushed morning.

Nobody else was in sight when she landed at the smithy. Shadows stretched westward from sparse grass, brush, and wildflowers. Dowa Yalanne dreamed in the offing, red-and-white, rugged, mighty. A few insects buzzed. Somewhere a mountain bluebird cried *teww, teww*.

Fjalar having reclaimed the keys, she let herself in with the spare for the padlock, leaving the door open for light. Nevertheless the space reached cavernous and gloomy. Poised on her parking gear, *Owl* shimmered, beautiful. Ginny took the sword forth. Steel gleamed likewise. She laid the scabbard on a workbench.

"I say," Fotherwick-Botts exclaimed from her hand, "what is this farce, eh, what? Thought I was a guest of Graylock's. Suddenly he boots me out. After casing me before nine in the ruddy P.M. yesterday. Right in the middle of my describing that set-to on Barmby Moor."

"I'm sorry," she replied. "We arrived and caused him to interrupt. But that was an emergency. You understand."

"Emergency? Hah. He didn't say. Certainly I understand emergencies. What kind of weapon would I be if I didn't understand emergencies? Tell me that, eh? What are weapons for if not emergencies? Yes, display and taking of oaths and whatnot, true. But fighting's what it's about, egad. And after you'd gone, he didn't unsheathe me, that Graylock. Is this your American idea of hospitality?"

"He was exhausted. He had to sleep."

"Hrrumph, he was awake bloody early, I can tell you. Didn't so much as say good morning. Left me gagged. No other word will do. Gagged, by thunder. Hah! Bah!"

"I'm sure he was too preoccupied." Ginny set him on the bench, leaned against the wall. "He had hoped for leisure to hear you out later today."

"Indeed? Tchah! If he was really int'rested— How could he not be? There I was, telling how I clove that scoundrel from left shoulder to right hip. Tasted terrible, he did. Hadn't bathed in months, I'll wager, and shaggy as a dog. How could any thinking person wait to hear the rest of the tale? Anyone but a, a born-and-bred *civilian!*"

"But General, sir, I had dire need of you," she cried piteously.

His wrath puffed away. "You did? You do? Dire need, m'lady? Why didn't you say so at once? At your service, madame! Just bring me to the villains and I'll spill their rotten guts for 'em. I'll sending 'em yelping down to the Devil. If you'll pardon an old soldier's language."

"No, thank you very much for your kindness, but that won't be necessary. At least, not yet. We want—we request you to keep watch here for some days while everybody else is away. You're tireless. If someone tries to break in or otherwise make trouble, you'll sound the alarm and the Zunis will come."

Fotherwick-Botts grew suspicious. "Everybody else? Going away? The dwarf too? What for, ha?"

"Oh, er, various errands."

"Errands? What sort? Bad business, this, that we're in. I smell danger skulking about." The sword paused. "You—are you bound off on a—a quest?"

"Well, in a way."

"A quest! And I'm to hang behind like the tail on a ruddy cow? Bleat for help from a pack of natives? No, by Cross and Hammer both!" he roared. "If you suppose I will, little do you know what a Fotherwick-Botts is full of!"

Ginny thought fast. Though he had no power over her, a surly sword could well prove a sloppy sentry. "But this is different, sir. The quest is only for knowledge. More like a pilgrimage. Yes, that's it, a pilgrimage. Here is the stronghold the foe must take if he can. I wouldn't ask anyone who wasn't totally fearless to stand guard. You, ringed in by the forces of darkness, standing your lonely vigil—"

His volume dropped. "Vigil, did you say?"

"Come worst to worst, you will blow your horn, so to speak, like Heimdall on the walls of Asgard or Roland in the pass of Roncesvalles."

"Hum, ha, see your point, m'lady. A vigil, eh? And a call to rally the troops. And then I'll join in the battle."

"When this need arose, we thought of you first. You are superb at blowing your own horn."

Thus she won his agreement. She hung him by two pegs above the bench before she adjusted and tested the alarm system. It was merely an open phone to the pueblo governor's dwelling. Somebody was always there, doing housework if nothing else. That person could holler for the tribal police. A number of able-bodied men had been deputized to strengthen their tiny band. The system could also call for assistance from the sheriff's office in Gallup. Since those people hadn't been briefed— discretion—reinforcements might take a while to arrive.

However, we didn't expect any huge assault. The enemy could have only a few humans working for them, maybe only the slippery customer we were trying to find. As for demons and other Beings, the protective spells remained potent. Ginny knew better than to tell Fotherwick-Botts that we thought of planting him here as nothing more than a cheap pre-caution against an unlikely contingency, like buying a life insurance policy from a vendor before boarding a commercial flight. And it'd keep him out of Will's hair, which was plenty gray enough.

So we thought.

She went on to operations that involved *Owl*. Quick and easy for a witch of her skill, they did not demand any physical or goetic examination of the spacecraft. That wasn't unfortunate, it was much worse.

Having bidden the sword a ceremonious farewell and received a gruff godspeed, she flitted home. When she walked in I was about to fix breakfast for the kids. She took over and made it good. She always made everything good.

We were almost casual as we saw Val and Ben off for school. I was going on an excursion, sort of, and their mother wouldn't leave today. Yet I stood at the door and watched them till they were out of sight.

Inside again, I met Ginny as she came out of my study. Chryssa trotted at her heels. "I returned the smithy key to your desk drawer," she said, "in case you have use for it when Fjalar and I aren't here."

The reminder spoiled my mood. "Hey, didn't you figure your jaunt might be shorter than mine?"

"Might. I still have much to learn and do. In any case, we can't foretell how things will go." She smiled and patted my hand. Sunlight streamed down the hall where we stood, to make ripples of fire in her hair and ripples of shadow across the curves beneath her clothes. "Don't *worry* so, dear old woof. C'mon, I've got something for you."

She led me to the living room. From the jacket she'd taken off and left lying there, she drew a pair of flat rock crystal discs about an inch in diameter. I stared. There was nothing obviously special about them. Probably every working thaumaturge has blanks like this in stock, to carry assorted kinds of everyday spells.

"Communicators," she explained. "That's why I roused myself at an unsanctified hour. I got the idea last night, after—" She glanced down at Chryssa. "As I was falling asleep. It's simply a portable, untappable phone line. Naturally, it had to be made ready before you start off today."

Such a device wasn't "simply." I wondered just how long and hard she'd worked on it. Eagerness drove that out of me. "We can talk while you're in yonder universe?"

"No, I'm afraid not. Nobody's developed the capability." Transcosmic expeditions had been mighty few, I recalled. Some had never been seen again. " 'Untappable' is the operative word. I've sympathized both these to *Owl*'s communication globe, which is unique, you know. Through it, you and I can be in instantaneous touch across any distance—in this continuum—and nobody and nothing not in actual earshot should be able to listen in on us."

"Unless in possession of *Owl*. . . . But we've provided against that, haven't we?" I couldn't help thinking of the hopeful applications. "Say, this'll come in handy when she's in space. Ought not to need all that apparatus to transmit voice in airlessness."

"Yes, it's mind-resonant, though given air it does audio. In case one of us has to be aroused, for instance."

"Smart girl. Um-m, but Balawahdiwa and I are supposed to be in spiritual retreat."

"I realize that. Matters will get grim indeed before I yell for you. What I mostly considered was the situation after we both come home."

"Yeah, when we try carrying the war to the enemy. But it's nice to have this gadget already. Thank you, darling."

Chryssa clutched my leg. I rumpled her curls. "Hey, honey, nothing to be scared of. This is only a funny phone. We'll let you talk on it later, okay? The boogies are far away. As far as Moldylocks is from the soap works. Want to come watch us make jewelry?"

We took her along into the studio. Ginny kept a supply of rings, fine chains, and suchlike stuff. Best not let untrained hands put talismans in their settings. Mine were reasonably competent under her supervision, and we worked together. It didn't take long. Both crystals went into lockets, to hang around the neck. I placed Ginny's on her. If our daughter hadn't been there, I'd have felt around for the exact right arrangement.

As we came out we heard a bass bellowing. Fjalar was awake at last. He wanted to know where we and his breakfast were.

Noblesse oblige, or some damn thing to that effect. We fed him and left him as our babysitter while we flew to Zuni on separate brooms. We'd leave one there for me to return with. We didn't linger in the pueblo. Well-meaning though the dwarf was, neither of us cared to have him in charge for any length of time. For instance, out of the kindness of his heart he might conceivably offer the child a beer.

Landing by the church, we spoke a few low-voiced words, took a hasty kiss, held hands for a minute, and went our different ways.

38

AT BALAWAHDIWA'S COMMAND I'D BROUGHT A MINIMAL OUTFIT, BACKPACK FILLED with the usual gear and clothing, sleeping bag tied to the frame. It goes without saying that besides my new communicator I kept my wereflash under my shirt. When I'd asked about a pistol, he'd replied, "No. Wouldn't be any use, and might give offense."

He waited at his home, broom heavily laden. The food, which he'd said he'd supply, had little volume or weight, traditional Zuni fare. His priestly things were likewise deceptively few and simple. But water for several days filled as many large clay *ollas*, padded against breakage in a net lashed to the coffer. We boarded, lumbered into the air, and flew slowly east.

I mentioned Fotherwick-Botts' presence at the smithy. "Good," Balawahdiwa said. "We really can't spare even a boy any longer to stay in view. Busy time—the regular duties of the season, the Doll Dance coming up, and preparations for the Shalako under way in earnest."

The casual-sounding words gained power from the grave tone. He and his people lived their religion. Not for the first time, I wondered if my family and I should do likewise with ours. Had not a veritable saint once come to our aid? But he didn't seem to have been—dispatched; he'd heard our appeal and responded, being the kind of spirit he was. And the business had had some ridiculous mixups. And if we'd been, oh, Shintoists, might it have been somebody like Susano-o? And in, say, the Kaiser's War both sides had called on the same Christian God. And if He really wanted anybody's prayers, why was there so much pain and evil and outright horror in the world? . . . If you trace such questions no further back than the prophets of Israel, I'd still have to set my poor wits to pick and choose from three thousand years of thinking. That wasn't my natural bent. For now, at least, I'd take the guidance of this old medicine man.

"Where are we bound, please?" I ventured to ask.

"Same place where Kokopelli met us," he answered.

My belly muscles tightened. The aftermath of that encounter—

"They're different, those I'm hoping will come to us now," he added. "You'll need your courage."

After a moment, while the air flowed warm and the uplands lifted stark ahead: "It's permitted that we land on the site and unload our stuff. But then we have to fly down and walk back up." He glanced at me. "Don't worry about being attacked on the trail like last time. The enemy don't repeat their mistakes. Also, Virginia isn't with us. I think they wanted most to eliminate her."

"And you," I replied around a thickness in my throat.

"That's not for me to say."

Nor may I say what followed, unless in words so bare as to be nearly meaningless. Let me try, though, within the limits laid on me.

By the time we'd returned to our things, the sun was low. I unpacked and made camp while Balawahdiwa gathered dry wood, kindled a small blaze with a fire bow, and blessed it. After he'd given me basic instruction in the proper prayers, we ate and drank frugally. I did the cleaning, as befitted an acolyte. We both made reverence while sunset burned away in enormous gold and red. Later we sat watching the stars come forth, impossibly bright and many. He told me of much. We hailed the rising moon before we went to sleep.

Understand, I wasn't being converted. My puzzled, partial religion stayed the same. It wasn't incompatible with his. I just had to make myself worthy.

Tuesday was hard.

On Wednesday I began to use a little of what I'd learned and, more important, to feel it.

This went on through Thursday. That night they came to us.

The moon rose gibbous, only half an hour later than before, for it was waning down from Harvest, to be reborn as Hunter's. Against the icy brilliance of Milky Way and crowding stars, its glow barely touched the soil, rocks, and sparse growth around us with gray. Below our ridge the mountainside plunged into a darkness that upheaved itself on the other side of a dry arroyo. Embers in our banked fire lay like drops of blood. Balawahdiwa and I had stripped down to kilt, sash, and paint. A breeze stroked my skin with a chill that seemed far distant. It fluttered the feathers of our prayer sticks. The silence in which we stood belonged to the rite we performed, and the rite had taken possession of me.

Beyond this, I can't really tell what happened, what was said, or how. Even if I were free to, I wouldn't be able to. Words, images, ideas don't reach to it.

Did the wind go from a whisper to a whistle, or was that a flute at the lips of a hunchback? Did thunder roll through these unclouded hills, or was that a drumbeat?

I felt them approach, without knowledge of how they did. Balawahdiwa scattered sacred meal from a bowl he held onto the ground they would tread. Then it was as if the night thickened there and became the pair of them.

Short they were, but hugely muscled and cougar-lithe. Ugly they were, but flintily majestic. Clad like hunters they were, in skin tunic and leggings, bow and quiver slung behind the shoulders, but gourds in their belts rattled the measures of a dance, plumes nodded tall above leather caps, each right hand bore a spear and each left hand a shield. The markings on the shields glimmered with tracings I could not follow, lines and curves and emblems in which my gaze lost itself till I ripped it free. The priest had taught me well and I knew them—once the Divine Twins, now the Twin War Gods.

We spoke with them.

—The Beloved Ones know what is our need and our prayer.

—*We know what the Fluteplayer told. We know that Coyote has consorted with strange Beings. What is that to us? Again and again have we raised the hearts of our peoples. Again and again they were crushed.*

Their war cries resound no more. Their lands have fallen to those who love not Earth our Mother, but flay her alive. Why should we help the invaders?

The Twins were not only gods of the pueblos. Folk venerated them across our whole West and far into the South. The Maya told how in the underworld they once played ball with the Lords of the Dead. Everyone told how they had led the ancestors of humanity from below to the sunlight. There could be truth in that belief, the same kind of symbolic truth there is in Genesis.

—Forsake us not, we pray.

—*How faithful do* you *remain? After the Fluteplayer revealed his news, we searched. Yes, terror is on the moon, and this is unholy. But may it not scourge the world clean, as terror did over and over in the ancient past, and purify those who live through it, that they may begin anew?*

—What threatens is worse than death, worse than pain and loss. Hear what my friend has to tell.

The Twins looked coldly upon my soul.

And somehow, I don't know how, I found—not the facts; those they scanned at once—but the will to speak up, clumsily, foreignly, but as honestly as ever I did.

—Sirs, if you please, is this the worst of all possible worlds? Are my people really such monsters? A long time before us, wave after wave of newcomers crossed over from their old countries. Did they always mingle peacefully with those they found? Who wiped out the mammoth, the giant bison and bear and sloth, the sabertooth, the American horse and camel, any big game that didn't learn fast enough to fear them? Who, in these very parts, stripped the land till at last they had to move out? Did one tribe never come with slaughter, torture, rape, and enslavement to drive another from its home?

—And today, how dreadful is it to have eyeglasses when your vision weakens, books to read, teeth in your mouth for life, no more hours and hours spent over a metate to grind the corn, an excellent chance that a woman will live through every childbirth and every child live to have children?

—Sure, we whites have done horrible things and made horrible mistakes. We're still at it. We're human, after all. But more and more of us are trying to do better; and we've worked out a few guidelines, like the Bill of Rights; and—

—And, God damn it, we're not about to fold our hand and quit the game! I said it, we're human too. Best would be if we had you and your people at our side in this mess. It makes sense. The disaster would also fall on them. If we win together, they'll have more say in what to do with the victory. If we lose—we'll go down together, and you won't have sold out to Hell.

I straightened before the Twins.—Sorry, sirs. But with respect, that's what I mean, and I'll stand by it.

—He speaks truth, as well as he grasps it, Balawahdiwa said.

—*We see that. . . . And, yes, a monstrous evil is indeed gathering here in our motherland and upon the moon, the holy moon. The Fluteplayer did not believe but could not long keep still. Then we made medicine, we sought, and we learned. At this meeting we have learned more.*

—*We will speak with Others.*

Can gods feel anxious, even afraid? That's not for me to judge. What I imagine I remember, and retell as a shadow-scrap of the reality, is:

—*We will call Coyote to task and hear him out. He is mischievous, sometimes stupid, but he is not at heart evil. And he is among the Creators.*

—*But all of us together cannot by ourselves fend off the demons who are abroad. They are too strange to us, and too strong. Once more, humans will have their part in upholding the world . . . if you and we can . . .*

Presently the Twins left us. The air blew frosty, the stars gleamed keen.

"We, we aren't sure how they'll help us, or when, or anything?" I stammered into the stillness. My breath smoked white under the moon.

"It depends on what happens, which they can't foresee either. I'll hope for another dream, come the time." Balawahdiwa laid a hand on my shoulder. "Let's turn in, Steven. It's been a long day and a longer half a night."

Suddenly I felt how wrung out I was. I barely made it to my sack.

My dreams were weird, though not as terrorful as I'd expected. Slowly they settled down into normal gibberish. One almost roused me, a formless fear. My eyes opened. I saw stars, heard silence, felt the cold on my cheeks, and toppled back into sleep.

Medicine outfit or no, I'd kept the locket Ginny gave me on my breast. Now it woke me for keeps.

"Daddy, Mother, help!" the girl-voice cried, small, remote, desperate. "Please, can you hear me? Anybody? Help!"

39

FOR THE NEXT THREE DAYS AFTER SHE SAW ME OFF, GINNY WORKED HARDER THAN you'd dare work a mule. Transit to another continuum—another cosmos, another reality—isn't like flitting cross country or even paying a call on Dr. Fu Ch'ing, especially if you'd prefer to come home alive and sane. Fjalar provided important information, plus manual skill and muscles when matters got that far, but she had to do the goetics all alone, research, planning, preparation, everything.

True, he'd made the journey before. However, that was long ago, when the sympathetics of human belief kept the connection close and the passage fairly easy between the Nordic region and that universe. Besides, he'd gone with a bunch of his kind, led by their chief wizards. Most dwarves lived yonder, as they presumably still did. Those on our Earth went to persuade the gods to send more business their way.

When the Christians took over their stamping grounds they were left stranded here. In his rough-hewn style, Fjalar was pathetically eager to see the old scenes again. It made him do his damnedest to help. It also made him discount any dangers.

Along with a lot else, Ginny obtained a complete file of Nornwell's tax records and papers pertaining thereto. She didn't tell Barney why she requested it, because he didn't need concern about her on top of the woes already besetting him, but he trusted her. She added the same from Operation Luna and the Matuchek household. Thereafter she tapped into the public lorebase for the United States tax code. Transmitting that took about twenty-four hours and, despite the modern miracle of atomic-level recording, presented her with a lorestone weighing two pounds.

Meanwhile she flew to Albuquerque. In a big hardware store she bought a disassembled tool shed. Collecting Fjalar at our house, she took him, his kit, and her purchase to a spot she'd discovered. She left him there to assemble the structure and prepare certain items for it, returned home, and cooked dinner. That was Wednesday evening.

Thursday morning she sent Val and Ben to school as usual. Though she had assured them and their sister that everything would be quite safe and she expected to come back in a day or two, she hadn't gone into detail. The dwarf had likewise kept mum. They did their best to believe her. Nevertheless, I can imagine that stoic little "So long" scene. I can't make myself write it.

Will arrived shortly after she phoned him, suitcase in hand. She made it an occasion to smile. "You'll hardly need that, I hope," she said. "With luck, this jaunt of mine will only be an overnighter." She paused. "If it does run a bit longer, don't worry . . . and don't let the children worry . . . or Steve, if I'm not here to meet him."

"Won't you give me an emergency line?" he asked.

She shook her head. "I'm sorry, Will. I can't. You know our family doctor and the police and— I'd better be on my way."

He followed her to the garage. Chryssa tagged anxiously along. Several containers were secured on the rear of the Jaguar. His thumb gestured at them. "The coffer must be full," he observed. "Rather a lot of baggage for an overnight trip, isn't it?"

"Professional apparatus."

"That much, to cope with the tax collector?" He saw her lips tighten and shrugged. "As you wish. I'll look forward to hearing about it someday. Bon voyage."

"B-b-bye, Mommy," Chryssa gulped.

Ginny hunkered down for a hug and a kiss. Edgar hopped from her shoulder to the broom and perched there in a marked manner. He disapproved of sentimentalism unless it focused on him.

When Ginny straightened, Will bent toward the child. "Let's go inside, sweetie," he proposed. "How would you like a brand-new story? Perhaps later, if you want, we can go to the park playground." Ginny signed the garage door to open. She boarded the broom and slipped out. Her brother and daughter waved farewell.

It was a lonely flight to Mount Taylor and a lonely place, high on its northern flank, where she landed. There was nothing illegal about camping here, and nothing against bolting a temporary shelter together from corrugated steel panels. Nobody did, because no trail ran anywhere near, nor was water to be had. No Beings were likely to come by, either. But she had more on her mind than secrecy. The public menace afoot was great enough without her adding to it.

Like every licensed thaumaturge, she knew her physical sciences, including the conservation laws. Nature keeps exact accounts—well, pretty exact, say the quantum mechanics experts. If mass goes to a different continuum, an equal amount must go the opposite way, plus or minus whatever balances the energies. As Ginny, Fjalar, Edgar, and their gear crossed over, several hundred pounds of Old Norse stuff would appear where they'd been and stay till they returned.

No telling what form it would have, except that a load of plain dirt and rocks was ruled out. The second law of thermodynamics must be satisfied as well as the first. It's more lenient; surrounding matter, such as air and soil, can take up considerable entropy slack. In fact, since a demon's basic structure is chaotic, junk will serve. She knew, all too well, of one that had exchanged with the contents of Svartalf's catbox. But true life is highly organized. There was bound to be at least some living matter from the other side. It wouldn't necessarily consist of vegetation and bugs. The books mentioned pretty formidable creatures.

Ginny had studied those books in college, along with belief systems from around the world, history, and anthropology. The more esoteric a symbolism a witch employs, the more powerful are her spells. In an irreverent mood once, she and a classmate had composed a ballad to the tune of "Jesse James." They called it "The Childish Edda." The chorus went:

> "Yggdrasil, where nine worlds flash,
> Is a noble piece of ash
> That shelters Norns and gods and all that crew.
> There's a dragon gnaws the base
> Of an eagle's resting place,
> And a squirrel and four harts complete the zoo."

Fun. But who knew what else might happen to be running around in the vicinity?

As for it, given Fjalar's recollections and the rheatic effect of his presence, Ginny had figured out a scheme that ought to land them reasonably near the well of Mimir. She had a certain amount of control over the time parameter too. If they made it back, they might have spent some hours more or less than had passed in our world, but the difference shouldn't be major. If they made it back.

First they needed the shed for a cave in which she'd cast her crossing spell. Afterward they'd need it to contain whatever exchanged for them. Its isolation added a trifle to a safety margin that was thin at best.

"Hail," hailed Fjalar as she got off her stick. He doubtless enjoyed the sight, though she was dressed for the field in heavy shirt, jeans, and boots, with her hair falling loosely gathered from beneath a battered old hat. Belted to her left hip was a canteen, to her right a pouch for things she might want in a hurry. A light backpack carried the remaining essentials. The dwarf's outfit was similar, in a medieval fashion. "You brought visky?"

"I left a fifth with you yesterday," she said.

"That vas yesterday. Vat if ve meet poison snakes?"

"I've a first aid kit," she told him firmly, "sandwiches, meat pies, and two thermoses of hot coffee." Relenting: "Oh, and candy bars. Here, have one now. You've done a good job, I see." She took it from a shirt pocket and handed it over faster than Edgar could snaffle it. "We'll ration the rest. They supply quick energy."

For a moment she stood still, looking out at the sky and down the mountain to the land below. Junipers rustled darkly green in a wind whose coolness they sweetened. Clouds loomed like snowbanks against an unending blue. Desert reached subtly colored to ocherous cliffs afar. Two or three vultures hovered on broad wings. Here and there she saw human works, very small. She sighed and turned about. "Let's get going," she said.

Fjalar helped her unload and arrange what she'd taken along. It amounted to considerably more than what we'd had on our Hell expedition. Mainly it was to safeguard the shed against attack from within or without. The occultics of the destination universe bore scant relation to ours; a pentacle surrounded by blessed candles wouldn't contain an angry monster from there. Besides, Coyote or one of his alien buddies just might happen by, spot the setup, and investigate. It had to withstand the kind of forces they could bring to bear.

I don't know what she deployed, nor what she used and did to make the crossing. I do know better than to ask. I can guess at a spear; rods of oak, ash, and thorn, carven with runes; chants, gestures, horse blood splashed from a horn onto the ground—guesses.

The gloom of the locked shed deepened. Lightning flared, thunder cracked, stones shivered underfoot, waves ran wild before a sleetful gale, a noise of galloping hooves and hawk-shout of female voices passed by, a maelstrom raged, the wayfarers whirled down and down to the bottom of night.

40

THEY STOOD BENEATH VASTNESS. FOG DRIFTED IN LOW, SMOKY STREAMERS. LIGHT seeped wan from an unseen sky. Silence brooded.

"Quark!" screamed Edgar and rocketed from Ginny's shoulder. He flapped to and fro above them, hoarsely expressing alarm, indignation, and doubts about this whole business.

"You come back," Fjalar called to him. "Vat kind of familiar ban you, getting scared by a little frighteningness? You shicken or something?"

Edgar braked to a hover, glared, and returned. On his way he gave the dwarf a smart beak-rap on the head. "Ow!" Fjalar bawled. "Surt's fires sizzle you black, you foul fowl!"

Ginny refrained from pointing out that the raven was already black. The ruckus had diverted her, steadied her shaken mind and body. She looked around.

A root rose slightly above the soil. That part of it loomed like a curving silver-gray cliff. The moss underfoot, wet and cold but a green richer than she had ever seen before, grew halfway up the bark. Where the root met the trunk, sight ended. Too broad for eyes to make out any curvature, the bole ran right and left until it faded into the mist. Upward it reared, as if forever. Somewhere aloft the boughs began. She glimpsed one through a twilight of leaves on branch above branch, overshadowing all.

And yet she felt a warmth, a sense of life like a tide, of strength and abidingness. Did her ears capture a ghost of the soughing where a wind blew between the worlds? Did she glimpse a gleam, brighter than gold, a dwelling of gods? She had found Ash Yggdrasil, the Tree whose roots go deeper than death and whose crown is among the stars. The Earth she knew seemed remote, unreal, a half-forgotten dream.

Fjalar drew her back from helpless awe. "Look," he rumbled. "The traces of vat vas svapped for us."

"Oh, yes." She peered through the mist. A wide, shallow depression showed where turf and sod had been torn away. "But what about animals? Did the transition force scoop up some birds that happened to be flying by?"

Fjalar squatted. He had lived close to nature throughout his many centuries. "No, see here, tracks. They come but don't go." Now she could identify them, faint in the resilient moss though larger than her own. Not human—claws— "Yumping yiminy," Fjalar breathed, "Ay think we caught Ratatosk himself."

Her mind wobbled at the thought of a giant squirrel bouncing around and chittering in the tool shed. Well, for that while he wouldn't be carrying nasty words between the dragon under the Tree and the eagle on its heights. . . .

"This ought to scare off volves and bears and drows and such," Fjalar opined. "They von't know vat happened, or if it can grab them too. This patch ought to ban pretty peaceful till Ratatosk gets back."

"But we'd better not waste time anyway." At first her voice sounded strange to her. She ordered her strength to the forefront. "Let's find the well. It should be somewhere near."

Reaching into her pouch, she withdrew her wand and extended it. The star-tip lit and strewed brightness through the dusk. "Gruk," said Edgar, obviously encouraged. "Good bird. God damn."

They trudged along the root toward the bole. A hole gaped where those joined, the mouth of a tunnel. Fjalar indicated a trail, hardly more than a slight flattening across the bark, switchbacking down the root from above. "Ay think this ban the path Odin takes ven he goes to speak vith Mimir. *Ja*, ve should keep moving. Ay vould not like to meet him, especially in the dark."

So much for the benevolent All-Father of the kiddie books, Ginny thought. The real Odin had hanged himself on the Tree and swung in the wind for nine nights, as the price of gaining the runes of power. That was how it got the name Yggdrasil, the Horse of the Terrible One. That was why the human sacrifices to him were hanged, and he known as the Lord of the Gallows. Pagan gods weren't very nice people.

Well, maybe those of the Pueblo Indians—some of them—

And she had her part to do. She entered the opening.

A passage sloped downward. Rootlets matted its sides and hung from above, snaky, dead-white. Water dripped, runneled, puddled the clay floor. Soon only her wand gave light. It leaped in and out of monstrous shadows. A cobweb as big and thick as a carpet draped halfway across the corridor. Fjalar, in the lead, brushed against it. The spider that scuttled into view was the size of a dog. Edgar shrieked and flew to attack. His wings snapped, his beak jabbed. The spider retreated into the dark. Edgar settled again on Ginny's shoulder.

"Brave bird," she said. "Noble bird." He gave her a stare and presented his bill. Sighing, she handed him a candy bar. He held it in his beak while one foot clawed the paper off. She stopped to collect those scraps. Even pagan gods think ill of littering.

Winding ever deeper, the tunnel burrowed into rock. She heard water clink where it hit and chuckle where it ran. An underground chill gnawed through her clothes. Breath gusted white in the forlorn radiance she carried.

"How much farther?" she asked.

"Ay dunno," Fjalar replied. "Ve dvarves don't never come *here*. Ve got better sense." Nonetheless he stumped stoutly onward.

The star-point of the wand seemed to pale. Likewise did the murk around. Light had begun to glimmer from ahead. Ginny's feet quickened with her heartbeat. The tunnel dipped, curved, and opened.

A cavern lay before her. She could not tell its size, only that it was huge. The rock itself shone, to make a bluish gloaming, shadowless and windless. Some distance off, black moss ringed silvery water, a pool, no, surely the well. A squared-off block of stone lifted man-high beside, with one side a ramp leading down to it. Something rested on top.

Fjalar jarred to a halt. After a paralyzed moment, he took off his woolen cap. Edgar hunched down where he sat. Ginny's wand flickered.

She needed none of these tokens. Witch nerves shivered with the knowledge that she had reached her goal.

Slowly she advanced, the dwarf now at her heels. The silence grew and grew. As she neared, she saw runes graven in the block, but could not read them. She drew as close as she dared, stopped, and met the gaze of the head.

Had it somehow turned on its altar to confront her? Larger than human it seemed, though she could not give a measure to it. Hair and beard fell white over the stone, around livid skin tight across jutting bones. Eyes deep-sunken under the brows did not gleam like living eyes; they had had no tears since Mimir died. Odin embalmed the head and called the awareness back, to counsel him with insight from the Otherworld; but nothing was left that wept or laughed, feared or loved.

Ginny heard Fjalar's teeth clatter. He set them and trod gamely forward, bowed till his own beard brushed the ground, and stuttered a salutation in Old Norse.

Lips parted. A dry tongue stirred behind them. The words that rolled forth were deep, iron-hard, with an eerie hiss. Ginny did not try to wonder how that throatless, lungless thing formed them. She knew a sword that did likewise.

Nor had she spent scarce time filling her brain with this language. The words and phrases she used professionally had given her a hook on it, which she expected Mimir could seize. From her pouch she drew a crystal into which his speech and hers had been 'chanted. She held it in her left hand, waved her wand around it, and uttered the activating charm.

Light blazed briefly out of it. The grating sibilance became English: "I have learned. Put that toy away."

She obeyed. "Hail and honor to the Wise One," she said, faintly surprised at how steady her own voice was. "I am Virginia Graylock Matuchek, witch, come from across space and time to seek your help."

She'd considered using a johnsmith but decided it would be useless here. Mimir would surely realize it was false and might well feel insulted—that she'd imagine he'd stoop to casting a nymic spell. She dared tell him nothing but the naked truth.

Naked. . . . An impudent thought sparked. She barely choked back a giggle. At least the disembodied head wouldn't mentally undress her. She supposed.

"That you are not from any of our Nine Worlds, I see, I hear, I smell," answered the harshness. "But do you think me a mere corpse, to be raised and questioned?"

"No, no, no!" yelped Fjalar. "There ban nothing mere about you, sir!"

Ginny made a shushing gesture. "Of course not, my lord," she said. "My kin and friends are in desperate need. Enemy wizards have made a riddle no man in our homeland can solve, and laid it on us. Unless we find the answer, and so unbind ourselves from it, we and our works will go under; and what we're waging is a fight against wicked trolls. Recalling how Odin himself seeks to you for advice, I trusted you might grant it to me. Then the name of Mimir and the fame of his great-heartedness—er, his intelligence will always be remembered in our country."

"Hm." The uncanny stare shifted. "You do bear the bird of Odin with you."

"And gifts, sir, such as a guest should bring." Ginny emphasized the word "guest" a trifle, a reminder that hospitality was sacred. "May you find them worthy."

She took off her backpack, opened it, and lifted them out. Considerable thought had gone into the choice. Gold must be plentiful hereabouts; the head couldn't put weapons or fine clothes to use; what then? Well, the Zunis carved beautiful small images, mainly stylized animal figures, in assorted gemstones and minerals. Though many were fetishes, they were often made for sale. Ginny had acquired several fine specimens, a jet buffalo, a pipestone buck sheep, a dolomite deer, a black marble fish, a serpentine snake . . . She spread them on the block before the head.

Mimir studied them. "Yes," he admitted. "Handsome work. And foreign indeed. Contemplating them should pass time for me. You must tell me more about them."

"Gladly, my lord, since you will so generously counsel us."

For the first time, the dead face showed expression. At least, it raised its brows. "Counsel? Did I say that? What you have given will probably oblige me to grant you safe conduct out of here, after you've satisfied my curiosity."

It didn't describe how it proposed to stop her if it wanted to, and she didn't ask. "The fame of your wisdom will reach farther than the boughs of Yggdrasil," she urged. "And I truly believe you'll find the riddle interesting. A challenge nobody in our whole world can meet, a word-skein no mortal man or woman can unravel. I came because I had no doubt that Mimir can," she finished slyly.

The head considered. Silence pressed inward, except for Fjalar's repeated gulps. The dwarf had never seemed daunted before. Ginny wondered if he sensed, still more than she did, how formidable their host really was.

"Well," murmured Mimir after a gape of time, "you have traveled far, with tidings new to me. None else but Odin has ever dared. That deserves something too. I must admit, existence can get tedious, all alone here. . . . Yes-s. Sit down, tell me about it, and I'll see if I can help."

Gladness danced. "Thank you, my lord, thank you!"

"Of course," Mimir said, "I charge for advice."

Fjalar moaned. Edgar bristled his hackles. The cold struck deep into Ginny's bones. "Charge?" she faltered. "What is the price?"

"An eye is customary."

Shock staggered her. "No! I mean—you're joking, my lord."

The head scowled. "I never do."

Yes, Ginny thought at the back of her mind, *it must be hard to keep a sense of humor when you've lost your body.* She grabbed after words. "Is it honorable, my lord, to, to set a price on prowess?"

"Odin paid it. I can take no less from you."

"Awrrk!" croaked Edgar. "Lawyer!"

The retainer Mimir demanded did seem excessive. However, Ginny felt that that line of argument would lead nowhere. She heard: "His eye lies here in the well of wisdom. Each day I drink from it."

How? she wondered wildly. An unpleasant vision arose, of the head rolling down to the water, the eyeball rising, the tongue lapping. . . . And how did Mimir know day from night? . . . "I, I'm not prepared—"

"If your fingers tremble, your raven can pluck it out for you," Mimir suggested. "Right or left, whichever you prefer," he added with fine old-world courtesy.

The images before her became ridiculous. "Edgar? He'd swallow it."

Her wits leaped. "Lawyer!" the raven had cried. She hadn't trained him as a familiar for nothing. The nonhuman life in him strengthened her in her sorceries. And sometimes he *knew.*

She recalled the hairsplitting legalisms of the Icelandic sagas. "But Odin wanted more than I ask for," she protested. Through her rang a verse from—how long ago?—"The Childish Edda."

> "Odin said to Mim, 'I think that I would like a drink.'
> Mim said, 'That will cost you your left eye.
> You have come so very late to the well at wisdom's gate,
> And the setup prices after hours are high.' "

Not exactly lines to sing in this presence. Yet poetry was potent among the Old Norse.

Poetry. Shakespeare. *The Merchant of Venice.*

She rallied, clutched her wand tighter, and told the head: "Besides, if you must have an eye, that doesn't include any blood, does it? Impossible."

Was Mimir actually taken aback? "What warrior counts a little blood loss?"

"That's beside the point. A deal is a deal. You've named it, you should stick by it. Furthermore, I repeat, I don't need any of your water. Just your words."

"What words can you give *me*?" asked the oracle sullenly.

She had made ready for that. A poem of praise was itself a valuable gift. "I am no skald, my lord," she said, while hope rose within her, "but I did do my best to make staves that puff—that compliment you."

The tone brightened a trifle. "You did?"

"The form is different from any that your bards use," Ginny explained. "It is short and end-rhymed. But my people consider it their most powerful way to express the generative force of life."

"I listen," said Mimir almost eagerly.

Ginny took stance, drew breath, and recited:

> "Mimir who dwells by the Well
> Is the wisest 'twixt Heaven and Hell.
> Since his head lacks two hands,
> A heart, and some glands,
> It more thoroughly thinks, I can tell."

Fjalar braced himself against he knew not what. Ginny waited.

"That is . . . unusual," Mimir said.

After a moment: "Nobody ever made a poem for me before."

Abruptly: "Yes, you shall have your skald-gift, witch. I'll read you your riddle."

She fought down a gasp and a wave of weakness. If necessary, for her children's sake and mine, she would have paid the price. It was not necessary.

"You are my guests," Mimir said. "I have no food to give you, but sit down and let us drink together."

Oh, no, you don't, Ginny thought. Once she'd partaken— And yet shared mead or wine sealed the bonds of hospitality. If only she'd packed along some Scotch, as Fjalar wanted. "We are not worthy of this water," she replied. "May we offer you something from our homeland?"

Mimir grunted. Probably he was disappointed that his trick had failed. He might still go temperamental and refuse to cooperate.

She broke out a thermos bottle. "Would my lord like to taste?" She unscrewed the cup, pulled the stopper, poured a serving, and held it out to him.

Did his nostrils dilate at the aroma?

His tongue reached forth. She tilted the cup to his lips. Where the coffee went, she didn't know, but it went fast.

"Aahh!" The stony voice had gone soft. The lips—by every god everywhere, the lips curved into a grin. "This they quaff not in Valhalla! Where's it from? Do you have more?"

"Oh, yes, two jugs."

"Good, good," Mimir purred. "I'm sorry I've no bench to seat you, but do make yourselves comfortable. Ask what you will, my dear. And we'll drink together, won't we?"

"*Ja*," Fjalar muttered, "Ay should have known."

Ginny realized that she too could have foreseen. Mimir was a Scandinavian, after all, a Scandinavian who had just had his first cup of coffee. Naturally he grew quiet and refined.

From then on, events proceeded with the utmost cordiality. The only trouble was that it took so long. Mimir needed to be filled in on the situation. That involved many searching questions and complicated explanations. As hour and hour and hour went by, living flesh wearied. Mimir was tireless; Ginny wouldn't risk upsetting the mood by calling a break; he didn't mind when his visitors ate, and declined a share, but he drank every drop of the coffee; Edgar could tuck head under wing, Fjalar could stretch out his sleeping bag and snore; Ginny must keep on. Exhaustion dragged ever more heavily. The stones beneath her bottom got harder and harder.

Much of the time, the part that felt infinite, she didn't even talk. She sat waiting, or rose to stretch and pace, while Mimir pondered the playout of the tax code. He admitted it made the ultimate Eddic question—"What did Odin whisper in the ear of Baldr when Baldr lay on his pyre?"—look easy. He mumbled and muttered and gnawed his beard, which he caused to float up to his mouth for the purpose. Maybe he'd have been baffled, were it not for her sustaining brew.

In the end, though, the end of endlessness, he worked out the answer. He told her the basics of it—her spirit sang for a minute, before sinking back into ashen weariness—and spoke the technicalities—which took quite a while itself—into the three recording stones she'd brought.

By then she could find nothing to say but, "Thank you, my lord."

"A pleasure, my lady," Mimir replied. "I'll throw in a warning. You war with Powers unknown here; but what you have told shows me they are mighty and crafty. I think one of them has possessed one among your band, hiding too deeply for any skill of yours to find it. Beware—and seek stronger help."

Ginny shuddered.

"I further counsel you to be well rested before you return home," Mimir continued. "There is no foresaying what awaits you, yet I feel some great onslaught is nigh." His solemnity turned amiable, maybe slightly wistful. "You are welcome to sleep here."

"Thank you, my lord," she said, "but, well, I think we'd rest better above ground."

"Yes, this is a hard and cold floor," Mimir agreed. *And a spooky place in general*, she did not remark. "Fare you well, then. Do feel free to come back if you have any other little problems. You'll bring coffee, won't you?"

41

UAL'S DAY AT SCHOOL BECAME A DISASTER. HER ATTENTION KEPT RUNNING AWAY, hounded by fears for us. I was supposedly on a safe errand in strong and knowledgeable company; but what if something went wrong, like a bunch of evil Beings getting on my tail? Her mother claimed she'd be all right too, but hadn't really said much about what she intended, had kind of glossed over her destination. . . . Those squarehead gods were *violent*. Every day at that Valhalla place, a drunken brawl. And the reasons for our gitzy expeditions—hostile demons, the Internal Reaming Service— negative plus! Meanwhile she herself, Valeria Matuchek, was supposed to sit and listen to Miss Prickett dissect *David Copperfield* like the book was a frog in biology class. Unseelie!

So when Mr. Nakamura in history period asked who had been the Spanish conquistador of Mexico and called on her, she blurted, "Coyote." In gramarye Mrs. Kaltfuss sprang a pop quiz and Val totally mangled the conjugation of *venefacio*. In goetics lab, which she'd always loved, they did an elementary pyromantics experiment, mainly to learn safety. Her flame sputtered bilious green. She blew on it and spoke the controlling words, but scrambled those as well. The flame rose, took the form of a clenched hand with an upright middle finger, and vanished.

That broke her. She couldn't hold back the tears any longer. Every- body stared. Larry Weller moved toward her. She waved him back as if she were striking him. Half of what caught at her was rage.

Mr. Escobedo drew her aside. "Are you ill, Valeria?" he asked gently. "You've never made mistakes before."

"I, I, I'm sorry," she gulped, knuckling her eyes. "No, I'm not sick, but—" She couldn't go on.

Being a wise and compassionate man, he didn't inquire further. "I think you should take the rest of the day off," he said. "No blame, no fault of yours. Everybody feels overwhelmed now and then. I'll inform your other teachers." He smiled. "We'll hope to see you happier tomor- row."

"Th-thanks." She walked out with her cheeks wet but her head high.

Bicycling home through indecently cheerful sunlight, she won back her self-control, sort of. Too bad she'd miss geometry period. They were studying Pythagorean significances, which was fascinating. But probably she'd also have cowfooted there today. At least she was free of sex education. That sex could be made boring had been beyond belief till Mr. Tupper started in on the subject.

Stewing and fretting were no help to anybody. Might even cause trouble for the people she loved—bad sympathetics, maybe— She wasn't sure. So much she didn't know. At her age, that thought came as a shock.

Well, she'd take shelter in her room and try to uncoil. How about rereading a Magister Lazarus book? And, after dinner, playing some music to fall asleep by? Who knew but what Daddy and Mom would both be back when she woke, carrying the strange treasures they'd gone in search of?

A breeze blew fragrant off flowerbeds about the neighborhood. They were still brilliant and leaves had not begun to fall. Yet somehow a breath of winter reached her. It conjured glistening blue-shadowed whiteness, snow men, snow angels, snowball fights, sledding, skiing, a fire in the fireplace where chestnuts roasted, and if she and Larry went on a hike and he stole a kiss—she'd make like it was his idea, of course—how extra warm and cider-spicy!

Though not exactly blithe when she reached our house, she felt better able to cope with herself. Dismounted, she wheeled the bike to the garage, whistled the door open, and entered by the adjoining storeroom. Her sneakers made no noise and she wasn't in a mood to shout, "Hi." In fact, she'd have some explaining to do to Uncle Will. He'd understand, the old darling, but she didn't want to bare her soul or anything like that. Pondering what to say, she passed through the kitchen into the hall.

His voice drifted from the living room. "—caution your agents not to fly it off. The ergodics are known only to the designers and builders, but powerful forces are obviously latent. Furthermore, at the moment I don't know where any key is for either vehicle or building. Let me suggest that two men carry it out and put it on a truckrug—"

Val came in. Will sat at the phone. The face before him was Alger Sneep's.

"Oh!" burst from her.

Will twisted about. His features, briefly slack and bloodless, froze. A hand made a chopping gesture. He turned back to the other man. "I think that covers the situation," he said fast.

"We appreciate—" Sneep began.

Will cut him off. "Pardon me. I have to disempath. An urgent personal matter. We'll talk later." He cut the resonance and swung again toward Val.

She quivered under the impact of a world falling apart. "What's that about?" she cried.

"What brings you home so early?" His tone could have slashed chaparral.

"I, I felt bad—they excused me—but, but, Uncle Will—"

"This is unfortunate," he said across the distance between them. "Are you sick?"

"No, I was just worried and scared and— You and *him!*"

"I see." Will stayed mute for a minute. She watched his face soften. Somehow, though, it and his voice never quite became what had cheered and enlightened and comforted her in the past.

He rose, approached, stopped a yard off as if wary of seeming to press himself on her. "I meant to keep this from you, Ben, and Chryssa," he said dully. "Why load bad news onto the fears you already suffer? Your parents will know best how to break it, after they return." He sighed. "Well, you've overheard. I can't be other than honest with you. But will you promise not to tell your brother or sister?"

She had no choice. "Yes, I do."

Will constructed a smile. "Very well." Once he'd have said something like, "All right, then, soldier," and made a gesture, such as knuckles barely touching her shoulder. "The IRS called. The examiner wanted to speak with your parents. When I explained that they're out of town, I don't know where, it apparently catalyzed the agent's suspicions. His office is putting a lien on the property of Operation Luna. Tomorrow they'll seize the spacecraft."

"They can't wait a couple of days?" Val wailed.

"Evidently not. I suppose their superiors have ordered direct action."

"How'd they even *know?*"

He shrugged. "Your parents and their associates haven't tried to keep things strictly secret. Agents may have put two and two together and instigated inquiries. Or they may simply have asked of the FBI. It has me under surveillance, remember. In any case, seizure of a crucial article from a small group like ours is easier than proceeding full tilt against a company like Nornwell."

"And it hurts everybody just as bad! Or worse! Why were you *helping* them?"

"What use, an attempt to lie? Yes, I did volunteer a warning, as you heard. Not that I know precisely how the spacecraft works, but the test flight suggested it can be, hm, tricky. Best play safe. Suppose an agent did try to flit with it and came to grief, perhaps was killed. Wouldn't that prejudice our cause? Also, he wouldn't be a devil, merely a civil servant, probably with a family of his own, doing a job. Let us not be malicious, Valeria."

"And, and not meek either." She whirled and ran from him.

I can't say what went on in the next several hours. I'm a man, not a girl. I no longer feel the storminess of youth. No doubt she wept for a while, alone in her room, raw, racking sobs. Probably Svartalf went "Mneowrr" at her door till she stumbled over and let him in. He'd have joined her on the bed and butted his big black head against her till she curled around him. Then maybe he groomed the disheveled hair. Not that he was ever what you'd call sentimental. Tomcats aren't. However, time had somewhat mellowed the arrogant old bastard.

Unless—well, for most of his life he'd been a witch's familiar. He'd known sorcery, combat, dealings dark as well as bright. Once, for a while, he was the vessel of a spirit who in life had been as rowdy as himself; and together they'd gone along on a harrowing of Hell. Anyway, he wasn't in full retirement. He partnered the witch's and werewolf's daughter as step by step she moved toward her own mastery of the Art.

Maybe he foresaw something. Or maybe he lusted after one last piratical adventure. His purring presence may have done more than console and encourage. It may have generated an idea. Val would only have been aware of the turmoil in herself and a resolution that slowly—or lightning suddenly?—crystallized out of it.

At dinner time she washed her face, combed her hair, and came to the table.

Will had cooked his usual good meal. It went stonily. Ben and Chryssa sensed the tension in the other two. It kept them short-spoken, stiff. Will tried to jolly the party up and failed. He lacked the whimsy they'd formerly enjoyed. His remarks fell wooden, his jokes as flat as a frightened soufflé.

"I'm sure your sister would like a bedtime story from you, Valeria," he said at last.

"Sorry," Val answered, staring at her plate. "I don't feel inspired."

The cloud in Chryssa's eyes threatened rain. "Please," she begged.

"Well, I'll do my poor best," Will offered.

Val raised her head. "No, I guess I can," she decided.

The tale she invented was fairly sinister, Moldylocks getting chased by a vampire. She'd have won to safety by crossing a brook, but was unwilling to wade through water. Barely ahead of pursuit, she came on an Italian restaurant and ducked in. The vampire couldn't pass the crucifix over the door. He lurked outside. After eating a large meal, Moldylocks stepped forth and breathed on him. He started to flee, turning himself into a bat. In his panic he got it wrong and became a baseball bat. Since now he could neither speak nor gesture, this condition was permanent. Moldylocks gave him to a bush-league player she met on her way home to belch. Chryssa fell asleep reasonably content.

Val joined Will and Ben at the farseer for the "Alice the Goon" show. Though it was pretty funny, nobody laughed. She said goodnight before it closed.

In her room she set the alarm clock for silent awakening at four, changed to pajamas, and crept into bed. Svartalf crouched beside her. His eyes gleamed yellow in the gloom. She didn't fall asleep soon, and then fragments of dream gibbered.

It was almost a blessing when the clock sprouted an arm and shook her. In spite of the uneasy night, she woke keenly alert, charged by excitement. Stealing forth—she could always claim an errand to the bathroom—she found the house lightless and soundless. Returning, she switched on an edison; no unnecessary, revealing goetics. "Shh, Svartalf," she whispered. The cat arched his back and bottled his tail.

She dressed quickly: underwear, warm shirt and jacket, Levi's, wool socks, again the sneakers, a hat to shade her after sunrise. A wallet with some allowance money went into a rear pocket. Svartalf padding behind, she entered my study, where she took the keys to smithy and spacecraft that she knew about but Uncle Will didn't.

Nothing stirred. Poor man, he slept so much and so heavily these nights. Not to rouse him. He'd have to forbid her enterprise. This way, he, like her parents, would be uninvolved.

They'd get terribly worried, of course. Having shut off the kitchen and illuminated it, she scribbled on the reminder pad, "I'm sorry. I had to try and save your moon boat. The broom will be at the workshop. I will be okay. You will hear from me real soon. I love you. Val." Her vision blurred. She blinked fiercely. No, damn it, she would not cry anymore.

Food. She constructed sandwiches, wrapped them, and stuck them in her jacket. Candy would be helpful too, when her strength flagged. For a moment she grinned. The best excuse in the world to scarf down some Venus Bars and Elf Mounds. Never mind if they gave her a few zits.

From the storeroom she fetched a saintelmo and a couple of canteens, which she filled with water and belted on her flanks. Dousing the kitchen light, she tiptoed out into the garage. Svartalf ghosted alongside.

Both Matuchek brooms were elsewhere. The saintelmo picked Uncle Will's staid Völve out of the murk. She lifted the cat—he felt heavier than before—and put him on the front seat. "Okay, fuzzface," she murmured. "You know what I want. Do your stuff."

She set up the conditions for him with a simple cantrip such as she'd learned in school. It was quite insufficient, especially since her inhibitions about misuse weakened it. Svartalf wasn't burdened with morals. He'd acquired some powers during his long association with Ginny. Given a preliminary charm, he needed just a short meow-song and a gleeful gesture of his tail to hotspell the vehicle.

The girl quelled her conscience and boarded. A skulky trick to play on Uncle Will. She'd considered using her bicycle, but thirty-odd miles over bad road in the dark would have wiped her. Nor could she be sure of arriving at the right time, dawnlight to pilot by and nobody around to notice. She was only borrowing this stick. Uncle Will could easily get a lift with somebody and retrieve it. He was bound to forgive her as soon as he understood why she must go. Wasn't he? And the police would overlook the fact she didn't have a flyer's license. Wouldn't they?

She definitely had the skill. Very quietly, she commanded the door open and steered the broom forth.

What about the Fibbies? If they were watching— But their detectors would show it wasn't Uncle Will leaving the house, and her mother's wardings blocked them from seeing or hearing anything that happened inside. She didn't expect they'd trail her. Regardless, her heart thuttered.

She left the town behind. It was as if her doubts and fears stayed there. More and more exultant, she flew south. The moon stood high, well-nigh at the half. The Milky Way swept crackling bright among uncountable stars. The land below intermingled shadows, dim grays, and ruggedness. Each cold breath she drew sparkled through her blood.

No, she swore, the IRS monster wasn't going to grab *Owl* away from her folks and trample on their dreams. She'd flit her—*her*, by the Aegis, not *it*—to a safe hiding place. That obscure canyon where they'd enjoyed a span of peace. . . . She could leave the spacecraft tucked beneath trees, hike out, and take a bus home. Unless she phoned. . . . No, probably better not. Keep the location as secret as possible. Meanwhile Dad and Mom and Uncle Will and honorary Uncle Barney could seek court orders or something. They'd be clearly innocent of this removal, and who'd persecute—prosecute a kid for a, well, a prank? Possession was nine points of the law, she'd heard. She was buying time in which nobody had possession, above all the monster.

Everything is so clear-cut, so certain to work out happily, when you're young.

The east was faintly paling as she passed over Zuni pueblo. Dowa Yalanne sheered across it. Val slowed. Her breath smoked into a tremendous silence. There, the smithy! She slanted to a landing.

Svartalf jumped straight off and relieved himself, unless he was putting his sign on a clump of rabbitbrush. Val dismounted and pulled the keys from her pocket. Numbed, her fingers fumbled before she got the door unlocked.

She stepped into utter blackness. Her saintelmo limned *Owl* against it, lean and taut. Scattered light flashed off the blade hanging nearby.

"Who goes there?" she heard. "That's '*Qui vive?*'if you're Norman. Stand and deliver!"

"Me," she called shakily. "Don't sound any alarm. It's a-a-all right."

"Eh? You, princess? What the devil are you doing at this unsanctified hour? Risky for young ladies, let me tell you, risky, traipsing abroad unescorted after dark. I mind once on Stromsay—became the occasion of a rather pleasant battle, it did—"

"Hush, please hush, sir." She groped toward Fotherwick-Botts. "Later we'll talk. B-but right now we've got to escape."

"What?" roared the sword. "Leave my post? Slink off like a, a, a slinker? Isn't done, I'll have you know. Not British. Or Norwegian."

"You're supposed to guard the spacecraft," Val pointed out. "We've been, uh, betrayed. The enemy'll soon come to steal her. I want to—to—"

"Forestall them. Yes, that's the word, forestall. Unless 'outmaneuver' fits better. Which d'you think, 'forestall' or 'outmaneuver'?"

"I think we'd better get away from here."

"I see. Strategic retreat. Of course I must accompany you."

"Sure. They won't snatch you either, you good old fighter."

"P'r'aps we should make a stand instead?" wondered Fotherwick-Botts. "Your mother wielded me well, except she wouldn't go for the kill. Let me drill you till the villains arrive, and—"

Val sheathed him.

Slinging him at her side, she looked around for the medicine bundles. Just in case. She wasn't about to shoot for the stratosphere. Anyway, probably she couldn't get that high when the pilot stone was just a boringly ordinary piece of local rock. Curtice and everybody said that in low-level flight the craft wasn't much different from a regular broom, aside from being able to go a lot faster if you wanted.

However, Dad had often told her that engineers thought well of—what was the word?—redundancy. Following his principle would feel a tiny bit like having him at her side.

She found the bundles and buckled one onto her back. Another, a miniature, caught her eye. Yes, Svartalf ought to have redundancy too. Abruptly she remembered Balawahdiwa's remark about this, that a small person might need it. Caution, guess, hunch, or something unconsciously heard from someone or something unknown? Eeriness walked the length of her spine.

Therefore she took time to locate the jewel Curtice had used to link herself with the communication crystal and slipped its necklace over her head. Be prepared.

Svartalf didn't object when she fastened his packet on his back. He sprang readily to the rear saddle. His whiskers stood stiff. Did he feel a hunch of his own? She verified that the go-force would provide a steady one gravity beneath him no matter what. It was almost an afterthought to check her own.

She climbed onto the forward saddle. Fotherwick-Botts clunked against a canteen. She inserted the key. "Rise," she pushed past the knot in her throat. "Go straight ahead." *Owl* glided out the door. "Park." She got off, relocked the building, and remounted.

Her hand flicked for a northwest course at a hundred-foot elevation. Once aloft, she'd evoke a map in the control crystal and aim properly at her goal. The broom lifted.

The broom tilted heavenward and took off.

"Hey, wait!" Val screamed. "Stop! Back!"

There was no sense of acceleration. That made the headlong rush all the more horrible. Air boomed around the screenfield. Its noise dwindled to a whine, ever thinner. Stars that dawn had been drowning crowded again into sight. The moon stood hard-edged. Sunrise blazed suddenly behind her. Earth fell away as if down a hole.

She tugged at the key. It stayed frozen in position. No gesture, no command worked. Tumbling upward through terror, she roused the communicator. "Daddy, Mother, help!" she cried. "Please, can you hear me? Anybody? Help!"

42

"VAL!" I SHOUTED. "THAT YOU? WHAT'S WRONG? WHERE ARE YOU?"

"I, I don't know— The broom's gone runaway."

"Huh?" I scrambled from my sleeping bag. "The hell you say!" *The Hell indeed*, I thought. "You mean—oh, no—"

Balawahdiwa was already on his feet. He gripped my hand. Steadiness flowed into me. I became aware of the world. Stars glistered in blackness, but eastward the sky was lightening. The air cloaked me in cold, the dirt gritted beneath my soles.

"Okay, honey," I said. "Calm down. I'm here. Are you in any immediate danger? Aside from your problem, that is. Are you hurt? A prisoner?" I choked on a killing fury. If some creature had dared— "Tell me everything you can, and we'll go to work on it."

"No, I—we—we're alive and, and well. Svartalf and me and . . . the sword." I heard how she swallowed. There was a silence of an infinite half minute or so. When she spoke again, her voice was low, almost a monotone, as if she talked in her sleep. "Earth's big, huge, but shrinking so fast. Mostly it's dark. I can still make out bunches of lights, cities, I guess. Some strung like pearls. . . . A thin bright curve, all blue and white. The sun's just above it . . . beside it. . . . I can look straight at the sun and it doesn't hurt my eyes. Like looking through a filter. That's the medicine pack protection, isn't it? Everywhere else I look, more and more stars. I've never seen so many. And they're *around* me. The Milky Way goes clear around the sky."

"Jesus Christ!" I yelled. "You're in space?"

"Y-yes. Moving faster and faster, I think."

"You're aboard *Owl*? Bound for the moon?"

The voice gathered strength and clarity. "No, we're heading straight away from Earth and sun. The moon's falling behind too. I have to turn my head back to see them."

My mind, gone quick and sharp, detached from the fear and grief in my heart, drew a diagram for me. My tone flattened. "Then you're bound into really deep space. Probably your acceleration vector points straight outward. Your speed's increasing second by second. Don't panic. Think hard. What made this mess, and what have you tried to do about it?"

She replied straightforwardly and to the point. *That's my girl*, thought the feeling part of me. "The IRS was going to seize your spacecraft and all the other stuff before you or Mother came home. Wouldn't that ruin everything for you? I decided I'd fly her to a hiding place. Then you'd have time to figure out what to do. But as soon as I took off from parking stance, she zoomed straight up. The steering crystal is blank. Nothing responds except, I guess, the communicator."

My soul groaned, wanted to turn her over my knee, wanted to hug the valiant lass close to me and weep. Any of it, a waste of time. "That should certainly not be. You ought to've been able to fly her the way you intended. Or if for some reason she did run wild, she ought to've headed for the moon. Something's radically wrong. Okay, let's try this. Listen and repeat back to me."

I led her through what spells and other procedures I knew that she could do without special equipment. They should have restored control. They didn't. The sun rose over me. Earth dwindled behind Valeria. I had her estimate the rate from the constellations the disc occupied. By then she was cool—I shied back from that word—and, within her limits, competent. About two gravities of boost, I reckoned. *We* hadn't planned a moon flight that hot.

At least the part of the system that kept a steady one gee on the normal to the long axis was still working. Otherwise—no, I would not think about that.

"All right," I told her. "One or more major parameters have changed, and I've got no way where I am to discover which. Balawahdiwa and I are off in the Zuni Mountains. Our only outside link is with you. Your mother hasn't returned yet, or we'd have heard from her through her connection. Our stick is miles from here. I'm going after it as fast as possible, which means wolf shape. It'll take an hour or more." By which time she'd be approaching the orbit of the moon. "Evidently your medicine bundle is preserving you. Hang on, sweetheart. I can't answer you while I'm running, unless you'd like a yip now and then. But put together an account of what's happened and how, and give it to me as I go. The more information we have, the quicker we can bring you home."

If ever we do stayed unspoken.

"Sure," she replied. "I'm awful sorry about this. Thanks for everything, Daddy. Love you."

"Love you right back."

"I'll wait," Balawahdiwa said quietly. "I'll pray as best I can."

"Thanks," I mumbled.

"Before you transform, Steven, let me suggest you drink a quart or two of water. Even werewolves can overexert and dehydrate."

"Good idea. Thanks once more."

Having gulped a bellyful, I crawled back into my bag, pulled the cover over my head, and changed. Balawahdiwa stroked me as I emerged. His other hand made a sign of blessing. I loped.

Brush, rock, soil fled past. Sometimes a jackrabbit bolted. The sun climbed. Odors of growth awakened. Air warmed. Toward the end it was like a furnace blast in and out of my gullet. I paid no heed to anything but the running.

Valeria told her tale. My wolf brain couldn't follow it closely, but stashed it in memory for later attention. My wolf body wanted to rip throats. My wolf spirit wanted to howl for my mate. Pointless. Nor had I breath to spare.

When at last, nightmarishly at last, I reached the stick, I fell on my side and struggled for air. My heart hammered. A were recovers fast, though, from whatever doesn't outright kill him. Soon I could lurch up, crawl into the coffer, and transform.

"How're you doing, Val?" I croaked.

"The same," she said, "except Earth and the moon, they've really shrunk, and they're both the thinnest crescents, with the sun between them. Everywhere else, stars." After a moment: "Space is beautiful. More beautiful than I imagined." Did I catch the ghost of a laugh? "Even Svartalf looks awed. He jumped from his saddle to me. I caught him and put him on my lap. He sits there and stares out of big, round eyes. How are *you*, Daddy?"

"About to set things in motion, I hope."

"Mother?"

"Not yet. We'll know it when she does report in."

"Oh, won't we! And Mr. Sneep and NASA and everybody." The forlorn gaiety faltered. "If she—"

"No ifs," I decreed. "She will. Now I've got to fetch Balawahdiwa and analyze what you told me and start calling around. Break in anytime, if anything changes. Understand?"

"Yes. I understand."

"I'll check with you every chance I get. Not to make a pest of myself, but—"

"You can't. It's lonely here." Again she paused. "I'll be fine. Honest, I will."

"If you grow desperate for conversation," I said absurdly, "you can draw Fotherwick-Botts." Since the sword, lacking a mouth, spoke by goetic generation of sound waves, he should be able to affect the communication crystal, which would act on the jewel mike, which in turn would vibrate her eardrums. My locket should pick it up also. Not an elegant system, from an engineer's viewpoint. No matter. *Owl* was what we needed to make work—right.

Her answer came grave. "I guess I should. It must be lonely for him too."

I had no better response than, "Okay, pony. I'm on my way. Hang tight."

The flit to camp was quick. I considered what Val had told and sketched plans. On landing, I drank a lot more water. Balawahdiwa gave me some jerky and Zuni-style bread. I realized, dimly surprised, that I was hungry. He'd arranged our things. We didn't stop to load most of them, just what was sacred or otherwise essential. I dressed. We lofted.

"Ha!" brayed on my breast. "Bound from the flinkin' mortal world, are we? Hardly for Heaven. No offense, young lady, but I doubt you've made sainthood yet. Besides, how the deuce could I and the cat? And we have evil at work. I sense the traces of it on this steel steed. Stinks like the dead horse I once saw a trebuchet throw into a besieged city. Well, well, courage. Keep up the side. We won't likely crash through any crystal spheres. What say you practice with me? Against enemy ambuscade, y'know. Good for morale, a round of drill, if it's not punishment drill, and even that teaches a lesson, what? We'll begin with presenting arms—"

I lowered the volume to bare audibility. If Val needed my counsel, she'd yell loud enough for me to hear and tune up.

As if seeking a moment of shelter, my thoughts stayed with Fotherwick-Botts. Originally Ginny and I meant to return him to St. Oswald's, the same clandestine way we'd borrowed him, assuming either of us got through this brannigan alive. But having learned what his nature was, we couldn't condemn him to lie in solitary confinement, gagged, for more decades, maybe centuries.

Events might bring our role to light regardless. Then we'd have to confess, plead necessity, and hope for leniency. No doubt we'd be fully pardoned if the kuei had been exposed and expelled. If.

Victorious, we'd rather not endure the publicity. The aftermath of our Hell foray had shown us what that meant. Well, we could lay the sword back in his case as we'd first planned. Then Frogmorton could claim a scholarly interest and request to examine him, which would surely be granted. We'd have gotten the promise of both not to say anything about us.

However the revelation happened, Fotherwick-Botts' future was guaranteed. He'd be a treasure for historians. I visualized him going on the lecture circuit—where he wouldn't have to eat creamed chicken—before accepting a professorship. The only question would be whether he chose a famous university or a military academy.

Provided, of course, that he survived and our cause did.

The subject dropped out of me as Zuni hove into sight. We set down at Balawahdiwa's house. He anticipated my words: "By all means use the phone here, Steven. Don't lose time, go straight in. I'll take care of the stuff."

Tribesfolk in the lane on their early morning errands gave us curious glances. I ignored them and opened the door. "Excuse me, Mrs., uh, Adams," I said to the lady. I couldn't remember her native name. Ought to be ashamed of myself. No, under the circumstances, who could blame me? Anyhow, maybe the Anglo one was more respectful, coming from a *Melika*. Never mind. I went to the phone and called home.

Will's face appeared. He didn't look well rested. "Oh . . . Steve. What's this? You woke me."

"None too damn soon," I snapped. He'd have had to leave the feathers shortly anyway, to fix breakfast and otherwise start the kids on their day. Unless he relied on Val. No, negligence wasn't like him. Not that he'd been much like himself very often of late.

The possibility that Ginny and I had recognized and denied, with the psychoscopic results to give confidence, rose again. Half of me struggled to hold back a sickness. Couldn't be, mustn't be! The other half somehow went on: "Emergency. Rouse Ben and Chryssa. Pack clothes and teeth-breesh for them. I'm asking the Goldsteins to come take them in."

Instant alertness peered back at me and demanded, "Why?" in as cold a voice as I'd ever heard.

"No offense, Will. But there's hell to pay, and I don't want the bill collected from my children."

"A demon? This house is secured, I'm told. They should be safer here than anywhere else. Particularly if it's under federal observation."

"I'll decide that. Neither you nor those Fibbies are trained to know every trick evil can play. Besides, we may need your help." If this man was harmless—*Please, God, let him be*—his knowledge could be valuable. If not—against that *if*, the youngsters must damn well clear out of there.

"I notice you didn't mention Valeria," he said.

"Tell you later." He was bound to find the note she'd left. I guessed he'd guess her vulnerability was what terrified me, not anything concerning him. "Take too long right now. Make Ben and Chryssa ready. Sam or Martha Goldstein should arrive in a few minutes. Or somebody else, if I can't raise them. The police, if need be. Move, man! And then sit tight. You'll hear from me again. Savvy?"

A stiff nod replied.

I disempathed and touched our friends' glyphs, Martha answered. "Why, good morning, Steve. How are you? Frankly, you look terrible. Something is wrong, maybe?"

"You bet it is," I grated. "I can't explain, not right away, but Ginny's not here and our two younger ones need a place to stay. Immediately."

"You had a fire or—" The plump features steadied, the tone firmed. "No. I can see. A guest bed we have, and the crib from when Esther was little is in the attic. I'll tell Sam. He'll be right over. Don't worry, Steve. We'll be delighted. Danny especially, having his friend Ben here."

"Don't send mine to school or the nursery. Keep them indoors. It should be just for a day or two, or less, till Ginny gets home and things straighten out."

She regarded me closely. "They are very tangled, *nu*? I won't say this is what comes of dealing with the Darkness—"

"We didn't, Martha. It, well, it wished itself onto us."

She raised a hand. "Hush, Steve. I know. You and Ginny would never make bad. What I'm saying is, if you don't mind, we will ask Rabbi Levinson to come and give our house a new *barucha*."

"Do I mind? Y-y-your God bless you," I stammered, blinking back tears.

This was why I'd turned first to this family. Not only were they goodhearted and reliable; they believed, and practiced their belief. I didn't see how wicked spirits could pass through the holiness that guarded those doors.

They might lay siege. But they wouldn't, I calculated. That would expose their game too blatantly. Ginny's and my house, however well antihexed, wasn't the same case. Its defenses were purely goetic, and technology can outwit technology. Moreover, it was a focus of the enemy's interest.

And maybe it had already been invaded.

No, I would not accept that notion, not yet. *Not ever, please.* Was my wordless agnostic prayer worth anything? If only we too could sincerely believe. But we were what we were; in our minds, belief was a powerful force if you really had it, with no doubts or reservations, an attitude we'd never managed to reconcile with a slew of disturbing questions. Intelligence had nothing to do with that. Sam, for instance, was smarter than me, more widely read, better at math, and so on. It was a matter of psychology.

Enough! What next? Recalling Val from the outer deeps. Which I should approach as an engineering problem. Else helplessness and hysteria would grab me.

I glanced at my watch. Amazingly, the hour was still too early for anyone who mattered at Cardinal Point to be on hand. Not that much help was available there. Sure, everybody would be sympathetic, in the emotional sense of the word. But how many of them had knowledge, let alone experience, of Operation Luna? Not Incanted Here. They'd call meetings, at which I'd have to appear, and—

Al-Bunni was supposedly in Washington, where people weren't quite ready to go to lunch. I unscrolled the national directory and reached an office where they might be in touch with him. They weren't. Having testified before Congress (again!) and done whatever other lobbying he'd come for, he'd taken a long weekend off, leaving no information about his itinerary. Not unreasonable. I'd probably have done the same.

But by Monday Val would be half a billion miles or so from us, among the farthest comets, her speed maybe at a point where the medicine bundle could no longer fend off the hard radiation of collision with atoms and dust. Before then, she'd have run out of food and water.

What use calling al-Bunni, anyhow? He'd given Operation Luna ideas that made all the difference. However, by now I understood them as well as he did, if not better. Cut-and-try experience counts for more than theory. Jim Franklin had contributed, but mainly to communications, which were functioning well in spite of everything. Ginny and Fjalar were those we most needed. How much longer would they be out of touch?

A thought hit me.

First I checked back with the Goldsteins. They'd collected the kids, who were bewildered and sort of scared but well on their way to being comforted. Then I called Will.

He'd found the note. I saw him white, shivering, appalled. "Valeria actually did it?" he whispered. "Yes, my broom is missing. But she— What have you heard from her?"

I'd had my fill of pussyfooting. "The spacecraft went crazy. She's bound for outer space. I mean outer. Any ideas for getting her back?"

"No . . . no. . . ." Face and voice stiffened. "This is incredible. How may I help?"

"For the time being, stay put. We don't need your Fibbie shadows while we try to cope with this." A reminder, just in case, that they were there. "Think. Pray, if you're able." After a few more words, I cut off.

Balawahdiwa had entered the house. He stood above me like an image of its austerity. "My fellows and I will seek knowledge," he said. "Maybe the Beloved Ones will speak to us."

Why utter more thanks? He knew how I felt. "Good, I expect I'll be in the smithy. That's where everything is that we Anglos can use, plans, records, apparatus. I might find a clue to what's wrong and how to turn that damned shaft around."

"Your technics won't be all that's necessary, I suspect," he said. "But they won't be useless either. Yes, go and work on them," and find what consolation I could in the work.

"One more call from here, if you please."

I got hold of Curtice Newton. "Hi," she greeted. "You caught me barely in time. I was about to take off for the Point and yawn my way through another day." Like Martha before her, she looked closer. The image of the red head leaned toward me. "Hey, this isn't fun anymore, is it?"

"No." I explained. By the end, I was gulping and stuttering. "Y-you know things about *Owl* nobody else does. And, uh, and you're a good technician. Could you come and, well, help me figure this thing out?"

"Judas priest, Steve," she exclaimed, "why did you suppose you had to ask? Sure. The workshop, you said? I'll be there pronto. Fast as I can finish in the kitchen."

"Huh?"

"Poor man, I'll bet you've forgotten about lunch. I'll pack a basket for us, and coffee and such. You want a clear head, not a growling stomach. Wouldn't hurt if I stuck a couple of beers in the cooler, too."

43

THE SUN WHEELED HIGHER. THE LAND WARMED, BUT NOT MUCH MORE, BECAUSE A WIND blew from the west. Clouds were massing on that horizon. Drifts of them passed overhead. Light and shadow played across Dowa Yalanne, as though the rock of it stirred.

Curtice and I hardly noticed. Even before she arrived, and she'd burned the air on her way, I'd been occupied. Besides Fjalar's tools, forge, runestones, and whatnot, the smithy was loaded with the scientific and engineering equipment that had analyzed, measured, and tested as the spacecraft came into being. Strain gauge, voltmeter, tarot, polarimeter, dowser, reckoner, mummy dust, microscope, you name it, probably you could find it here. I set about arranging things for use.

Curtice strode in. She spent one second giving me a smile full of compassion, then asked, "How can I talk with the girl?"

"Through this." I took off my locket, tuned it up, and handed it to her.

"—slantwise," we heard. "You've no shield, y'know—bally carelessness—so my blade'll have to defend as well as attack. I'm no la-de-da rapier, but it is possible. Yes, like that. Now, a slicing cut. . . . No, don't hew. Draw across. A feint, but with luck you might take off his nose. Again. Again. Hup, hup, hup—"

Curtice stared at me. "What in the jumping blue dickens?"

"She's got a talking sword along," I explained. "And our old tomcat."

"Well, I knew it's weird out, but I didn't expect—" The woman shrugged, brought the locket to her lips, and said crisply: "Hello, Valeria Matuchek. Curtice Newton on the line. Stow that drill and listen." Her tone softened. "How are you, honey?"

Fotherwick-Botts sputtered to silence. Val's reply trembled. "You, Captain Newton? W-we're alive. Still speeding away. Earth's nearly lost in the sun-glare. B-but you—" I pictured a few tears breaking forth, tears of sudden joy. She idolized the celestonaut.

"Good. Your father and I aim to turn you around and haul you home. For openers, we need to discover what's caused this. Stand by to answer questions as they occur to us. We may ask you to make some observations too, as best you can. Okay?"

The voice rang—thinly, but it rang. "Yes, ma'am."

"Keep on with what you're doing, Steve," Curtice told me. "I want to get the details for myself." I obeyed. My hands and most of my mind made a complex of instruments ready. With half an ear I heard inquiries more incisive than any of mine.

"All right," Curtice said at length. To me: "I have a hunch of sorts, but we need confirmation and more exact data. You know better than I how to handle most of this gear."

"And you know better what to look for." I leaned close to the locket, which she'd hung about her neck. The scenery was admirable, but I didn't stop to enjoy. "This is a technical problem, Val. It may take a while to crack. Don't think we've gone cold and unfeeling. Time enough to hug you—" My words stumbled. "—when you're back with us."

"Sure, Daddy. Er, General Fotherwick-Botts, sir, excuse me, please, but I think I ought to sheathe you. Svartalf, if you don't stop kneading my lap you can go back to the rear saddle!"

I won't describe the next half hour or so. To you it would be a dry list of procedures, tests, readings, calculations; to me the recollection would be hurtful. That's twice true of when we had to call on Valeria. An eyeball estimate from her seat wasn't worrisome. However, when she must crawl along the shaft, both backward and forward, to lay hands on straws and on nose cap, gathering impressions that the resonance sent for us to interpret— No. I see her too clearly, silhouetted against the unforgiving stars. One blunder and she'd drift free, to fall among them forever.

Oh, sure, she made light of my fears, and Curtice vowed that any agile young person could easily manage. "Do you suppose I'd have asked her to, otherwise?" Nevertheless—

The report stabbed: "I'm unscrewing the cap. . . . Reaching in. . . . The stone— Yow-w-w, I'm dropping!"

"Keep your legs wrapped around the shaft as I told you to," Curtice answered. "Don't lose that hold, whatever you do."

"But what's happening?"

"Free trajectory. When the pilot stone's removed, acceleration stops. You've still got the field giving you a one gee pull, but when the shaft is all that's under you, you can too easily slip off. In fact, most of you is bound to be out of line and feeling the weightlessness. Are you all right? Any nausea or dizziness?"

"N-no. I was just surprised. It feels. . . . it feels fun." *What a girl*, I thought dazedly. "I almost let go of the stone, but curled my fingers in time."

"Well done. Look at it. Describe it."

"The sunlight and shadows here, they're kind of confusing, but— It's blackish, lumpy. When I look close, I see. . . . like little grains embedded."

Curtice's face had become a bloodless mask. "Very well. Put it in your pocket and return to your saddle. Better fasten your safety harness."

"Svartalf's first."

Panic grabbed. "Hey!" I yelped. "That's not a—"

Curtice waved me to keep mum. "I'm back," Val called after a few minutes. The sweat on me reeked.

"Good," the celestonaut said. "I didn't want to risk startling you so you lost your grip on the stick. That's probably a chondrite. It's positively not terrestrial or lunar."

I leaped to the cabinet, unlocked drawers, yanked them open and slammed them shut again. Yes, one of the samples was missing. Its identification label mocked me.—*believed to have come from a collision in the asteroid belt, but there are some indications of an origin more remote, possibly the Kuiper belt*— The ring of comets beyond the orbit of Neptune.

"That bit of Earth sandstone was supposed to be still in the nose," I moaned. "Somebody switched it for—for—" My throat seized up on me.

Curtice nodded. "For a rock with an outwardness so great it overrides all ordinary control. A counterspell would have curbed it, but no one imagined any would be needed yet. The next test flight, you remember, was only planned to check maneuverability at low altitudes. Chances are, our pilot wouldn't have bothered with a medicine bundle. Death within seconds, as the craft shot beyond breathable atmosphere. With no living person aboard, we'd have no hope of recalling her. End of Operation Luna, very likely of Project Selene too."

"But who—"

"Later. Valeria, did you hear? Don't be afraid. You *are* alive and well. We *can* get you back."

"I know," said the brave, dear voice. "Daddy and Mother got me back from Hell once, didn't they? This should be a, a cracklesnap."

"Not exactly," I must confess. "We don't know offhand how to do it. But we'll find out, by God. Hang in there."

"At least she's no longer adding to that huge velocity," Curtice muttered. "As for reversing it—"

A new sound broke in from the locket on her bosom. "Steve? Fjalar and I have returned. What I heard— What's the matter?"

"Ginny!" I exploded. "You're okay?"

"We're fine, except hungry. But what's wrong here?"

Valeria, Curtice, and I told her. Well before we finished, she and the dwarf were demolishing speed limits in our direction.

"Oh, if only I'd come back sooner." Never before had I heard her wail. She mastered it and continued steadily. "Our mission was successful but exhausting. We decided we'd do best to arrive home rested, and slept the night through beside Yggdrasil. If I'd known, if I'd even guessed—"

"You couldn't have," Valeria said.

"Nor could you control the exact time when you'd return," I reminded.

"Or vat Ratatosk, or whoever it vas, did to the shed," Fjalar added. "It held, but it vill never be mush good again."

As always when the chips were down, Ginny became straight business. "We'll see you in about half an hour. Phone Balawahdiwa and inform him."

I tried, but as well as I could understand his wife, she said he'd left for a while. Making medicine, I supposed. "Shall I let Will know?" I asked.

"*No.*" Ginny's tone was like sudden midwinter. The suspicions that had been nastily floating in me congealed.

Before my guts quite felt the weight and chill of them, Curtice said, "Uh-oh. We've got visitors."

I looked through a window. Tatters of cloud sent shadows scything across the desert. Brush stirred to the breeze. A broom and a truckrug had set down by the other vehicles. Dust puffed and blew away from their extended legs. Each carried two men. Three were big, neatly dressed but like laborers, the fourth small and in a business suit. He had a briefcase along.

Memory rammed through my tension. "Yeah." Words I'd once seen on a tombstone in an old New England graveyard: "I expected this, but not so soon."

"What?" Curtice asked.

"Our wonderful government. Its income tax tentacle. Precisely what we need."

"They'll be disappointed!" laughed Val from her aloneness.

Anger put a good, clean taste in my mouth. I opened the door. Alger Sneep jarred to a startled halt. His companions stopped more slowly. They carried a sledgehammer, a crowbar, and a spell checker. The air that sighed around them seemed to have gotten a touch less warm than when I arrived.

"Mr. Matuchek!" Sneep yelped. "What are you doing here?"

"I'd like to hear the same from you," I replied.

He drew himself up to his full, negligible height. "I have an order to seize this alleged spacecraft and any other relevant material, and sequester the site."

Ginny was bound for us. She'd said her expedition had succeeded. I'd better play for time. Lounging in the doorway, I drawled, "Would you mind telling me the reason? I'm kind of curious. Maybe you'll agree that's natural."

"You have received notice that you, your associates, and your business are under investigation—"

"Have we?" I interrupted. "Sorry, but some troubles have driven a lot of things out of my head, Let me think a bit." I made a production of running fingers through my hair, rolling my eyes, and similar foolishness. "Um-m . . . yes, I do seem to recall something like that. But really, we're honest, law-abiding citizens in these parts. We might not always agree that our taxes are remotely in proportion to what we, or anybody except the favored few, get in return, or that the founders of this nation would condone the method of collection, but our returns are complete and accurate."

"That is what is in dispute, Mr. Matuchek. Please let us by." Sneep's plug-uglies, who'd been obviously disgruntled that they weren't going to bash their way in, began to look hopeful.

"Of course, of course. I wouldn't dream of obstructing justice. Assuming it is justice. Actually, my objections to the system are basically, uh, philosophical. Plato doubtless wouldn't have shared them. But he was a totalitarian, as his *Republic* makes plain, and an idealist, meaning he imagined the world around us is all in our heads and only his abstract archetypes actually exist. Those positions often go together, you know. The idea that our experience of reality is more direct leads to the concept of the human being as a, uh, maybe not a Cartesian monad, but a separate individual with individual rights. For instance, Locke—" I was fudging it from a couple of vaguely remembered college courses.

Sneep suppressed a yell. "I am not here to discuss philosophy!"

I nodded. "Or, as Anthony said to Cleopatra, 'I am not prone to argue.'"

"Will you step aside, Mr. Matuchek, or must I invoke the law?"

Before his troops could lick their lips, I made an expansive gesture and declared, "Far be it from me to interfere with an officer in the performance of his duties. That's what I was trying to tell you. Come right into our humble shop. Make yourselves . . . at home, I mean. But first, just so you won't suppose we aim to spring anything on you, let me introduce the lady. Curtice, would you step out for a minute?"

She did. "How do you do," she said. Her voice implied she was not remotely interested in the answer.

"Curtice Newton, please meet Mr. Alger Sneep of the Inquisition for Revenue Securement. I'm sorry, I don't know you other gentlemen. If you'll give me your names, I'll do you the honor of introducing you, too."

"Never mind," snapped Sneep. "How do you do, Miss Newton."

"Captain Newton," I corrected him. "The distinguished celestonaut. You must have seen her on the farseer. Her record goes back to well before the space program. She was a test pilot with Boeing, and set a still unbroken record for—"

"Yes, yes. Let us *by*."

"Certainly. Curtice, would you go back inside? And now me. This is a pretty narrow door, but then, we're on a tight budget, as you doubtless know. I should explain that Captain Newton is here to give advice on a problem. We're always getting surprises in this business." I winced. "Some are unpleasant."

Did I hear Valeria gulp and Ginny snarl?

The agents entered. For a moment they blinked. In spite of the cloud-rags, the outside was brilliant compared to the interior. Fjalar liked his workplaces gloomy.

"But—but where is the spacecraft?" Sneep said.

"That's what we're trying to learn," I told him, not untruthfully. We didn't have an exact fix.

"Somebody busted in and stole it?" growled one of the bruisers.

"No," I said. "She was taken out—" My glibness broke down. "For damn good reasons. Now she's lost."

Sneep's eyes needled me. His followers glowered. "Is this an attempt to forestall seizure?" he demanded.

"How could it be? No papers had been served on us. And by the way, I want to see those you've got."

"Do not raise more obstacles, Mr. Matuchek. I warn you. And you, Captain Newton. We shall have to investigate your involvement in this matter."

Even in the dimness, I saw her tauten. Rage flamed through me. I struggled to keep it down. "Ever hear of the Fourth Amendment, Mr. Sneep?" I rasped.

"That is for a tax court to interpret. Thus far, judgments have generally been in favor of our service." Sneep turned to the others. "Load as much of this material on the carpet as you can. I'll be asking questions meanwhile." He produced a minirecorder from his jacket. "You will be well advised to give prompt and correct replies, Mr. Matuchek, Captain Newton."

My eyes went toward an upright cabinet in the rear. It had room to hold a man. Curtice grabbed my arm. "No, Steve!"

"I'm here," Ginny called, maybe barely in time.

She stalked through the doorway. Edgar hunched black and ominous on her shoulder. Fjalar stumped behind, hair and whiskers bristling like a porcupine, nose a crimson beacon of fury.

"Ah—Mrs.—ah, Dr. Matuchek." Sneep retreated a step. His thugs stopped in their tracks. "Welcome. We have come to—"

"Kindly do not bid me welcome to my own property," she said. "And

I know what your wretched errand is. Listen, Sneep and the rest of you. Listen well. You'll regret it if you don't."

She thrust a lorestone into his shivery hands. "I have just returned from a long session with a very special advisor. He analyzed our case not only item by item, down to the last cent, but from every aspect of the entire United States tax code. Take this back to your office and play it. I will dispatch a copy to Mr. Sturlason of Nornwell Scryotronics and retain one for myself. It will take you some time and effort to go through the calculations and logic, but I assure you they are steel-clad. You will find we are absolutely in the right. I do not claim we followed every jot and tittle of the technicalities. That would be impossible for any mortal. Furthermore, as this report demonstrates, there are numerous contradictions. But it turns out that none of us owes a thing. Rather, the Nornwell company has, over the past three years, overpaid by a total of approximately fifteen thousand dollars. This includes Operation Luna, which under the regulations is a legitimate subsidiary. My husband and I, as individuals, have overpaid by approximately nine hundred dollars. Refunds will be expected, with interest."

"Y-you assert this," he stuttered, "but until we, we have gone through the analysis, it's only your word." He stiffened. "Meanwhile—"

She smashed him flat. "Meanwhile, sir, you are delaying the rescue of our daughter, an innocent child." Did I hear Valeria squelch a giggle? "Your overbearing tactics drove her to desperation. She took the spacecraft. No papers had been served, no official notice of any kind given. Therefore the sole possible charge against her is flying without a license, which is not within your jurisdiction. It is trivial. In fact, it's debatable, because this is not an ordinary vehicle. If the charge is considered at all, you know perfectly well it will be dismissed."

"What, what, what do you mean?"

She told him no more than that the flight had gone out of control and astray. Her words were few but whetted. He cringed. His threesome mumbled and bunched their muscles, till Fjalar took his favorite hammer from a bench and tossed it to and fro, rippling his thews at them.

"Our Congressman and both our senators will hear of this," Ginny finished. "We would prefer to keep it from the news media. However, I suggest you think what the consequences will be if we can't. Here you are, as I said, endangering a child's life the more for every minute you inflict yourself on us. I do believe that if we must resort to forcible measures—" She had drawn and extended her wand. The star flared wickedly. I bared teeth, wolf style. "—a jury will find we were justified. Best you return to your office at once and study what I have been kind enough to bring you."

"But I—I didn't know," Sneep half sobbed. "I'm so sorry. I have children too and— I'm sorry!"

Ginny gestured at the door. "Good day, sir."

"Grech, kh-hui," added Edgar.

They shambled out. The sunlight glinted off tears in Sneep's eyes. I almost sympathized. There's little doubt in my mind that the Sixteenth Amendment was inspired directly by Hell, but its agents are human, most of them decent at heart. The jobs they have were the best they could get.

The stick and the rug took off.

Ginny gusted a long breath. The ice fell from her. "They're gone," she said low. "How are you, darling?"

"I'm okay," Val called across the gulf, "but, oh, Mother, I'm sorry too. For giving you this trouble."

"*No importa.* What matters is to free you from it. I think we can, but let's not waste time on sentiment." Ginny turned to Curtice. "Pass that locket back to Steve, please. I'll tune mine down. You and I have work to do. He can keep her company."

"*Ja*, me too," Fjalar boomed. "Ay vill give her heart, songs and stories and visdom."

"No, we'll want you on tap—" He perked up for a split second, then saw what she meant. "—ready to fill us in on any technical questions that may arise. You're the wright, Curtice is the pilot and, in a way, engineer, I'm the thaumaturge. Between us, we'll find an answer. How lucky that Svartalf and Fotherwick-Botts are with her. Both carry a strong ergodic charge. That should give us a handle on the forces, in the absence of a proper lodestone."

Edgar flapped to a stool. The trio went into a huddle around him. I found a corner, sat down, and talked with my daughter. I won't write what we said. She was too gallant; I was fighting too hard to keep up a light and optimistic front.

Ginny interrupted a few times and spoke directly—for instance, when a sortilege revealed that Val should toss away the piece of meteor. May the damned thing orbit into the sun.

Light went down as a man-shape filled the doorway. I surged to my feet and went to meet Balawahdiwa. He'd returned to Zuni and gotten my message. Ginny explained to him that this wasn't his kind of goetics, but begged him to stay because we really would need his help soon. I joined him outside and we continued the conversation with Val. He spoke of beautiful, secret places he'd guide us to, once our troubles were past. The clouds piled higher in the west, snow-bright on top, blue-black in their depths. The wind piped louder and colder.

Brilliance flared in the shed. Something sang like a trumpet. "Hey!"

Val shouted. "The . . . the boat's turning. . . . The sun, Earth, they're *ahead* of me! Daddy, Mother!"

Curtice emerged from the shed. "We've done it," she gasped. "Reversed acceleration— She's coming home, Steve."

Ginny appeared behind her. She didn't whoop and dance like everybody else. Her expression brought us to a dead stop. "It'll take seven or eight hours, if not more," she said. "There's a matter we must deal with immediately. Curtice, Fjalar, will you hold the fort here? Steve—Balawahdiwa, sir—will you ride with me?"

44

THE WIND OF OUR PASSAGE BRAWLED LOUDER THAN THE WIND OVER THE DESERT. ROAD, heights, brushy flats unreeled around us. Edgar crouched on Ginny's shoulder, beak forward, spearlike. Balawahdiwa and I crowded together in the rear of the Jaguar. His fingers clutched a medicine bag, which he had brought along from Zuni, with needless tightness.

When the stick was steering itself, Ginny twisted around and regarded us. The look of her terrified me. "My fault," she said. Each word fell like a stone. "I should have seen from the first. But no, I let wishful thinking take me over."

"Me too?" I mumbled. My vision blurred; I tasted salt on my lips. "Will seemed impossible."

"Everything pointed to him."

"No, but—that time somebody tried to kill us— He isn't capable of any such thing! For sure he couldn't have left his house and returned unobserved, hotspelled that carpet, or shot so well. I— Remember when I took him out on the target range once? Just once. The other guys were laughing too hard."

"The evidence—"

"Frame-up."

"The physical evidence is *there*. Oh, yes, Will never would or could have done any of it. The thing that's possessing him did."

"He passed the psychoscopic exam."

"It's no ordinary demon. I think now it's not strictly speaking a demon at all. It lies deep in him, intertwined with his whole being like a latent virus. When it goes active, it takes him over, body and brain. *He* isn't aware of what happens then, and afterward he doesn't remember."

Balawahdiwa nodded. "Indeed he cannot," he said, "or he would have revealed the truth, or taken his own life if he saw no other way out. Only his spirit knows. Horror and heaviness are upon it."

"Yeah, that depression," I admitted. "But when the thing's using him, it does a great job of faking his real self."

"No demon could control him that cleverly," Ginny said. "This is an infection of the very soul."

Whatever the thing was, I thought, *it needed some practice to begin with. When it entered him, and when it first really used him, it left traces in the form of nightmares. Not anymore.* Desolation gripped me. "It must plant false memories of those times, now that it knows its way around in him."

"Obviously. Harking back, I realize how vague his accounts were. To his conscious mind, whenever the possessor is lying low, it must feel like some kind of mental lapse. That alone would worry him sick." Ginny shook her head. "But he's not one to dump his fears and woes on others. Not Will."

The grief in me was turning to vengefulness. It was as if I heard a clangor and a shrilling inside my skull, a blade forged and honed. "That thing—yes, plain to see—now—it switched lodestones the day we test-flew *Owl*. When he ducked into the smithy. Later on, though—"

"I think it decided to try an alternative approach. It could acquire skills like shooting and evading surveillance from demons that know how. But they and it are not native to America. In many respects it must be naive about this country, learning gradually and piecemeal from Will's brain—who's pretty naive himself—and by observation. It came to understand that if *Owl* took off and killed her pilot, investigation would incriminate him. He's too useful to abandon until it becomes absolutely necessary. Nor would anyone else with such potentials be as easy to invade as he was. Another kind of infiltration looked more promising. I neglected to quiz Sneep, but it seems clear that, when Valeria caught him on the phone, Will—his body—wasn't simply responding to an IRS initiative as he claimed. He had tipped them off and proposed that they sequester the boat."

Ginny had left her communication locket with Curtice. I'd kept mine, and hadn't reduced the gain. Our daughter's voice wavered from afar: "Yes, he, he—*it* warned Mr. Sneep they shouldn't try flying her."

"Uh-huh," I grunted, the way a wild boar might. "Doubtless it could've persuaded them to dismantle her in the course of bankrupting Nornwell and us."

"But Uncle Will, old Uncle Will, how could something that wicked get into him?"

"Because he was—in his heart still is—so innocent," Balawahdiwa answered. "His studies, his previous contact with your Fair Folk, drew the attention of the enemy. He was one they needed to subvert, for his research strongly aided the space program. Possessed, he could be a major force in undermining it. Besides his trustfulness, the work itself had made him vulnerable."

"He never thought to have protective spells cast," Ginny added. Agony: "I never did."

"For God's sake, don't blame yourself," I begged. "Who outside of Hell could have known? Just cure him!"

The steel of her stood forth. "I mean to try, with the help of you two."

Balawahdiwa leaned over, halfway across me. "Valeria," he said gently, "you'd better not hear the rest of this."

"I wouldn't yell," the girl protested.

"No, but it would be hard on you. Besides, you'll likely need to exchange information with Captain Newton from time to time. That would come through to us and be distracting."

"He's right," I said. "Hang in there, punkin. We'll call as soon as possible."

For that instant, Ginny's tone was tender. "Yes, so long, darling. Fare luckily. We love you."

I snapped the off switch on the locket. Part of me wished it were somebody's neck.

"Do you believe we can exorcise the thing?" Balawahdiwa asked. His question sounded stupid to me till I realized how it probed.

"I think that between us we have a chance," Ginny replied. "But first we must secure him."

Gallup appeared ahead, tiny when we glanced at the cloudbanks on our left. She slowed to a legal speed. Getting pulled over and ticketed would eat time.

No doubt the spirit's controlling him at this moment, I thought. *Probably it's been continuously in charge for at least the past couple of days. And we left the kids alone with it.* A knife twisted.

But harming them would've been pointless and could've given the game away, I told myself. Ben and Chryssa were safe now, Val distant a couple of million miles and homebound, homebound. She'd taken his broom. Anyway, the FBI maintained watch on him. True, the possessor had outspelled and eluded them before. However, that was at Will's house. I supposed the charms on ours would complicate, quite possibly forbid any such stunts. And it didn't know what we, Ginny in particular, had been up to. And although I'd removed the kids, I'd left the impression that I trusted Will same as always, because in fact I did . . . then. I imagined it'd figure its best bet was to lie low, alert.

Lightning flickered in cloud-caverns. We landed at our place and dismounted.

"I'll go ahead and catch his attention," Ginny said. "You follow a minute later, Steve, and grab him. He'll resist. Try not to hurt him."

The Medusa mask of her dissolved. She tossed her red locks back as if casting off a burden. Her smile beamed. I don't know how she managed that, sorcery or an innate gift. Balawahdiwa stood impassive. I had all I could do not to howl and attack.

Feather-lightly, Ginny ran up the walk and the front steps. She flung the door open. "Hallo, Will!" she caroled. "I've got news!"

Counting seconds under my breath was better than staring at my watch. One hippogryphius, two hippogryphius, three hippogryphius . . .

The door remained ajar. Words drifted to my tight-strung hearing. "—we routed the tax pack. We're in contact with Val—"

Sixty. I moved. *Easy, easy. Don't rush. Amble.*

Will confronted Ginny in the living room. He saw me enter and nodded absently, his mind on her. "—not sure what the trouble is," she was saying, "but I have a guess. I expect we'll want your help."

Did the brush of gray hair faintly bristle, did the green eyes flare behind the innocuous spectacles? Approaching, I caught a stench of anxiety and . . . malevolence? He nodded. "Of course," he said. "Anything I can do."

Anything the spirit can do to ruin the undertaking and leave our girl adrift.

Balawahdiwa came in, cat-footed, and closed the door. I found my position and pounced.

At Will's back, I caught his arms. I brought them together, pinned them with my left, and swept my right around his throat till that hand joined its mate in a choke hold.

"What—what's this?" He sounded so shocked and bewildered, so Will, that I nearly relaxed and apologized.

Ginny restored my strength: "Stand fast, Steve. Goryo, we are here to drive you out. Will, if you can hear me, if something of you understands, we mean to set you free."

He shrieked, a horrible saw-toothed noise. He threw himself to and fro against my grip. He kicked my shins; the heel of his shoe bit and raked.

Try not to hurt him. The fury became unbelievable. Enough to tear bones from their sockets. I hooked an ankle in front of his, pushed his shoulders, and hung on to keep him from falling too hard. I followed him, though, and lay on top, using my weight to control the writhing, jerking, raving mass.

Ginny had darted off to the storeroom. She returned with a length of stout cord. Tears whipped down her cheeks. Balawahdiwa helped me hogtie the prisoner.

"Be quiet," I growled. "You want the Fibbies to hear and bust in?"

He choked the racket off. The air whined in his gullet. Spit drooled into his beard. He'd lost his glasses. Nothing stood between us and the utter hatred in his gaze.

Ginny squared her shoulders. "All right," she said, "Take him to my arcanum."

Balawahdiwa and I carried him. Edgar, who'd flown to his perch, descended and click-clicked along the floor after us. Ginny, in the lead, drew the blinds. We laid the body on the couch. Its frenzy had passed. The sweat was drying on skin grown cold. Only the ribs moved, and those terrible eyes that followed us.

Ginny spread books and certain other things on her worktable, Balawahdiwa unpacked his bag beside them, the raven settled on the edge: shapes dark and strange in the dimness. I waited aside, listening to my heart knock. My mouth had gone dry as a dead man's.

"What do you think the possessor is?" Balawahdiwa asked hushedly.

"A goryo," Ginny answered as low. "I began to wonder a while ago. Things Will had told us at times when he was himself—I threw the idea from me, but it wouldn't stay gone. Mostly for reassurance, I read some Japanese lore. Parts of it fitted hideously well. Still I denied. But Mimir seems to have done more than solve a secondary problem for me. One like that—" Her voice faded.

"I too have met with Powers," he said. "You don't come away unchanged. What is this you speak of? A kind of—shen, kuei, do they name them in China?"

"Not quite. It could perhaps become a kami, a tutelary spirit, but its malice locks it into what it is. A vicious ghost, oftenest a woman's, self-tortured, trying to avenge the miseries of its past life on the living. Goryo have driven people to madness, violence, suicide. Like the rest of the paraworld, they were helpless during the Long Sleep, but old tales remembered them. Since the Awakening, a few seem to have reappeared—or newly come into being."

And the demonic conspiracy co-opted them, I thought.

Ginny went on, Fimbul-bleak, iron-hard. "I suspect we have here the late Princess Tamako. We'll find out, I hope."

I'd never before seen Balawahdiwa hesitate. "Necromancy is vile."

"Necromancy is rubbish, at least as my civilization defines it. But the soul, the spirit— Yes, I admit we don't know much more about it than that it exists." Ginny's manner went professional, impersonal. There was an odd comfort in that. "I favor the theory that it's formed by the living organism, an energy structure within the universal web of forces, and outlasts its matrix. You may consider this crassly materialistic. But surely you'll agree that it, like everything else, is subject to the great law, whether you call that the law of nature and logic or the law of God and morality. Demons have been exorcised. Between us, you and I should be able to expel a ghost."

Balawahdiwa nodded. He murmured in Zuni and crossed himself. They got to work.

Again I won't tell of the next two hours. I mustn't, and I couldn't. While I watched, frozen, they studied, conferred, planned, prepared. Sometimes they drew on Edgar, in ways I am not sure of—he, a member of the nonhuman natural world, kin to the birds of Odin and to the mighty Creator and Trickster of our Northwestern Indians. Once they laid hands on my head, and for a moment I whirled off into infinite abysses.

It passed. I sat in the shadows and waited. Inside, I felt as lonely as Valeria. Maybe more; she had company, yonder in the void.

They lighted sticks of incense and a bowl of dried herbs. The smoke drifted bitter through the dusk. Ginny's wand glowed star-fierce. Balawahdiwa chanted. A small drum throbbed beneath his right hand, his left shook a feathered rattle. Did I also hear the notes of a cedar flute, the beat of dancing feet? The sorcerers went to stand at Will's side, her familiar again on her shoulder. They began an incantation.

His throat shrieked. His face contorted to a troll's. He writhed, strained against his bonds, would indeed have broken himself while he wrecked the room if he hadn't been restrained. I tensed for a battle.

No need, thanks be. The songs joined, Latin and Hebrew, Zuni and Shoshonean; fingers beckoned; the raven spread wings as if to fly to the Underworld. Blue fires blazed icy and died. A wind that smelled of thunderstorm whistled by. The floor quivered. And the spirit passed.

I glimpsed it go. Did I see the image of a woman, faint and tattered as fog in that wind, robe and hair streaming wild, mouth drawn back from dreadful teeth? Did I hear her scream, did I feel the wrath and spite and despair? I don't know. I don't want to know. Enough that she was gone.

Will collapsed where he lay. His eyes closed, his breath shuddered and steadied, his face became his, and he slept. Edgar flapped to the bookshelf and sat a-droop, exhausted. Ginny sank to the floor and wept. I groped my way over to hold her close. Balawahdiwa stood above us while he spoke his final prayers. Glancing up, I saw that there was not yet any real peace in him.

A long while afterward, a short while by the clock, Ginny and I with our arms still around one another, we watched Will rouse. He sighed, blinked, looked nearsightedly around. She disengaged and bent over him. "How, how are you?" she stammered.

"Free," he whispered. "The horror . . . no more . . . like escaping from a fever nightmare, back to . . . reality. . . . I can never thank you. . . ."

She kissed his brow. "No need to, old dear. Take it easy. Rest. Sleep. Or what do you want?"

"First, I suppose, to be untied," I said. Prosiness was a blessing. "Can you roll over, Will? I'll undo those knots. Sorry 'bout them, and if I was kind of rough."

"No, you saved me, you called me back from Hell—" I took the cord off.

He stirred. His head lifted. "Take it easy, I said," Ginny urged. "You've been through an ordeal as bad as cancer. Give yourself time to recover. Would you like some food or drink, maybe some broth? You should certainly take plenty of water."

"Wait, wait," he pleaded. "I have . . . memories . . . not suppressed anymore. . . . What *she* thought and did. What she told *them*, and heard from them."

"Later, Will. You're free. Val's returning to us. That's all that matters right now. That, and healing you. Lie down. Rest."

"I can't," he gasped. "Not till— You've got to know. *They've* kept track of you. Not everything. They don't know where you went, Virginia, or what you did, nor the dealings of our shaman friend with his gods, nor—But they know plenty else. Already they're reacting. Valeria—"

His words trailed off. He lowered his head, completely wrung out.

Balawahdiwa stepped forward. His own voice chopped. "He speaks truth. In my Seeking this morning, I felt a hint. While we worked our spell here, the Beloved Ones spoke again, more clearly, and I begin to understand what they said. The demons can't keep your daughter from returning toward us, but they can set their strength against her."

They can apply a vector to the forces, I thought. Sickness rose in me.

"I do not see how we can counter it," Balawahdiwa finished. "She will not land on Earth, but on the moon. They will be waiting for her."

45

"OH, NO," I BEGGED.

Ginny turned on the priest. "You're quite sure?" she demanded.

He nodded. "I wish I weren't."

Same as earlier, she had become all business, like a sword drawn in anger. "We might have foreseen." She spoke flatly, except for the barest quaver, while her lashes blinked away drops that sparkled in the dusk. "It makes sense. They want to destroy *Owl*; Val's incidental. They can't stop her in her course, but the original mission, a lunar landing, gives them the goetic leverage to redirect it that much. Can we change it back?"

"That's your department. But I'm afraid the answer is no."

"Can your Beings help at all?"

"I will go out beneath the sky and pray." Balawahdiwa gathered his things and went from us. After a minute, while our eyes and Will's met in silence, I heard the door to the back yard open and shut.

I shook myself and managed to say, "Maybe it has an engineering solution."

Ginny touched my cheek. "Always the engineer, aren't you, Steve? Still, yes, we'll see what we can do."

"We and Curtice."

"Absolutely." She stepped to her desk and resonated the phone. The celestonaut's image shone at us, pale and expectant.

"Will's rid of the ghost," Ginny said. "The possessor, I mean."

"Why, wonderful!" Curtice cheered. "Did you hear that, Val?" The girl shouted jubilation.

"We have bad news as well," Ginny went on. "I'm sorry, darling, this has to be confidential. We'll explain soon. Turn the communicator off, Curtice."

The other woman obeyed. Ginny gave her the facts. She let loose several words that shocked me, then steadied. "Yes," she agreed, "we must break this to the child as calmly and optimistically as may be. But break it we must."

"Have you any ideas?" I asked with scant hope.

"Not really. Without navigational instruments, Val can't give me the data to determine her position and path any closer than a ballpark estimate. I'll try for a fix here, groundside. If that succeeds, and assuming your Zuni partner got the straight goods from his gods, maybe we can work some trick. I honestly don't see how, but— When can you join me?"

"As soon as my broom can manage." Ginny's glance fell on her brother. "No, I'm sorry. Not immediately."

"Eh?" he wheezed. "Go. Don't delay. I'll be all right."

I looked down at the drawn face and replied, "Nonsense. You're convalescent, son—yeah, and in the earliest stages of it. You've got to have rest and care. Not to mention protection from any attempt to repossess you."

He shuddered. Either he was too scared or too weak to argue further. "We have to wait for Balawahdiwa anyway," I remembered. "We'll call you later, Curtice." I disempathed and touched the glyphs for the Goldsteins.

Martha saw me, sucked in a breath, and asked compassionately, "All right, Steve, so what's gone wrong now?"

"I can't explain yet, but—I'm sorry, it is an imposition, but can you take in another refugee for a day or two?"

"Refugee? This sounds like a war or a pogrom." She wasn't joking. "You bring whoever it is straight over. We will be very hurt if you don't."

"Thanks and—and God bless you," I wished once more for her and hers.

"God help you, Steve, Ginny. Sam's at work, but I will be making up a cot we have. Before you ask, yes, your children are fine, though naturally anxious. They will be glad to see you. I will too."

Doing something, anything, was a relief. We collected Will's pajamas and stuff. He leaned heavily on my arm as I led him to our broom and helped him onto a seat.

Martha, Ben, and Chryssa waited at the Goldsteins' front door. Their uncle's condition frightened the kids. I said he was sick but recovering; their mother and I had to take off for another little while but ought to be back shortly with everything made right. I'm skilled at hiding my feelings when necessary, legacy of wartime and of countless poker games. I convoyed Will to his bed, got him into his bedclothes, spread sheet and blanket over him.

"You're kind," he whispered.

"I'm family," I said.

"Yes. The Graylocks are honored." He smiled a wee smidgen. "Excellent chromosomes you've brought us."

Martha promised as I left: "The Sabbath begins this evening. We will pray for you." She gave me a quick hug, kissed my cheek, and let me go.

I returned home. Ginny was at her books. The look she threw me was desperate. "I've found nothing that might work," she said.

Balawahdiwa came back in a few minutes later. My pulse jackrabbited.

He regarded us gravely. "Behind my eyelids I have had a vision," he declared. "Within my head I have heard. The Beloved Ones, yes, with Coyote himself, will do what they can against this thing that menaces all Earth."

He paused. "What they can. They are not the Single True God, you know. Their powers are not unbounded. We too must give what we are able, we humans, everything we are able to.

"They can't stop the spacecraft from landing on the moon. But once she has, they can sing her home—if she has a living pilot, if Valeria escapes the trap laid for her. The demons will surely pursue. The Beloved Ones will try to give her the speed or the trickiness to keep them from overtaking her. If the chase goes clear to Earth, the Beloved Ones will fight. But they can't do it alone. We must be there ourselves, in body and in soul, prepared to stake our lives."

Through my pounding blood I heard my voice recite the rough calculation that was all I had at this hour to offer. "At two gees, braking, Val should reach the moon about, oh, about nine or ten o'clock. If she can then take off again, same acceleration to midpoint and equal deceleration, well, roughly an hour and a half to here."

"She probably can't leave at once or go that fast. The demonic forces will drag on the vehicle."

"Wouldn't a new lodestone help? An object from Earth. Like a coin, a pocket knife, anything?"

"Yes, after a fashion," Ginny said. "It would be much better if she had a paranatural or poetically charged thing. Perhaps the Fair Folk can give her something of theirs."

I scowled. "Dicey. But we'll have time to talk with her. Maybe somebody will get an idea. Where do we meet our allies, Balawahdiwa?"

Sternness responded. "On the sacred mountain. There the Beloved Ones have their greatest strength."

"Well, that figures, I guess. When should we flit?"

The priest shook his head, a slow weaving to and fro. "You don't understand, Steven. Dowa Yalanne is holy. We don't set foot atop it casually or even easily. That would be sacrilege. For us, our mission, it would damn any hopes we ever had. This isn't a simply practical matter. It's also spiritual, and sacrifice is always required in an appeal. It may be as little as a pinch of meal, it may be as much as your whole life, but it is what you must give to become, for a while, one with a Power higher than yourself, and what the Power must have for this to happen.

"We'll walk up the mountain. A small beginning to whatever sacrifice we must make. How great that will be in all, I do not know."

A stiff six- or seven-hour climb, I'd heard.

Balawahdiwa hadn't been preaching a sermon, just telling us how it was. Nevertheless I badly wanted some plain old practicality. Ginny beat me to it: "When shall we start?"

He frowned. He wasn't entirely used to the white man's scissored-off concept of time. After a moment he replied, "We should take a particular route. I'll tell you how to find the trailhead. Suppose we meet there at three-thirty. You see, it looks as though we'll have trouble along the way. Did the demons brew this weather? Or is it an accident? Or a test, a part of our sacrifice? I don't know."

"Very well," I said. "Three-thirty P.M. Meanwhile, uh, no disrespect, but we'll try to redirect *Owl* ourselves."

"Go ahead," Balawahdiwa answered starkly. "However, I believe this is our only chance."

"Let's go!"

Ginny shook her own head. "Be sensible, Steve. I wasn't at first, but that was an impulse. We're starved, we're tired, we'll be worthless without some food and a nap. You too, sir?"

Balawahdiwa nodded. "We're mortal."

We made sandwiches in the kitchen and swallowed them while we discussed details, carefully keeping them mundane. We called Curtice. She told us her observations seemed to confirm the priest's warning. She'd been searching for an answer herself and gotten nowhere.

"Bring Valeria in," Ginny said.

I haven't the heart to write exactly what went on between us and our daughter. She took the news like a trooper. I suggested she draw Fotherwick-Botts and continue the swordsmanship drill. She said Svartalf was already sharpening his claws on his saddle. We bade farewell for now.

Ginny laid a sleep-and-arousal spell on the three of us. We stretched out and toppled.

Someone spoke to me in my dreams, someone good. I don't quite recall.

Much refreshed by that hour of siesta, we prepared for the trek. Food and extra garments, including rain ponchos, went into backpacks, sleeping bags onto the frames, water into canteens. Ginny foresightedly borrowed Val's and Ben's back-country gear and did likewise for it.

Edgar with us, we reached the workshop about three. Balawahdiwa took off on his own stick. He needed to fix a pack, too. I suspected he meant to do more than just that. Ginny, Curtice, Fjalar, and I conferred, briefly and without result.

"If there is a straightforward method, we'll never find it soon enough, and probably there isn't." Curtice sighed. "Okay, we'll go the religious route."

"You're coming?" I asked, not surprised.

"*Ja*," the dwarf boomed. "Ay'll ask Thor he hammer those trolls."

"Why not?" Curtice said. "And I'm a Christian. Not awfully devout, but I do attend Congregationalist services most Sundays. I'll be praying."

And the Goldsteins, I thought. *And Fotherwick-Botts, who's a Catholic of sorts. And Will and Ginny and me in our uncertain ways. And Balawahdiwa, powerfully. And Valeria out of her innocence.*

We locked the workshop, mounted our brooms, and set forth.

46

BALAWAHDIWA WAITED AT THE TRAILHEAD. HE WAS AS PLAINLY OUTFITTED AS US, EXCEPT for a weblike pattern of paint on his face and a prayer stick tucked in his belt. I guessed that his backpack held other sacred objects and that he'd spent his time here blessing the way we must walk.

Naked red rock loomed steeply from the desert scrub. Up and up it sheered, buttresses, ravines, cliffs, crags shaped into fantasies by a million years of weather. Beyond glimmered the pale strata, then layers again ocherous, on to the final heights. From the bottom we could only glimpse jumbled great fragments of what reached ahead of us.

The sky also hindered sight. Clouds covered it, gray and blue-black, the lower ones scudding like smoke. What light seeped through was turning an eerie brass-yellow. Wind whistled and boomed. It thrust around us, stronger, louder, colder every minute.

Balawahdiwa addressed me through the noise. "I think you should come along as a wolf, Steven. We may well need that strength and toughness on the climb and in whatever happens afterward."

Disappointment flickered. I'd be under animal limitations. Ginny laid a hand on my arm. Resolution and an odd, savage glee drove off any qualms.

I gave her the communicator locket I'd worn. She kissed me. I kissed her back. I'll carry those few seconds with me through my life—but probably not Edgar's beak grooming my hair from her shoulder. He meant well.

"You guys start," I suggested. "I'll catch up."

Curtice nodded. "Yes. We're in for a tough stretch at best, and the weather may make it worse than tough." She glanced at Fjalar. "Will you be okay?" she asked. When the dwarf tried on Ben's rain poncho, the smallest we had, he'd said it was too long for him to do any scrambling in.

"Oh, *ja*," he replied. "Yust Thor making merry."

He didn't know how violent Southwestern thunderstorms can get. Often outright cloudbursts, they generally hit in summer but are not unknown as late as October. I doubted today's conditions were pure chance.

My friends began their ascent. Winding among rocks, they were soon lost to view. I stowed the pack I wouldn't be able to use in the coffer on one stick and laid my garments beside it as I stripped to my skinsuit. Chill ripped at me. I crawled into another coffer and made the changeover. Maybe that wasn't needful, as murky as the scene had grown.

Wolf pelt and wolf vigor warmed me. I bounded out and yelped defiance at the wind. It still bore faint scents of blowing grit, wildly tossing brush, deer. . . . I quelled an urge and loped ahead.

Nothing but feet had carved the trail, century by century. A greenhorn could easily lose it. Narrow, strewn with stones, pitted and gullied, it twisted skyward like a snake about to strike. Maybe the Zunis usually took a different, better path. Maybe this route, the difficulty and danger, were part of our sacrifice. I didn't know. In my present state I wondered only vaguely. The question slipped from my wolf mind. I ran on my hunt.

Soon I overtook the party and fitted my pace to theirs. They all knew how to move on a mountain, long, slow strides, aware and wary of everything that might make them slip or stumble. Fjalar's short legs had to swing faster, but he seemed unweariable. His right hand clutched a heavy hammer he'd taken along from the shop. Token of religion, lucky charm, or just a comforting reminder of tasks less uncanny? He grinned at me. Ginny stroked my head, Curtice ruffled my shaggy neck, Edgar cawed a hello from Ginny's shoulder, which he must hang onto tightly. Balawahdiwa, leading, turned his head to give me a smile. We climbed on.

Occasionally my companions stopped to rest, drink from their canteens, munch on a handful of raisins or other trail food. Ginny would pour some water into a depression for me to lap up and give me a piece of jerky. The interludes were brief, in that bitter, tearing wind. At the priest's signal we'd rise and resume the hike, ever higher.

The sky went black. Lightning flared, over and over. Each white blaze showed the mountainscape in shadowless sharpness. Thunder rolled like monstrous wheels, down and down across the world, echoing off scarps, shaking our bones. Wind roared, skirled, keened.

The rain came, a cataract around us, upon us, against us. Hail mingled, slingstones to bruise and draw blood. We couldn't make out Bala-wahdiwa's shout, we barely saw his gesture through the flying silver, but we did as he did, cast ourselves flat on the slanted ground, lesser targets for the lightning. First Fjalar brandished his hammer aloft. "Fun ban fun," he bawled, "but, Thor, this ban ridiculous!" I suppose he used English to inspire us. Edgar took refuge under a concave boulder.

Water runneled in the trail. Its stream swelled, a torrent, mere inches deep, yet a force that clamored, foamed, dragged. The sudden mud gave way beneath Curtice. She slid aside and downward. Runoff plunged over the edge of a nearby bluff. Jagged rocks lurked below. She flailed after a handhold to stop her skid. Whatever she caught pulled free.

I sprang up and bounded. My pads and claws kept an uneasy grip. I reached her, grabbed her poncho between my jaws, and hauled. We stopped on the brink. I fought to keep us there.

That kind of berserkerdom seldom lasts long. As abruptly as it had exploded, the chaos ended. Rain and hail ceased, wind dwindled, the sky lightened as clouds broke apart, the spates gurgled away to naught. Both of us on all fours, I helped Curtice back to firmer footing.

She clambered erect. Her hand caressed my drenched head. "That's another I owe you, Steve," she said shakily. "I hope you'll be best man at my wedding someday—the groom's bound to ask you—and, later on, godfather."

Even wolf, I was touched. Even human, I couldn't have mumbled more than, "Aw, shucks." I wagged my stump of a tail. Ginny came over to lift my muzzle and kiss me right on my black nose. "Yumping yiminy, Grettir the Strong never did any better!" Fjalar exclaimed. Balawahdiwa signed a blessing.

We labored onward. The dwarf and I were a sight, my pelt and his hair and beard waterlogged, both of us black with mud. We could take it, though. Wind chill might have been too much for the others, but their ponchos had kept them from being soaked and now gave some protection. However, neither Ginny nor Curtice were at their glamorous best.

The going became marginally easier. With just the thinnest small patches of soil on the high slopes, the trail was again solid underfoot, aside from where the rain had washed scree across it. The clouds scattered, opened an infinite blue to us, at last were quite gone. The wind died off. Only the scrunch of stone beneath soles and the often harsh sound of breath remained. The cold deepened, but it was a quiet cold, which exertion held at bay.

The sun set behind Arizona. We lost sight of the lowlands as night fell quickly, glorious with stars. They gave light enough to travel by, through a world gone dim and shadowy. With my other animal senses to help, I could have gone faster than any human. But I stayed close to the women and listened.

From time to time they had spoken with Valeria. Hitherto the girl had been hopeful, almost cheerful. When you're her age and healthy, you don't really believe you can die. She'd caught naps, supported by her safety harness, taken food and water, attended to Svartalf's needs, and dutifully practiced wielding Fotherwick-Botts. As Earth and moon waxed, blue and gray-white, her excitement had mounted.

Now, though, the lunar disc hung huge, a blackness cut out of heaven, edged with dazzlement where steeps and craters stood brutally forth. "She's coming in for a landing," Ginny told us. Her words trembled beneath the stars.

"Sooner than we estimated." I heard the anguish in Curtice's voice. "Oh, if only we'd had exact data—"

"Yingle, yingle, yingle," Fjalar moaned. "How mush longer ve got to go?" Edgar added a croak.

"About two hours, I'd guess, if we can hold to this pace." Balawahdiwa's answer tolled iron-steady. "Once on top, we have to continue to where the Beloved Ones are gathered. When the maiden has landed, they'll sing their recalling song. They don't know when she'll actually be able to depart; and without a lodestone of Earth in her craft, she will fly slower than otherwise. I'm not sure how effective an ordinary, uncharmed object out of a pocket can be."

"I've been advising her," Ginny said. "If she can't avoid setting down on the moon, she can steer, choose her spot. In daylight there'd be nobody but demons. She's aiming for the dark side, well beyond the sunset line."

"In any case, we ought to reach our goal before she arrives here." Balawahdiwa's tone had turned equally, deliberately commonplace. "We couldn't help her right now, wherever we were. If it comes to a fight, that's when we'll be most wanted.

"Keep going."

47

AGAIN I HAVE TO RECONSTRUCT THE STORY FROM BITS AND PIECES, WHAT I HEARD AT THE time and afterward, what I myself experienced, and—because witnesses' memories are notoriously unreliable—what I rightly or wrongly infer. How much of history do we really know?

Owl slanted downward across a moon that was no longer ahead but below. The terrain reached gray and black under the soft bluish light of Earth. Our planet stood high in the western sky, slightly gibbous, altogether beautiful, clouds a swirled and banded white marbling azure ocean, glistery polar caps, greenish-brown Asia. Its brilliance drowned most stars out of Val's eyes. She wondered whether she glimpsed lights like them, city lights, sown on the night half. Maybe an illusion, a glint of tears caught in her lashes.

Joy warred with fear. First lunar landing ever! And, God willing, the nastards, taken by surprise, wouldn't reach her before she'd fixed the craft and left for home.

Mountains, gentler contoured than Earth's, fell aft. She swept above a lower stretch of stone, where craters peered from shadow, down toward a darkling plain. "Mare Tranquillitatis," said Curtice's voice from Dowa Yalanne. "The name a good omen? Anyhow, safer to settle on than the highlands westward, and farther from the sun."

"Yes," rang the command of Valeria's mother. "Take it."

Owl handled easier than in an atmosphere. Of course, allowing for the low weight was kind of gitzy. . . . She'd show them. Too young for a license? Ha!

Savagely braking, *Owl* hawk-swooped at her goal. Her liberation. When she touched yonder soil, the spell that compelled her was ended. Val need simply put a piece of terrestrial matter in the nose cap, and the Zuni gods would call her to them.

"Yee-hi!" she shouted. She stole a glance aft. Svartalf arched his back and bottled his tail. She didn't hear him through the vacuum, but she well knew that yowl from of old. *Here I come! Make way, rabble, or I'll gut you for fishbait.*

The broom slammed to a halt, yards above ground. Val lost her saddle.

Ashen desert and luminous Earth spun across her vision. The stick rebounded and toppled. She struck. Black dust billowed.

"Val!" Ginny cried. "Are you there? What's happened?"

Dazedly, the girl sat up. She'd fallen next to the vehicle. For a second she noticed only how fast the dust settled, no air to lift it, and that it'd gotten all over her, a fine powder that clung, an unseelie mess. Svartalf had sprung clear. He trotted toward her, equally disarrayed, furiously indignant.

"Valeria, Valeria—" And, less loud and clear, she heard her father howl.

Her sense came back. She rose to her feet and stared. "We hit something. Something invisible, I guess. We dropped."

"Are you hurt?"

Val moved arms and legs, twiddled fingers and toes. "No, don't seem to be." She was most conscious of how light she had become. The collision had occurred at perhaps five miles an hour, while the forces held the riders secure. Given lunar gravity, the fall had corresponded to a couple of feet on Earth. It was well, though, that she'd unbuckled her harness before starting her descent. The broom would have hit ground with her astride. That mass would probably have broken any bones caught underneath it.

Ginny swallowed a sob before she asked, "The spacecraft?"

"Lemme take a look." Val stooped, peered, and felt. "Okay, I think."

"Sure she ban fine," Fjalar snorted. The whole gang must be clustered around the locket bearers. "Ay do honest vork. Volund the Smith could have took lessons from me."

"The fact you can still communicate, that the crystal wasn't knocked out, yes, that's encouraging," Curtice said. "Think you can fly?"

"Well, she's lying on her side," Val reported, "but I don't expect she weighs too much here for me to right her."

"Have you any idea what you struck?" Balawahdiwa inquired.

"N-no, sir." Val gripped the hilt of the sword at her hip. "I, I can try feeling of it."

"Don't linger," Ginny ordered. "The demons must have tracked your path. They'll be on their way. This could be a barricade or a trap of theirs. Get out!"

"I wonder—" Balawahdiwa mused.

"Oh!" Val gasped.

A touch, light as a breeze, tender as a kiss, on brow, eyes, lips, bosom, hands. And there *they* were, at hover before her and around her. Seven figures, male and female, less tall than her, slim, big-eyed, features grave and exquisite, long silvery hair and translucent billowy garments afloat though there was never a wind. . . . Earthlight shone through their locks and robes; it seemed almost to pass through them. Above them reared a wall surmounted by slim towers, ivory-hued, playfully filigreed, a high ogive gate at its middle that shimmered like mother-of-pearl. To the left of this gaped a hole. The shards showed how thin the wall was, how delicately formed.

Svartalf halted his prowlings. He settled down on the ground, alert but much as he would have at a fireside.

"The Fair Folk," Val whispered. "It's got to be. They've appeared to me."

"Hush," came Balawahdiwa's word to his companions. "Don't disturb the meeting. Listen, only listen. Let's us keep on."

Valeria gulped. "Hi," she breathed. "Can you hear me, people? I'm sorry I damaged your building."

She heard the reply within herself, dream-speech, a melody, a bird-song, a running brook. —You are not at fault. How could you have known? Welcome, welcome.

"*Are* you—"

—Yes. And now we know who you are and what your need is. A fate is in this. What it may be, we know not. May it bring deliverance.

"You, once you showed yourselves to my Uncle Will."

—Your kinsman, aye. For we saw that humans might well follow us to the moon. We wished that someone would give them forewarning. Then perhaps when they came they would show us mercy. We could not speak for ourselves. Few are the haunts remaining on Earth which have not become horrible to us. Nor do we understand anymore the souls of most men, who no longer walk in awe and worship, but question everything and seek ways to bend the whole world to their will. Here was a youth as pure in heart as any son of Adam can be, his yearning already turned heavenward. We hoped he would be our friend.

Val shuddered. "He was. But later those scabrous demons went for him."

—With sorrow did we learn this from your mind, and with gladness that he is again free. But you, child, are in terrible danger.

She gulped. "When w-will they get here?"

A male frowned. It was not natural on a face meant for carefree happiness. —We cannot say. But we think that if they have lain in wait for you, they are not together. For they must know that while they could command you to this sphere, you, wisely counseled from Earth, could find harbor wherever you chose. Thus they would not gather at a single place, but spread themselves over great distances. Is that not what hunters would do?

Val nodded.

—The number of them is not large. No more than a hundred, belike fewer.

"What?"

A female, with unwonted grimness: —We have found out much in the years since they first arrived.

Well, passed through the girl's head, *that figure must be about right.* Besides what observation had shown, it just wasn't reasonable that China, Japan, Mongolia, Tibet, any country had ever been overrun by fiends. Most Beings were benign, or at least neutral, or at worst sort of mischievous. Didn't the old stories say so? How could the world have survived if good didn't always outweigh evil?

Then how could these devils, kuei, oni, spooks, hoodoos, and screaming meemies have caused the grief they did?

Because it doesn't take many, she thought. Anywhere in the human or nonhuman worlds, nature or paranature. One stalking murderer can terrorize a city. One self-infatuated dictator can turn entire nations into prison camps and torture chambers. One warped prophet can preach a creed whose fanatics butcher millions of the harmless. Why, one honest but pushy bureaucrat—

Her tension and fear erupted in laughter. She had remembered Alger Sneep.

She grew aware of the Fair Folk's puzzled regard and realized that her merriment was half hysteria. But it had rallied her like a dash of cold rain.

A female told her: —That is why they have not destroyed us and our homes. We withdraw from their warlike bands, as we withdraw from the sun. Being too few to ransack widely, they seldom discover our dwellings, whether we take shelter there during the day or depart for others.

She gestured. The gate swung open. Val saw gardens where flowers glowed beneath arching argent trees, fountains soared in white plumes, a pool shimmered full of twilight. One building stood amidst them, as fragile as everything else, wholly strange yet in its way as lovely as the Taj Mahal.

—We make our homes and ourselves invisible to all who menace us.

That shouldn't be hard for Beings so ethereal. Indeed, this couldn't be ordinary, material matter. What was it composed of? Starlight and enchantment, perhaps?

—Sometimes the wicked, casting about, come upon a place by chance, as you did . . . if your advent truly was by chance. They wreck it. Sometimes they sorcerously find traces of us and hunt us down and . . . we will not say what then happens. Give the demons time, and they will slay the last of us.

Like humans hounding whole races of animals to extinction, Valeria thought.

—And always, from their lunar stronghold, they will wreak harm on your kind.

No, they needn't really be many. Plenty of mortals are, well, easy marks for them, Dad would say. Some would choose to be their allies.

—We will do what we can to aid your escape, before we too must flee.

Her blood throbbed. "Oh, thank you!"

—You bear not only your own hopes, but ours.

Svartalf jumped up, squalled, and spat. She couldn't hear him. He tugged at her jeans. She looked down and saw him crouched for battle, eyes and teeth agleam in the stiff-standing ebony fur. Sparks snapped through its dustiness.

Her gaze swept west. Over the near horizon, across the pockmarked plain, under serenely shining Earth, three forms bounded toward her. They went in flat leaps, hurtling like cannon shells. A hairless giant, nude but for a loincloth, blunt horns sprouting from a narrow brow, fangful mouth agape; a fish-scaled monkey with a split head and an obscenely erect phallus; a human skeleton, clattering its jaws: nightmare become as real as a gallows.

"They're at us," Valeria cried to father and mother and friends, unreachably distant. "The nearest of them—they didn't wait for more—"

She heard me bay. There was no time for terror. It was as if she stood aside and watched. She drew the sword.

"Haro!" Fotherwick-Botts trumpeted. Him she could talk with, more bluntly than with the Fair Folk, who scattered back appalled from the oncoming enemy. "God send the right!" He began scolding her. "None too soon, young lady. D'you think I liked sitting in that confounded sheath, mute while plan after plan came to me? Bally insubordination, I call it. Never have happened in the Widow's army, I'll wager." His attention went outward. "Bloody heathen, those. Not even natives, are they? Let 'em break themselves on us. Remember, no roundhouse swings, no silly overhead cuts leaving your belly wide open. Slantwise. Go for the neck, the arm, the thigh. If you must stab, strike below the rib cage. . . . Yoicks! Tally-ho!"

The demons arrived.

Svartalf sprang, hooked claws into the giant's skin, climbed up him and set about tearing out his eyes.

The monkey was more agile. It bounced to and fro, dodging the blade. Its muzzle leered and soundlessly gibbered what its phallus threatened.

"Fight, Val, fight!" Curtice shouted from Earth, as if she were still a college cheerleader. I could not yawp anymore, merely, in my dumb animal way, implore. Fjalar futilely shook his hammer. Edgar flapped and screamed. Ginny's wand wove spells, Balawahdiwa lifted his prayer stick to the stars and chanted—to what avail?

The skeleton attacked on Val's left side. Its fingerbones grabbed her and jerked her around. Its teeth clapped.

The monkey leered and doubled its legs for a pounce.

Three misty shapes blew over to swirl around and blind it—Fair Folk, with the desperation of the timid when they are cornered. It swatted at them. They wavered like a fog.

"Backbone," Fotherwick-Botts directed.

Val hewed. The blow shocked through her. The skeleton's vertebrae parted company. It fell in two pieces. They sprattled for a minute, then lay still. Kicked-up dust settled back onto the bones.

"Now that beastly little ape, while it's hampered," Fotherwick-Botts said. Val clove it. Blood gushed onto the ground, black under the blue light, and seethed off into vacuum.

"The big fella," barked the sword. He was clearly enjoying himself.

The giant staggered, groping for Svartalf. The tomcat clung but shifted to and fro. Val summoned what force remained to her. She sliced across the abdomen. Guts spilled, blood spouted. The demon collapsed.

"I—we whipped them," Val choked aloud. She knelt and vomited.

"Good Lord, m'lady, what's wrong?" Fotherwick-Botts wondered. "You slew 'em, didn't you? A shield maiden, by Jove! I've never seen a woman do neater work. Nor many men. My compliments."

Svartalf raised back and tail. He caterwauled his triumph into airlessness.

"Val, how are you?" her mother pleaded. "Pull yourself together. You've got to get out. They'll be after you in a horde."

"Uh-huh." Strength returned from deep inside the girl. She lurched to her feet, steadied, and approached *Owl*.

"I, I have to right her and put an Earth thing in to guide her back," she told the returning Fair Folk. Her throat burned, her mouth was foul. Well, once embarked, she'd swig from her canteen, spit the puke into space, and—and—

—Yes, quickly, before more of them come, she dream-heard. —But they will pursue. We believe every last one of them will pursue.

Bound to, she thought. For the demons it was now or never. If she came home bearing her news, exorcists would soon land here. But if she didn't, how many people would take our unsupported word? There would at least be endless argument and shilly-shalling. Meanwhile the demons could sap all space enterprises beyond revival.

—It is your cause and it is ours, the Fair Folk sang.

"If you must sheathe me, first wipe me clean," Fotherwick-Botts interrupted. "Military neatness, y'know." Numbly, she took a handkerchief from her shirt and obeyed.

"Now don't hesitate to draw me again," the sword added. "We've won a skirmish, not the war. I've seen battles lost because of overconfidence. F'r instance, once when campaigning with the Varangians—"

She slid him into his scabbard and dropped the handkerchief by the slain. It fell slowly.

—Make haste.

She bent her knees, took hold of the shaft, heaved the broom off its side. A push on the rune key released the parking legs. *Owl* stood.

Val fumbled in her pockets. What did she have for a lodestone?

The Fair Folk gathered around her. —Whatever you carry has not been long in space. Therefore it has little power. The Beings on Earth cannot by themselves move you swiftly. The enemy will overtake you in midpassage.

She looked upon death and said, "I've got to try."

—But we, we are also children of Earth. Thence we came. There we go back from time to time, renewing ourselves at what is left of her springs and streams, her wildwoods and wild meadows. She is our mother too.

The girl unlatched and unscrewed the nose cap. She had decided on a silver dollar, a birthday gift from long ago which she still carried.

Beauty drifted close. —I am Rinna, it sang. —I will give myself to this. May we both outlive the flight.

The Being went small. She slipped into the cavity. Val had no words. She replaced the cap.

The rest of the fays hurriedly kissed her, one by one, a token of love she barely felt.—We must go now. Fare you well. Fare you always well.

They vanished from Val's sight. She swung to her saddle. Svartalf jumped to his post behind her.

Ghastly shapes swarmed over the horizon.

Val took off like an upward meteor.

48

BY THEN WE WERE ON TOP OF THE MESA. WE STOPPED FOR A FEW MINUTES TO OFFER tears, prayers, wishes. The air went hoarsely in and out of us. Otherwise it lay still, thin, freezing cold. Stars gleamed in their thousands, the Milky Way as a river of frost.

"Our girl is free." Curtice's sigh trembled.

"No, she ban Steve and Yinny's," Fjalar corrected.

My wife shook her head. "Tonight Valeria is everybody's."

"Well spoken," Balawahdiwa agreed. "Everybody of good will. Deliver her from evil. Come, we'd better move."

Again he took the lead. Though the growth was fairly sparse, piñon, juniper, low bushes, it made the going gloomy. Ginny didn't give us witch-sight or even light a saintelmo. Balawahdiwa had not told her she might. This was holy ground. That didn't stop Fjalar from ripping out Old Norse oaths when he stubbed his toe on a rock; and with wolf-keen ears I caught occasional muttered words from Curtice that weren't ladylike.

I found my own way easily, by cues captured in nose, ears, hairs. Ginny did likewise; though not kindled, her wand thrilled in her hand. But this freed our minds to be afraid for our daughter. I felt almost grateful for the limitations on my intelligence in my present form. I could only hurt, inwardly rage, and mutely try to keep courage. Ginny could visualize, calculate, weigh odds all too clearly.

Val had blurted an account of herself after she was spaceborne. Later Ginny called and asked how things were going. "Fast," she answered. "I can nearly *see* the moon shrink and Earth grow." After a pause: "I d-don't see . . . anything else . . . behind me."

"You wouldn't, across that many miles," Curtice told her. Unspoken: *Yet.*

"She rides at a mounting pace," Balawahdiwa said. "Maybe the demons can't match it."

"Thanks to that little spirit who came along," Ginny couldn't help observing.

"True." Balawahdiwa's tone reproached. "Nevertheless, do you imagine this was happenstance, that the Beloved Ones had nothing to do with it?"

"I'm sorry. Their inspiration— But Rinna, she accepted, didn't she? How can we ever reward her?"

Memories from humanity passed through me. I heard my father's voice: "Some good turns you can't pay back. What you do is pay them forward." I thought of cleansing the moon for her people—the image was wolf, snarls that challenged, fangs that tore—and, necessarily vaguely, of afterward starting a movement to restore woodlands and flowery meadows on Earth, so the Fair Folk could visit their mother more often.

"Now hush," Balawahdiwa commanded.

"We'll call again when we can, darling," Ginny finished. "You call if anything goes wrong. But don't fear. We love you." I licked her hand, as if somehow she could transmit a caress. Edgar made a sound like a rusty purr.

We traveled on.

It took about three-quarters of an hour. At last the trail entered a thicker stand of evergreens, you might call it a grove, which ringed a broad open space with its low boles, gnarled boughs, and murky needles. Starlight fell hoar on grass, a few shrubs, scattered rocks, and the remnant of a stone house. I could still remember that the whole Zuni tribe had taken refuge from their foes for years on Dowa Yalanne. As they had done in the mythic age of the Great Flood. . . .

Silence, cold, emptiness brooded over us. Balawahdiwa halted and made a sign of reverence. We had arrived.

Edgar's cheekiness got away from him. "Wot, no gods?" he croaked. I don't know where he picked up that British gag.

"Quiet, you!" Ginny rapped. "My humble apologies," she added to our guide.

He smiled. "They are not humorless, you know." Solemn again: "They watch and wait. Calm your hearts, open your spirits, receive." From his pack he took kilt and sash and donned them.

We grew very still, under the galactic arch and the wheel of heaven. Ginny bowed her head—yes, and Edgar too. Curtice folded hands over breast and murmured. Fjalar took off his stocking cap, bent a knee, put the cap back on but held the hammer as a Christian might a cross.

I also felt it, awe, awareness of a vast presence, like communion in a cathedral—no, not really that. They were not One but many, not infinite though ancient and strong, friends and guardians of life, to which they gave a meaning that went beyond it. As I was, I could not fully feel, nor understand at all; but I lowered my head and stumpy tail in submission to an alpha.

The feeling passed. "They have withdrawn a small way for this while," Balawahdiwa told us softly. "We have to do our own work, our own thinking, before we can play whatever part will be ours."

Fjalar was first to go pragmatic. "Ve can't help the girl vile she flies in space," he growled. "If the trolls and drows ban far behind, somebody like you, Herr Ballavalla, can take her to a safe place. Ve others, vell—" He hefted the hammer. "Ay'd like to crack a few skulls, Ay vould."

"If Valeria escapes, I doubt they'll attack us," Ginny replied. "Not worth the risk, when they've lost the prize."

Curtice scowled. "But I'm afraid it'll be a near thing at best," she said. To the priest: "What do you think?"

It was dismaying to see him taken aback. "I . . . don't know. I should imagine—moving as fast as before—"

"If the spacecraft is boosting that hard now. I don't have the data to say for certain. However, from what Val's told us, probably she is. It's pretty much her performance limit. Can the enemy match that, Ginny?"

"I don't know either," the witch said raggedly. "Their powers are limited too. If Fu Ch'ing were here, he could give us an estimate. But I'd guess, from my own slight knowledge, they can, or better. Otherwise, why would they give chase?"

"Vich they maybe are not," Fjalar proposed.

She struck down his note of cheer. "We don't dare assume that. We can simply hope and pray that Val has enough head start and enough capability that they won't overhaul her."

"She has to make turnover and decelerate," Curtice reminded. "About a two-and-a-half-hour flight, total. No, worse. The moon's not in this sky yet. The only refuge for her is right here. To reach us, she has to apply vectors—curve around, in effect. I'd better advise her soon."

"Can the pursuit cut across that arc?" Balawahdiwa's question was not quite even.

"They may well," Ginny said. I bristled and bared teeth.

"Maybe we can do somethin' about that thar problem," drawled a new voice. "Maybe we jest can."

We stared. A man sauntered out of the woods and across to us. While clad in Western clothes—ten-gallon hat tilted back on his head, fancy bandanna, plaid shirt that would have been loud in a light that showed colors, silver-buckled belt, crisp jeans, tooled-leather boots—he was an Indian. Or was he? He seemed too lean for a Southwesterner, if not a plainsman. Certainly his features were too narrow, his nose too bladelike for any full-blood anywhere. And was it a trick of shadow, or did his outline somehow waver, like smoke or a desert mirage?

Balawahdiwa's firmness broke apart. "Suski!" he cried.

The stranger nodded. "The same." With a glance at us: "Otherwise known as Coyote. At your service, ladies and gents."

And he wasn't there. In his stead posed a canine smaller than me, gaunt, prick-eared, sharp-muzzled, with a scruffy pelt that we knew was sandy-brown and with eyes that mocked us as they had done a flicker ago. He lolled his tongue and grinned.

Balawahdiwa lifted his prayer stick, Ginny her wand, Fjalar his hammer. Edgar cracked his wings up and down and cawed, I tightened my muscles. Curtice alone kept aside. She brought her locket to her lips and in an undertone told Val what was happening.

Coyote flashed back to human appearance. "Whoa, podners, take it easy," he said. "Didn't mean no harm. Jest innerducin' myself."

Ginny exchanged a look with Balawahdiwa. He nodded. She stepped forward to challenge the demigod. Loosened and tangled by the storm, her hair seemed to crackle with the starlight it captured. I stalked at her side.

"No harm?" she retorted. "You, sir, brought this trouble on us. You allied with the common enemy of man, the creatures of the Adversary. You helped them wreck the Selene spacecraft. That no lives were lost wasn't your doing. That a maiden's life and soul are now in mortal danger traces back to your mischief. And you don't give a curse, do you? What more evil have you raised?"

"Hey, you really are mad." He didn't act remorseful or even apologetic. "Calm down, why don't you? We're different, that's all. You're you and I'm me."

He switched to animal shape, I suppose to underline his point. I drank in the feral smell and bristled my ruff.

He changed back to man. "I was jest havin' some fun," he went on. "Though I got to say, if you'll excuse me, you folks been crowdin' in mighty hard on my range." His speech continued slow and amiable. "How'd you like it if squatters moved onto your spread, yay, right'n your garden, and brought along their prairie dogs to burrow through it and their buffalo to graze and trample it? My folks ain't too happy with what you done to their country. Or to them."

"We were never your people, Suski," Balawahdiwa declared. "You never belonged to or cared for any but yourself."

Coyote gibed by swapping forms back and forth for a minute.

Human, he replied, "Wall, now, they do say as how I had a little somethin' to do with the Creation. 'Course, the *Melika* claim that's a kid story, and I reckon they've got most of you believin' so. Truth's a tricky maverick, though, like I was tryin' to demonstrate jest now."

"You said it yourself. We are what we are, which is what history has made us. You have betrayed us to the enemies of everything rightful."

"Aw, that's puttin' it purty stiff." Coyote held up a palm. "But okay, mister, I made a mistake. Not my first, I admit. You folks never made any?"

Recollections rose in me, easy for a wolf with a half-human brain to grasp, some of the countless old tales about him. If he was the Trickster, he was also the Bungler, the schemes he thought so clever ending more often than not in a pratfall—or in death, from which he always arose, apparently unable to learn any lesson whatsoever.

Ginny must have remembered too, for she smiled starkly. "Are you here to try setting things right?" she demanded. "Dare we let you?"

He fished in his shirt pocket, brought out makings, rolled a cigarette between his fingers and struck a match on his heel. "I did have a session or two with the Beloved Ones," he replied, unabashed, after the first drag. "Yep, turns out those waddies are a real mean gang, and shore, none of us wants 'em in charge. I come up with a notion they'll go along with if'n you agree."

A scream sounded from Ginny's and Curtice's lockets.

Startled, the newcomer changed shape. Not entirely. I'd never before seen a coyote with a cigarette in its mouth.

"I spy them!" Valeria cried. "I think I do. I looked behind and . . . like dust-glints over the dark side of the moon—Daddy, Mother, is that them?"

Ginny looked straight at doom and stared it down while she said, "I can't imagine what else it might be."

I howled. Edgar screeched.

"Darling, keep going," Ginny urged. "Don't give up. We're here, we have friends greater than they are, we'll save you."

"A minute." Curtice turned off her communicator. She signed Ginny to do the same before she stated, "If they've become naked-eye visible, that means they're boosting faster than the spacecraft is. I don't have figures to work with, of course, but I expect they'll intercept her before she arrives, especially if they shortcut across her change of direction."

Coyote had resumed man shape. "Beg pardon, ma'am." Suddenly he showed excitement. His eyes flashed starlight. "The little lady don't need no two hours. I reckon she can get here inside of one more, even allowin' for that thar switcharound you talk of."

"In God's name, how?" Ginny exclaimed.

"Why, she don't need to slow down till the very end. Tell her to keep tumbleweedin' along, faster'n faster. The gang can't match that nohow, can they?"

I barked a protest. Curtice voiced it for me: "The whole distance at two gravities? Have you any concept of what her speed will be? If somehow she stops within a few miles, our forcefields can't withstand such a deceleration. She'll be smashed like a beetle under a boot."

"*Ja*," Fjalar added heavily, "Ay guess the boat vill crumple and break in shunks. It's good steel, none better, but the sword of Sigmund the Volsung shattered against Odin's spear."

"The demons will for shore have to put on the brakes," Coyote said. "I reckon they can do it faster'n a human could stand. But it's bound to take them a while, and that's when they lose ground. For your gal, though, why, we've got the Beloved Ones handy. You reckon they can't cradle her to a soft landin', easy as turnin' a flapjack?"

I saw Curtice frown. In my dim way, I wondered too. Nobody short of the True God can repeal the conservation of energy. Those gigajoules would have to go somewhere, damn near instantly.

But Coyote *was* smart. And he doubtless knew what his superiors could or would do. And—

"The gang may be close on her tail, mind you," Coyote warned. "But I got a notion about that." His laugh yammered. "Oh, but I got a notion!"

Ginny's chin lifted. "We'll try it," she said, as impersonal as the sky. "It seems to be our only chance."

"I think it is," Balawahdiwa answered.

49

FOR A SHORT SPAN OUR HEARTS ROSE. SOMETHING WAS BEING ACCOMPLISHED. THE REST of us listened while Curtice talked Val through the maneuvers that would aim her at America and us. Formerly I'd have claimed that such piloting by second-hand eyeballs, with neither instruments nor reckoners to help, was impossible. But Ginny had judged that the combined influences of the Beings here and the spirit aboard made a crucial difference.

Then once more the agony of waiting set in. The shift in path would give the pursuit opportunity to shorten its own. What we couldn't predict was whether the two would meet.

And then Val told us, and we heard in her voice and felt in her bones how she shuddered: "They've gotten close. M-maybe a mile. I can't stand to look at them. But I'll have my blade ready."

"Into Thy hands, O God, we entrust our souls, in the name of our Lord and Savior Jesus Christ," her weapon said. "Remember, cut right and left both, or they'll be at your undefended side. Whatever the outcome, I wager those scoundrels won't soon forget who they dealt with. St. George, haro!"

And *then* Val: "They . . . they . . . yes, they're dropping behind. They are! S-slowly, but . . . they are, they are!"

I howled. Coyote yipped. "Khr-r-r, quark!" Edgar gloated. "Good bird. IRS nevermore."

"They've got to start deceleration," Curtice said like a machine. The demons couldn't tap this line of communication. "But they'll take for granted it's to prepare for a course change. They can't expect you'll dive straight at Earth. They must suppose you'll apply a vector to slip past, and they'll line out after you."

"You won't," clanged Ginny's word.

"If you stop instantaneously and they're on the same track, they may not be able to sheer off," Curtice cautioned. "They may have no choice but to follow you down."

"Still hoping to catch you," Balawahdiwa said.

"Yup, that's how I figured," Coyote bragged.

Fjalar chewed his whiskers. "If it vorks," he muttered. "Ay dunno. Ay yust dunno. A gale, a riptide, and a lee shore."

"Yes, go ahead and cry for a while, dearest," Ginny called to the sounds of weeping. "You've earned the right."

Time crawled.

In an eyeblink, time was no more.

"Earth's enormous," Val said from the stars agleam over us. She didn't sound altogether calm—who would have?—but she was done with tears. "Fills half the sky. Dark, dark, the seas and clouds like silver, there's a kind of blue rim—the air, I guess. No sun, but the half moon's off yonder. Earth growing, faster and faster."

When she hit the outermost atmosphere at that velocity—

She knew. "You better stop me soon, I think." A gulp. "If . . . if you can't, make a wish on the shooting star."

No wishes would be left that were worth making.

The Beloved Ones appeared.

Their host filled the meadow. They were as if gently luminous, yet blinded no sight of heaven from our vision. Balawahdiwa made reverence. We companions gave them the honors we had earlier given an unseen nearness. Their presence overwhelmed. Coyote himself took off his hat.

The Twin War Gods glowered at the forefront, squat, ugly, shields and spears to hand. Kokopelli stood offside, the hunchbacked wanderer, flute to his lips. Some of the rest I knew from books, pictures, dolls, costumes in ceremonies that whites may watch.

The warrior Salimo:beya, face hidden in his collar of crow feathers, yucca-bundle whip in his grasp, guarded the Longhorns. Hu:dudu, also masked, strung his bow. The ogres of discipline stood like stones. The torch of the tiny fire god burned close to six bird-headed Shalako, each twice the height of a tall man. Grotesque, heads plastered with mud, the sacred clowns kept unwontedly still. And more kachinas and more, rank upon rank, not human to behold but intertwining with human lives and the life of the land, had come to save what they preserved and blessed.

The Ko:koshi, earliest rain dancers of the year, raised their rattles and evergreen boughs. Kokopelli's music piped. Somewhere drums and a chant both shrill and deep-throated made response. Feet moved. All were now dancing, most of them gravely and in place. The Mudheads capered and somersaulted, ululating. The ground thundered.

Valeria hurtled at our planet. Her forcefield clove the outermost wide-strewn molecules of air. Incandescence blazed around her.

Something like tremendous invisible hands closed on it. They took the shock into themselves. Val found herself hardly more than a mile above the mesa, flying hardly faster than an eagle upon its prey.

That energy did have to go somewhere. Sky roared, earth shook. The Mudheads got much of it. They flew on high in every direction. Their gleeful shouts pierced the boom and bang. This was fun! They crashed on treetops, tumbled to the ground, skipped back to their pranks unhurt.

Owl arrowed from aloft. The spirits must have helped Val steer. Her own skill, though, gave aim; her own dear form was silhouetted on the broom with Svartalf's, a Hallowe'en figure athwart the stars. She still clasped the drawn sword.

"Flit for yonder house," Ginny told her beneath the music. "Land inside. Stay."

Balawahdiwa had said an altar for prayers and sacrifices stood there. The ruin was holy. Bounding toward it, I watched her glide to a near halt and through the doorway. Balawahdiwa advanced to stand in front. Two kachinas flanked him.

"Yahoo!" Coyote yelled. "Here comes the stampede!"

It was he who had proposed, "We shouldn't ought to jest disappoint them. Let's see if we can't bushwhack them." His overlords had evidently agreed.

Svartalf darted forth between Balawahdiwa's legs. His pelt and tail stood straight, his eyes were a tiger's, he yowled the challenges of his tomcat youth.

From within the house a basso blustered, "What is this farce? I demand my bally honor. There'll be questions in Parliament if I'm confined, there'll be courts martial, and you'll jolly well deserve to lose your confounded fight!"

"He's right," Curtice said. She sped to the doorway. "Pardon me." She edged past the sentries. I'm sure she grabbed a moment to hug and kiss our girl before she returned brandishing Fotherwick-Botts.

"That's better," the sword grumbled. "Were you concentrating on the drill I gave the lass? Should've been, damme. Well, keep your head, obey my orders, and by all the merciful saints, woman, strike to *kill*."

"I went in for saber fencing in college," the celestonaut replied. "This isn't the same, but I can get the hang of it."

Fjalar tossed his hammer, limbering up. The star-tip on Ginny's wand kindled to a hellish blue-white. Edgar flew to perch alert on the head of a Shalako. The giant didn't seem to notice. I unreeled my tongue, cooling off against the heat to come.

Something like a sheaf of lightning bolts burned lurid aloft. —*It is they*, went through our minds.

> —*ma' lesi tewanane*
> *a-winakwe*
> *awan tse'makwin aka*
> *tetse'makponolkwina*—

"The prayer before war," Ginny whispered.

The demons streaked at us. Curtice and Coyote had guessed truly. Not foreseeing that Val would plunge directly to Earth, they hadn't decelerated enough in that direction. Superhuman though their power of goetic movement was, it couldn't check them before they hit the atmosphere. So, wild with the chase, the blood lust, they followed her onward. If they caught her on the surface, they'd tear her to rags and carry away our craft.

I wished for an antiaircraft battery—rumor claimed the Army had developed some firearms that shot more than silver bullets—but Val would've been dead and forever lost before we'd gotten through the bureaucracy and clearances and politics and—

And here we were: mortals, who are nonetheless born with the power to resist evil; weapons and tools charged with paraforce to match its own; gods of the land and the people.

Too late, the demons saw.

They attacked anyhow. Their numbers were close to a hundred, and scorn for others dwells at the core of the satanic. I glimpsed the grisly and the graceful, the crazy and the cruel, mingled together in a swarm that stank of death and corruption. I felt the bow wave of their passage, cold, cold. And they were upon us.

Nobody ever sees a combat whole. It's clamor and confusion, fear and fury, stab and stagger, shoot and take shelter, the world narrowed down to you and your nearest foes or friends, sometimes a flash from a scene elsewhere that sears itself into your memory for as long as you live, which may be only till that unawaited dull shock and amazed understanding. Maybe I, wolf, sensed more of it than my civilized self would have; but it was in fragments flying by.

A man shape came at me. For an insane instant I thought it was Fu Ch'ing, tall, thin, stooped, solemn, in mandarin robe and cap, with mandarin nails as long as a finger joint. No. When I rushed in, those nails slashed me like whetted steel. My were-flesh knitted. My teeth raked. They closed on a fold of the robe. It was not clothing, it was the very body of the Being. Blood gushed icy. The features never changed, the throat never cried out, as we fell to the ground and struggled.

The wounds he gave me went deep. I barely felt them. They healed while I tore him open. After a time he sprawled, empty. I coughed a vile taste from my mouth and glared across the field.

Nearby, a short, squat demon in a coat of mail might have been a benign temple guardian. But his pop eyes and grinning gape radiated hate. He swung a curved sword at Fjalar. The dwarf's hammer met the blow in midair and turned it. He smote the wrist behind. Bones cracked. Fjalar waded in and beat the creature to shapelessness.

Svartalf sprang at a cat twice his mass. *Off my territory, you!* They mixed it up, a tumbling, spitting whirl. Fur and blood flew. Our old guy got the worst of it. He hung in, though, and worked some havoc of his own. I ran over and bit through the devil's neck.

Svartalf crawled free and threw me a dirty look. What'd I mean, butting in? His injuries didn't seem too bad. A couple of rat-sized horrors scuttled by. Svartalf took off after them. Edgar joined him.

A man shape seven feet tall and broad to match charged Curtice. Its head was like a wild boar's. Hunched over, it went to gore her. "Ha, swine to hunt!" exulted Fotherwick-Botts. His blade whirred. It shortened those huge tusks. The monster reeled back. Curtice took a two-handed grip and stabbed it in the lower body. It sagged, threshed, and went limp. "Excellent," Fotherwick-Botts approved. "Modern pigsticking."

A different sort assailed Coyote. Like a deformed woman with needle teeth and claws at the end of webbed hands, the rear half a shark's, it swam through the air as it had swum in space. Coyote leered. It raked at him. He became a coyote, lower case. *Duh*, it maybe thought. Coyote turned man again. And beast. And man. And beast. When he had it thoroughly confused, he worked his way around, got onto its back, rode as he'd have ridden a bronco, and broke its neck.

Farther off, Ginny's wand swept to and fro. She dueled something I could not see from here. I loped toward her. Terror grabbed me. That misty, ghastly phantom, hair and kimono tossed by no wind I could feel, mouth stretched open, the silent shriek— I cringed. The racket of battle elsewhere rolled over me.

I recalled that this was my mate who fought. I forgot everything but rage and bounded forward.

Too slow. Just as well. I'd have been no use in such an engagement. Ginny's left hand gestured. She spoke words of power. Her wand smote. The goryo wailed one last time and blew apart like fog before a dawn breeze.

I joined my witch. Sweat ran down her face and soaked her shirt. She breathed hard. The wand shivered in her grasp. But she spoke gravely. "I believe I've given peace to Princess Tamako."

We stared around us. Demons dashed again and again at Valeria's refuge. Always they recoiled from the priest and his companions. However, those were having an awful time keeping her where she was. She wanted to get out and join the fracas.

With spear and shield, the Twin War Gods raged. Arrows whistled and struck. The fire god darted about, the touch of his torch setting foes aflame. The ogres of discipline clubbed. The kachinas pressed in, smiting. The Mudheads bounced like rubber balls; they let no bunch of our enemies rally. The Shalako ponderously trod the wicked underfoot.

And it was as if others loomed behind, above, as if every well-wishing spirit of Earth and Earth's life was with us. Six arching legs across the stars and a body at the zenith where they met—Water Strider? A hint of a web that bound the stars together—Grandmother Spider, mightiest and most caring among the Hopi? Edgar, silly Edgar, was something of the Northwest's Raven in him? Even Coyote—

My wolf sight blurrily saw the half moon rise over the trees.

I saw the demons break. Panic swept through the survivors. They scattered aloft as sparks fly from a dying fire when you stamp on it.

Arousal drained out of us. Weariness and awareness of the cold crept in. Ginny put away her wand, clasped her shoulders, and shivered. I nuzzled her while calling up the last of what heat was in me. Fjalar strutted, Svartalf limped to us across the hideously strewn field. Edgar landed and sat, wings drooping, as if glad to be again no more than a bird.

Curtice followed. Fotherwick-Botts hung low in her shaky hand. "Jolly good show," the sword deemed. "Milit'ry lessons. Yes, by Jove, this should go into the textbooks."

Curtice slumped down beside us. "Chilly con carnage," she sighed.

Did a trumpet peal, did a chorus sing? A radiance filled the sky. His wings reached across constellations. The glory around his head lighted his face, his eyes, the wisdom and compassion. His great hand moved. The slain and the blood vanished from the sacred meadow. The final fleeing devils became nothing.

And he was gone.

"Cambiel," Ginny breathed. "The fifth archangel. He who watches over discoverers."

Did our deeds and our dreams mean more to the cosmos than we had known?

—*Farewell*, we heard. *Blessings.* Coyote, kachinas, and the Beloved Ones vanished. We rested alone on Dowa Yalanne.

Balawahdiwa led Valeria out by the hand. "It's all right if *Owl* flits us to our brooms," he said. "Let's go home."

I sat on my haunches and howled my happiness at the pure moon.